OTHERS AVAILABLE BY DK HOLMBERG

The Dark Ability

The Dark Ability
The Heartstone Blade
The Tower of Venass
Blood of the Watcher

The Cloud Warrior Saga

Chased by Fire
Bound by Fire
Changed by Fire
Fortress of Fire
Forged in Fire
Serpent of Fire
Servant of Fire

The Lost Garden

Keeper of the Forest
The Desolate Bond
Keeper of Light

THE HEARTSTONE BLADE

THE DARK ABILITY
BOOK 2

ASH Publishing
dkholmberg.com

The Heartstone Blade

ISBN-13: 978-1523442133
ISBN-10: 1523442131

ASH Publishing
dkholmberg.com

THE HEARTSTONE BLADE

THE DARK ABILITY
BOOK 2

CHAPTER 1

Rsiran Lareth looked at the hard lump of lorcith sitting unshaped on the gleaming anvil of his shop, thinking of all he had been through to get that single hunk of metal. He no longer noticed the bitter bite to the air of the smithy from the lorcith, not like he once had. There were many things he no longer noticed. Since leaving his family, he had changed much. Nearly dying did that to a person.

He crouched in front of the anvil, studying the lorcith and wondering where in the Ilphaesn mines it had come from. Each nugget he worked made him think back to the time his father had forced him to serve there, the attacks he had endured while serving penance for his ability, even from the boy Rsiran had left behind who shared one of his gifts.

He could already feel the lorcith pulling at him, demanding a shape. He had to patient, though, and wait for it to tell him what it wanted to become. That was one of his abilities, a gift of his bloodline: he could hear the lorcith sing to him.

With a sigh, he set the lorcith aside, knowing he couldn't give it the time it needed. As much as he longed to heat it to glowing red, slowly work the shape from the ore, a nugget of this size could take nearly the entire night to forge, and he didn't have time, not if he was to meet with the others as planned.

Yet… something about this piece drew him.

Knowing he should not take the time, Rsiran could not help himself. Lorcith was in his blood. And the others knew he would be late; he rarely arrived at the same time as Brusus or Haern. Before he fully knew what he was doing, he heated the small lump of lorcith and began working it with the hammer. The ore sang to him with a quiet voice, and he quickly folded it into a longer shape as he listened to it. As usual, Rsiran didn't fight what the metal demanded of him, letting it fill him with a vision.

His father had spoken of controlling the ore, of learning mastery over lorcith. That had been part of the reason he had sent Rsiran to Ilphaesn, as punishment for his inability to control the lorcith, rather than succumb to its demands. Instead of learning how to master it, Rsiran allowed it to speak to him and became more attuned to it, *better* able to listen. Some might say the roles were reversed, and the lorcith controlled him.

The work did not take long. A pattern emerged that delicately spiraled in a lacy sort of charm that reminded him of the flowers Jessa wore. Under the influence of the lorcith, he envisioned it hanging from a necklace. After it cooled, he brought it to the long table cluttered with his other forgings. This would not have the same market as the knives or the sword he'd made, but he had another purpose for it anyway.

Then he checked the dwindling stack of lorcith near the forge. Eventually, he would need to Slide for more. Doing so meant visiting the mines and risking the others who mined at night, including the strange boy. After everything the boy had done to him, Rsiran still feared him, but would not put him in danger; nor would he risk being discovered by others who mined at night, He'd heard them, but did not know their location. And taking from anywhere else in Elaeavn would shine attention on himself that he didn't need, attention from the miner or smith guild, or worse, the ruling Elvraeth family.

He glanced at the forge. Coals glowed a cool orange, but he didn't bother to extinguish them. There was a time when such a thing would have terrified him, but having lived under the fear of his father's berating, the constant reminder that he wasn't quite good enough—that he would never be good enough, he'd had to find his own way to survive. Had he listened to his father, he would never have listened to the singing of the lorcith, never learned the lessons the ore itself taught him about forging, skills many of the master smiths had not even learned. Perhaps his listening was the reason his forgings fetched such a premium.

Never in Elaeavn, though. He did not dare risk that, not after what he had been through. Besides, Brusus managed to export most of what he forged and Rsiran could keep his cut. An arrangement that had worked out well for all of them.

The rest of the smithy looked little like it had when he first acquired it. The hole in the roof had long been fixed; one of Brusus's contacts had spent days patching the hole so that water no longer dripped into the smithy when it rained, threatening to damage the iron and copper he had stored here. Rsiran had swept and mopped the floor, repairing the few floorboards that had splintered over time. Brick painstakingly repaired left the walls sturdy. Had the smithy been in any other part of the city, he knew it would have been busy, journeymen and apprentices working the forge, the sounds of hammers on metal filling the air, a heavy smoke hanging over everything like it once had in his father's shop. But had the smithy been anywhere else in the city, they would never have found it empty.

Even the shelves had been cleaned, wiped down and now cluttered with his work. Pieces that he had forged over the last few months, each carefully made and inscribed with his mark. It still felt strange to him to think of it as *his* work.

"Are you coming?"

Rsiran turned and saw Jessa leaning over a long table near the back wall, closely examining his recent forgings. Some were crafted from lorcith, but Rsiran preferred not to use the metal too freely. He had not heard her come in, but he never expected to. Jessa was one of the most skilled sneaks in Elaeavn.

"I am."

"You don't sound convinced." She smiled at him as she brushed a loose strand of her shoulder-length brown hair behind her ear. A flower with long petals colored grey and green tucked into her shirt. Her head tipped forward slightly as she smelled the petals.

Rsiran suspected he was the only one who noticed how she did that. Of course, with all the time he spent with Jessa, there were many things about her that only he noticed.

He wiped the sweat from his brow and waved a hand toward the bin of lorcith. "I could stay here all night and work if I wanted. Brusus wants…" He trailed off, trying to decide what it was that Brusus wanted. Knives were easy to sell, and they had an established market, but lately Rsiran hadn't been able to make many knives. Decorative items were valuable, as well, but not nearly as much as weapons. Elaeavn smiths would not make weapons; doing so was not only forbidden by the guild, but by the Elvraeth council. "He wants more," he finally finished.

Brusus hadn't revealed *why* he needed the knives, only that he could sell them. That made Rsiran worry about his friend. Who did he owe? And how much?

"If it's too much, you should cut back. This was never supposed to be hard on you. Besides, Brusus has his debt paid off."

Rsiran wasn't certain that Brusus had, but Jessa often had a blind spot when it came to him. "Not hard. And nothing I don't enjoy." Rsiran found peace while working the forge. A place where he *knew* he fit. Strange that his father had tried for so long to keep him from it. "Just that Brusus has committed to more than I've been able to manage. You know I don't want to disappoint him."

Jessa laughed and stepped toward him. As she neared, he smelled the light scent of the flower she wore, the sharp scent of the soap she had washed with, and the other scent that he recognized as her. Somehow, in spite of no longer noticing the bitter scent of the lorcith, he always managed to notice how she smelled.

She grabbed his hand and squeezed. "You don't have to do this yourself. I don't think anyone expected you to do as much as you have."

He shrugged. "I haven't done anything I didn't want to."

Jessa watched him, reading more into the comment. Both knew the toll the last few months had taken on him. Not just in learning how to use his abilities, deciding that his gift of Sliding was not the dark ability his father wanted him to believe it was, but in learning how to listen to the lorcith, learning that he could *move* it through that connection. That gift had saved them both, but Rsiran still hadn't fully dealt with the consequences of what he'd done.

A man had died because of him. Because of his ability. And not just any man, but one of the ruling family of Elaeavn. An Elvraeth. And another had seen him, one he suspected part of a rebellion. Only... nothing had come from that attack yet.

That part was the most important. The thin man from the mines, the one with the scar on his head. Why had *he* been in the palace? And with Josun?

They were questions that plagued him, and no answers came.

If not for Jessa, Rsiran didn't know how he would have gotten through it. Of course, if not for Jessa, he would not have been in the same situation.

At times, part of him wondered if perhaps his father had been right. Had he spent more time in the mines, he might have learned mastery over the lorcith, might have better learned to ignore its call. Instead, he learned to listen, to use its song to help him create forgings that he would never have managed on his own. But had the price been too high? What did it matter if he learned to create such works if he sacrificed the life of another to do so?

"There was no other choice," Jessa said softly. She touched his arm, running her hand down it in a comforting way.

Had he not known better, he would have suspected that she Read him. But Jessa's gift was Sight. Perhaps she saw the tension Rsiran felt in his jaw, the way the muscles in his neck clenched every time he thought about what had happened over the last few months. He wondered if he would ever get over it, or would he forever struggle with those memories and the nightmares that came with them?

"I know."

"You should see Della. You look tired. She might be able to give you a draught that can help you sleep."

He shrugged. "Just the work. It feels like there is so much to get done."

Jessa frowned at him, her deep green eyes flaring brighter as she studied him. Her brown hair hung around her shoulders, longer than when he had first met her. A face he had once thought angular and harsh now looked beautiful as she worried about him. "Have you thought of bringing on help?"

He smiled, pushing away the dark thoughts that plagued him. He would need to do a better job hiding that from her. Some things he just had to deal with on his own. "Are you offering? I *could* use an extra pair of hands..."

Jessa punched his shoulder, relaxing as she seemingly decided that he had moved on. "The Great Watcher knows you do well enough with the hands you have," she started. Rsiran flushed, but Jessa didn't seem to notice. "But I meant something different. Someone you could teach."

"An apprentice?" he asked. Jessa just shrugged. Rsiran shook his head. "I'm in trouble enough if the guild ever learns that I have an unsanctioned forge. If I were to take on an apprentice..."

Rsiran didn't want to think of what would happen. He didn't need any more attention drawn to him. It was not just the unsanctioned forge that would draw attention to him, but using lorcith in ways that the Elvraeth didn't approve would do it too. Of course, were the Elvraeth ever to learn of what Rsiran had done to one of their own, his sentence would be much harsher than simple banishment.

"Besides, if we produce much more, we'll run out of the supply of lorcith. The way it is, I won't be able to continue much longer with what I have."

"You think taking lorcith from the mines isn't enough to get you into trouble. To get *all* of us into trouble?" Jessa asked. She didn't say what they knew, all of them including Brusus, about what would happen were the ruling Elvraeth to learn about their access to lorcith. Banishment. Exile. They would become one of the Forgotten.

But the worst would happen to him. That was part of the fear that kept him up at night. "I haven't been back to the mines since..." He trailed off, finishing the thought in his mind. Since he'd escaped with the sack of lorcith. Since before they had entered the palace. Since before Jessa nearly died.

Jessa pulled him toward her and looked up at him, her green eyes flashing darker for a moment. "You worry too much, Rsiran." She kissed him on the cheek and stepped away. "Besides, when have the Elvraeth *ever* concerned themselves with what happens here in Lower Town?"

There was some comfort in that. Della claimed the Elvraeth fought only amongst themselves, with no concern of happenings outside their walls. That had been Brusus's justification for explaining what happened with Josun Elvraeth, the man Rsiran had killed. Since then, there had been no sign that the Elvraeth suspected that anyone had entered the palace, much less that they'd lost one of their own. There was no evidence that Rsiran had ever been there.

Yet... he still couldn't shake the uncomfortable way he felt. The Elvraeth might not worry about what happened in Lower Town, but after the friendships he'd made over the last few months, *he* did. And anything that might put those friendships at risk bothered him. What had happened in the palace had been his fault—his decision—and by revealing that he could Slide, he put the others in danger. And regardless of what Brusus and Della believed, Rsiran had seen the other man, one who might recognize him.

At least the smithy seemed protected. The entire time he had used this shop as his own, he had never seen even a sign of the constabulary. Only poverty and sickness. But that didn't mean things couldn't change.

And Jessa was right. He *was* tired; exhausted as much from the work he had been doing at the forge as from not sleeping well. He just didn't want to think about adding another person who might learn his secrets, but maybe Brusus would know of someone who could help. Brusus seemed to have connections to everyone in Lower Town.

"Should we go?" Rsiran asked, trying to lighten the mood. "I'm sure Brusus is waiting for you to take more of his coin."

"I can't help it that he's terrible at dice." Jessa squeezed his hand. "And I made sure the door was locked."

Rsiran snorted. "As if that matters."

"Well… not to me. But most aren't like me."

Rsiran forced a smile. In spite of having Jessa alongside him, he couldn't shake the uneasy way he felt. Since the palace break-in, they hadn't heard anything, but how much longer could that last? How long until the Elvraeth—or worse, those who had been in the rebellion with Josun—came looking for him?

He knew what he would need to do. Rather than let the others suffer for him, he would need to disappear. If the Elvraeth found him first, they would want the person responsible for Sliding behind their walls. They would not care about simple thieves. If it was the other… Rsiran didn't want to think about what would happen.

Jessa frowned at him, as if Reading his thoughts again.

It was a good thing she couldn't. He wouldn't let her worry any more than necessary. Already she worried about things she couldn't control, that he wouldn't *let* her control.

Taking a deep breath, he Slid.

CHAPTER 2

THE FEELING WAS ONE OF TAKING A SINGLE STEP, but during that single step, wind whistled past him, blowing through his ears, and flashes of color washed over him. When they emerged from the Slide, Rsiran and Jessa stood in the alley outside the Wretched Barth, the tavern that had become a second home to Rsiran. After all the practice using his ability, he no longer felt the same overwhelming fatigue as he had when he first learned to Slide. Just a hint of weakness this time, and he attributed that to Jessa Sliding with him.

She squeezed his hand but didn't let go. "And you thought your ability useless," she whispered.

Not useless, but still dangerous. Still something he didn't dare use openly. How many others felt like his father felt, that Sliding was a dark ability from the Great Watcher, one meant only for thieves and assassins? How many others would immediately think him cursed? "Still can't see in the dark."

She laughed softly. "Yeah. You're like a baby."

They stepped out onto the narrow street running in front of the Wretched Barth. He had been so uncomfortable the first time here, practically dragged by Brusus. Now, the Barth was a familiar place, comfortable and easy. A place where friends met.

This close to the bay, air smelled of the sea, a mixture of salt and fish with an undercurrent of rot that Rsiran somehow found reassuring. A pale streetlamp burned nearby, casting a soft glow of light and intended to aid those not Sighted. A few other streetlamps glowed farther up the street, but they were spaced far enough apart that shadows pooled between them. Rsiran saw a man in a faded cloak drifting up the street, likely one of the Servants of the Great Watcher, judging by the cloak, but otherwise, they were the only ones out. He heard a cat nearby and waited, but didn't hear another. Two meant luck, but only one…

Jessa pulled on his arm. "I heard two," she said.

Rsiran listened for a moment before following her.

Inside, the tavern was awash in light. Candles burned on a few tables, their flames flickering with sudden life as the door opened. A crackling hearth near the back of the tavern glowed brightly. After working the forge for the last hour, Rsiran didn't need its heat, but it still gave the tavern a different kind of warmth. A bandolist played near the back of the room, a man Rsiran recognized from other performances. Likely a friend of Lianna's, the owner of the tavern.

Jessa led him to a table along the long wall. Brusus sat atop one of the stools, a cracked, brown leather satchel tucked between his legs. He wore a navy shirt heavily embroidered and simple black pants. There was a bright shine to his boots. Everything about the way he dressed screamed that he belonged in the palace rather than down here in Lower Town, but as far as Rsiran knew, he had lived his entire life here.

Haern sat next to him. A dronr drifted across the tops of his fingers, flicking quickly from one to the next. The other hand held the cup of dice. The long scar on his face tensed as he dropped the dice onto the table.

Firell sat next to Haern, dressed simply in a plain, olive-green shirt with matching pants. The pointed beard on his chin had lengthened since the last time Rsiran had seen him. He smelled heavily of fish, though it was more a ruse than anything. Firell was a smuggler.

Brusus looked up when Jessa dropped onto one of the stools. "Do you have to do that?" he asked. His voice was gruff, but a smile drifted across his face, reaching his eyes.

"Do what?" she asked.

Rsiran sat next to her, still holding her hand under the table.

"Flaunt yourselves. The Great Watcher knows we don't want to see it."

She glared at Brusus. "Just because *you* can't be happy doesn't mean the rest of us can't."

Brusus looked past her toward the bar as one of the servers brought over two mugs of ale and set them on the table. She was heavyset and wore a wide apron. Her eyes glanced around the room before settling on Brusus.

"Don't worry, Jessa. Brusus had never been happy," Firell said. "Not so long as I've known him, at least."

Brusus ignored the barb. The server chuckled before walking away, not mindful of the way Brusus glared at her. "Thought we'd see you before now," he said, looking to Rsiran. "Anything new? Firell will only be in port a little while."

Brusus wanted more forgings, and not of iron or steel, though he managed to move those just as easily as the lorcith. After all the time Rsiran spent working lorcith, listening to it as it guided his forgings, he had improved his skills to the point where much of his work was indistinguishable from that of the master smiths. He felt a quiet pride in his burgeoning skill. As far as he knew, few of the other master smiths could match his skill with lorcith. And soon, he suspected, the same could be said about other metals.

Why had his father never told him that lorcith could teach as well as any master smith?

"A few items. A hook. A lantern," he said. He had been particularly pleased with how that had turned out, but knew it was nothing like the lantern he had seen in the palace that glowed with a blue light. If he only had one to study, he might be able to copy it. He didn't tell Brusus about the charm he'd just made. There seemed no use in selling simple jewelry. "A couple of knives."

"What am I going to do with a hook?" Brusus muttered. He grabbed the dicing cup from Haern and shook it more vigorously than he needed before dumping them out on the table.

"Fish. At least, that'll be what I claim if I'm caught with it," Firell said.

Haern laughed and grabbed the coins stacked in front of Brusus, sliding them in front of him. His eyes drifted for a moment, and Rsiran wondered what he Saw. As a Seer, Haern had visions, glimpses of the future, though Rsiran had never worked out how far into the future those visions went. Some Seers, like the great Seers of the Elvraeth, could see far into the future and used that to help guide the rest of Elaeavn. Or so the Elvraeth claimed. Most had a more limited field, able to only See moments into the future.

Rsiran shrugged. "Can't always help what I make," he said, though that wasn't quite true. With iron and steel, he could be intentional. Grindl could be forged well and fetched some value, but they struggled getting enough of the pure ore to be useful to Rsiran. And he didn't dare steal any from the other smiths. Anything that brought more attention to him, he avoided.

"Hasn't he done enough?" Haern asked. He set another coin in front of him and shook the dice cup.

Brusus sighed. "He's doing enough. But I know we can do more. Just need the supply. With what we're fetching for those knives alone…"

"I don't want to sell the sword, Brusus." Selling the knives bothered him more than it should. He didn't want to think about the sword.

Brusus looked over. His pale green eyes flashed briefly, for the barest moment. Rsiran was one of the few people who knew Brusus's secret, that he carried Elvraeth blood in his veins and with it, he had their abilities. Abilities that were more than Rsiran could manage. Rsiran felt the crawling sensation as Brusus tried to Read him, and he fortified the barriers in his mind using the image of lorcith. Another lesson he had learned while nearly dying in the Floating Palace.

Brusus nodded slowly. "If you ever do—"

"If I ever do," Rsiran agreed.

So far, he hadn't forged another sword blade. Either because the metal had not wanted to become a blade or he somehow exerted his own influence over it, though he didn't think that he did. He'd never truly *tried* to push the metal to become something it didn't want to be. That struck him as too much like what his father did, a power he felt uncomfortable wielding, especially considering the connection he had with lorcith.

More likely, he had not chosen the right nuggets of lorcith to become a longer blade. Rsiran had no doubt about how much a lorcith-forged blade would fetch, but part of him was glad that he possessed the only one he had ever fully forged. After learning of his *other* ability, the one that Haern of all people had drawn out of him, he felt somewhat unnerved to forge anything too large to control.

Brusus looked at him, and some of the edge faded from his face. "None of this can come back to you, Rsiran. That's the whole point of moving everything outside the city, getting it to places like Thyr and Asador so you aren't at risk."

"But his mark," Jessa said.

Firell looked to Brusus before answering. "That mark is what makes it even *less* likely Rsiran will be tagged. None of the master smiths have marked their work in over a century. And none has worked lorcith like Rsiran in much longer than that."

Rsiran nodded, knowing that they were right. The mark identified forgings made by him—placing the mark on them just felt *right*—but he hadn't seen anything made by the master smiths working in Elaeavn with a mark. Some of the oldest and most revered works carried the marks of the smiths that had forged them, but the guild felt doing so took away from the work. Still, if someone ever did learn that it was his mark, there would be no way he could deny how much he'd made. Since leaving his father and his apprenticeship, he'd marked everything he forged.

"Even moving his work out of the city, are you certain the Elvraeth can't learn of everything Rsiran has made?" Jessa looked from Brusus to Rsiran as she spoke.

Rsiran hadn't told her of seeing the other man in Josun's room before they Slid. He hadn't wanted to worry her, not yet at least.

Brusus shook his head, running a hand through dark hair streaked with silver. "Not the way we're moving it. Firell ships it out, moves most of it through Asador—"

"And Thyr. But Asador prefers the knives. Everything else moves more easily through Thyr," Firell said. He took a long drink of his ale.

"And you don't think word gets back to Elaeavn?" Jessa pressed.

Rsiran had not realized she worried so much about the Elvraeth. Back at the smithy, she had not seemed as concerned as she seemed now. Did she ask because she feared he wasn't concerned enough or because she worried more than she let on? Did she know what he feared—that the Elvraeth would learn what he did, making it necessary for him to choose between staying and hiding, or running, leaving the only friends he'd ever had?

"Easy, Jessa," Haern said. His eyes flared green for a moment. "I've not Seen anything to indicate that Rsiran risks himself."

"But you can't really See him that well, can you?"

Firell looked from Jessa to Haern. He was the only one who didn't fully know of Rsiran's ability to Slide.

Haern stared at Jessa for a long moment, his jaw tensing, before nodding. "Not as I can others," he agreed. "But what I can See tells me that we are safe. I have warned Brusus of the dangers."

Brusus shot him a look, and he cut off.

"What dangers?" Jessa asked.

Brusus waved his hands and tipped the dice cup toward Jessa. "Set out your coins and play."

She didn't reach for the cup. "What dangers, Brusus?" she pressed.

Rsiran squeezed her hand, trying to soothe her, but when she got like this, there was not much that he could do but sit back and let her work it out. Besides, she knew them better than he did, had much more history with them.

"No, Rsiran," she said, looking over at him. "If there are dangers that Haern has Seen, I think we all should know about them. We are in this together, you most importantly, especially after what happened—" She caught herself and lowered her voice. "—what happened the last time. If the Elvraeth come looking for any of us, it will be you, Rsiran. I won't have them risking you again," she said, giving Brusus and Haern a look of warning.

"Do not confuse me with *that* Elvraeth. I did not risk Rsiran." Brusus stared at her, heat in his gaze.

Letting go of her hand, Rsiran pulled Jessa over to him and put his arm around her shoulders. "Let it go. If Haern says that we aren't in any danger, then we aren't."

"Like last time?" she asked. "When you almost died?" Looking at the others, she seemed to punctuate her point. "When Rsiran tried to do the job by himself to protect the rest of us?"

Rsiran noticed she didn't comment on how *she* almost died. And thankfully, she didn't mention what he had done to keep them safe.

"That was different. Josun was different," Brusus argued.

Jessa sniffed but set a stack of dronr on the table anyway. Finally, she took the dice cup from Brusus and shook it, upending it over the table. As the dice spilled across the rough wood surface, the door to the tavern opened. Brusus looked over and something about him changed. Tension seemed to leave him as Lianna entered.

Long black hair pulled back and twisted into a bun. A pair of slender rods seemed to hold it in place. She strained under the weight of a heavy basket. Green eyes, not as deep as Brusus when he didn't hide his ability, but darker than even Haern's, flickered around her tavern. The other servers stepped a little more quickly when their mistress arrived.

Lianna smiled when she saw them and stopped at their table. "You've been busy, Brusus."

"Busy?"

Lianna nodded. "I know you wanted to move some of those crates along with Rsiran's work, but I don't know why you would leave one stacked out on the docks like that. Never seen other crates like that before, so it must be one of yours."

Brusus frowned, not saying anything. Rsiran noticed that Haern's eyes flared deep green for a moment, and then the scar on his cheek started to twitch. He looked at Firell. "Those crates should not have been left on the dock."

Firell frowned. "They weren't, at least not when I left. Just my transport. Besides, you've not been removing full crates from the warehouse. Don't know how you could, really. Too heavy."

"Someone has," Lianna said. She frowned as she sensed the mood. "And if not you, then perhaps you should go check on that crate. Told you not to get involved in something like that." The last comment was directed at Brusus.

"And I told you I had it handled."

Lianna laughed lightly, shifting the basket she carried. "Not sure you do. And you put these others—"

Brusus stood, grabbing his coins off the table with a sweep of his hands. "What I'm doing is *for* the others," he said softly. "Come on. We need to move that crate before someone finds it."

"Sounds like someone *has* found it," Firell said, smiling.

"Someone else." Brusus started toward the door.

Haern looked from Lianna to Brusus as his friend left the tavern. The dronr he held flipped across his knuckles, sliding quickly. The long scar on his cheek tensed. His eyes took on the faraway expression Rsiran had come to recognize as him trying to See some future vision.

The worried expression on his face made Rsiran nervous, but it was the sudden fear that they might have been discovered the sent fear tingling along his spine.

CHAPTER 3

RSIRAN FOLLOWED THE OTHERS TO THE DOCKS. He could Slide there, but did not have the strength to take them with him all at once. He'd never taken more than one with him—Jessa, and even doing that for short distances strained him. And besides, since Firell didn't yet know about his ability, he preferred to keep it that way for as long as possible. That part of him had been influenced by his father over the years.

Brusus walked quickly through darkened streets. Once, Rsiran would have wondered how he managed so easily, but that was before he had learned of Brusus's heritage. The dark bothered Brusus no more than it bothered Jessa; both were strongly Sighted. Rsiran wondered how many of the Elvraeth could Slide, but had never gotten a satisfactory answer. As far as Della knew, the ability was incredibly rare even among the Elvraeth.

Haern trailed alongside Brusus, silent. One hand went to his pocket, and he left it there. He had a distant expression, one Rsiran recognized as him using his ability to See. Since leaving the Barth, he continued to frown, the corners of his mouth working as if struggling through a puzzle.

Firell hurried ahead, his thin black cloak flailing behind him as he jogged through the street. Rsiran had yet to learn what ability the Great Watcher had given Firell. Whatever it was likely helped him captain his ship, either Sight or Listening. Even Reading could be useful, Rsiran decided, if the Reader were powerful enough to step past the barriers others built within their minds. Maybe Pushing, like he'd learned Brusus could do, influencing another's thoughts, but that seemed tied to Reading.

Jessa pulled him off to the side of the road, drifting into shadows. The others continued ahead. Only Haern noticed that they had stopped and nodded once to Rsiran before continuing forward.

"I worry about Brusus," she whispered to him.

"Why?"

She looked down the street. The others had turned a corner and disappeared. Neither Rsiran nor Jessa worried about losing sight of the others. Rsiran could simply Slide them the rest of the way. "I haven't seen Brusus like this in a while. He's… he's obsessed with this."

"With what?" Rsiran had not known Brusus long, but the man always seemed somewhat obsessed. First, it had been the knives Rsiran made; then it had been the strange cylinders they found in the warehouse. Recently, Brusus's newest obsession seemed about raising money, using whatever Rsiran could create.

"The crates in the warehouse. The lorcith knives. You." She shook her head. "Something is going on that I can't explain. And it's making me uncomfortable."

Rsiran had learned to trust Jessa's instincts but didn't share the same anxiety. For the first time in his life, he was doing what *he* wanted to do. Running a forge. Spending time with friends, feeling cared about—loved even. If he had to risk himself to help Brusus, then he would.

"When I first met him—all of you, really—I thought you were part of the rebellion."

"There is no rebellion, Rsiran," Jessa said. "Josun wanted power. Without him… well, there's nothing without him."

He glanced down the street and thought about the anxiety he'd seen from Brusus and the way Haern looked. "What if there is?" He sighed, realizing that he had to tell Jessa. "When I Slid, before we left the palace, there… there was another. A man I knew from the mines. I don't know if he saw me, or if he recognized me, but…"

Jessa bit the inside of her lip and leaned to sniff her flower. "Brusus would have heard if there was something more. I don't think he would keep that from us."

"Like he did with Josun?"

Jessa sighed. "I know what you intend to do. Just—"

"I'll be careful," Rsiran promised.

She took his hand and squeezed. "I've… lost a lot of people I've been close to. I can't lose you too. Not now that I've found you." She whispered the last and looked down at the ground as she said it.

His heart fluttered, realizing just how close her fears were to his. Rsiran didn't *want* to have to leave them, but if doing so kept the others—kept Jessa—safe, then he would do so. After everything they had been through, after the way Jessa had made certain to pull him into her world, prevent him from getting isolated, he owed that much to her.

"I'll be careful," he said again.

She looked up and let out a long breath. For a moment, he thought she might say something more. Rsiran would wait, would delay anything if Jessa needed him to, but she said nothing more, only nodded.

21

Jessa so rarely spoke of her past. He knew it haunted her, but more than that was a mystery to him. He never pushed her to share, suspecting that she would open up in time. Now that she feared losing him, he wanted her to know he felt much the same. He had lost his entire family only to gain a new one. And he would do anything to keep it together.

Strange as it seemed, he owed his father for the fact that he had met Jessa in the first place. Had he not been sent away by his father, sent to the mines in Ilphaesn where he had to run away or die, he would never have grown as close to Jessa. Really, Rsiran would never have met any of them.

"We shouldn't keep them waiting. They already tell stories."

"What kind of stories?" he asked.

Some of the anxiety left her face, and she offered him a playful smile. "The best kind."

Holding tightly to her hand, Rsiran Slid, emerging in the darkness near the docks. It seemed harder than when they had Slid from the smithy to the tavern, as if he pushed against something, but he'd had little rest over the last few days.

He stuttered forward before catching himself. Jessa gripped his hand tightly and looked at him with a worried expression. Rsiran patted her hand, hoping to make it seem reassuring, and looked around.

At this time of night, the docks looked like long shadows of darkness, little more than a series of wooden fingers sticking out and away from the rocky shore, jutting into Aylianne Bay. Rough wooden boxes lined most of the docks, meant to collect the day's catch before moving to the market. Waves crashed along the rocks, sending spray and the scent of salt into the air. Even now, gulls circled overhead, cawing occasionally. The bustle that normally filled the docks had died to nothing.

A single lantern lit the entirety of the docks. On the nearest, a small portage boat was pulled up to the dock, and Firell stood alongside, motioning toward it. Brusus stood staring where Firell motioned, but Haern looked past them both and out over the water.

Rsiran followed his gaze and saw the outline of a large twin-masted ship moored out in the harbor. Firell's ship, he suspected, though he would need to wait until it was lighter to know for certain. But why would Haern look at it with a troubled expression?

"What is it?" Jessa asked as they approached.

Brusus looked up and frowned at them. A wide grin spread across Firell's face.

"I thought Lianna said she saw one of the crates down here. Where is it?" Rsiran asked. From what he remembered, the crates were massive, too large to easily move without the help of several people. If Lianna had just come from the dock, the crate should still be here. He glanced at the other docks but saw no sign of the crate there, either.

Brusus motioned to the dinghy. Rsiran looked into the boat as he neared but didn't see anything. "This your transport?" he asked Firell.

"Nothing there, Brusus. You know I wouldn't keep anything out like that."

"Then where is the crate?" Jessa scanned the dock, using her Sight to see where the crate might have gone.

"How would it have even gotten down here? Those were—"

"Just a shipping crate," Firell finished. "We get them all the time in places like Cort and Asador. Not so much here. The docks aren't set up for that type of crate to come off easily. These are fishing docks, not shipping docks. Have to load them into transport boats to reach the shore."

Rsiran hadn't known that before. But those shipping crates filled the warehouse, stacked from floor to the ceiling, massive rows of them.

Somehow, they had been brought off the ships. It seemed strange that they would have to load and unload in such an inefficient manner.

"You can't just sail all the way into the docks?" he asked.

"Not my ship. Water is too shallow."

"But the other ships dock here." Farther down, two medium-sized ships were tied to the docks. Both had faded paint and rolled sails. They didn't look the same as Firell's ship—his seemed quite a bit larger—but bigger than any ship he'd been on in his life.

"Flat bottomed, all of them. Have to travel close to the shoreline. Deeper keeled boats like mine can handle rougher water." Firell smiled. "Better for my line of work."

"Are you finished giving sailing lessons?" Brusus asked.

Firell shrugged. "Not sailing lessons, but you wouldn't know anything about that."

Brusus's frown deepened. "Just because I've never sailed with you doesn't mean I don't know how."

Firell arched an eyebrow and then laughed. "But never willing to come with me? As many times as I've tried getting you out on the water, now I hear it's just *my* ship you don't like."

Brusus's face clouded. "Damn, Firell! There's not time for this. Lianna said she saw one of the crates. Then what happened to it?"

Rsiran hadn't seen Brusus this agitated before. Maybe Jessa was right. *Something* was clearly bothering him, but Rsiran didn't know what. That he would get so upset over one of the crates surprised him.

Firell raised his hands and backed away from him a step. "Easy, Brusus. Just having a little fun. Nothing to worry about if it wasn't your crate, anyway, is there?"

"That's my concern," Brusus said. "You know how we've been moving those crates, so you should know that I would not have brought it to the docks that way. What I need to know is what happened? Why would it have been here?"

"Could someone else have brought it in?" Rsiran offered.

Brusus waved toward the water. "No other ships use shipping crates like that around here."

Haern finally turned away from looking out over the water and met Brusus's eyes. "Lianna spoke truly, Brusus. That was one of the Elvraeth crates. I can See that much." He shook his head. "But nothing more than that."

"I still don't understand what the problem is, Brusus." Jessa had one hand planted on her hip as she glared at him.

"The problem is that the Elvraeth have left those crates alone for years. Some for *hundreds* of years. And, as far as I know, there haven't been new crates added to the warehouse in at least a hundred years. So everything has been sitting untouched." He looked out over the water, shaking his head. "And now, in just the last few months, we see activity? First with Josun. The Great Watcher alone knows what he intended. And now this." He swept his arm around the dock.

Jessa glanced over to Rsiran. "Who then?"

Brusus shook his head. "I haven't seen any other Elvraeth in the warehouse other than him. Haven't seen anyone, really. Patrols around the warehouse haven't changed. Nothing has changed that would make me think we needed to be more careful. And nothing from the palace, either."

Rsiran didn't say anything. Since they had infiltrated the palace, he'd feared some repercussions. Since none had come, he'd allowed himself to slowly relax. Now, learning this—that one of the crates had been moved to and then quickly off the dock—that tension suddenly returned. He was the one who had Slid them into the palace. He was the one who'd stolen lorcith from the mines, using it to forge weapons.

He was the one who'd killed one of the Elvraeth. He was the one who had been seen.

And if they had been wrong, if the Elvraeth learned that he was the one who had been there, the others were in danger.

Worse, it was clear Jessa was right. Something other than the crates was bothering Brusus. He was hiding something from them. After what they'd all been through, Brusus owed it to him to share, but if he didn't want to say anything here, Rsiran wouldn't push—not yet—but he needed to know.

"What can we do?" Rsiran asked.

Jessa looked over at him, but he ignored her. Thankfully, she didn't let go of his hand.

Brusus sighed, blinking slowly. He ran a hand through his hair and scratched at the back of his head. "Would you take Jessa and go look in the warehouse? Let me know if you see anything?"

Firell looked at Brusus and laughed. "You sure it's smart to send those two? I mean, they had to take a stop off on the way down here! Great Watcher knows I remember what it was like to be that age, first in love…"

Jessa stiffened. "How many flippers did she have?"

Firell frowned and pinched his chin. "I can't remember, but I'm certain that it was no more than two."

Haern laughed softly before turning to Brusus. "You don't think you should go yourself?"

Brusus shook his head. "Jessa can see better than I can," he started. "And there is something else I need to do."

Not for the first time, Rsiran wondered how much any of the others knew of Brusus's secret heritage. Jessa knew. Della too. But did Haern? Did Firell? The secret was not his to share, any more than his own secret should be shared by them, but Rsiran was learning to trust the others, learning to accept that they would keep him safe. If he still kept secrets from them, dangers that Haern had Seen, he wondered when Brusus would feel the same?

"What are you going to do?" Jessa asked Brusus.

"There is something else that I need to check on. Haern will come with me."

Haern hesitated a moment and then nodded. The long scar on his cheek twitched.

"And me?" Firell asked.

"Find Shael. That damn man knows practically everyone along the docks. If anyone knows what might be going on, it would be him."

"Shael's not in Elaeavn," Haern said. His eyes took on that faraway expression again.

Brusus frowned. "I saw him two days ago. No transports since then. He's here."

Haern's frown deepened.

"I'll see if I can find him. He owes me, anyway." Firell said. He looked at Jessa for a moment, a wide smile crossing his face, and then started away from the dock at a quick pace.

Brusus looked after him for a moment and then pulled Rsiran aside. "Need you to Slide to the warehouse. Look for anything that might be missing or out of place. See which crate might be gone. I've been through quite a few, but there are too many there to sort through all of them. But if one of those crates was here," he started, flicking his eyes to Haern, "then we need to know which one. And why. Jessa will help."

"I don't know that I will even recognize if anything is missing, Brusus. You've been handling the transactions there. I've been focusing my energy on the forgings, trying to get enough for you."

Brusus rested his hand on Rsiran's shoulder and squeezed. "And know that I appreciate what you've been doing. You'll get your cut soon. Jessa has been there enough that she should be able to tell if something is out of place."

"That's not what I'm getting at." Rsiran didn't want Brusus to think that he wanted only the money.

"I know, but I don't want you to think that I'm taking advantage of you."

Jessa stepped up next to him and grabbed is hand. A playful smile split her lips. "No. That's my job."

Brusus just shook his head. The urgency never left his eyes, not like it once had. Rsiran didn't know what it meant, but it was significant somehow.

"Don't worry, Brusus. We'll help you figure out what's going on."

Brusus's eyes flashed deep green for a brief moment. "Probably nothing," he said, "but with what we've been doing, can't be too careful."

He turned away from them and made his way toward the shore. Haern followed after, watching Brusus's back rather than walking alongside him.

Rsiran waited, worried about when the Elvraeth would learn of him, learn how he Slid into the palace, killed one of their own, and now used lorcith in ways they had forbidden. Or whoever remained of Josun's rebellion discovered he had killed their leader. Unless they already knew. And then it was too late to do anything but run.

Jessa studied his face, almost as if Reading him. He forced a smile as he squeezed her hand, but didn't say any of that to her.

CHAPTER 4

THE SLIDE TOOK THEM TO THE OUTSIDE of the warehouse. Rsiran had been here only a few times before and never alone. The first time he had come, Brusus had nearly died. It had taken Rsiran exposing his abilities to save them. And, because of that, he had learned Brusus's secret, one that was more shocking than what Rsiran hid. The second time he'd come, he had met the Elvraeth Josun. He had not known it at the time, but he had just met the only other person he knew about who shared the ability to Slide.

Since then, he had come here only a handful of other times. Each time, he'd come with either Brusus or Jessa, and often both. Because of his earliest experience, a gnawing unease chewed at his stomach as he emerged from the Slide, a sense of immediate fear that *something* would go wrong, or worse—that one of the Elvraeth would find him. The last few times had been uneventful, but that didn't mean his luck would hold.

The energy required for the Slide taxed him enough that he wavered for a moment. From his experience, he would regain the necessary strength to Slide with a little more rest, but he wouldn't be fully restored without a good night's sleep. Nothing like the nuanced ease he'd seen Josun manage.

They stood just on the other side of the door to the warehouse. His Slide could have taken them anywhere inside the building, but he didn't dare push his luck too far in case there *was* someone else inside the warehouse. Besides, he didn't know what would happen if he went too far and plunged into one of the crates.

Jessa started forward. From here, she would lead.

"Let me know if you see anything," he whispered.

"Don't worry. I'm not letting go of you."

Only a little light streamed into the warehouse from windows cut into the massive roof overhead, but nothing more than the light from the crescent moon filtered through. Rsiran would have an easier time searching the warehouse when it was lighter, but he had not argued when Brusus asked him to come, willing to do whatever was necessary to help his friend.

Shadowed walls rose up around them. Dozens of crates stacked atop each other, some reaching as high as the ceiling. A narrow walkway separated the stacks of crates. The farther they went, the older the crates became, until some were at least as old as the city of Elaeavn itself. Near the center was where Brusus had first shown Rsiran the warehouse, had demonstrated the oddities and fantastic items that could be found hidden within some of the crates.

"What do you see?" he asked.

"Nothing here. Just footprints in the dirt. Most are old. The newest look like ours. Crates look undisturbed."

Rsiran felt himself relax. Without Jessa, he would not have risked coming at night. Too many with Sight could surprise him. Though he could Slide to safety, a single blade or arrow could injure him enough to prevent him from moving anywhere. But with Jessa guiding him, he felt a sense of ease, knowing that she would keep him safe, just as he would do anything to keep her safe.

They went on. Fumbling through the dark with Jessa leading him by his hand, he felt every bit the babe she often teased him of being. Worse, he could not help but remember the other time he knew such darkness, when he wandered the mines of Ilphaesn. At least there, he had the sense of the lorcith in the walls to guide him, almost drawing him forward. Here, he felt only distant sensations of the ore.

Rsiran paused. Had he always felt lorcith here? He couldn't remember. The first time he had come to the warehouse, he had not been as acutely aware of lorcith. The second time, he had been more focused on Josun Elvraeth and the fact that he had stolen the sword Rsiran had forged. Any other times he had come had been light, so he'd not had the same sense of the darkness as he did now. Maybe that mattered.

"What is it?" Jessa whispered.

He shook his head. "Probably nothing."

"But it might be something?"

"It's just… I sense lorcith. I don't know if I've always sensed it when we've come. I never really paid much attention to it before."

She squeezed his hand and continued forward more slowly. "Let me know if it changes."

"Changes?"

"Moves."

Rsiran tried to focus on the sense of the lorcith, but it felt muted. As if distant. Usually, he had a more distinct awareness of it, even from distances. Were he to focus, he could feel the sword hidden in his smithy or the knives he had recently forged. He had the constant awareness of other lorcith, like that found in the Floating Palace, but this felt different.

His awareness of lorcith gave him another ability, but one that only seemed to work on items he had forged, granting him the power to push or pull the lorcith. The pair of knives hidden in his pockets felt like a gentle presence in his mind. Were he to have the need, he could send the knives spinning away from him. This ability had saved his life once already.

"Up ahead," Jessa whispered.

"What?"

"Clearing. Crates look like the last time Brusus was here a few days ago. Side split open. Most of the contents gone."

He hadn't known that Jessa had been to the warehouse a few days ago with Brusus. Not that he knew where she went all the time, but it seemed strange to him that she hadn't mentioned it. More reason to question Brusus about what he planned.

"Can you tell if anything is missing?" Trying to determine if one crate was missing out of the hundreds stored here would be nearly impossible. How would they know if just one had moved? And, without carting a wagon down to the warehouse, how would someone take one of the crates out of here in the first place?

"Not yet. Come on," she urged, moving forward.

When she let go of his hand, he felt a moment of panic. The lost connection meant he couldn't Slide her away from the warehouse, not without knowing where she was. He heard a rustling of cloth and tensed. A soft blue light suddenly filled the warehouse around them.

"Where did you find that?" He recognized the lantern as one of the Elvraeth lanterns. He had seen one when Josun had been here and again when they had Slid to the Floating Palace. The steady blue light was like nothing found anywhere else. The only thing he could compare it to was the orange lantern from the Ilphaesn mines.

"Brusus found it. One of the crates."

"How do you work it?" he asked.

She shook her head, leaning over the lantern. "No working. It's either on or it's not. The cloth keeps the light covered."

Rsiran took the lamp. Made of a strange metal, it took him a few moments to realize that part of it was made of lorcith, though not entirely. An alloy, and one he had only experienced one time before—when he had Slid into the palace. Until that time, he had not known that lorcith could be forged as an alloy. He still didn't know how it had been done.

Rsiran ran his hand over the lantern, admiring the craftsmanship. The metal was shaped in such a way that it seemed to draw the light out but left the lantern itself cool. There was something to the forging that he could almost understand. Could he recreate it if given enough time? If he concentrated, he thought that he might be able to *feel* how the lantern had been made.

"You should bring it with you," Jessa said with a laugh. "Neither Brusus nor I need it."

He looked up and smiled. "How did you know?"

She shrugged. "You get this intense concentration across your face and your eyes sort of squint."

If he could make another lantern like this… he wouldn't have to worry about the dark. Eventually, he would need to return to Ilphaesn to mine more lorcith; he'd used almost all of the supply he'd taken from the boy. Better to have some lighting than to risk injury in the dark, or worse, to worry about a mining pick or hammer suddenly slamming into his back, leaving him too injured to Slide back to Elaeavn.

"They had a lantern like this in the mines," he whispered.

"Like this?"

"Well… not quite like this. More of an orange light. The only time I have seen this blue light was when we were in the palace."

"I remember." Jessa said it with a hint of bitterness.

Rsiran swung the lantern so that he could see the rest of the warehouse. It appeared little different from the last time he had been here, though bright sunlight had streamed through the dirty skylight overhead that time. A wide clearing of the crates created a sort of circle where they stood. They were stacked at least three high, reaching high over his head. A few stacks reached the ceiling, and not for the first time, Rsiran wondered how they had been lifted into place. The crates in this part of the warehouse were older than the others. Most no longer had anything written on them, and on those that did, the writing was in a language he didn't understand.

"Can you tell if anything is disturbed?" he asked.

Jessa took a few steps around the clearing, peering at each crate for a moment. She returned to where he stood and shook her head. "Nothing that I can tell. Most of these have all been opened by either Brusus or myself. Can't tell if anyone else has been here, but nothing I see would make that likely."

"Maybe we should look outside. For a crate that size to be moved, you'd need some way of hauling it to the dock."

Jessa shook her head. "Not at night. I can see well at night, but don't want to get caught by one of the sellswords. Sight has limits."

"Everything has limits," Rsiran said.

Jessa laughed. "Some more than others."

Rsiran looked at the stacks of crates around the center of the warehouse. The time he'd come with Brusus, he'd seen a strange crate, one that they'd opened by peeling away the sides to get at the contents inside. Now he didn't see it anywhere. "Where is the crate Brusus opened?"

Jessa shook her head. "He took that away a few weeks ago. Wanted to be able to work through those cylinders on his own. And he liked the wood from the crate."

The metal used to create the cylinders was valuable. Some were made of gold or silver, enough that Brusus could likely sell them for a significant profit. But he hadn't. Considering how focused Brusus had been on money, there had to be a reason.

"How did Brusus move the crate?"

"Just a piece at a time. Not the whole thing. You're right—that would be too hard to move without getting caught. I think one encounter with a sellsword was enough for Brusus."

Had Rsiran been willing to expose his ability sooner, Brusus might not have come so close to death. But then again, had Brusus shared *his* secret, he might not have come so close, either.

"Are there any others that he has been particularly interested in?" Rsiran asked. Jessa had slipped over to stand next to him, close enough that Rsiran could smell the sharp perfume from the flower she wore. "You saw how he reacted when Lianna told him about the crate she saw on the dock, but we don't even know for sure if the crate was from here."

"Haern seemed to think it was."

Rsiran nodded. "And Brusus seemed convinced. Something has him worried, more than he's letting on."

"I don't think it's the warehouse," Jessa started. She bit her lower lip, hesitating.

Rsiran touched her hand and pulled her close, brushing her hair back behind her ear. For a moment, standing in the warehouse with her like this, he could pretend that they didn't have a care in the world. And most times, they didn't.

"You don't know him like I do, Rsiran. Brusus has been different since the attack. I think he feels that he should have been the one to deal with Josun. Or maybe he worries that he put us too close to danger." She took a deep breath. "I don't know, but I think it's more than just what's in this place."

35

"But it's a part of it," Rsiran said.

Jessa nodded. "It's who he is."

She didn't have to explain more. Neither of them spoke about Brusus's bloodlines. Neither needed to. It was not their secret to share, but both knew that he was descended from the first Elvraeth, the founders of the city. His mother had been banished from the city—Forgotten—taking the infant Brusus from the palace. Rsiran didn't know much more about Brusus's past than that, but that secret would be enough to drive anyone to obsession. He could not imagine what it must be like for Brusus to live knowing what might have been, how he could have been different, if only the Elvraeth had not banished his mother. Since Brusus did not speak openly about that time, Rsiran did not even know what she'd done to warrant banishment.

"What do you think he intends for all of this?" Rsiran asked.

"I don't know." He could tell not knowing troubled her.

Carrying the lantern out in front of him, Rsiran made his way to one of the crates. From what he could tell, most looked like they had been opened once and then closed, but he saw one that looked to have taken more of a beating. A line of nails held one of the side panels in place, the edges dimpled where they had been pounded back into place. The pale wood of the crate had splintered in a few places. No writing marked the outside.

Using one of his lorcith knives, Rsiran pried the panel back. He was not certain what he expected to see on the inside, but someone had taken the time to open this crate more than once. Likely Brusus. Rsiran felt a little uncomfortable opening this crate without him here, especially if he had something in mind for the crates. As one descended from the Elvraeth, Brusus had more right to what was stored within these crates than Rsiran.

"We should inspect other parts of the warehouse," Jessa suggested.

Rsiran nodded as he laid the panel on the floor. "Just want to look inside this one," he started.

As he did, he suddenly had a sense of lorcith flare around him.

Different from before, this was not something distant and difficult to place. This came from behind them. Close. And moving.

He grabbed Jessa and pulled her down.

She didn't argue or fight. That probably saved her life.

A knife came whistling past to sink into the wood of the crate just above where they had been standing. Lorcith made, and one of his.

Rsiran Slid back three steps, pulling Jessa with him. He didn't want to linger but needed to know who would try to hurt them. The lantern didn't cast enough light for him to see anything other than shadows near the fringes. Sliding shifted the halo of light, but he still saw nothing other than darkness.

"Can you see anything?" he whispered.

Jessa jerked her head around before shaking it. "Nothing."

She grabbed his hand and then threw the cover back over the lantern, plunging him into darkness that she didn't share. Her Sight created an advantage. Unless the other with them in the darkness was also Sighted. Which, given the fact that they were here at night, Rsiran thought likely.

He let his senses feel for lorcith. Somewhere in the darkness, he felt the sense of another knife and recognized it as his. Whoever was here had acquired his forgings. As far as he knew, Brusus had moved everything out of the city. Either he hadn't… or they had made their way back.

He sensed the knife move a few steps. Something about the way it moved felt odd. Rsiran didn't have time to contemplate for very long. He *felt* the knife come flying toward him.

Definitely Sighted then.

With a *push*, he slowed the knife as it neared and grabbed it out of the air.

Not daring to linger any longer, he *pulled* the other knife out of the crate and caught it as well. Then he Slid them away from the ware-house.

CHAPTER 5

Rsiran emerged in his smithy, his body shaking. He clutched the strange lantern in one hand, Jessa in the other. A sheet of thick grey fabric covered the lantern, looking very much like the clothes he had been forced to wear while in the mines.

He pushed the lantern away from him so that it rested on the ground near the table. He would examine how it was made later, when he had more time. With enough study, he hoped that he might be able to recreate the lantern. Now *that* would be useful, and something he would not fear having his mark attached to.

He knelt down and let the knives drop to the wooden floor. They spun for a moment, his mark on them clear. Neither looked like recent forgings, lately the knives had taken on a smoother hilt than these, but they were both definitely his work.

"Did you see who was there?" he asked as he studied the knives.

She lay back and sprawled across the floor. Rsiran lay next to her, propping his head up on his elbow as he looked down at her.

"I didn't see anything. Didn't hear anything. Had you not been there, I don't think I would have made it out."

Jessa took great pride in her ability as a sneak. That she hadn't noticed someone else in the warehouse with them bothered Rsiran. "It was the lorcith. I sensed it moving."

"Not a sellsword."

He shook his head. The sellswords were skilled with the blade, but none had gifts like those given to their people by the Great Watcher. None were Sighted.

"These are my knives, Jessa." Knowing that, and knowing that Josun had been interested in his sword, frightened him.

"Are you sure?"

He handed her one of them. Only his forgings responded to him pushing and pulling. He hadn't fully tested whether he could push lorcith forgings from other smiths the same way, but so on those he'd tried, he'd not managed to make it work for him.

Jessa looked at the knife, her finger running over his mark. "I thought Brusus shipped all your work out of the city so the Elvraeth didn't discover us."

"That's my understanding."

She looked around, studying the smithy, before her eyes finally settled on the table covered with his recent forgings. "Could someone have broken in like the last time? I mean, if Josun could do it and steal that sword blade you'd made…"

"But he could Slide." Rsiran stood, deciding to check if the sword was still where he'd hidden it. But the small space beneath the floorboard still held the sword, the jeweled hilt added by Josun making it more formal than anything that Rsiran forged had a right to be. He returned to Jessa and sat alongside her. "I think I would have noticed if something went missing."

She nodded toward the table. "With as busy as you've been, how do you know what you've made or what's been given to Brusus to move?"

Truth be told, Rsiran realized that he didn't. Most of what he kept on the table had value, but not the same type of value as the lorcith he forged. He couldn't deny that the quality of his work had improved dramatically the more he worked with lorcith. Ever since he stopped trying to ignore the way it pulled at him, instead choosing to listen.

"I guess I don't," he admitted.

"I'll keep my eyes open and see if anyone is watching the streets around the smithy," Jessa suggested.

"And if there is someone watching?"

She punched him again. "You think I don't know how to keep myself safe? What do you think I did before I met you?"

Rsiran smiled. "I don't know. How many times did you nearly die before you met me?"

"None." She laughed. "Maybe I *should* stop spending so much time with you!"

"As if you could," he said, pulling her toward him.

Jessa laughed again and let herself be drawn into him. "Brusus has been going there for months. Other than Josun, we haven't seen anyone else ever enter the warehouse. Why attack tonight?"

The same night the crate had been seen on the dock. All these months thinking that they were safe. Could it be the Elvraeth or the others in Josun's rebellion finally noticed? Could it be they finally determined who killed Josun?

Jessa squeezed his hand reassuringly, but Rsiran couldn't shake the worry or the steady gnawing in the pit of his stomach.

* * * * *

They awoke early the next morning to the sound of pounding on the door. Rsiran looked over at Jessa sleeping comfortably on the thin mattress he had tucked in the back corner of the smithy and smiled at her. He pushed the lantern behind the table, making certain it was mostly hidden, before arranging his shirt and pants. Only then did he unlock the door to peek outside.

Shael's massive form filled the doorway. The smuggler had a deeply tanned face with a wide beard. Piercing blue eyes stared at Rsiran. "Good you be here, Rsiran." He peered past Rsiran, looking over his shoulder, eyes quickly scanning everything. "You be liking the forge I find for you?"

Rsiran nodded, smiling at the massive smuggler. He had only seen Shael one time since the first time they'd met, but the wide man made quite the impression. Shael had been the one to find the forge, had helped get him set up with his shop. Had anyone other than Brusus introduced him to Shael, Rsiran might have been more nervous around him. But if Brusus trusted him, then Rsiran felt he should as well. Still, having Shael suddenly show up at his door—and he considered the smithy *his*—put him on edge, especially after what happened the night before.

"You want to see it?"

Shael glanced up the street for a moment and then nodded. "I do be curious what you did with the space," he admitted.

Rsiran moved away from the door and Shael stepped inside. Appraising eyes scanned the smithy quickly, looking to the patched roof and the swept floor. Even the brick of the chimney had been patched so that it smoked properly. Rsiran had worked a damper into it so that it diffused the smoke out several different chimneys, making it look like several small fires burned here rather than one massive one. Less likely to be noticed that way.

"Cleaned up right nice, didn't it?" Shael said. "Never made you proper. No be havin' the time. But Brusus do be keepin' the constables away?"

Rsiran nodded. "Constables have left us alone." From what Rsiran could tell, the constables had no interest in coming into this part of the city. But Rsiran made a point of not walking through the streets to reach his smithy. He didn't have to. And none of the other people living along the street ever complained about the noise from his hammering. He wondered if the constables would take it seriously if they did.

Their voices had woken Jessa, and she rubbed her eyes as she came over. She frowned when she saw Shael and shot Rsiran a questioning look.

The wide man gave her a crooked smile. "So you two do be together now? Good for you, girl. Need a solid man in your life, don' ya?"

"Do I?" she asked dangerously.

Shael raised his hands. "Jus' want you to be happy, is all I be sayin'." He laughed and glanced over at Rsiran. "Can' say I didn't see it. Now you be takin' good care of her?" he asked Rsiran.

"Why are you here, Shael?" Jessa asked. She shifted the flower tucked into her shirt that had wilted overnight. Rsiran knew that she would be finding a new one as soon as she could. Jessa didn't like going too long with a faded flower.

"Touchy girl?" He laughed and ran a beefy hand through his wild brown hair. "You do be happy?"

She glanced at Rsiran with sleepy eyes and laughed. "I do be happy, Shael."

Rsiran suddenly remembered what he had heard last night. "Haern thought you weren't in Elaeavn."

Shael snorted. "Haern don't be knowing me travels, now do he?"

He looked around and his eyes settled briefly on the long table covered with Rsiran's forgings. Jessa stood partially in front of it, blocking his view. Rsiran realized that she did it so Shael wouldn't see the lantern tucked behind the table. Considering everything he had openly on the table, it seemed strange that the lantern was the one thing they most wanted to hide. While the forgings of copper or iron wouldn't cause him any issue, the lorcith knives resting on one end of the table would get him into as much trouble as anything else were they discovered.

"I be coming to see if you got something I can use, Rsiran. Brusus do be telling me of your forgings, and I have need of something I just can't be finding elsewhere. He say to come by here, see if you do be able to help."

"What sort of something?"

A wide smile split Shael's mouth, his yellowed teeth peeking through. He reached into one of his pockets and pulled a tightly rolled sheet of parchment. "Do be needing space," he muttered.

Rsiran led him to the table and cleared a section, shifting some iron and steel work out of the way. A few bowls, a short length of chain, and a narrow candleholder, all made as a way for him to test his skill, to see if the lorcith had truly taught him or if he depended upon the metal to guide him. Each turned out far better than he had expected. He had hidden his mark on each.

Unrolling the sheet of paper, Shael had to unfold it before its size could be appreciated. Shael took one of the steel bowls and set it atop the page to hold it down. Then he smoothed the rest of it flat with his thick hand. What Rsiran saw on the parchment surprised him.

Rather than a single item, it appeared to be schematics of some kind. Each piece labeled with dimensions, the shape carefully drawn. Notations along the side had no meaning until he realized that they indicated what metals should be used. Most he recognized, but there were a few that he couldn't quite place.

"What is it?" Jessa asked over his shoulder.

"I'm… I'm not sure."

He leaned toward the drawings, trying to piece them together in his mind, but couldn't. They were schematics; everything was diagramed in an exploded view, lines and arrows indicating how it should go back together. Rsiran had seen schematics like this before in his father's shop, but had never paid much attention to them. His father wouldn't include him with this detailed of work.

"'Course it do be a device! All these parts and fixed together like that?" Shael laughed and his belly shook. He pointed a pudgy finger at the page. "Can ya doing anything with it?"

Rsiran looked up. "There have got to be dozens of smiths that would be better able to help you with this. I'm not sure I can even follow these plans."

Shael laughed. "You don't know how good you be, do ya, Rsiran? Don't know how skilled you become? Just look at this bowl." Shael lifted the bowl that was holding the page down. When he did, the paper folded up and back on itself, closing as if to hide the diagram on the inside. "Not too many smiths able to pull the metal so thin, you see? Way you be doing it almost makes it transparent. You do be creating some curves here too. Trust me, nothing like this anywhere else." He shook his head as he set the bowl back down, not bothering to open the plans back up. "No other smith has the skills I need. Not here, at least."

Jessa grabbed his hand and squeezed, holding with just a little more pressure than was necessary. "Why does it need to be here?"

Shael glanced at her. "I'm here."

Rsiran resisted the urge to turn and look at Jessa. The pressure on his hand meant that she was warning him to be careful, though he did not need her to tell him that. "I'm not sure that I can help with this, Shael. If you needed something simple…"

Shael grunted and shook his head. "Simple don't be doing me no good, now. Just look over the plans a bit. Then you be telling me whether you can do this thing." He made a point of looking down the table to where the lorcith knives lay openly.

Rsiran nodded carefully, suddenly wishing that he had been more careful with how he stored his work. The pace at which Brusus wanted product from him had made him careless about putting things away. But it was more than that. Other than Jessa and occasionally Brusus, no one came to the shop. And Rsiran simply Slid there. "I'll look it over." He forced a smile. "Will you be in town for long?"

"Long enough," Shael said, waving his hand.

"Where can I find you?"

Shael's wide mouth split, flashing teeth. "You don't need to find me, Rsiran," Shael assured him. "I do be knowing where to find you."

He looked at the table again, eyes lingering longer than needed, and then turned, weaving around a few uneven spots on the floor before reaching the door. Shael pulled it closed with a loud *thud*.

Jessa released his hand and hurried to the door, locking it quietly behind Shael. She turned to Rsiran, a worried look on her face.

"What is it?"

"Probably nothing."

It was the same thing he had said in the warehouse. "But it might be something?"

"Just… I got a strange feeling when he was asking you to make that," she said, motioning to the paper still folded on the table.

"He said Brusus sent him here."

Jessa frowned as she bit her lip and leaned toward her flower. As she inhaled, her nose crinkled slightly. "Fine. But maybe we show Haern. Learn what he might See."

"Jessa—"

46

She threw up her hands. "Fine. I'm just being paranoid. But you can't say it's not earned."

Rsiran smiled, looking to the door. Shael might not be from Elaeavn, but he knew enough people in the city to get things. He'd gotten the forge and knew about the lorcith.

"Shael is a friend," Rsiran said. Wasn't he? Shael worked with Firell, and Brusus trusted him completely, probably why Brusus sent him to Rsiran.

Rsiran glanced back down to the rolled up schematics on the table. The least he could do for Shael was study the plan and see if he could understand anything from it. But not now. First, he needed to clear his head, and to do that, he needed to work the forge.

As he picked up a lump of lorcith, he wondered what it would compel him to make this time.

CHAPTER 6

JESSA RETURNED LATE THAT AFTERNOON with a loaf of dried bread and strips of jerky. Rsiran barely heard her as she entered, only aware because, at his insistence, she carried one of his lorcith knives.

"What have you been doing?" he asked between bites of bread. Until she's brought food, he hadn't realized how hungry he'd been. Now his stomach heaved uncomfortably as he ate. Other than lukewarm water, he hadn't had anything in his stomach since the night before.

She shrugged. Sometime while she was gone she had found a new flower. It had pale blue petals with streaks of yellow down each one. She leaned toward it and sniffed slowly, her eyes fluttering closed as she did.

"Went looking for Brusus and Haern. Stopped at the market. Came back here."

Rsiran frowned. "That can't be all you've done." She had been gone for the entire morning.

She shook her head. "Told you I'd be watching."

Then he understood. She had been keeping an eye on the smithy. "You think someone would watch this place during the daytime?"

She shook her head. "No. I just wanted to get a sense of *where* they might watch from so that I can see later."

"Anything you notice?"

She sighed. "Nothing. And I couldn't find Brusus or Haern. And what have you been doing?" she asked, looking at the cool forge.

"I can't tell what this is supposed to do." Rsiran pointed toward the Shael's paper on the table. One of his knives stabbed into each corner, holding it open. Studying the plans had not helped him determine what the machine did or even how the pieces went together. As far as he could tell, the plans didn't even really tell him how to make each piece, just a general description. Most were lorcith, though. That must be the reason that Shael brought it to him.

"It looks something like your forge."

He hadn't made the connection before, but nodded. "A little. But what forge is made from this much metal? And what forge would be this small?" He shook his head and laughed. "Shael should just tell me what it does. That might make it easier for me to make."

She shrugged and took a bite of jerky. "You can ask him next time we see him."

He looked up from the table. "I've never seen plans like this, Jessa. I wasn't lying when I told Shael that I'm not certain I can even make this."

Part of the plan made sense to him. There were a few components that he understood and thought that he might be able to make. A rectangular box of iron with fittings for a few side pieces looked easy enough that he could probably make it today, except it appeared that the plans also dictated *weight*, and he saw no way of making the box that light without making it hollow. And perhaps that was the point. Copper tubing that would run along one side. Copper was relatively easy for him to work with, but more difficult to acquire. Not only copper, but some of the other metals indicated in the plans were rare enough that he would have to spend time finding them. Or stealing, but the prospect of doing that bothered him. Taking lorcith from the mines was one thing, but stealing from the master smiths felt very different to him.

"Maybe you shouldn't, then."

"Shael said Brusus told him to come to me, only…" He sighed. He might have learned how to work with metal from the lorcith, but there was much about being a smith he still didn't understand. He folded the plans back up and reached behind the table for the covered lantern before turning to Jessa. "I need a change of scenery. Come with me?"

"Where?"

He held out his hand. Jessa narrowed her eyes but stepped over to him and grabbed his hand. Rsiran Slid.

He emerged in the warehouse. Light streamed through the glass overhead, giving it a filtered sort of light. The air smelled dusty and mixed with the ever-present scent of the sea this close to the water, that of salt and old fish. Rsiran felt for the sense of lorcith but did not feel anything unusual.

Jessa tensed immediately. "This isn't a good idea, Rsiran. We don't know what happened last night or who was here. What if they're not gone?" She stepped away from the door and scanned the warehouse, looking for anything unusual.

At least in this light, Rsiran's eyesight was not as poor as it had been at night. He touched the pocket of his pants, feeling the reassuring weight of the lorcith-forged knives he'd made today. They were different from some of the other knives he'd made. Smaller and easier to hide. He felt the connection to them and knew he could push them if needed. At least he would not be caught unprepared. Not like last night.

"I want to know who was here last night. I need to know if it's someone who knows what I did to Josun."

After spending part of the morning hammering, his mind had cleared enough to realize that he needed to know who attacked him last night. Without knowing, he would simply feel scared, nervous. All the time he'd spent fearing his father to finally emerge from it safely, he would not let some unseen person make him feel the same again.

"But whoever was here had your knives. They attacked us."

"I don't feel any sense of lorcith today. I think that we're okay. Besides, it's daylight outside. No one is foolish enough to break into the Elvraeth warehouse in the daytime."

"We are."

He took her hand and started between the rows of crates. "But we didn't really break in, did we?"

Jessa laughed, the sound low in her throat. They reached the clearing of crates in the center. Rsiran still didn't have the sense of lorcith, not even distantly as he had last night. He hoped that meant they were alone.

"Do you see anything?" he asked.

Jessa scanned the warehouse and then shook her head.

Had Brusus or Haern been with them, they would be better able to know if they were alone. Brusus could simply search for anyone to Read while Haern, as a Seer, would give them a different advantage.

Trusting that no one else was in the warehouse, Rsiran pulled the cloth off the lantern. Blue light spilled out, adding to the dirty, natural light coming through the skylight. As it did, Rsiran looked at the crates again, carrying the lantern in front of him. Jessa walked alongside, holding onto his hand. Rsiran felt thankful that she did; at least this way, if they encountered someone else in the warehouse he could Slide them to safety.

He guided them past the central area. From what he could tell, nothing seemed off with those crates. And he remembered the distant sense of lorcith from the night before, trying to track where he had sensed it. They wound between stacks of crates, these not nearly as old as those in the center, the writing still in a language he couldn't read, but faded rather than gone.

Jessa pulled him to a stop as they reached an intersection of crates. "Look here," she whispered. She pointed at one of the crates, biting her lip as she did.

Rsiran held the lantern out so that he could more easily see what she tried to show him. The crate looked no different from any other. It took him a moment to see what Jessa saw.

The crate reminded him of the one he had seen last night, where the wood had been pounded in from nails being replaced. He saw splintering around one of the side panels and pulled on the edge. It pried away with a soft squeal.

He set the panel on the floor and held the lantern up so that he could see inside, not knowing what to expect. The glint of light reflecting off metal sent his heart fluttering momentarily, until he realized that it was nothing more than pale green vases, the flowing lines clearly of grindl. Rsiran could use the metal, melt it down and reshape it, but the vases as they were shaped were probably just as valuable as anything he could make. Other than that, all he saw were a few rolls of cloth.

Still, he didn't understand why someone would have taken the time to open and reseal the crate. Nothing inside was valuable enough.

"I don't understand," he said, turning to Jessa still holding the lantern in front of him.

She pushed it down and away from her face. "Should I be surprised?"

"Take a look for yourself." He moved so that she could make her way to the crate.

She looked inside and pulled out one of the vases, twisting it in her hands. "This isn't valuable?"

"Not that it isn't valuable," he said. "But so much of what we've found here is *more* valuable. These are pretty enough, but I expected… something different."

"Because it's been opened a few times?"

He nodded. Rsiran had come here hoping for something of an answer, an explanation about who might have attacked them last night, or at least some evidence of what their attackers had wanted. But he didn't see anything that looked unusual.

Starting down the line of crates, he wandered away from their usual path. Each time he had been in the warehouse before, he had come to the main door—or Slid to it—and made his way to the center of the warehouse where the oldest, and presumably more interesting, crates were stored. He hadn't wandered farther through the warehouse.

"Where are you going?" Jessa asked.

"Just curious. I haven't been toward this end of the building before. The crates near the door keep us from it. Have you?"

Jessa frowned and shook her head. She followed alongside him, keeping a soft hand on his arm. "Never really had the need. I'm sure Brusus has explored the entire building. Think he practically owns the place."

Rsiran laughed softly. "In a way, he does. But you're right. I'm sure Brusus has explored the entire building." Only the warehouse was massive, and the crates created a maze that seemed to guide them toward the center, as if determined to keep them from making their way anywhere else in the warehouse.

They followed the crates until it turned again. Through the narrow alley of crates, he saw the vague dark outline of the far wall. A stack of crates rose nearly to the ceiling here, forming a secondary wall on one side. On the other side of the walkway, the crates stacked only two or three high.

Rsiran stopped. Swinging the lantern from side to side, he looked for an opening in the wall of crates but didn't see one. "Do you see any way to get through there?" he asked Jessa.

"Through where?"

He motioned at the crates. "To the other side. This path leads straight to the wall and then stops. But there has to be something on the other side. With these crates stack so high, I can't tell and don't think we can climb over."

Jessa released his arm and made her way down the line of crates until she reached the far wall. Then she retraced her steps back. "Not that I see. No spacing. They're just shoved too close together."

"That seems strange," Rsiran said.

Jessa studied the crates for a moment and then nodded. "None of the others have been pushed this close together. Just these. Almost like they were meant to keep us out."

"But not me," he said.

"Are you sure that's safe? You don't know what's on the other side. It could be nothing—just open space like at the center of the warehouse, or it could be more crates like these. You've told me that if you Slide and don't know where you'll end up, there's the risk that you could get trapped."

Rsiran nodded. That was one of the risks of Sliding. If he didn't have room to move, to take some sort of step forward, the Slide would trap him in place. "What's the worst that could happen? That I get stuck in one of the crates? I could hammer my way out if I needed to. But what if there's something hidden on the other side that we're not meant to see? What if the person who attacked us last night is over there?"

"How would they have gotten there, Rsiran?"

"There must be another way in," he suggested. A part of him wondered, though. What if the other side of the stack of crates could *only* be accessed by Sliding?

For a moment, Rsiran considered simply Sliding anyway. But he didn't want to risk Jessa not knowing what happened to him. And if he were to get stuck, there was nothing she would be able to do to help him. He didn't dare Slide with her and risk her too.

"All right," he agreed.

They started back toward the center of the warehouse. Jessa dropped her hand on his arm, holding him lightly. He sensed the tension beneath her fingers and knew that she guessed what he had been thinking. She would hold onto him just to make certain he didn't do anything she would consider stupid.

As they neared the intersection where he had opened the crate and found the vases, he felt something touch his senses.

Lorcith.

Rsiran froze. The sense hadn't been there before, but now he sensed it easily. Grabbing onto Jessa's hand, he made certain that she didn't move. He listened for the lorcith, realizing that it was another knife he'd forged. And close by, likely near the center of the warehouse.

How had he missed it before now?

Without waiting for another attack, Rsiran Slid away from the warehouse, pulling Jessa with him and back to the smithy.

CHAPTER 7

R SIRAN LINGERED IN THE SMITHY long enough to collect more
of his lorcith-forged knives. Had he a way to conceal it, he
would have taken the sword with him too. Suddenly, he didn't feel entirely comfortable leaving it in the smithy.

"What was that, Rsiran?" Jessa watched him for a moment, and
then hurried to the table to help. The few knives that he couldn't grab,
she stuffed into pockets in her pants. She started reaching for the other
items made of lorcith, a bowl and the hook, but he shook his head.
"Not those. Just the knives for now."

"Why?"

How to tell her what he feared? That there was someone else in the
warehouse who could Slide. And had his knives.

"My knives are returning to the city," he told her.

"You felt another one, didn't you?"

He nodded. "Just before I Slid us out of there."

"Where was it?"

"Close."

"Close? Like someone snuck up on us?"

Someone sneaking up on them would make him feel better, but he didn't think so. Even distracted, the sudden sense of lorcith had been hard for him to miss. One moment it hadn't been there and the next…

"Josun isn't the only one who can Slide," Rsiran said. "I mean, he even said that the Elvraeth tried to push down the ability, make it so that others wouldn't have it. But that means that others *do* have it." He looked over at her, meeting eyes that flared bright green. "I can't be the only one, Jessa. And with what he was after… whatever his rebellion aimed to accomplish…"

"It doesn't make sense! How would anyone else even learn about the warehouse?"

"Unless they're Elvraeth." Which made their presence in the ware-house—and with his knives—even worse.

"We need to talk to Haern. Maybe he has Seen something."

"Haern won't have Seen anything," Rsiran said. "For the same reason he can't see around me, at least not clearly. Something about the ability to Slide masks me from him."

Jessa frowned. "Brusus might know something. As connected as he is, he's bound to know if there's another Elvraeth who can Slide. And he can listen for word on what Josun might have been up to. He's connected, Rsiran."

"But if he doesn't know? Or can't learn? Then what?"

It was times like these that Rsiran simply wanted to turn to the forge, work over a piece of metal, just listen to the lorcith calling to him as he hammered away, turning a plain lump of lorcith into something else. But with this, he couldn't. He didn't dare let himself relax. If there was someone else in the city who could Slide…

"You couldn't find Brusus earlier?" he asked.

"I told you that. Not sure what he's up to, but I'm guessing it has to do with that crate that Firell saw on the docks last night. Nothing gets Brusus fired up more than thinking someone is interrupting his plans. You know how upset he was when he got hurt and couldn't do what Josun wanted."

"I think Brusus did exactly what Josun wanted of him."

"You know what I mean."

Josun had used Brusus to get to Rsiran. Unlike others living in Elaeavn, as one of the Elvraeth, Josun had pieces of all abilities. Rsiran remembered feeling Josun rifling through his thoughts, Reading him in a way that few others had ever managed. But it was the Sliding that Rsiran remembered the most. The easy way he moved, practically skipping with each step. Rsiran had never seen someone Slide so openly, though the way Josun used it, few would even recognize what he did.

But Brusus hated the fact that Josun had used him, and that the others were pulled into his plan because of Brusus. Rsiran suspected Brusus would do anything to keep that from happening again, even if it meant hiding something from them.

And then there was the matter of what Shael wanted him to make. What would the smuggler do if Rsiran simply *couldn't* make it?

First, they had to find Brusus. "I don't think we can wait until tonight to find him," he said. Most nights, he expected Brusus to show up at the Barth for dicing and eating.

"There are a few places I haven't checked. Maybe I do that—"

"Not alone. I'm going to come with you."

The knives tucked into his pocket pulled on his senses. He was aware of the others that Jessa had and felt reassured by them, knowing that as long as she carried them, he could find her.

The thought reminded him of something that he had been meaning to do but never got around to. Jessa had started toward the door. "There's something else," Rsiran said.

He rummaged around on the long table until he found what he wanted. Buried under a few bits of iron—a run of chain, a misshapen candleholder from one of his early attempts, a few heavy pots that he thought he might use for cooking but never had—was the small decorative piece of lorcith. The lump of metal from which he had forged it had been small, but he remembered how it had pulled on him with a seductive song until he shaped it into this spiraling pattern that reminded him of so many of the flowers that Jessa wore.

Grabbing a length of twine, he slipped the shaped lorcith onto it and reached around Jessa to place it around her neck. She watched him with a bemused expression at first. After he had tied it, she cupped her hand around the lorcith and pulled it out so that she could look at it.

For a moment, her eyes flared a bright green. "You made this?" she asked in a whisper.

He nodded. After he had made it, he had worried whether she would like it. Lorcith, even folded as this was so that the metal seemed to flow, was a dull black or grey. Nothing like the vibrant colors Jessa preferred to wear. "After I made it, I thought of you. I'll make a better necklace for it when I can…" Already he started thinking of what he would need to make the chain. A smaller hammer for delicate work, a smaller tong to hold the metal, and ideally, silver or gold, though for some reason, he could already envision how he could turn a certain nugget of lorcith into what he wanted.

She smiled. "It's perfect as it is." Jessa didn't look away from it, her bright green eyes telling Rsiran that she used her Sight as she studied it. "It almost looks like several colors come together. The detail is amazing." She looked over at him and frowned. "Can you even see the detail that you put into it?"

"Not like you, but I can *feel* it. I don't think I could have made that out of anything other than lorcith." He hesitated, fearing to ask the next question. "Do you like it?"

In answer, she leaned toward him and kissed him.

She took his hand and led him to the door. "We should walk. Might need you to Slide us later, and you'll want to save your strength."

In the alley outside the smithy, Jessa made certain to lock the door carefully. "Maybe I should just take back my key," he said.

She grinned. "I don't really need it.

"Me, neither."

"Still can't see in the dark."

"You still have to walk," he said as he took her hand.

"Not all the time," she said, pulling him down the alley.

They passed a few puddles of stagnant water. The air in the alley felt still and dank, stinking of rot in a way the rest of the city never managed. Buildings pressed closely together, most with crumbling stone faces and doors boarded over. Having the forge in such a location provided the benefit that he would be less likely to be discovered. Part of him worried about what would happen were someone from this alley to learn of the smithy and decide to see what sort of reward the constables would offer.

Near the end of the street, there came the whine of a distant cat. Rsiran hesitated, knowing that he was being superstitious, until he heard another. Only then did he relax.

Jessa glanced over at him. "You worry too much."

She pulled him onto a wider street. A few carters made their way along here, some coming down from Upper Town by their dress, but not as many people filled the street as they would find earlier in the day, after ships returned with the day's catch.

"You don't worry?" he asked.

Rsiran looked over and saw her holding one hand over the lor-cith charm. Somewhere along the line, she had grabbed a flower and tucked it inside the twisting shape. She sniffed at it softly, a distant look to her eyes.

"Worrying hasn't ever changed anything for me."

They made their way toward the docks. Rsiran let Jessa lead him, mindful of the twists she took as they went. He still didn't know the city—especially this part of Lower Town—as well as she did. And since he Slid most places, he hadn't really needed to know the streets that well.

As the road sloped downward, he caught sight of someone and paused almost imperceptibly. The face looked familiar, the set of the jaw so much like his sister Alyse, but she would not be down in Lower Town, and certainly not carrying a loaded basket of fish.

The woman disappeared as they turned a corner. Jessa caught him looking backward and punched him on the shoulder. "Don't think I didn't see that," she said, swatting at his arm.

When they nearly reached the shore road that ran along the bay, Rsiran saw Shael ambling toward the docks. His wide back was hard to miss, but his brightly colored shirt and pants would have stood out, regardless.

Rsiran pulled Jessa toward the line of buildings along the street. "Just saw Shael."

"You sure?"

"Who else wears such bright clothing?" It was the deep red shirt that drew Rsiran's attention. "Where do you think he's going?"

"Probably same as us."

"And where are we going?"

She tilted her head toward the water. "I wanted to check with Firell. Something about that crate last night still bothers me."

"He'll be on his ship. You won't be able to get there."

A smile played across her lips. "You sure about that?"

"You want me to Slide us onto the ship?"

He wasn't certain whether he could even do it. Usually Sliding required him to know where he was going, either by seeing it or having been there before. Trying to do it another way risked him missing his target. And if he missed the ship... they would end up in the water. Rsiran didn't know whether he could Slide them back.

"You don't think you can?" Jessa seemed surprised.

"I've never tried it," he admitted. "If I had better Sight, I might feel more comfortable trying it. At least then I could see my target. But what if I miss or overshoot?" At least there wasn't the same risk of ending up stuck in walls of rock like he'd had when Sliding in Ilphaesn or of ending up stuck in a crate as he would have had attempting to Slide in the warehouse.

As they neared the docks, Jessa pulled something out of her pocket and handed it to him. An amused smile crossed her face, pulling at the corners of her mouth.

"What is this?" What she handed him was made of a silvery metal, but not steel. Long and cylindrical, it felt cool and lighter than he would have expected. It reminded him of the cylinders he had seen when Brusus first took him to the warehouse, but didn't seem as long as those. One end tapered more than the other. "Is this..."

She shrugged. "Just a part. Look through it."

"Does Brusus know?"

They stood on the rocky shoreline, away from the docks but near enough that they could see them. Water splashed up around them, sending soft splatters of cool water onto their arms. Rsiran remembered the first time he'd come to the shore with Jessa, thinking how different things were now.

A half dozen ships were moored out on the water. A few smaller boats ferried people to and from the larger ships. At the dock, a single-masted ship slowly made its way toward the shore. Flat bottomed, from what Firell had said, and clearly from Elaeavn.

"Does he have to know everything?" Jessa said.

Rsiran laughed. "I know how he'd answer that."

"Just look," Jessa urged.

He held the cylinder up and turned it, realizing that a piece of glass capped each end. A spyglass, though he'd never seen one like this before. Rsiran smiled and place the narrow end up to his face and looked through.

Waves cresting on the bay suddenly jumped into view. Rsiran's smile deepened. The clarity surprised him. The only other spyglasses he'd used were blurry, with impurities tainting the glass. This was as if everything were simply magnified. He turned so that he could look through the spyglass at the other ships. Most of the ships in the bay sailed from Elaeavn, though a few came from other port cities like Asador and Thyr.

Without the advantage of Sight, he had never been able to really see the exotic ships up close. Elaeavn sailors stayed mostly in the bay where fish were plentiful, but the interesting ships were the ones that couldn't reach the docks. On one, a triple-masted boat with a sharp prow shaped like a massive bird, several men walked on the deck. Most had thick beards, and they worked the lines with experienced hands. Another ship had wide square sails, but Rsiran didn't see anyone on the deck. He turned with the spyglass and finally found Firell's ship.

Rsiran had never really seen it. The wood of the ship was painted a dark green. The prow had been carved into the shape of a woman, long hair flowing down her shoulders, before her waist melded into the rest of the ship. Thick lines ran from the two massive masts. White sails were rolled and stored. A long anchor chain hung off the side, disappearing into the water.

"I don't see him on the ship."

Rsiran lowered the spyglass and looked at Jessa. She stared out over the water, eyes flaring a deeper green. "Agreed. I don't see him, either."

"Is that what it's like for you all the time?"

She smiled. "Like I said… you're just a babe."

He laughed and searched the road for Shael, but the wide man had disappeared. There were dozens of shops along the shore he could have slipped into. Part of Rsiran wished he would have followed him just to see what Shael was up to, but there was no reason to worry about who Shael was talking to.

"Can you get us to the ship?"

"But Firell isn't there."

She shrugged.

"What is it you're not telling me?"

"Can you get us there or not?" Jessa asked.

Rsiran raised the spyglass and looked out to the ship and picked an open section on the deck. Fixing it in his mind, he grabbed her, and before he thought about it too much, Slid across the open water and onto the ship.

CHAPTER 8

THEY EMERGED STANDING ON THE DECK of the ship. Rsiran staggered, but didn't know if it was the effort of the Slide or the slowly rolling ship that sent him stumbling. Jessa clung to his hand. Her other hand gripped the lorcith charm he'd given her.

Jessa's face had turned pale white. "Okay. So maybe this wasn't the best idea I've had."

"You've never been on a ship?"

"And you have?"

Rsiran shook his head. "My first time."

Jessa swallowed again. She looked out over the water and started frowning. "Come on. Let's make sure Firell isn't here before we go snooping around too much."

The ship rocked slowly underfoot, rolling in a way that made Rsiran uncomfortable. With the deck empty, it felt like they were the only ones aboard. He had met others who sailed with Firell, but he hadn't seen Tagus or Jesin in over a month.

Lines were coiled neatly along the deck rails. Hooks and oars stored in open lockers, as well as other tools that he had no name for. Near the far end of the deck, stairs led below deck. Jessa started toward them.

"Will he be upset if he learns we're here?" Rsiran asked as they neared the stairs. He didn't know Firell nearly as well as Brusus did, though Rsiran had the sense that they had known each other a long time. But he knew how he would feel if someone suddenly appeared in his smithy without asking for permission first. It felt like a violation of privacy, of trust.

"Don't know."

She didn't give more of an answer as she started into the dark stairwell. The wide stairs creaked as they stepped down them. The air smelled different here than it did along the shore, cleaner, less of the stink of fish. Of course, he wouldn't smell fish on Firell's ship; he claimed to be a trader but specialized in contraband, forbidden items that he had to sneak past the Elvraeth inspectors.

At the bottom of the stairs, a narrow hall opened before them. Two doors were closed on one side of the hall. Midway down on the other side was a single door. Also closed. Jessa studied all three doors for a moment before trying the single door. When she found it locked, she unrolled her pick set and quickly opened it.

"And this is where Firell gets mad if he learns what we've done," Rsiran said.

Jessa smiled and pushed the door open. "Good thing he doesn't know that you can Slide."

The door opened into the hold. It was mostly dark, but the light from the hall streamed in letting Rsiran see rows of boxes, similar enough to the crates from the warehouse. Unlike those in the warehouse, these were small enough that they could be easily loaded onto the ship. Rsiran wished for the lantern so he could see.

"Close it," Jessa whispered.

Rsiran closed the door and was plunged into darkness.

For once, he'd like to sneak someplace with Jessa where he had the advantage, but here in the dark, unable to see anything, he felt as helpless as the babe she always teased him of being. He heard her moving in the darkness, heard a soft rustling and the quiet squeal of nails pried free from a box, and then nothing.

Just like the night before when they had been in the warehouse, the darkness raised his awareness of the lorcith. He sensed the knives in his pockets and those that Jessa carried. He felt the soft sense of the charm he'd given her. And something else.

"Jessa," he whispered.

He felt her coming toward him as an awareness of the lorcith.

"I know."

"There are some of my forgings here."

"I know."

Rsiran tried to remember when Brusus had last shipped a collection of his lorcith from the city. Had it been a few weeks? He sensed more than just bowls and decorative pieces. Knives were here as well. Each pulled on his senses in such a way that he could tell where they were in the hold.

But something else felt strange. Not just forged lorcith was here.

Rsiran listened, heard the soft call of the metal, different from the sense he had once he had shaped it. This reminded him of the mines, of the way the lorcith demanded he pull it from the rock surrounding it. There was not an insignificant quantity here.

Jessa moved away from him. In spite of the darkness, he felt the lorcith she carried with her and knew where she was. He heard her open another crate and then sucked in a soft breath. "Firell isn't supposed to have this," she muttered.

Rsiran wasn't certain she spoke to him.

He stepped forward, drawn by the lump lorcith. He felt the crate that stored it, ran his hands overtop the surface, wondering what it meant that Firell would have so much. Was this what Brusus planned? Was this some way of increasing his production?

But where would Firell have gotten so much?

Jessa moved along the wall, opening crate after crate. Rsiran wondered if she sealed them after she inspected their contents but didn't ask. Moving undetected in the darkness was her area of expertise, and he knew better than to challenge her. That he could sense her in the darkness comforted him. At least he didn't feel completely blind.

As she worked to open a crate near the door, a *clump* sounded above him.

Footsteps. Someone had returned.

Jessa rustled through another crate and then hurried over to him, taking his hand.

"We should go," he whispered.

"Not yet. Need to see if anyone is with Firell."

"Does it matter?"

"Yes."

He wondered why but didn't argue. He doubted it would do any good anyway.

Jessa pulled the door open silently and crept out the door and into the hall. He clung tightly to her hand. If he let go, their chance to easily Slide to safety disappeared.

She moved carefully up the stairs. Rsiran heard voices on the deck, but the wind carried the sound away so that he couldn't tell who spoke. He squeezed Jessa's hand, reassured by her calm movement. His heart fluttered nervously about being caught on the ship. Firell might be their friend, but what they were doing now—creeping around his ship without his permission—did not feel quite right.

Near the top of the stairs, Jessa froze, partly peering out of the darkness. Rsiran stood behind her, hand around her waist, ready to Slide if needed.

"You do be sure he don't know?"

Rsiran recognized Shael's voice and frowned.

"I do be sure," Firell answered.

"When can you be gettin' to there?"

"A week. Maybe longer, depending on the seas. No worries."

Shael laughed. "You know it be my nature to worry. How you be thinking I last so long in your city?"

"Are the right people in place to make this worth the risk?"

"The people be in place. They do be ready."

"Good."

Footsteps sounded closer. Strangely, Rsiran thought he sensed lorcith on the deck of the ship, not just in the hold below. But that would mean another crate of lorcith, one he hadn't seen or felt before. That would mean they were bringing lorcith *onto* the ship.

"And the other?"

"I do be workin' on that, too, as he asked."

Firell laughed. He sounded closer.

A few more steps and he would reach the stairs.

"You're careful, I'll give you that. Help me carry this to the hold."

They stepped closer, each step seeming to thunder across the deck of the ship.

Without waiting for them to near, Rsiran held onto Jessa and Slid.

CHAPTER 9

Night had come in full as Rsiran walked the streets of Lower Town. He hated that Jessa was not with him, but understood when she told him that she had to check on a few things that were easier for her to do herself. Rsiran understood the message. While he could Slide, she could sneak. Sometimes that was a more useful skill.

He walked along the road that fronted the bay. Waves splashed onto the rocky shore, the sound soothing him. No streetlamps lit the road here, but the nearly full moon provided enough light for him to see, bouncing off the water. The air tasted strange, almost bitter like lorcith, but he suspected that was more from the nausea rolling through him than anything real.

Lorcith pulled on him as a distant sort of sense, and he took the opportunity to listen for it. There was the charm he'd given Jessa. He felt the sword he'd made, hiding in his smithy. There was the soft sense of knives he'd forged, some on him, others with Jessa or Brusus, a few now scattered about Lower Town, hidden to serve as anchors, if he needed them during a Slide. A few reached out to him from over the water on Firell's ship. Now that he knew of them, he recognized what he sensed. Over it all, came the gentle pull of the unshaped lorcith sitting in Firell's hold.

Everything suddenly felt twisted to him. Firell had a cargo hold full of his forgings, but what was odder to him were the crates of unshaped lorcith. At first, he had thought Brusus had found a different supply of the metal so that he didn't have to risk himself in Ilphaesn, but if Firell had crates coming in from Elaeavn, that didn't seem likely. Especially if Firell planned on sailing for a week. But where would his supply come from?

Rsiran knew of two sources. Either mined directly from Ilphaesn— and if that were the case, he would not expect it to come through the city—or taken from the guild. And that was a riskier possibility.

He knew from his time in the mines that supplies of lorcith had dwindled. He'd also learned that someone controlled the supply, probably tied to the thin man from the mines. He didn't know why, and had not cared. Once he had left his father and his smithy, his ties to the guild were cut, along with his information source.

But something his father had said the last time he had found him in his shop replayed in his mind now. He had thought Rsiran had stolen some lorcith. Rsiran *had* stolen from his father; he had turned into the thief his father had suspected he would become when he learned of his dark ability. But Rsiran had taken tools rather than ore.

So—who stole the lorcith?

So many questions, but he was no closer to any answers.

Without really thinking about what he was doing, he Slid, emerging on the street outside his father's shop.

The street was empty. Lanterns staggered more regularly here, throwing a soft glow over the street and making it feel safer and warmer than any street in Lower Town. The air changed here, as well, smelling less like the sea and the daily catch and more of smoke and bread and all the work done here. In days past, those smells reassured him. Now, they just put him on edge.

Since escaping from the Floating Palace, Rsiran had spent all of his time in Lower Town. Since most of the guild shops were on the fringes of Upper Town, he hadn't even been near his father's shop. Standing in front of it felt strange after all this time away. It had once been a place of comfort. Even though his father had never let him do anything more than clean, occasionally act as striker, Rsiran had spent so many days here that it had been home. Now it felt like someone else's home.

The sign hanging in front of the shop, Neran Lareth, Master Smith, seemed faded. Had the lettering always seemed so small, or had his time away given him a different view? Rsiran tried peering through the windows, but couldn't see anything. He stepped up to the door and twisted the handle. Of course it would be locked.

He *should* return to Lower Town. That was his home now. But he couldn't. Now that he was here, he felt compelled to see the inside of the shop. The last time he had been here, his father had promised to report him to the constables. Rsiran wondered if he had ever done what he promised. Not that he would ever learn. So long as order was maintained, the constables didn't care what happened in Lower Town.

Closing his eyes, he Slid inside.

The smell of the smithy welcomed him, that of lorcith and hot metal and work, but the scents were faded and subdued, like a memory. As he opened his eyes, he realized that nothing looked as it should. Sunlight streamed through the windows, allowing him to easily see the interior. Walls once cluttered with tools and forgings now were empty. The long bench where his father had done much of his finer work had fallen away from the wall, two legs bent and broken. Bins that should have been full of iron and steel and lorcith stood empty. Even the forge looked as if it hadn't been used in weeks or longer.

Deserted.

Rsiran's heart thudded. What would make his father abandon the shop that had been in their family practically since the founding of Elaeavn? In his youth, Rsiran had assumed he would inherit the smithy, take over for his father as had been done for generations. That was before. But even after everything that had happened, seeing this made him ache deep inside.

He walked toward the back room where his father's office had been. It had always been locked, off limits to Rsiran, and as he passed through the doorway, he still felt a pang of guilt that he shouldn't be here.

The office was small, a dozen paces wide, perhaps as many long. An empty desk butted against the wall. A few sheets of paper rested on the desk, but nothing else. Where had the wall of journeymen projects gone? Where were the stacks of orders? The bottles of ale his father kept hidden?

Nothing remained. It was almost like the smithy Shael had found for him.

Rsiran looked at the papers on the desk, shuffling them together, and then tucked them into his pocket. His father might have banished him, but somehow, it was his father who ended up getting banished.

He stepped out of the office and looked around. When he had come the last time, taking grinding stones to use on the knives he made, he had not expected to ever come here again. But he never thought his father would no longer be here for him to find. That he wasn't here left him feeling emptier than it should. After everything his father put him through, sending him to the mines, demanding that he ignore the gift the Great Watcher gave him, Rsiran still struggled to hate him.

But questions still remained. What happened to the lorcith? Did his father's shop closing have anything to do with the dwindling supply? Or was it something simpler—just the matter of the ale finally catching up to the quality of his work. Even when Rsiran had still been with him, the quality had begun to suffer. The last time he'd seen his father, he'd been drunk.

He should find Jessa before he did anything foolish. What he'd done already—coming back to his father's shop—would anger her. But he didn't want to risk her. Not after what he'd experienced in the warehouse. Had he not been with her, one of those knives would surely have struck home, would surely have ended her.

And he needed answers. First, the strangeness with the warehouse, and then Firell's ship. And Shael? Where did he fit in? He wanted some device forged, but Rsiran didn't even know what he was making. Now, he learned his father's shop had been abandoned. Too much happened all at once. It could be nothing more than a coincidence, but he couldn't shake the feeling that everything was somehow connected, if only he could learn how.

There was one place he had avoided since the attack on the palace. One place where he feared going, until now. But answers were needed, and at least some of what was happening around him was connected to lorcith. Especially with what he'd found on Firell's ship.

That meant the mines.

Was he really ready to return? Could he dare not return?

But not without Jessa. Rsiran didn't want to risk her anger. More than that, she could help. Her Sight would make anything he needed to do that much easier.

Without thinking about it any longer, Rsiran Slid away from his father's shop.

* * * * *

He found her waiting for him in the smithy. She sat quietly hunkered near the table, slowly twisting something on the blue lantern. The light flickered on and off.

She looked up as he returned. "Where have you been?"

"Waiting."

Her mouth tightened, the frown that formed so familiar. "You need to be careful at night, Rsiran. After what happened…"

"I seem to remember that I saved you this time. And the last."

Had she been closer, she would have punched him. Instead, she tossed a small steel spoon he'd made at him. Rsiran ducked. Too bad his power over the lorcith didn't extend to other metals; then he could have simply slowed it enough to catch.

"So?" She flicked the lantern again, plunging the smithy into darkness.

Rsiran felt the pull of the lorcith on her. The knives. The charm. And was reassured. "I… I visited my father's shop." The sense of lorcith told him that she moved.

The light flicked on. She stood two paces from him. "Why would you do that? Didn't he say he planned to report you to the constables?"

"That's what he said. But he hasn't."

"You don't know that."

Rsiran shook his head. "No. I don't know that. But wouldn't Brusus or Haern have heard *something* if the constabulary sought someone who could Slide?"

"Not if the Elvraeth want to keep that secret. How many even know of your ability? Della did. But I'd never heard of it before meeting you."

Rsiran hadn't really pieced that together before. How had his *father* known about Sliding if it was so uncommon? "It was empty."

75

Jessa shrugged. "Well. It's late. Did you expect him to keep your hours?"

"Not like that. He's gone. All of his tools were gone. The forge looked like it hadn't been used in weeks. Only a few papers on his desk remained." Rsiran pulled the papers from his pocket and looked down at them. Numbers ran across the page. He'd seen notations like that before; his father's bookkeeping records. But with everything else gone, why had these been left behind?

"Do you care?" The light flickered out.

From the lorcith, he knew she slipped closer to him. But he didn't need to feel the lorcith to know that. He smelled the flower tucked into the charm that mixed with the clean scent of her sweat.

When he didn't answer quickly enough, the light flickered back on. She pressed against him.

"He's my father."

"After everything he did to you?"

How to explain to Jessa what he felt? "Without him, would I have met the others? Would I have met you?"

Her eyes darkened. "Without him, would you have nearly died twice?"

Rsiran swallowed. They were hazy memories, either blocked or remembered through the fog of his injuries. "You're right. I… I just wanted to see the shop, to see what happened to him…"

"And now that you do?"

Something in her tone made him pause. "You knew," he realized.

She watched him and then nodded slowly. "I knew. After what happened in the palace, and what you told me, I've been keeping watch. I didn't want any sort of surprise."

"Then what happened?"

She shook her head. "I didn't see. One week he and his journey-man were working as usual, the next the smithy had been cleared out."

When Rsiran frowned, she continued. "I didn't watch every day, Rsiran. Just enough to keep tabs for you. I wasn't sure you were going to go back, but I was afraid that you might."

"Why were you afraid?"

Jessa set the lantern on the floor next to him. "After what he did to you? After how he hurt you?" She shook her head. "You're still not healed from that. Not really. Your injuries might have healed, but inside?" She took his hand and hugged his arm. "I didn't want him to do anything else that might hurt you. You saved me from the palace, and I'm not going to let *them* hurt you again."

The passion in her voice made him smile. Rsiran tucked the pages of numbers back into his pocket, remembering why he'd come back to the smithy. Not just for Jessa, though that was part of it, but because he needed her.

"There's someplace I think we need to go."

"The Barth? I already know Brusus will be late. He had another engagement."

Rsiran frowned. "What kind of engagement?"

With one hand, she touched his cheek. "The kind he wouldn't want me talking about."

Rsiran didn't push. When Jessa became coy like that, he knew it wouldn't help anyway. "Not the Barth. I started thinking about what happened in the warehouse and what we found on Firell's ship. It reminded me of how lorcith seemed to be missing from the mines, lorcith I *know* still lives within the walls. It's just that miners don't take it. And now, with the supply of lorcith so low in the city, Firell suddenly has a massive collection?"

Jessa stepped away from him. Her eyes flashed a deep green as they narrowed. "I don't think it's a good idea."

"What?"

"Don't think I don't know what you intend, Rsiran Lareth. You want to Slide to the mountain. After what we've already seen…"

"That's just the problem. You've seen. I've only felt. And I can't get past the idea that the mines are part of whatever is happening."

"Rsiran…" She didn't finish. Jessa just studied his face, her eyes Seeing enough to practically Read him. Then she sighed. "Not without me. And not without your knives."

Rsiran patted his pocket. "I have three. And you have two."

"How did you…? You can feel it that well?"

He nodded. "If I made it, I can. Otherwise, it's less sensitive. But I can still feel it. It's stronger the more I focus on it." All around him, he felt the sense of his lorcith forgings pulling on him, the sword most strongly. For whatever reason, that always pulled on him. He could only guess that either his forging of the sword or the fact that he'd used it as an anchor when he infiltrated the palace and rescued it from Josun had connected him to it more strongly than to anything else he'd made.

Jessa squeezed his hand. "So… maybe not a complete babe in the dark."

Rsiran laughed and then stepped into the Slide.

CHAPTER 10

RSIRAN AND JESSA EMERGED ON THE ROCKY BLUFF outside Il-phaesn Mountain. Wind blew around them, cooler and with a hint of damp rain, so different from Elaeavn, even though they were only a few days' ride from the city. The moon hovered behind a few clouds, but enough light filtered through to let him see. Nothing like the utter blackness he'd experience in the mines. At least he'd have Jessa with him.

And the lorcith. Always the lorcith.

Dark bars blocked the entrance to the mines. There had been a time he'd let those bars keep him barricaded inside. But there's also been a time he'd feared using his ability. Now... now he believed that he had a gift. If only he knew more about it.

Even more than in his smithy, the bitter scent of lorcith filled his nose, his entire body aware of it. Were he to focus, he could sense his forgings all the way down the mountain in Elaeavn. From here, the city seemed dotted with them.

Rsiran frowned. Most of the lorcith-made items were sent from the city, shipped with Firell or Shael. But here, he sensed them all throughout the city. And… some even within the palace.

"What is it?" Jessa whispered.

He shook his head. As a skilled sneak, she knew better than to speak too loudly. Here, outside the mines atop Ilphaesn, there was little chance they'd get caught by the Towners. But the men still in the mines might hear.

"You feel something?"

"Later," he whispered.

Jessa didn't let go of his hand. Her eyes narrowed as she looked around, searching with her Sight for what might have drawn his attention. "What now?"

Rsiran didn't know what he intended to do now that they were here. In the tunnels, all he had was the ability to sense the ore. At least with Jessa, they could see throughout the mines. They would have to work together, but that wasn't new to either of them.

"Are you ready?" he whispered.

She squeezed his hand, and he Slid into the mines.

Had he not been in the mines before, he would never have dared. A Slide, especially blind like he did, could be dangerous. But years of mining had turned Ilphaesn into a series of tunnels. The weeks Rsiran spent mining had given him a familiarity with those tunnels.

Darkness engulfed him. For a moment, he had the same anxious sense he'd felt the first time he'd been in the mine. The sense of the mountain pressing down all around him mixing with the sense of the lorcith pulling on him. Only at then, he hadn't known exactly what it was that he felt. Now, standing in the darkness with Jessa clinging to his hand, a sense of reassurance worked through him. As long as he had her with him, he didn't need to fear the darkness.

"Where are we?" Jessa spoke in a soft whisper. She pulled on his hand, leading him down the tunnel.

"Deep inside Ilphaesn and near the mines."

Had he Slid where he intended, they should be standing where the foreman guided them to the tunnels. Rsiran remembered the last time he'd been here, after the pick pierced his neck and he began bleeding heavily. Had he not risked Sliding, even as wounded as he was, he wouldn't have survived.

"It's so… bleak."

To him, it was little more than shades of blackness. What must Jessa see? "The council feels this is a fitting punishment for some." He didn't remind her how his father felt it was an appropriate punishment for him as well.

"How long were you forced to mine each day?"

Rsiran shrugged. "Most of the day. I usually lost track." His days had been spent trying to ignore the call of the lorcith. Worse were the days when he didn't. Then he became caught up in the flurry of mining, pulling the lorcith free from the rock.

"And you feel it?"

He nodded. "All around." Even here in this cavern came the sense of lorcith. The ore pulled at him, drawing him. After months spent working with lorcith, he felt even more attuned to it than he had ever been before. Each nugget had a distinct feel, and he suspected that he could search based on size.

"How is it that supplies have dwindled?" Jessa asked.

"That's just it. The supplies *haven't*. The ore is everywhere. After I told Brusus I would make knives for him, I never feared finding an adequate supply. As long as I avoided the mining guild and took the lorcith from the mountain itself, I would always find enough." Thinking of Brusus gave Rsiran a strange thought. "But to keep from finding lorcith in the walls, the miners would have to almost avoid it."

Could someone be Pushing the miners to avoid the lorcith?

The idea seemed too impossible to believe. Miners were split into groups, usually three separate groups, and led to where they worked. If there were someone like Brusus Pushing on them to avoid the lorcith, it would have to be more than one person.

But what about the man he'd overheard in the mines, and the way the thin man had reappeared in the Floating Palace when they infiltrated it? Rsiran *knew* there was more going on than he'd learned, but what exactly?

Jessa interrupted his thoughts. "Maybe the guild."

Rsiran thought that unlikely. The guild would *want* lorcith to flow so they could sell it to the alchemists or to the smiths. "Not the guild. Either way, Firell is carrying more lorcith than he should."

"That's what we're doing here?"

Instead of answering, he moved toward one of the caverns. The soft breeze of the mines blew on his cheeks, its touch familiar. The breathing of the mines had saved his life once, alerting him that someone was there in the darkness. At least now, he had a different advantage. Jessa could keep him safe.

He listened. Always before, there had been the steady tapping at night. Only later did he learn where it came from. Either the boy or another, a mystery person that he had never discovered, worked the mines, peeling lorcith from the tunnels. At first, no sound came. Just the soft sense of the wind blowing across his face.

Then he heard it. A soft tapping, steady and distant.

"Do you hear that?" Jessa whispered.

"I noticed it when I first came here. Happened every night. Only when the boy attacked me did I fully understand I wasn't the only person mining at night."

"Still can't believe you let some boy attack you."

Rsiran pulled on her hand. "Still can't believe you made me save you."

She squeezed back. "Me either."

He started toward the tunnel where the tapping seemed to come from.

Jessa pulled against him. "Not that way. Down here."

"Where?"

She chuckled. "To your right."

Rsiran went with her, but thought she had it wrong. The tapping didn't seem to come from the tunnel on the right. He sensed the opening—it felt like a space where lorcith should be—and listened again. Now the tapping seemed to come from here.

"I don't know where it is," he admitted.

The tunnel Jessa indicated was one he rarely had mined. For whatever reason, Rsiran had always avoided it, choosing instead more familiar places. He tried to remember how the tunnel shifted and opened, but couldn't picture it clearly enough to safely Slide them deeper into the tunnel.

"I think I'll have to lead from here. Let me know if you see anything."

"I'll squeeze your hand?"

"That will work," he said.

Then he led her into the tunnel. As he did, it felt stranger than simply returning to the mines. Now that he had a better sense of the lorcith, he used it to practically light his way. He might not be able to see in the darkness, but he could essentially see the lorcith in the walls and ceiling of the cave, the tunnel burrowing through where lorcith *should* be lighting his way.

Even Jessa seemed to move hesitantly. She pulled against his hand, and he had to urge her forward. Rsiran turned, following the bend in the tunnel that he felt, before finally slowing to let Jessa keep up more easily. What was the advantage of having her Sight with him if he didn't wait to let her use it?

"How much can you see?" he asked.

Jessa sighed and her warm breath whispered practically in his ear. Another time, and he would have wanted to take advantage of the darkness. "Just shades of grey here. Even a little light would help. How are you moving so easily?"

"The lorcith."

"I still don't understand how you sense it."

"I don't, either. Della said it was a part of my blood. She seemed to know that the ancient smiths had the ability to hear it." He paused, listening for a moment. The tapping still came distantly. At least he believed he was headed down the right tunnel. And from here, he could Slide back to the upper mines or even out of Ilphaesn altogether. "My father could hear it, but controlled it. He wanted me to learn to control it too. That was part of the reason he sent me here when he did. But instead, being here taught me to listen to it. There's almost the sense of a song…"

"You know you sound crazy when you talk of listening to the metal?"

Rsiran laughed softly. "I know. About as crazy as the fact that I can Slide."

They walked further into the tunnel, finally reaching the end of where the miners had reached. Lorcith lit the walls all around him. But there was no sign of whoever mined here. The steady tapping continued.

Could it be somewhere else? He knew of only these tunnels, but hadn't the boy alluded to other access? Maybe there was a different set of tunnels and a different person mining.

"The tunnel just sort of stops right here," Jessa said.

He sighed. "There isn't anything beyond here. Just more rock the miners haven't cleared."

"Then what?"

In answer, he Slid them from the mines. They emerged back outside on the flat rock before the barred entrance to the mines. Sudden moonlight seemed bright, bathing everything in a soft glow. Even without Sight, he could easily see the outline of the rocky shape of Ilphaesn, the stilted scrub trees growing on the mountain around them, and the flickering lights of Elaeavn far below.

Jessa punched him lightly on the shoulder. "A little warning? My eyes *do* need to adjust."

"Sorry."

"Why did we leave? I thought you came here for answers?"

Rsiran sighed in frustration. "That *is* why we came." He walked around the clearing and looked up at the rocky face of Ilphaesn rising above him. The massive mountain spread out and around, pushing off toward the plains north of Elaeavn and then west before falling steadily off into the sea. "I need you to help me see if there are other ways into the mountain. Maybe another cavern, some other way to mine the lorcith."

"This is massive, Rsiran. Even in good lighting, it could take me weeks to search for some other way into the mountain. And searching at night creates other disadvantages. At least in the daylight, I can search for changes in shadows, flickers of movement. Here, at night, all I will see are gradations of grey."

She didn't need to explain any more. He understood the limitations. Just like his ability to Slide was limited by what he could see—at least to do it safely—her Sight was limited by the amount of light. It just never seemed that way.

"Then we'll have to come back tomorrow."

Jessa laughed. "You're serious?"

He shrugged. "We have to see if there's another reason for Firell to have all that lorcith. It can't be coming from the city. Their supply is already limited, and the quantity he had aboard his ship would practically drain the guild." But how would Firell get a supply from the mines? And why? Only Elaeavn smiths could work with lorcith.

Jessa studied him for a moment before nodding. "You know I'll help. Whatever it takes."

There was another place he needed to investigate, one he knew wouldn't please Jessa. The area behind that wall of crates in the warehouse was intentionally blocked. Rsiran *knew* there was something more to that space, if only he could reach it. And he knew *how* to get there, only... Jessa would worry. Maybe he would leave her behind for this one.

She squeezed his hand firmly. Not for the first time, he felt as if she could practically Read him.

CHAPTER 11

R SIRAN STOOD ON THE FACE OF ILPHAESN. Though bright sun-light streamed around them, there were spaces where shad-ows still lingered. Near the top of the mountain, a trace of white snow remained, only visible as a faint reflection of light. They finally stood protected from the wind that had been howling around them earlier in the morning, threatening to push him from the narrow slope they stood upon.

Jessa scanned the rock, her face intent. She bit her lower lip as she did. "I still don't see anything."

This was the third place they'd Slid to, and each time had been the same. Even now, Jessa couldn't see anything but shear rock. They didn't climb, just stood on a narrow rocky path that wound up the edge of the mountain. Finding the path had given Rsiran even more reason to believe they would find something.

"Next stop," he said. He looked ahead, searching for the next place along the path he could Slide them to. He would take them where he could see and no further. Otherwise, they risked emerging to tumble down the face of the mountain.

"Rsiran—"

"I'm not ready to return."

"How many more times can you Slide us safely?" She leaned toward the deep indigo flower tucked into the charm and inhaled. A slight smile spread on her face as she did.

He felt the effects of the Sliding he'd done so far, but not nearly as he once would have. And with Jessa, at least he had the comfort of Sliding with someone. The years of isolation within his family had made the closeness he shared with his new friends all the more important. Especially with Jessa.

But why did he feel so strongly about discovering another access to lorcith? Would he really risk entering the cave if they found one? And if they did, what did that mean for the supply of lorcith that Firell had?

"I can return us to Elaeavn, if our safety is what you fear."

She turned away from scanning the mountain and studied his face. "That's not what I fear. At least, not for me. But you have warned me what happens when you push yourself too hard. How you risk a Slide going astray. You told me how difficult it was Sliding us from the palace."

"I had an anchor. Just as I do now."

"You can feel your forgings in Elaeavn from here?"

He nodded as he pulled the spyglass from his pocket and looked through it. Jessa laughed lightly, but he ignored her. Had he her Sight, he wouldn't need the spyglass. There were many times he wished he had a different ability, but lately, he had been growing increasingly comfortable with what he *could* do.

He scanned the face of the mountain as he'd done at each stop. Through the spyglass, the stones and rocky prominences high above him looked almost close enough to touch. And he could touch them, if he chose to Slide. Jessa may be able to see everything more clearly than he could, but he could actually go to what he saw through the spyglass.

Scattered along the rock were a few stunted plants. Browned leaves drooped toward the rock. Some green moss smeared across other rocks, and after nearly slipping more than once, Rsiran had learned to be careful when stepping near it. An eagle soaring overhead made a shadow that fell across the rocks. Otherwise, nothing stood out.

Rsiran stepped forward in a Slide, and they emerged farther up the narrow path, about midway up Ilphaesn, now positioned almost directly above the mining cavern. At this time of day, none of the Towners walked along the path leading down to the village. He made certain to Slide them behind a massive rock pile that concealed them from below. He didn't want someone from the village seeing him wandering up the mountainside.

Jessa looked up. She surveyed the upper slopes of the mountain for a long time before slowly shaking her head. "Nothing here, Rsiran."

He sighed. How much longer would he continue? As much as he wanted to believe there was another access into the Ilphaesn, another mine buried here, what if there wasn't? Maybe the tapping he'd heard came from a part of the prison mines that he knew nothing about.

Jessa squeezed his hand. "I'll come back with you at night and explore again."

"I know you would. I just thought…" Staring overhead, he trailed off. Why would he have continued going *up* the mountainside? The mines all worked deeper into the mountain, sloping ever downward into the depths. But he'd Slid them up the face of the mountain. If there were going to be another entrance, would it be *higher* than the one the miners used?

Rsiran frowned and crawled around the massive boulder blocking the path. The wide base of Ilphaesn spread beneath him. On this side of the mountain, if he looked far enough into the distance, he could see the end of the Aisl Forest as trees slowly faded into the plains. Higher up the mountain, he wondered if he could see all the way to Asador. But they had looked all along this side of the mountain. So far, Jessa had not seen anything that looked like it could be a cavern entrance. Each Slide had carried them higher up Ilphaesn, ever closer to the peak, but what if they'd been looking in the wrong direction?

He squeezed Jessa's hand in their sign that he planned to Slide.

They emerged near the miner's entrance to the caves. The path here was wider than higher along the mountain but still treacherous. A single wrong step could send them slipping off the rock and falling down the side. Rsiran had been careful to bring them back to one of their previous Slides.

From where they stood on the path, they were shielded by the gentle curve of Ilphaesn as it wound back toward the mines. A short walk for any of the Towners who might be standing guard. Rsiran relied on Jessa's Sight to keep them safe here.

"What are we doing?" she whispered.

"Going the wrong way."

Rsiran dropped to his knees and crawled to the edge of the path. A soft pattering of rocks fell from the edge, bouncing below him. Ilphaesn dropped off steeply here, no longer spreading out as it did on the other side. Instead, the rock seemed to have been shorn from this side as it plunged down toward the sea. Frothy waves crashed far below. A wave of dizziness struck him and he backed up.

"There's nothing down there," Jessa said.

"Nothing you see?"

She leaned over the edge, ignoring the dangers he felt. "Just nothing. Flat rock until it reaches the sea."

"There has to be something."

"Why? Why must there be something?"

Rsiran sighed and came to his feet. How to explain what he heard every night he lay alone in the tunnels? That tapping—the soft and steady sense of dread that he'd felt hearing it—lived in his mind, not imagined. And the boy hadn't been responsible for all of it. He couldn't have been. Rsiran remembered clearly times he'd heard it when the boy had been with him.

"Because I know there's someone mining here."

"You already told me it was the boy."

"There's someone else. I don't know who, but I don't think it's in the same mines."

"Can you not just…*feel*…for the opening in the mine?" she asked.

Rsiran hadn't even considered trying that. Taking a moment to focus on the lorcith, he realized he *did* feel the opening to the Elvraeth mines. It felt like an emptiness where the lorcith should be. Otherwise, the sense of lorcith was all around him, pressing on him with a gentle awareness. As he focused, he realized he could even sense the tunnels working beneath him by the void they created in the continuous sense of lorcith.

Pushing that sense outward, plunging deeper into the rock, he searched for a different sense, one where he could feel the absence of the lorcith, but try as he would, he couldn't feel anything different.

"No."

"Then maybe there isn't one." Jessa shrugged and then looked up and down the face of the mountain. "This is dangerous. Being out here, *Sliding* along this path. Damn, Rsiran, I'm uncomfortable enough just standing here. What would have happened had you taken us just a little too far?"

"But I didn't."

Jessa smiled. "I know you have control of it. I've seen you Sliding. You don't know it, but you sort of… shimmer… when you

Slide. Everything around you sort of bends. It's easier to see when you Slide alone. When I go with you…"

"What do you see?"

When he Slid, he saw flashes of color and had the sense of wind rushing through his ears. He had grown accustomed to it, and the sense barely registered anymore, unless he Slid great distances and even then, only when Jessa came with him. The Slide to Ilphaesn itself had been like that. A sense of movement whistling around him. Flashes of color that seemed like he could see something moving at the edge of his vision. Even the bitter scent present when Sliding—so reminiscent of forged lorcith—seemed lessened when traveling short distances.

"Nothing," she said. "I don't really see anything. It's like my vision fails when we Slide."

He had hoped that she might be able to better describe what happened in the space between, in that place he considered as stepping between planes. But she couldn't help him. Probably since she had no ability to Slide, had no control over the Slide.

Rsiran sighed again and crouched carefully to lean over the edge of the path. Taking the spyglass from his pocket, he peered through it and down the rock face. All he needed was a flat stretch where he could stand. Somewhere they could reach and look up the mountain and try to see other openings.

For a moment, he thought he wouldn't find anything that would work. The rock ran nearly vertical most of the way down to the sea. But near the bottom of the mountain, near where the water frothed around the base, a flat stretch of rock jutted from the mountain, curling around. It *should* be just wide enough for the two of them to stand upon.

"Do you see that?"

Jessa followed where he pointed. A deep frown crossed her face.

"And here I thought I needed to worry about you Sliding us safely along the path."

"Don't you see it?"

"Yes I see it. I just don't think you're thinking clearly about this, Rsiran. That's nearly in the sea. How much spray do you think has built up there? And you thought the patches of moss were slick."

"I just need a place where we can look up at the mountain."

Jessa took his hand, shaking her head as she did. "Just know that I think this is a terrible idea. And I should know. I've had many of my own."

Rsiran stood and held tightly to her hand. This would be different from some of the other times he'd Slid. The spyglass could help, but he needed to fix the location firmly in mind. That far down the face of the rock, he couldn't be certain that he could. And if he missed… they wouldn't just go slipping down the side of the mountain. They would end up falling into the ocean. The way the waves crashed there told him they wouldn't have much chance of survival if that happened.

He hesitated. Did he really need to do this? Was there another way to discover what he needed? But he didn't think so. Lorcith was being brought out of the mines in enough quantity to fill those massive crates on Firell's ship. They wouldn't have come from the prison mines, or more than just the mining guild would have known. The Elvraeth would have known. That meant another source. Another mine. And he needed to know *why* there would be another mine before he could confront Firell with *why* he had so much of the ore. To do that, he had to learn where it was.

Without thinking about it much longer, he Slid.

As soon as he emerged, he knew he'd missed.

Rsiran clung to the lip of rock. It jutted out barely two feet and, as Jessa had predicted, it was wet from the spray. His boots slipped, and he flung himself back against the rock.

Jessa wasn't so lucky.

She fell forward, away from the rock. Only because Rsiran held so tightly to her hand did she not fall into the waves. As it was, she dangled, leaning out and away from the mountain, his hand her only tether to safety. Had he not spent so much time working the forge the last few months, he might not have had the strength needed to pull her back.

With a jerk, she came away from the water, and he cradled her in his arms. Jessa trembled softly. Her breath came in shallow gulps of air. Rsiran's stomach seemed to flutter and a rolling nausea washed over him. He'd almost lost her.

"There are better ways of getting me into this position," she said.

"I'm sorry."

She shook her head but didn't move for a long moment. The waves were much closer here, crashing loudly against the rock. Occasionally, massive sprays would strike, splashing them with a fine salty mist. The rock behind him felt damp and cool, but he didn't dare turn.

"Take a quick look and then we'll go," he said.

Jessa didn't push away from him as she craned her neck to look up the mountain. She stared for a while and then her mouth twisted in a tight line. "I think… Yes. Up there." She pointed with her finger, her hands gripping him tightly around the shoulders.

"What is it?"

She shrugged. "Can't really tell from here. Shadows are different enough that it looks like the opening to a cave." She laughed nervously. "Took you almost killing me to prove you were right."

Rsiran tried to laugh, but the thought of what he'd almost done made his heart flip painfully. He twisted her so that she could lean against the stone and turned to look up the face of the mountain. With the spyglass, he stared up the rock face. High overhead, he saw a wide opening that looked much like the cavern the miners used.

He swallowed. At least that should be easier to reach.

"Hang on," he told Jessa.

She grabbed his hand as he started to Slide to the cavern.

And failed.

Rsiran met resistance, like a barrier blocking his access. He'd experienced it only once before, when trying to reach the palace. This felt much the same, as if something pushed back against him.

He tried to step out of the Slide, but the footing along the lip of rock was too slick. He started to slip. Jessa gasped, as if sensing what was happening. At the last moment, Rsiran changed the direction of the Slide, praying to the Great Watcher that it worked.

CHAPTER 12

RSIRAN EMERGED IN HIS SMITHY, shaking and weak. The effort of Sliding all the way to the smithy from Ilphaesn after all the Sliding he'd done through the day had almost been more than he could manage. Had it not been for anchoring to the sword, the one thing he reached for when he needed to Slide such a great distance, he might not have made it. As it was, he had even come a few steps short of the sword.

Jessa barely held onto his hand. Moisture—either sea spray or sweat—slicked their hands, threatening to pull them apart. Her eyes were wide, and she looked around before falling to the floor in a heap.

What would have happened had he not made it all the way?

Rsiran shook off the question. Too often, he had been risking himself with Slides like this. One of these times, he would fail. And if Jessa were with him, he would be the reason she got injured. He would not let that happen.

"What was that? Why did you bring us back here?"

He shook his head. "I don't know. I saw the cave through the glass but when I tried to Slide us there, I couldn't reach it."

"Like with the palace."

He nodded.

"That would mean there's something there intentionally keeping you back."

At the palace, it had been bars forged with the lorcith alloy. He hadn't focused on the opening enough to know if there was something similar there. But if lorcith alloy blocked access to the cave, that meant something was there.

But it was more than that. Whatever was there needed to be kept from someone who could Slide. Someone like Rsiran.

Rsiran let out a slow breath and looked around the smithy. The air smelled strongly of lorcith, so different from the fresh sea air that had blown around them while standing aside Ilphaesn. He smelled something else but couldn't quite place it.

Jessa turned to the mat in the corner. As she made her way across the floor, she glanced to the charm he'd made her. The flower that had been inside had fallen out somewhere along the way. She bit her lip. For a moment, he thought she might simply leave the smithy in search of another flower, but she stumbled to the mat and lay down.

Rsiran considered joining her, but his heart seemed to pound too rapidly to let him settle. After what had nearly happened, he couldn't slow it down. Normally, he would turn to the forge and begin work on a project, but he wanted to let Jessa sleep. As he watched, her chest began to rise and fall slowly.

So instead, he sat on the floor in front of the strange lantern they'd taken out of the warehouse. He might not be able to work the forge, but there were some things he could do to keep his mind off what had happened. The fact that there had been a barrier present at all told him he was onto something. But not what. And digging deeper risked more dangers like this one.

How many times did he have to put Jessa in danger before he learned better? How many times until he failed? What if the next time, he couldn't get them back safely? Or if he simply Slid too far and she went tumbling away from him? He couldn't help her if he couldn't reach her.

The thoughts nauseated him. Better to hold a hammer in hand, pound at red-hot lorcith, feel the pull and draw of the ore as it guided his shaping. If he closed his eyes, he could almost feel the steady pounding, feel the metal drawing its shape out of the coals, the lorcith guiding him…

A strange thing happened as he visualized it. As he did, he felt himself calm, almost as he did when working. In that state, he felt a connection to the metal. And then… he felt the lantern.

He sensed what had been done to the lorcith. It was unpleasant, something the lorcith had not wanted, but had been willing to do. Whatever had mixed with the lorcith changed it in some distinct way, made it different enough that it became something else. An alloy, though he had no idea what kind, and the metal did not offer any clues.

It seemed strange to think of the metal with a sort of sentience, but how else could he describe what he felt? As long as he had worked with it, it had seemed to guide him. But he'd never really wondered why. Always he'd felt content just taking from the lorcith. First taking the shape out of it that it had wanted and then lessons from it that had forged him into a better smith. Yet… he'd never given anything to it in return.

But that wasn't *quite* right. He'd freed the lorcith, given some of the ore the release it demanded when he felt it buried in the walls of Ilphaesn. Had that been a fair bargain? Did the lorcith even have a sense of such things?

Maybe it was simply his tired mind that made him think such thoughts. How could the metal itself have desires? But how could the lorcith demand he form it into a particular shape—and there was no doubt in his mind that it had demanded certain shapes. Yet there were times when he had asked it to take a shape, though not yet with the knives, and the lorcith had complied. Is that the same as what happened when it agreed to become an alloy? Was the request part of the process to form the alloy? Maybe that was why no smith had been able to form an alloy. Before entering the palace, he hadn't thought it even possible.

As he sat there, he thought he understood *how* the alloy had formed, if not what was used to create it. And from that... he could make the shape of the lantern, if not the blue light.

Sitting and sensing the lorcith soothed him, and in return, his strength began to return. Rsiran stood and looked over to where Jessa slept, curled now into a ball, her knees bent and tucked into her stomach and her chin bent as if to smell the flower that was no longer there. He should stay with her, perhaps lie down and rest along side her, but questions remained that he had no answers for.

If only the mines had offered answers, yet they had not. Only additional questions. If only he could push past the barrier preventing him from reaching the cave on the face of Ilphaesn high above the sea. The last time he'd faced a barrier like that, he'd had one of his forgings he'd managed to use as an anchor. The sword had given him something to latch onto, to pull both him and Jessa forward. Without that, he wouldn't have been able to reach Josun's quarters. Even with it, he'd barely made it. And then, barely made it back out again.

Answers. To keep Jessa safe, he would need to find answers. Brusus didn't have them, or if he did, he didn't share. Probably thinking to keep them safe, just like he had when faced with Josun. Maybe Della would have answers, but he hated the idea of imposing on her, especially since the last time he'd really seen her, he and the others had nearly died. But at least she had decades of knowledge, the possibility of answers where he otherwise had none.

But before he reached out to her, he had to search that space behind the wall of crates in the warehouse. Now that she slept, he could slip in and out, barely be gone long enough for her to awaken. By the time he returned, he might have more answers.

Or, just as likely, more questions.

She would hate learning that he'd gone without her, but it might be better to ask forgiveness later than to ask permission now.

Rsiran stood and checked to be sure he had a few of his knives still tucked into his pockets. He sensed the knives and knew where they were. The slender blades fit easily into his pockets, but he couldn't help but think they might be longer than what he needed. If only the lorcith would allow him to forge smaller blades. Then he grabbed the lantern off the floor and Slid.

He emerged in the warehouse, standing near the center of the building. Late afternoon light worked through the dirty windows overhead. Rsiran hesitated, listening for anything that might seem out of order, but didn't hear anything. Then he listened for lorcith.

Just like the last time he'd come here, the distant sense of lorcith pulled at him. He didn't know where that sense came from, but began to suspect it was an alloy he sensed, rather than pure ore or something he forged. Otherwise, there was no sign of anything forged from lorcith in the warehouse.

Rsiran let out a breath. Before moving, he lit the lantern.

Under the blue light of the lantern, the crates looked no different from the other times he'd been to the warehouse. He looked for signs that something had changed in the days since he'd last been here, but there was nothing to show that it had. Even the musty odor of the air seemed the same.

He crept slowly away from the center of the warehouse, moving carefully, determined to walk as he'd seen Jessa when sneaking. Somehow, she managed nearly perfect silence.

Reaching the intersection of the crates, he hesitated before turning. Again he listened for lorcith but still heard nothing to indicate anything had changed. That, at least, reassured him.

Then he made his way down the long alley between the towering stacks of crates, skimming over the indecipherable markings on the crates. As the stacks grew taller, pressed almost purposefully together, he paused again.

He'd reached the area where he wanted to step to the other side. Somewhere past these crates would be answers. Rsiran felt certain of that. But reaching them was dangerous. Sliding just far enough to get past the crates put him in danger if two crates were stacked back to back. He could be trapped inside the crate—or worse, caught somehow in between the crate and outside.

There was another option. Rather than attempting a blind Slide with unpredictable results, he Slid to the top of the nearest stack of crates. Standing there, he looked out toward where the crates stacked higher, creating the wall. If he could find an opening, he wouldn't have to Slide blindly. But he saw nothing.

Holding the lantern out, he looked for some way past. The crates stacked all around. For all he knew, the stacks were solid all the way through. He Slid to the next crate over and then again, each time looking for a way to get past the wall. There didn't seem to be any clear access.

Rsiran Slid back to the long corridor and walked down until he reached the wall. The crates there didn't quite reach the ceiling, but he'd come almost all the way around and still hadn't seen a way past. Either the crates framed a clearing like was found in the center of the warehouse, or the crates were stacked so densely together that there would be no way to get past.

And he had no way of knowing the difference, not without tearing the crates apart. Rsiran didn't know if he could even manage that, and if he could, there would be no way to hide what had been done.

Rsiran wanted answers, knowing that he needed to if Josun's rebellion had begun to move, especially if they learned of him. Not only that, but something was happening with lorcith. With his connection to the ore, he needed to understand what that might be. Why did Firell have the crates of lorcith? And why had Rsiran been barricaded from the hidden mine?

Somehow, it started with the warehouse. Lianna had found the crate sitting on the dock. Rsiran and Jessa had been attacked here. And this wall of crates blocked him from a part of the warehouse. What did he risk by *not* Sliding to the other side?

Not knowing. That was what he risked. And something more happening to his friends. To Jessa.

Rsiran thought about the distance. Just far enough to get past the stack of crates, but not too far that he risked colliding with another stack. If another stack was pushed up against the first, he had to coordinate the Slide to ensure he ended up inside a crate if possible. At least, if something went wrong, he had the possibility of Sliding free.

Crouching just in case, he Slid.

When he emerged, he held his breath, body tensed for what might happen.

But he was unharmed.

A narrow gap opened around him, crates stretching to the ceiling, blocking off all natural light that would otherwise come through the overhead windows. Without the lantern, he would have had no way to see anything. The gap was barely wide enough for another row of the crates, almost as if crates that had been here were pulled out for this purpose. The air tasted stale and bitter, with a hint of dust filling his nose from the hard-packed ground, but another odor lingered, one of sweat and the tang of blood.

Someone had been here.

That either meant some hidden access existed or someone reached it the same way he had.

Not wanting to linger any longer than needed, he looked for anything that might explain what was happening. They could return later with Brusus and Jessa. Now that he'd been here, Sliding back would be easier.

Near one end of the space, a collection of metallic items rested on what appeared to be a side panel from a nearby crate, lying on the ground. Rsiran Slid there, not wanting to make anymore prints in the ground than needed. Not until he knew who had been here.

Close up, the objects each had a strange sheen to them. Made of some grey metal, they almost shimmered in the blue light of the lantern. It took him a moment to realize they were lorcith made.

But that wasn't quite right. Not lorcith—at least, not the same type of lorcith he worked with—but an alloy. Like the lantern.

One of the objects looked like a simple wide-bottomed pan. This was not lorcith, but something else. A deep black metal that he didn't recognize. Resting up against the side of a crate were a set of small tongs, the same as he'd use to pick up glowing metal heated at the forge.

Rsiran frowned, considering what else he saw.

A small, simple rectangle made of iron sat near the tongs. Other than the black pan, it was the cleanest shape. The other shapes scattered on the wooden side panel looked like crude forgings. Something that wanted to be a loop of chain. A too-thick length of metal that seemed to be a knife. And a deformed hunk of silvery metal that he couldn't identify.

With a growing curiosity, he lifted the panel, careful not to let any of the pieces fall. Again, he wanted minimal evidence that he'd been there. The ground underneath was scorched and covered in ash. His frown deepened.

What was this place?

He would have to come back. Brusus needed to see it. He always seemed to have answers. Grabbing the strange lump of metal, he turned it in his hands. Not silver, but something else he didn't recognize.

Rsiran set the panel back down. As he did, he felt the pull of lorcith suddenly strong on his senses. Without waiting, he Slid away from the warehouse.

Chapter 13

RSIRAN RETURNED TO THE SMITHY. Only after he'd returned did he realize that he still held the strange lump of metal. Cursing himself, he slipped it into his pocket. If he had more time, he would learn what it was. Maybe then he would understand why it had been hidden between the crates.

He looked around the smithy, but Jessa was gone.

Rsiran needed to find Brusus to fill him in on what they'd learned, and learn if he'd found anything from his sources in the palace. Too much had happened since they'd seen him, but it was growing clearer to Rsiran that it all tied together somehow. If only he could make the connection.

His mind still hadn't slowed since returning from Ilphaesn. Studying the lantern helped, but didn't put him at ease like working with the hammer would.

Deciding to take some time, he moved to the coals and began heating them to a red-hot glow. Once satisfied, he sorted through the remaining lumps of lorcith until he found one that called to him. He set it in the coals, letting it gradually heat to an orange glow. Lorcith could take more heat than most metals and had to be much hotter than even steel to work easily.

Then he set to work.

Rsiran began hammering the metal, flattening it. As he worked, he considered trying to influence the shape the lorcith took. So often when working with lorcith—and lorcith only—he listened to it and let the metal dictate what direction the forging took. This led to Brusus's frustration that Rsiran did not make nearly enough of the knives that fetched so many coins. Now Rsiran wanted to make knives, but for a different reason. He needed something small enough to easily pocket.

The lorcith responded. As he worked, he split the metal, turning the single lump of lorcith into three separate pieces. He hammered each of them, slowly turning them into small knives that he flattened, slowly shaping. Before finishing, he worked his mark onto the end.

When they were finished and cooled, quenched in the bucket of stale water resting near the anvil, he lifted them. Compact and balanced, but unlike the other knives he'd made. They barely fit in his hand. These would not be marketable, but they suited his purposes, fitting nicely into his pocket.

With a *push* on the lorcith, he sent one of the knives flying across the room. It sank into the wooden wall plank with a loud *thunk*.

Rsiran *pulled* it back and felt some resistance as he did. When the knife came flying back to him, he slowed it and caught it out of the air. These knives would be useful.

After sharpening them on his grinding wheel, he pulled the other knives he had in his pocket and set them on his table, replacing them with the small knives he'd just forged. They did not weigh so heavily in his pocket. The others could be hidden throughout the city as anchors. If there was someone out there for him to fear, he needed to be prepared.

Like it so often did, working the forge had cleared his mind. He considered what they had seen, about the stores of lorcith on Firell's ship. His own collection had diminished, and he had to address how he would obtain more. He could return to Ilphaesn late at night and mine the ore himself, but doing so would be risky. What if he took some from Firell?

The first person he worried about was Brusus. Would he mind Rsiran stealing from Firell? Brusus wanted more shaped lorcith items. Better to sell. While there was value to the unshaped lorcith, it was much more valuable when forged. And Brusus would likely have wanted Firell to bring the lorcith to him anyway.

And Firell? Rsiran didn't know him as well as the others, but Firell had been nothing but kind to him. Would he really steal from a friend?

If he did, what did that make him?

Nothing more than the thief his father had always expected he would become. Sliding, the dark ability, but one that had saved him so many times. And what Rsiran had used it for had not been dark, at least not the way he saw it. Could saving Brusus be a dark ability? Could saving Jessa? How could the Great Watcher *not* want him to use his ability?

But he didn't have to use it against his friends. First, he needed to understand why Firell had the lorcith. Then he could decide what to do. But doing that meant he would need to reach Firell. Too much delay and Firell would leave the city, travel up the coast to Asador, and whatever he intended to do with the lorcith would be complete.

But… he would have to reveal his ability to reach Firell. That was the only way he could think of reaching him. Given that everyone *but* Firell knew, it did not seem that much of a problem.

A loud knock on the door to the smithy startled him.

Rsiran Slid to the door, one hand resting on the hilt of the knife at his waist, ready to flick it toward whoever might be on the other side of the door. Jessa wouldn't knock. Brusus might. And Haern? Haern never visited. Since the attack on the palace, Haern had been distant. Rsiran preferred it that way.

He hated the idea of a surprise, but the heavy knocking came again, shaking the door practically from its hinges.

"Damn, Rsiran. I do be knowing you're there!"

Shael.

After what they'd seen on Firell's ship, what they'd overheard, he wasn't sure he wanted to talk to Shael. The smuggler likely wanted to see how much progress he'd made on the device, but Rsiran hadn't done anything with it yet. Nor had he decided if he wanted to.

Rsiran twisted the lock and pulled the door open. Shael looked at him, his wide face and deep blue eyes mixed with amusement. He pushed through the door and slammed it closed.

"You do be a hard one to reach, Rsiran. I be seeing Brusus this morning and he be telling me you be here."

He frowned. Why would Brusus have told Shael that he was in the smithy when Rsiran hadn't seen Brusus in days? Maybe Jessa found Brusus?

"I was actually just leaving," he told Shael.

Shael's eyes darkened and his brow furrowed. He scrubbed a massive hand across his face. "So... can you be making the device for me, Rsiran? That be the purpose of my visit."

Rsiran glanced over to the table where the sheet for the schematics lay folded up. He hadn't given it much more thought since Shael's first visit. "I haven't had a chance to try—"

"I know you be thinking this is more than you be wanting to do, but I can pay you well. Those plans… they be valuable to the right person, you know."

He didn't, but Shael knew that too.

"Jus' like the knives you be making for Brusus." He smiled a wide smile, but it didn't quite reach his eyes. "You do be making such fine knives for Brusus. And I hear you be making a sword? I no see a lorcith sword in… well, not for a long time."

Sweat suddenly slicked Rsiran's palms. His heart thudded once. How did Shael know of the sword? Brusus wouldn't talk of it, would he?

Rsiran shook his head. "No swords. And even the knives have been harder to make. Working with lorcith is difficult. The metal doesn't always take the shape I want it."

That last, at least, was true. But he wouldn't share with Shael that he kept the sword in the smithy. That he felt it calling to him even as he stood across from Shael, the sense of the blade so finely attuned to him. Since its forging, he'd always been able to sense it well, more so than any of the other items he'd made. Rsiran did not understand why.

Shael leaned toward him. "Don't be worrying about lorcith," he said. "I do be able to find it for you now. Told you the last time you asked I couldn't but found me a source, I did. So if that be your concern…"

Rsiran swallowed, afraid to say anything that might reveal he knew about Firell's ship and the lorcith collected there. "That would help," he said carefully. Having more lorcith, no matter how he acquired it, would help. At least then, he wouldn't have to return to the mines, work in the dark, and try to free the lorcith. The idea of returning haunted him more than he cared to admit. And he wouldn't have to steal from Firell.

And maybe Shael's source was the same one that Firell shipped, but to where? Who other than the Elaeavn smiths could use lorcith?

Shael's smile deepened and he stepped over to Rsiran and clapped him on the shoulder, nearly knocking him forward. Working with metal all these months, finally learning the secrets of forging, taking the lessons imparted by the lorcith, had changed more than just his skill. Rsiran had grown stronger too. But Shael still seemed to tower over him, easily able to overpower him.

"I be bringing a small supply to you tomorrow. Then you be working on my project."

Rsiran glanced again at the schematic. "I'll do what I can," he started. "But—"

Shael shook his head. "But nothing. You be one of the best smiths I meet in Elaeavn. If you no be able to do it, then who?" Then he stepped out the door and pulled it closed with a loud thud.

Rsiran stood, staring at the door. His father might have been able to help, but he was gone. The shop shuttered. Generations of Lareth master smiths would end. Rsiran may be able to work with metal, but he would never have the same respectability that his family had known for years. And he'd always felt fine knowing that until seeing what had become of his father's shop.

Now... now he didn't know how he felt. Only that it felt empty and strange to see the place that he'd always expected to take over abandoned, left empty. Would it one day fall into the same level of disrepair as the smithy he now worked in?

Rsiran sighed.

He made his way to the table and pulled out the schematics, unfolding the parchment so he could examine it again. The diagram looked like nothing more than parts, and he had no idea how to piece it together. Without knowing how to follow a schematic like this, he would never be able to make what Shael wanted.

He sighed again. What would it have been like to truly work as an apprentice? What would it have been like for him to learn from his father—or other master smiths—rather than taking whatever lessons the lorcith provided? He didn't deny that the lorcith had guided him well, as evidenced by his improved skills, but even the lorcith couldn't teach him certain things.

And without knowledge, he'd always be a second-rate smith. Never able to become a master smith. That shouldn't bother him, but it did. Did he really want to spend the rest of his days worrying about the guild discovering his unsanctioned smithy? Did he want to fear the Elvraeth learning how he worked with lorcith? But without an apprenticeship, he'd never be anything but what he was now.

That should be enough. He had Jessa. A sense of safety. A place where he felt at home and welcomed.

Why was it, then, that he felt something was missing?

CHAPTER 14

RSIRAN CHECKED THE KNIVES IN HIS POCKETS and looked over his smithy again. The unfolded parchment rested atop the table like a taunt, reminding him of how little he knew. He folded it back up so that it fit into his pocket. Maybe Brusus would understand how to read it. At least Brusus should know what Shael wanted from him.

At this time of day, he should be working. A forging of some kind—anything of value—that Brusus could move. And if Shael truly intended to supply him with lorcith, he didn't need to fear running out of his supply. Yet, he didn't feel like standing in front of the hot forge. Not that it wouldn't relax him. He knew it would. But doing so would only remind him of what he'd become. And he didn't know how he felt about it yet.

What else could he do? Search for Jessa? She could be anywhere in the city. Likely, she went prowling on one of her own tasks, something she wouldn't tell him about. Though they shared a deep bond, he knew she had her secrets. For the most part, he didn't mind.

And if not Jessa, then should he try to find Brusus? That man was more difficult to find than Jessa. Rsiran suspected he spent much of his day in Upper Town. At least, by the way he dressed, it seemed he did. Always decked out in some finery, heavily embroidered or with the perfect cut, almost as if he wanted to believe he didn't truly live in Lower Town. Not that Rsiran could blame him.

But he would not find Brusus. And after Shael's visit, he didn't want to stay here. Besides, there was much he needed to find out, not the least of which was an answer as to why Firell smuggled lorcith. That, at least, was something he could do.

He should leave a message for Jessa, but decided the knives sitting out on the table would serve. Then he Slid.

It was late afternoon and the sun was starting to sink toward the horizon, leaving streaks of orange in the sky and just enough light to finish up the day's tasks; the docks were flush with activity. A few shallow-keeled boats floated toward the docks. One was tied to the far dock. Men worked quickly, unloading buckets of fish that sloshed as they carried them. These would be carted to the Lower Town market, which would be a flurry of activity until late in the night.

A tall twin-masted ship was moored out in the bay. Rsiran recognized it as Firell's ship, anchored in a different location from before. Would its new location make it more difficult to Slide to, or would the fact that he had been on the deck before ease that transition? Had he only left one of his forgings on the ship, he would have an easier time reaching it.

But he remembered there *were* forgings of his on the ship. How many knives had he sensed when he first reached the ship? And he had practiced feeling for his work. Standing atop Ilphaesn had given him plenty of practice listening for the tiny pull of his lorcith forgings.

As he focused, he felt the sword in his shop… the knives resting on the table nearby… the various other items left throughout Lower Town in the Barth or Brusus's house… and at least two different knives. He could use that awareness to pull him, as he had when Sliding away from Ilphaesn earlier.

Rsiran hesitated before Sliding. Was he prepared to confront Firell about the lorcith on board his ship? Was he prepared to answer the questions he would get in return? Would he admit that he sensed lorcith? That secret, almost more than Sliding, seemed one worth keeping to himself. But how else would he explain his appearance on the ship? He could lie, say that he watched as Firell loaded the crates, and followed him onto the ship to confront him, but what would happen were Firell to catch him lying?

He didn't know. Had Jessa been with him, she might have an answer. But if Jessa had been with him, he doubted she would let him even attempt this. Not after what they had been through today.

There were answers they needed. Waiting did nothing other than put everyone at more risk. How long before one of the Elvraeth came after them—if they weren't after them already? Rsiran needed to find out what Firell intended to do with the ore.

Grabbing hold of the sense of lorcith on the ship, he Slid.

He emerged in the cargo hold. No light made it into the hold, leaving him standing in near darkness. All around came the sense of lorcith, both from forgings he had made and from the crates lining the walls. The ship rocked under his feet, and he struggled to stay with it. A wave slapped against the ship and sent him flying.

Rsiran had the sense of being back in the mines. Standing in the dark like this made him feel that way. These were times when he wished for Jessa's gift. Sight had so many uses.

Sliding was useful, too, but in a different way. And he could not deny the fact that he used the attachment to the lorcith, but that seemed different to him somehow, not the same as his ability to Slide. Using that gift did not require the same amount of energy. Sensing lorcith never fatigued him like Sliding did.

Or used to. How many times had he Slid today? Multiple times while making his way around Ilphaesn, and each of those with Jessa in tow. And then to the warehouse and back. Now to the ship. The only time he'd really felt exhausted had been returning to the smithy from Ilphaesn after nearly failing the Slide. Had his energy improved so much? Or was he so accustomed to Sliding with Jessa that when he traveled alone, he didn't feel the same strain?

Now he only felt mild effects from the Sliding he'd done today. He knew he could return to shore easily if he needed to.

Another wave sent him skittering across the floor. Catching himself on one of the crates, he wished he had thought to bring the lantern. At least then, he would have been able to see what Jessa had seen in the hold. Instead, he was left with the image the lorcith created in his mind and the song he heard. With as much as the ship held, he had the sense of light all around him from it.

Rsiran tried to orient himself to find the door. Strangely, it was the lorcith that let him find what he needed. Listening to the lorcith, he recognized a space where there was nothing. He made his way slowly to that spot, walking rather than Sliding. Without seeing exactly where he wanted to go, he didn't want to risk himself. Again. Already he had taken more risks today than he should have.

When he reached the door, he twisted the handle slowly, opened the door just a crack, and peeked out into the hall. No lanterns burned, but some of the fading daylight came down the stairs to the hall, giving him enough light to nearly see.

He crept down the passageway. He shouldn't need to hide—especially if he planned to announce his presence to Firell—but he wanted to make sure he was alone first. And Rsiran hadn't seen the others Firell worked with for some time. Were they even still with him? Once, when he first met Brusus, they had come to the Barth and diced, but since then, they hadn't returned. Likely as not, that meant nothing. But what if they learned Firell was smuggling something they weren't comfortable with?

Rsiran shook the worry from his mind as he reached the stairs. But as he did, the sound of voices came from behind him.

He frowned. There hadn't been anyone there before. He remembered two other doors along the hall when he had come with Jessa, but nothing more than that. Perhaps they were sleeping quarters?

That meant Firell, if here, would not be alone.

He debated simply returning to shore. Last time he'd been here, Shael had been with him, but Shael couldn't have beaten him to the ship.

Moving carefully, he paused at the first door. Not here. At the next door, voices drifted out, slightly muffled by the door but loud enough that he could hear.

"You should not be here."

This from Firell. He seemed agitated.

"And yet here I am."

He didn't recognize this voice, but something about it sounded familiar.

"Why? Why have you come to me here on my ship?"

Soft laughter. "Your ship? Like so many others, you think yourself so in control."

Something pounded angrily, like a fist on wood. "Damn you, this *is* my ship. You might be able to twist me into your plans, but do not think I am powerless against you."

More soft laughter. Then another loud thump. This time, a soft grunt followed. "And do not think I fear what you can do, smuggler."

Rsiran should leave. He *knew* he should leave, but if Firell was in trouble… Besides, he needed to know why Firell had the lorcith. If he could learn that by simply listening, then he wouldn't have to reveal that he can Slide.

"Have at it, then." Firell spoke with a tight strain, and his voice turned slightly high pitched. "But if you do this, then you will have to find another to replace me. You will struggle to find a ship as capable as the *Winding Sails*."

"You think I wouldn't take your ship?"

"You think I would leave it for you?"

For a moment, neither man spoke. Rsiran worried they would step into the hall—and then he would have no choice but to Slide away—but neither did.

"You can still be useful."

"What is it you want from me? We are almost finished loading your cargo. Then I will sail for Asador, as you've directed."

"Yes, Asador this time. And then next will be Thyr."

"Do you know how much trouble I have getting this onto my ship? And each time you send more and more."

"I have more working now. Your job is to move it for me. This is something even I cannot do."

"And I have told you how difficult it is to move. Each one has to be loaded individually before it can be brought here. That takes time! Already I've been in port much long than I prefer. How much longer do I risk being caught by the constables?"

"They will not bother you."

Firell laughed bitterly. "Of course they won't. And that doesn't draw attention either?"

"I have told you before that I do not care about your troubles. You know the terms."

"If my ship is torn apart carrying your supplies, your terms won't do you a damn bit of good, will they?"

The other man laughed softly. "Then you had best use more caution. I thought you claimed you were the most skilled smuggler out of Elaeavn."

"You have ensured that I am practically the only smuggler out of Elaeavn. That is why you used me."

"That is not the only reason."

"No. That is not," Firell agreed. "He is better connected than you know. How long do you think you can keep this from him?"

Another laugh. "I only need to keep it from him a little longer. After that… well, then I will be ready."

"Ready for what?"

The other voice laughed softly but didn't answer.

A chair scooted back and slammed into the wall. "And after this is over? Then you will return her?"

"Only then."

"Unharmed?"

"You should focus on your task before worrying about your payment."

"Damn you!"

"Can't you tell? I have already been damned. Now—don't make me return here again."

The soft sound of something scraping across wood filtered through the door before fading. Then he heard Firell whisper. "You were supposed to be dead."

After what he heard, Rsiran didn't wait to see Firell's uninvited visitor. He Slid away.

CHAPTER 15

Night had fallen as Rsiran sat atop Krali Rock, looking out over the city and the water. From up here, everything looked peaceful. Moonlight trailed along the water, creating a pale silver line leading past Firell's ship and out into the open water of the bay. Far below, lights flickered in windows throughout the city. All except the palace. There, floating away from the rock as it did, steady blue light glowed in several windows, its light so different from that across the rest of the city.

He hadn't wanted to return to the smithy just yet. Not after what he'd heard. Rsiran didn't know who Firell had been speaking to, but clearly the smuggler was not happy with what he was doing. It was a feeling he understood well. How long had he labored under his father feeling the same way? Living with the dread that came from fearing what he was and the abilities the Great Watcher had given him?

But this was different even from that. Firell seemed to be in trouble. Rsiran had considered taking the unshaped lorcith off the ship, but now he was not so sure. He was certain that the person Firell worked for was the one responsible for the mining of the lorcith. Those crates were what Firell had been struggling to load on his ship. For Rsiran to take any of the lorcith would put Firell in danger. Whatever else was happening, he didn't want to do that.

Who would it be? Someone who could influence the constables. In the time that Rsiran had known them, he had seen Shael speak of bribing the constables. That was how Rsiran had his smithy. But this seemed more extensive. Enough to keep their attention off his ship as it moored outside the city. Enough that this other person did not fear his crates would be in danger by sitting in Firell's ship.

Only one answer made sense to him: the rebellion Josun had been a part of.

But why? Lorcith might be valuable to the Elvraeth, but it was valuable to others only after it had been forged. How many smiths knew how to forge lorcith? Who other than someone from Elaeavn could hear the lorcith's call to have the skill to shape it?

He sighed. Too many questions without answers. Jessa could help, but he feared admitting to her what he'd been doing. When he told her how he'd left her sleeping on the mat in the smithy while he Slid to the warehouse, she would be angry. But when he told her about Sliding to Firell's ship? Envisioning the assault he could expect did not require much imagination.

But he had no choice. He needed her help. And Brusus's too. They needed to work through who Firell worked for. But more than that, they needed to help him. Firell was their friend.

At least he had an answer to the lorcith, even if incomplete. Someone *was* mining lorcith from Ilphaesn and smuggling it from the city. There really hadn't been any doubt, but having that confirmed, even if not the reason why, made him feel saner.

But how did they reach the lorcith? The quantity on Firell's ship was significant. Enough to keep the smith guild stocked for several months. Whether they used the prison mines or some other access remained to be seen. And this person implied to Firell that he had others working now. Did that mean additional prisoners or something else? Did more people mine at night in the secret tunnels?

Questions, all without answers.

He sighed again. It was time for him to seek help. That was the benefit of having friends like Brusus and Jessa; he didn't have to push through this on his own. If the last few months had taught him nothing else, he now knew that working alongside someone else was better than struggling through on his own.

As much as a hint of dread worked though him at the idea of admitting to Jessa what he'd done on his own, she needed to know. Besides, she might be able to see something he couldn't. They could return to the warehouse, Slide to the space between the crates. What might she see that he had missed?

But he wouldn't Slide her back to Firell's ship. Not until he understood what he was doing. And which Elvraeth was involved. He'd almost lost her the last time they rushed in when an Elvraeth was involved.

Taking another look out from Krali Rock, he breathed deeply. Up here, the salt of the sea mixed with the flavors of the Aisl Forest, almost as if this was where old Elaeavn met the new. Standing atop the rock was the only time he felt like an extension of the Great Watcher.

Lingering a moment longer to gaze over the city, eyes drifting past the Floating Palace, he barely saw any activity along the streets. Just small circles of light burning through windows. Waves crashed distantly and steadily, a sound often lost when standing within the city.

Somewhere, an owl hooted. Even though he knew it was not, everything felt at peace.

Rsiran Slid away.

* * * * *

He emerged in the alley alongside the Wretched Barth as he had so many times before. The sudden change from Krali jarred him more than usual. The stink of fish cloyed the air, pushing away the scent of the Aisl that he'd appreciated when looking down at the city. Waves splashing seemed less soothing, almost thunderous. Somewhere, a cat yowled.

Rsiran waited, but none came after. Bad luck.

He hurried from the alley and pushed through the heavy oak door of the Barth. A flutist played tonight, the song dancing from fingers and lips merry. A fire blazed in the hearth, pushing back the chill of the night. A young couple he didn't recognize sat at one table. A thin, wispy-haired man sat at the bar. He had a familiar face. No one else he recognized sat in the tavern.

Rsiran made his way to their usual table. Arriving first did not suit him. Usually, he would come after working through some forging to find Brusus and Haern several rounds deep, dice already dancing across the table. These days, Jessa usually came with him, though that hadn't always been the case. A few others Brusus knew would occasionally join them—and Firell when he was in town.

Lianna hurried to the table with a mug of steaming ale. She set it on the table with a wide smile that set her bright green eyes dancing. Her long hair twisted in a bun with what looked to be a fork stuck through it. "Not used to seeing you here so early."

Early. After everything he'd been through today, it felt late. First Ilphaesn, then the warehouse. What had he been thinking to Slide to Firell's ship? How many times had he Slid today? Enough that he should be exhausted. And, finally sitting and resting, he realized that he was.

"A long day."

Lianna smiled and pulled out a stool. She waited for him to nod before she sat. After coming to her tavern as often as he did, she practically felt like one of the group. "Some are like that. Great Watcher knows some days test us more than others. But you're a strong one, I think. No test too much for you."

He took a sip of the ale. Had there really been a time when he hadn't appreciated the flavor of ale? But that had been when he watched his father drinking to excess every night, a time when he feared the heavy-handed strike across his face. Now… now ale simply made him think of relaxing with friends.

"Have you seen the others?"

A playful smile crossed Lianna's lips. "Haven't seen your girl yet."

"Not my girl."

She arched her eyebrows. "Oh? So someone else gets to play with her then? Might not want to tell Firell that. I think he'd be interested in chasing her. Man practically has a woman in each port, from what I hear. Though not Elaeavn."

Rsiran laughed. "I don't think anyone could claim Jessa as theirs."

"Might be right about that. She's a spirited one, she is. But suits you, I think. Great Watcher knows she seemed to pull you out of your shell." Lianna leaned in and lowered her voice. "And if you ask me, I think you take a bit of the edge off of her. But don't you be telling her I said that."

He laughed again. Jessa's edge was part of the reason he liked her so much. Had he an edge like hers, he might have stood up to his father sooner. As it was, he waited until it was too late. And then lost

3333333

his family. At least he'd had the opportunity to find friends that had become a different kind of family.

"Don't worry. I won't tell her, but I think she wouldn't necessarily mind being told she has an edge. Too often, people assume she's soft because..." He trailed off and looked up at Lianna.

But Lianna laughed. "Why? Because she's girl?" She snorted. "They thought the same of me when I took over my father's store. Turned it into the Barth. No woman can run a tavern, they tried to tell me, but what do *they* know? So long as I'm happy and my customers are happy, well... my tavern be doing just fine."

"And you're happy?"

A flicker of darkness passed across her eyes. "Don't you worry about Lianna. That Brusus will come around."

That wasn't what he intended, and her answer took him aback. He knew Lianna and Brusus had a history, but not much more than that. Brusus kept so much of himself secretive. Had Rsiran not saved his life, he doubted that he would ever have learned that Brusus had Elvraeth blood.

"I wasn't trying to pry..."

Lianna shook her head. "No. I know you don't. Sometimes Brusus thinks to hide too much. Doesn't like to let people get too close. I know he wants to protect them, but I don't think he even knows what might hurt them. As if he needs to protect me! My family has been here for more years than I can count. Nothing going to change that."

Brusus's mother probably thought the same thing. Maybe that was why Brusus was so cautious with Lianna.

"Besides, I've chased off more than my share of drunks over the years. Most just need a firm hand." She plucked the fork out of her hair and slammed it down on the table. It pierced the wood and stood on its own. Lianna smiled. "Ah... I'm sorry, Rsiran. Such nice craftsmanship. Should be more careful with that."

He looked more closely at the fork before realizing it was one he'd made, and not really a fork. Another of the decorative forgings the lorcith had demanded of him, though early on when he had just begun working with lorcith regularly. Even at that time, he hadn't fought against what the lorcith wanted; let it guide his hands. Those earlier forgings had taught him skills he needed to work more complex shapes.

"It takes more than that to damage lorcith," he said. He pulled the fork out of the table and handed it back to Lianna. She took it and began swirling her hair back into it, twisting it around the tines. "It's harder than most."

"Even the hardest can break. Just have to find one weakness. I'll be more careful with it. Too pretty to do otherwise. Not like those pots you made me. Those I just abuse!"

Rsiran laughed. Brusus had been the one to come to him asking if he would make Lianna new pots. A way of thanking her, he'd said. Pots were easy, and better out of iron. At the time Brusus had asked, Rsiran's skill at the forge had improved to the point that he added a few flourishes, giving each a notch to pour out the liquids, and made certain to temper them well. Lianna had loved them, but strangely, she had appreciated the decorative fork he'd given her more than anything else.

"Let me know if you need others. Iron is easy to find."

Lianna touched her hair and nodded. "Keep an eye on Brusus for me. I think he does too much. All this worry about coin, having you make all those knives. That sort of work is bound to get back to someone."

Neither of them needed her to say that someone would be the Elvraeth. The Elvraeth learning of his forging lorcith his biggest fear. Not only did he use ore they would consider stolen from their mines, but he used it to create knives and a sword. Weapons. If discovered, too much attention would come down upon everyone he cared about.

"He's being careful," Rsiran answered. But as he did, he wondered if that was true. If Firell moved the forgings and lump lorcith from the city, did that really mean he was careful?

"Never really cared so much about coin before. Oh… he cared enough, mind you. Always looking to make a little extra on this deal or that. Always willing to steal from Upper Town." She said the last in a softer voice, leaning forward again. "Never worked Lower Town, you know. Figured those of us down here by the sea have enough trouble. Probably kept him safe too."

Rsiran hadn't known that Brusus never worked Lower Town. And it wasn't exactly true. The warehouse was in Lower Town, though to Brusus, it belonged to the Elvraeth so might as well be in Upper Town.

"I'll do what I can, Lianna."

She smiled and reached across the table to pat his arm. "I know you will. I know you saved him once. I just hope you don't have to do it again." She leaned back on the stool and stood. "And I've been chatting with you too long. All my other customers might get jealous." She looked around the tavern. "At least, they will when I get more customers. I'll let you get back to your ale. Figure Brusus will be here soon. About the right time, you know."

Lianna made her way back through the bar and into the kitchen. Scents of roasted fish and baking bread drifted out as the door opened. Rsiran took a long drink of his ale and listened to the flutist, a growing warmth working through him as he finally relaxed.

A cool breeze pushed into the tavern when the door opened. Instinctively, Rsiran made sure to reinforce his mental barriers, fortifying them with the image of lorcith. Somehow, they made it so Readers could not pass through.

"Damn!"

Rsiran turned. Brusus hurried in, Firell with him. Brusus wore a long, dark brown cloak, heavily embroidered and looking out of place in Lower Town. The indigo stone on the ring he wore caught the light from the fire. Even Firell looked well dressed, his shirt clean and tucked into simple brown pants.

"Either you ran out of work," Brusus started, eyes scanning the tavern as he lowered his voice, "or you just needed a drink."

Rsiran flickered his eyes to Firell and back to Brusus. "Just needed a drink."

Brusus looked at him, brow furrowing as he sat on the stool next to Rsiran. After a moment, he looked over to where Lianna stood in the kitchen. Wrinkles on his face flattened as the frown disappeared. For a moment, his eyes flared bright green.

"So you're not working?" Brusus finally asked.

Rsiran tried to force a smile on his face. "Jessa and I had few other things we were looking into."

Firell watched him with a neutral expression.

Brusus turned and the frown returned. "What sorts of things? Did you find anything in the warehouse?"

Had it really been that long since he'd seen Brusus? But it had. So much had happened in the time between, and he hadn't had a chance to catch Brusus up on any of it. Now, with Firell here, he hesitated saying anything. Until he knew what was happening with Firell, he didn't want to say anything that might make Brusus angry with him.

"Nothing really," he answered. "Crates looked pretty much untouched. Well, except for what you've taken out of there."

Brusus laughed. "Still can't believe all that the Elvraeth leave untouched there. Most of it is hard to move, but there are a few things…"

Firell nodded. "Thyr likes the ceramics you've found. You make me skirt around the issue of *where* they came from, but I *am* a smuggler."

"So you're saying you're good at lying?" Brusus asked with a smile.

Firell spread his hands. "Guilty."

Rsiran watched but said nothing. What would Haern see if he were here? Apparently, nothing if he hadn't said anything to Brusus yet. Somehow, that didn't make him feel any better about it.

Lianna came over to the table and set mugs of ale in front of Firell and Brusus. "Was worried you were going to leave this poor boy alone at the table."

Brusus smiled at her, eyes sparkling. "Boy? We'd never let a boy drink ale!"

"But saving your arse is fine?" Firell nudged Rsiran and laughed.

Rsiran tried to smile back, but knew it didn't spread across his face. If Firell was such a good smuggler that he could lie easily, what else had he lied about?

CHAPTER 16

RSIRAN SAT IN THE SMITHY HOLDING the small lump of metal on his lap, turning it over in his hand. He still didn't recognize the metal, but had accidentally discovered how soft it was. One of the lorcith knives in his pocket had pressed against the long side, leaving a long indent where the knife had been.

He didn't know many uses for metal so soft that you could practically deform it with your finger. Even the gold in the Elaeavn coins was too soft for his liking.

Standing, he made his way to his bench and set it atop the table. Next to forgings of iron and steel, it looked out of place. Next to the lorcith, it practically shimmered. Even the polished steel pan nearby looked dull in comparison.

"Was it worth it?"

Rsiran turned. Jessa stood behind him, one hand on her hips. She wore an olive shirt and tan pants with embroidery that matched what he'd seen Brusus wearing yesterday. The lorcith charm hung from her neck, a milky white flower tucked into it. Now that she stood so close, he felt the lorcith from the charm.

When she'd come to the Barth last night, he made a point of keeping her from saying too much in front of Firell. He'd managed to hold off explaining what he'd done until this morning. He'd only gotten as far as telling her about the warehouse before she'd stormed out.

"I'm glad you came back." He knew she would eventually.

"Now you're concerned with hurting me?"

"I'm always concerned with you getting hurt."

She punched him on his shoulder and let out a soft sigh. "I know you are. But you shouldn't be."

"Why not?" he asked.

Jessa opened her mouth and closed it again, as if considering her answer. "Because it makes me nervous," she finally said.

Rsiran laughed. She glared at him and the laugh died off. "Why would that make you nervous?"

"Before Brusus, no one ever really cared what happened to me," she said. She didn't meet his eyes.

He pulled her toward him, realizing that it was her past that bothered her most. "Do you care about the fact that my father banished me to the mines?"

"Of course not," she said, shaking her head.

"Or that I have a dark ability?"

She glared at him again. "You know that's not true. If not for what you can do, both Brusus and I would be dead."

"Then what would you have to say that would scare me away?"

At first, he didn't think she would answer. For so long, she had avoided talking about her past. All he knew was that she had *something* she hid from him. That she would open up to him now that she was angry with him surprised him.

"I haven't always lived in Elaeavn," she said.

"Where else would you live?" Few of their people ever left Elaeavn. She had told him that Haern had. He suspected that Brusus had.

"Many places," she answered. "Cort for a while. And then Ilian."

"I don't understand. How did you live outside the city?"

Jessa started to turn away from him, but he wouldn't let her.

"I'm like Brusus."

At first, he thought she meant that she had Elvraeth blood. But he knew that wasn't true. Jessa was Sighted, but had no other gifts. At least, none that he knew of. What she meant dawned on him slowly. A child of the Forgotten. "Who?"

"My father." She swallowed and looked up to meet his eyes. "He was a thief. A sneak. That's where I learned."

"But thieves are sent to the mines first."

She smiled bitterly. "Not if they try to break into the palace. But all that was before my time. When he was exiled,"—Rsiran noted how she didn't say Forgotten—"my mother chose to go with him. I was born outside the city."

"But why would you think I would care about that? I mean—my own father tried to exile me to the prison mines!"

Jessa didn't say anything.

"That's not it, though. Is it?"

She shook her head.

"Then what? What don't you want to tell me? And how did you get back to Elaeavn?"

Jessa pushed away from him, and he let her go. He wouldn't hold onto her if she wanted some space. "I told you that Haern used to be…"

"An assassin. Yes." He didn't mention how Haern had tried to kill him once. He might deny his intent now, but Haern had been pretty clear that he would do whatever was needed to protect Jessa."

"You never asked how I knew. It's not something he shares with everyone."

"How did you know?"

"I was young. My father was in a prison in a small town in Gran-lon. Barely more than a village. The local constable thought he'd been trying to break into the jeweler. Knowing my father, he probably was. Mother was working with the constable to buy his freedom when they came for me."

He didn't understand. "Who came for you?"

A tear formed at the corner of her eye. "Outside Elaeavn, there can be great beauty. Some of the other cities spread out in ways Elaeavn will never know. But there is ugliness too." She paused and swallowed, wiping away the tear that had escaped her eye. "The men who abduct-ed me took me to Eban. Said there was a man who liked girls like me. They tried to... They tried to do things to me, but I kept fighting and kicking." She shook her head and swallowed again. "I don't know what would have happened had Haern not found me."

A silent sob passed through her. Jessa forced herself to smile. "He rescued me from that ugliness. Said he would bring me to Elaeavn. At first... all I wanted was to be with my parents. But then I learned what the jailors did to my father. How they took his hand for stealing and left the infection to fester. I never learned what happened to my mother."

"Jessa... I am so sorry."

Rsiran began to understand why Haern felt so protective of Jessa. Why he hadn't wanted anything to happen to her. What she'd already been through was more than anyone deserved.

He crossed the distance to her and pulled her close. She didn't fight. "Nothing you've said will scare me away." He squeezed her tight. "Well... maybe Haern could if he tried to kill me again."

She rested her head against him and laughed. "Haern sees me as his responsibility. Not as much anymore, not since we reached Elaeavn and Brusus took us in."

"Jessa…"

She shook her head. The sense of vulnerability faded, disappearing as if it had never been there. "So after what I've been through, it would take more than what you can dish up to hurt me. What *does* hurt is you thinking you need to be protecting me. If working with Brusus over the last few years has taught me anything, it's that we're stronger when we work together." She pointed at his chest. "And that goes for you and me too."

Rsiran began to understand her anger. Not all of it. There were things she hadn't shared, but he had the sense that she would in time. "I wouldn't have been able to take you with me when I went."

"No? So you just had to go Sliding off to the warehouse by yourself? And if something had happened to you… if you didn't Slide far enough or too far and got stuck somehow? You've told me how you need a sense of where you're going to make sure the Slide is successful."

He reached toward her again, hoping to pull her back into his arms, but she shook her head. The moment had passed. Her irritation with him had returned. Short brown hair flicked angrily.

"No."

"Jessa—I didn't leave to upset you. I *knew* there was something there. And there was!" He turned and lifted the soft metal off the bench and held it out for her. "I found this."

Jessa took the metal and turned it over, frowning as she did. When she reached the indentation from the knife, she looked up at him. "Where?"

"Where I told you I needed to look. In the space between the crates."

Curiosity melted some of her anger. "Just this?"

"There were some other things. What looked like crudely forged metal. Looked like someone trying to work with lorcith." As he said it, he remembered that they weren't just crudely formed items, but items made of a dull silver that reminded him so much of lorcith. Yet unlike most lorcith, he hadn't *felt* it. "This is meant for an alloy," he realized.

He took the lump of metal back from Jessa and pressed his thumbnail into it, watching it indent. But what kind of alloy? And at what ratio?

Were he a member of the smith guild, he could have gone to the alchemist guild and asked. Likely, someone there knew the answer. Possibly his father would have as well. He had known more about lorcith than most of the other master smiths. But he didn't have that option.

Jessa frowned at him. "An alloy of what?"

He turned to the forge. Without an alchemist, would he be able to work that out on his own? Would the lorcith guide him in this as it had helped his forgings? But, remembering the sense he had from the lantern, that of coercion required to make the alloy, he didn't think that likely. The ore hadn't *wanted* to become an alloy. Doing so changed its purpose. Changed what it was. And in spite of that, it had still agreed. That had been the key to creating the alloy.

"With lorcith. This must be the metal used in the alloy that blocked me from reaching the palace. And Ilphaesn."

And if he could learn how to make the alloy, could he learn how to bypass it? Maybe then, he could reach the hidden mines in Ilphaesn. Learn who Firell worked for within the rebellion. Get some answers about what they were after.

"What is it?"

"I don't know. I've never seen this metal before. It's soft. Pretty much useless for forging anything, except for making an alloy." He looked back to Jessa. "I should have realized that sooner. That was what they were trying to make."

"Who? What are you talking about?"

"In the space between the crates at the warehouse. There was a pan, ground scorched as if heated. A rectangle of something that looked like silver, and this lump of metal. I thought someone was trying to create a makeshift forge, but maybe that wasn't it at all. Maybe they were just trying to create an alloy using this metal."

"With lorcith? How could they have gotten it hot enough?"

Rsiran smiled. "You've been paying attention."

She shrugged. "You get the damn smithy hot enough. Every time I complain, you just tell me that you need to get the lorcith to temperature. Different with iron."

He nodded. "And steel. Each metal takes a different temperature."

"So? You said you saw a pan and evidence of a fire." Rsiran nodded. "Then how would someone working in the warehouse get lorcith hot enough? Because it takes your entire forge blowing at blast strength to get it hot enough here."

She had a point. But he didn't have any other explanation. "I don't know."

"Show me."

"Show you how to make an alloy?"

She shook her head. Rsiran could tell she was getting annoyed with him. Or her anger was returning. The latter would be worse for him. After what she'd told him and how he'd snuck off on his own, he understood. And probably deserved it.

"Show me the warehouse. The space between the crates. Now that you've been there, you can safely return, right?"

Rsiran didn't really want to return to the warehouse. After overhearing Firell on the ship speaking to someone he assumed was one of the Elvraeth, he worried about what would happen if they were discovered.

"I told you. You need to stop worrying about me. I can take care of myself."

He smiled at her tightly. "I know you can. That doesn't mean I have to put you in danger."

"I do that pretty well on my own."

He didn't ask her to explain what she meant. "Jessa—"

"I will go whether you Slide me there or not. You're not the only one in this, Rsiran."

"How will you get past the stack of crates?"

She glared at him. "I'm a sneak. I've gotten past bigger obstacles than that before I ever met you."

"I know. You've made a point of telling me."

She looked at him as if she wanted to punch him again, and then laughed. She held out her hand, waiting.

Hating that they had to do this, Rsiran took her hand and Slid.

They emerged in the central clearing of the warehouse. He struggled with the sudden change in lighting. Though daylight pushed through the windows overhead, what light made it through was weak and dirty.

"I thought you were going to Slide us to the hidden space?" Jessa whispered.

"We'll walk there."

He hadn't wanted to Slide directly into that space. If he made a mistake in the Slide, he didn't want to risk her. Now that they were in the warehouse, the next Slide wouldn't be as great a distance, and he should have tighter control. But rested as he was, he probably *could* have Slid directly to the spot.

Jessa led him along the wall of crates hurrying toward where they stacked to the ceiling. At one point, she paused, looking at the ground. "You weren't subtle here, were you?"

Rsiran looked but couldn't make out what she saw. "I made sure to Slide as I moved. Went to the top of the crates," he said, pointing behind him, "looking for a different way in. Or at least a way to see where I was going. I didn't walk through here much."

She frowned, but didn't say anything. Every so often as they made their way along the crates, she stopped and stared at the stacks. Her lips tightened and her eyes narrowed. With more light, Rsiran suspected he would see her frowning. What did she see?

When they nearly reached the end of the warehouse, the massive brick wall stretching up before them, he pulled her short and squeezed her hand. Jessa nodded.

He knew a moment of fear as he Slid past the crates, making certain that they would emerge in the middle of the space. When they did, Jessa let go of his hand. The darkness around him left him uneasy. Here, standing between the walls of crates, his eyes struggling to see more than shadows, left him feeling as if he had plunged back into the mines. Why had he not brought the lamp?

Rsiran immediately knew something was different. The air tasted different. Stale. But something else as well.

It took a moment to realize what it was. Lorcith.

"Jessa—" His voice came as a whisper.

"We're alone."

Some of the tension he'd suddenly felt quickly dissipated. "Do you see the objects?"

"I see one object."

He frowned. "Just one?"

"Yes. Rsiran... you need to come here."

He made his way toward her voice, feeling her by the sense of the lorcith charm more than anything. When he reached her, he put his hand out and she took it. "What is it? What do you see?"

"You said you were here yesterday?" He nodded. "And there was a pan. Some metal objects."

"And a panel of wood. I think it came from one of the crates. The objects were set atop it. Underneath the panel was where the earth had been scorched." When she didn't say anything, he turned to her. The sense of lorcith in her charm pulled at him, but he'd made something else that was nearby, only he didn't know what it was. Or why it would be so close. "What is it, Jessa? What do you see?"

"There's no pan here. No deformed object. No plank of wood. I don't even see any evidence of the burned ground you said would be here. Nothing... other than this." She leaned away from him for a moment, but didn't let go of his hand.

When she stood back up, she pressed something into his other hand. It took him a moment to recognize what it was. Not a knife or something dangerous that he might have made. Instead, she handed him a small narrow cylinder. One that he'd made only a week ago. And one that he thought was still in his shop.

Why was it here? And where were the other things he'd seen when he'd come yesterday?

More than that, a worry simmered up within him. Whoever had been here was gone, taking everything that they'd worked on with them, leaving only the lorcith cylinder. Almost as if a message.

They might be gone, but they knew he had been here. And they knew who he was.

CHAPTER 17

Rsiran and Jessa tried finding Brusus that night but could not. When they reached the Barth, their usual table sat empty. No one diced or drank. The tavern was fuller tonight. Most sat along the bar or perched atop the stools scattered around tables. A bandolist played tonight, the song a slow dirge. The fire crackled with less energy.

Jessa waved Lianna over to them.

"You don't have to stand. Might be busier than usual, but still have plenty of room for regulars. Might even get a few to move if you want me to." A wide smile crossed her face.

Jessa shook her head. "Has Brusus come in yet tonight?"

"Not tonight. Been coming by later and later." Lianna started away but paused. "Something's got you worried."

"Just let him know we were here."

"And where should I tell him that you'll be?"

Rsiran thought about it. Not the smithy. They couldn't stay there too long. And after what he'd told Jessa about what he heard on Firell's ship, she wanted them to Slide there so she could see for herself. Finding Brusus had been the compromise.

"We'll find him," Jessa answered.

Lianna took Jessa's arm. "You be careful. I know he's got you messed up in something again. Don't want you getting hurt. Or worse."

Jessa smiled, though it didn't quite reach her eyes. "He's always got us messed up in something, Lianna. You should know that."

Lianna grunted. "I've told him he needs to give it all up. Too much could be lost."

Jessa gave Lianna a quick hug and pulled Rsiran from the tavern. Standing on the street outside, with only the single lantern lighting their way, she looked down toward the docks. A chill hung on the air and wind gusted down from the north. Waves crashed wildly along the shore, louder than usual.

"Not a good idea. Not at night," Rsiran said.

"You think daytime will be better? Why not go when he won't be expecting us to be there?" She lowered her voice and slipped an arm around his waste, steering him down the street. They passed a few people along the way, though none looked at them. "You're the one who said you thought he got caught up in… whatever Josun was a part of." She said the last as a whisper, as if refusing to acknowledge the rebellion that Rsiran was convinced existed.

Rsiran looked around the street before answering. "Either that of one of the Elvraeth. Who else can convince the constables to turn a blind eye?"

"Brusus. Shael. Haern. Me."

"Wait… how?"

Jessa shrugged. "Enough coin, and anyone looks the other way. That's how it works in Lower Town." They turned down one of the side streets. "Enough coin and others talk. Why do you think Brusus wants to move your knives?"

"Who is he trying to get to talk?"

"Don't know, but when I've seen him in Upper Town, that's what he's been doing."

Rsiran wondered why Brusus wouldn't have said anything to them.

"So you didn't see this person when you went to Firell's ship?"

"I didn't. And maybe we should just ask him."

"If he's working with the Elvraeth?" Rsiran nodded. "That's not going to get you anywhere. If he's not, he'll just be upset with you. And if he is, what makes you think he'll admit it to you? Better to search for a few more answers."

"You think Brusus might have had some answers."

She shrugged. "Something like that. Brusus is better connected than nearly anyone else. Moves just as easily through Upper Town as he does in Lower Town. You've seen that before."

Rsiran thought about it before realizing that he had. When he first met Brusus, it had been outside his father's shop on the outskirts of Upper Town. That night had been memorable for several reasons, not the least of them being that it was the first time he met Jessa.

"What do you think he might know?"

Jessa shrugged again. She turned again and this time, Rsiran realized where they were going.

"And you think just asking Firell is too dangerous?"

Outlined against the night was the long, low shape of the warehouse. Jessa kept them close to the walls of the neighboring building, moving slowly. Had he known where she wanted to go, he could have Slid them there just as easily. Though had he known, he likely would have refused. Jessa probably knew that, which was why she steered him here.

"We're not going in. Just looking for other signs."

"Like the sellswords?"

She shot him a look. "We're not going to see the sellswords. And even if we do, they have no reason to attack. We can walk the streets."

Rsiran wasn't as certain as Jessa. The time when Brusus had been attacked, the sellsword hadn't seemed terribly concerned about checking whether they were allowed to be on the street. But part of that might have been related to Josun's orders. Rsiran suspected he had been there that first time Brusus brought him to the warehouse, had Read him then, and decided to use him. Probably learned of the sword he'd made and decided to steal it.

"What do you want to see?"

Jessa pushed him against one of the nearest buildings. The stone pressed against his back, sharp and crumbling. Something moved behind him, slipping past his ankles. He shivered; too big to be a rat, it had likely been a cat. He'd hope a second followed.

She leaned toward him and whispered. "The crate Lianna saw on the dock has been bothering me. We all assumed it meant one of the crates had been taken from here."

Rsiran nodded. "But we haven't found any signs of a missing crate." The last few times he'd come to the warehouse, he hadn't really looked. But with as many crates as the warehouse stored, would they even notice? Just one missing crate would be nearly impossible to find.

"What if one wasn't missing?"

"Then what did Lianna see?"

Jessa leaned in closer, pressing up against him. As she did, he realized that a shadow moved past on the street behind them. Leaning as she did, they would look like nothing more than lovers out for a stroll. Which, most of the time, they were.

When the figure disappeared into the night, she let out a pent-up breath. "What if a crate wasn't missing? What if the crate Lianna saw was coming in?"

"But Brusus didn't think the Elvraeth had taken any new crates into the warehouse in a long time." He'd actually said it had been over a hundred years, but Rsiran found that difficult to believe.

"Just as it would be too hard to see one missing, how would we know if one was added? And what if it didn't go to the warehouse we thought it would?"

"Where else would it be stored?"

Jessa shook her head. "I don't know."

They stepped away from the wall. Jessa moved slowly. Rsiran imagined her scanning the street with her Sight, looking for anything that might explain how the crate had been moved. Something that size would not be easily transported. A wagon or massive cart would be needed, and both would have to be led by horse. And there weren't any stables in Lower Town.

"What do you think you're going to see out here at night? Wouldn't it be better to look during the daytime?"

"I already have. Didn't see anything."

They neared the stairs leading down to the warehouse door. This was the section of street where Brusus had nearly died.

Rsiran suddenly had a strange sense of awareness. Almost like something pulled on him, drawing him toward the warehouse. It reminded him of how he'd felt in the mines, before he fully understood how the lorcith pulled at him. In some ways, this felt similar.

"What is it?" Jessa whispered. She looked up and down the street. "Do you feel lorcith?"

He understood now that was what she wanted from him. Not that she would see anything more easily at night. She wanted to learn if he would feel lorcith and knew he felt the connection more strongly in the dark.

"That's why you brought me here?"

Jessa looked over at him. "Partly. After what you told me about Firell's ship, it got me wondering. What connection did we have to what we knew? Why would a crate from the docks be brought to the Elvraeth warehouse or someplace else?"

"You think it's lorcith."

"I think it's possible."

"But I didn't feel anything when we were here that night. Not until we were attacked. And then I almost missed it. The next day, I didn't feel any lorcith, either." And he hadn't each time he'd returned. Nothing other than the knives that were thrown at him.

"That's not entirely true."

He shook his head. "I didn't feel…" But he *had* felt a distant sense of lorcith, one he couldn't fully explain. Was that what he felt now? "I don't know what it is, but it doesn't seem to be coming from the warehouse. Not clearly at least." And so far, nothing ever really masked the sense of lorcith to him.

Were he to focus, he could feel the forgings he'd made scattered all about the city. The knives in his pocket pulled most strongly on him, but the charm Jessa wore had a distinct sense, almost like a signature. Close up, feeling those things was easy.

Even farther, he was aware of lorcith. That still buried in the mines tugged at his awareness like a distant ache, always there. Rsiran just had to close his eyes and Slide toward it, and it could guide him to the mountain. Then there was what Firell had on his ship. It was there, different and not as distant, but an awareness nonetheless.

What pulled on him now felt nothing like those others. It felt both close by and far removed. He could not explain any better, but the sense was indistinct enough that he wouldn't be able to anchor to it. Not like he could track the sword back in the smithy or the charm on Jessa's necklace.

Jessa squeezed his hand. "I had to know. With you, sometimes when you know what you're looking for, you tune out everything else. I thought it might help."

After how he'd kept her in the dark the day before, he deserved this. "Now what?"

Jessa led him back down the street until they reached the wide road running in front of the harbor. Three wide fishing vessels tied to the docks. The waves jostled against them, splashing softly and making the lines holding them creak. Farther out in the harbor, the bay was dark enough that he couldn't tell how many ships moored. Heavy clouds obscured the moonlight, making the night darker than any they'd had in several nights. A single streetlamp glowed distantly, back near the main road leading up from the docks.

Jessa turned to him and sighed. "Now? We don't know where Brusus has gone. Oh, I know he's been wandering Upper Town, but not *why,* unless he's giving more thought to this rebellion than he lets on. And Firell might be sailing for Asador with a ship full of lorcith and forgings you don't remember giving him. Whoever is involved has already tried to kill us once, and now they know we've discovered them. Does that about cover it?"

Rsiran nodded. Listing what they were trying to discover out loud made it seem nearly impossible. But he'd faced odds that seemed impossible before. When his father had sent him to the mines and he had been attacked, he'd not only felt helpless, but isolated. At least now, he was not alone. With Jessa, he didn't need to figure it out by himself.

She watched him and smiled tightly, as if Reading him. "I feel the same way."

CHAPTER 18

RSIRAN STOOD ALONE AT THE EDGE of Telvrath Square. The sun set behind him, pushing toward the expanse of water, almost as if sinking into the sea. The faded sculpture in the square looked out at him, one arm outstretched. Dirt and bird dung covered it, leaving the white stone speckled. A few corbal trees grew nearby, pale yellow flowers blooming on the upper branches.

From here, the palace floated over him. The large central area they'd used to break into the palace wasn't visible from where he stood. Little other than the face of the palace could be seen from below. But up on the palace wall, he would be able to see where Jessa had snuck them in. Where they'd almost been caught. Had it not been for his ability to sense lorcith, they would have.

He'd come for reflection while waiting for Jessa. All he had were questions.

They slept most of the day. When he'd awoken, she had already slipped away with a promise to meet him here later. She wanted to search for Brusus. After leaving the harbor the night before, Brusus still hadn't appeared in the Barth. Neither had Haern. That bothered him most of all. As a Seer, didn't he know what was happening?

Jessa figured she could find Brusus in Upper Town. Rsiran hadn't argued but agreed not to go along. The son of a smith, he ran the risk of being recognized. So he waited for her.

How much longer should he wait? Already he'd been here nearly an hour. The sense of the charm he'd made her felt... not distant, but not nearby. He could anchor to it, Slide to Jessa, but didn't want to interfere with whatever she had to do to find Brusus.

But he could return to the smithy to wait. When she arrived in the square, he would sense her and come to her. Besides, he wanted to try combining the lump of metal he'd taken from the warehouse with lorcith to see if he could create an alloy.

And he no longer felt comfortable leaving the shop unprotected. Not after Shael had done as he promised and delivered a crate of lorcith right to his door.

Rsiran checked to make certain no one was nearby. It wouldn't do for his ability to be seen so openly. Questions would be asked, but worse than that, there was the possibility that he would be connected to the attack on the palace.

Satisfied there wasn't anyone there, he Slid.

Bitter air whistling through his ears sounded different, though the smell reminded him of lorcith, as usual. Colors flashed past, twisting in the moment the Slide took. And then he emerged.

But rather than emerging in his smithy, he stood outside Della's house. Had he lost his focus during the Slide? The Great Watcher knew what could happen if he lost focus Sliding. He hadn't used one of his forgings to anchor; Sliding to the smithy had been so familiar to him that he didn't need to. How, then, had he appeared here?

Della lived in a cozy home buried in Lower Town, though the area she lived in looked like so many homes in Upper Town. No one walked along the street. The fading light from the sun cast long shadows here, giving her even more privacy.

When he first met Brusus, he had ended up at the healer's home often. Mostly for himself. Injured and bleeding from attacks in the mine, Della had healed him. And then for Brusus and Jessa. In all that time, the healer had never complained about the visits.

Had it really been since the palace break-in that he'd been to Della's home? The door opened, as if she waited for him.

Wrinkles around her green eyes softened when she saw him standing outside, and she stood with a straighter back than the last time he'd seen her. Then she'd had to use every bit of her ability to keep Brusus alive. A scarf made of indigo and violet wrapped around her shoulders. Grey hair twisted neatly into a bun atop her head. "You don't have to just stand there, waiting. Usually, you just come right in."

She disappeared into the house, leaving the door ajar. Rsiran took a deep breath and stepped into her home, closing the door behind him.

As usual, a small fire crackled in the hearth. Two chairs angled toward the fireplace. A table rested between them. A steaming mug—likely mint tea—sat atop the table. Everything looked familiar and felt more like home than the one he'd grown up in.

Della rustled behind a stack of shelves for a moment before reappearing. She nodded at the chair. "Sit."

Rsiran had learned not to argue with Della. A healer of considerable skill, there was more to her than that. She had saved his life at least twice. And she had healed Jessa when Josun had tried taking her life. For all that, Rsiran owed her everything.

"Where is your girl?" Della dropped into one of the chairs, waiting for him to sit. When he did, she motioned to the mug.

"She's…" He debated telling Della where Jessa had gone, but likely the healer knew. She had considerable skill at Reading. "She's looking for Brusus."

Della grunted and pointed to the mug again.

Rsiran lifted it and took a sip. It tasted of warm mint and left his mouth tingling. The flavor reminded him of the warm drinks she'd given him in the days after he'd managed to Slide from the palace, days spent watching over Jessa, waiting for her to be well enough to leave. Della had been weakened by healing Brusus, too weak to do much more than stabilize any injuries. That was a weakness he understood, one that came from pushing too hard with your abilities. As weak as he'd been just Sliding into the palace, he almost hadn't been able get them back out.

"How did you know I was coming?"

"Because I pulled you here."

She said it so nonchalantly that Rsiran almost missed the significance of what she said.

"What do you mean you pulled me here?"

Della turned away from the fire and met Rsiran's eyes with an iron gaze. "That is one of my gifts," she said.

"One of your gifts? You're a healer—"

Della took a sip from her mug. A playful smile twitched the corners of her mouth. "Just a healer?"

She was more than a healer but he didn't quite know what. "How is it possible that you brought me here?"

Della set her mug down. "It's unfortunate that you haven't had anyone around to teach you. Your ability has its uses, but like all abilities, it has a weakness."

"What weaknesses?"

She turned back to the fire. "Think of other abilities. Take Reading. You can build barriers in your mind to prevent Readers, yours more fortified than most. Sliding is like that. You have become particularly strong, Rsiran. Impressive how you managed that without training."

As she spoke of her abilities—not only healing, but Reading and now the ability to pull on his Slide, he wondered about Della. "Are you one of the Elvraeth?"

She laughed softly. "Many put much stock in how many abilities the Elvraeth possess, yet they forget that it matters more how each ability is used. I've known those with Sight who could do more with their ability than any who live in the palace."

Rsiran noticed that it was not a denial. "How did you pull me here?"

Della looked at the fire for a moment. Then she reached to the side of her chair to lift a pot of water that she poured into a cup. Steam drifted from it. Rsiran recognized the minty aroma as the same as his tea. Della cupped her hands around the mug and inhaled deeply. Her eyes suddenly flared a deeper green before fading back.

"When you Slide, you create a ripple." She shook her mug, swirling the tea. "Don't ask me to explain it any more than that, because I cannot. This ripple is what lets you move from one place to the next, what protects you from Seers like Haern. But it can be influenced."

"How many can do that?" Rsiran started thinking of all the ways that he could be in danger, how Sliding was no longer safe.

"Not many. Doing so requires a certain… strength… that most lack."

"How many know? How many can sense these ripples?" He had sudden visions of being pulled along when he Slid, taken to places he had not intended to go.

She shrugged, smiling at him. "No more than a few. But those who do will feel your Sliding, will feel the ripples. And yours have grown more powerful since I met you."

"Jessa often Slides with me."

Della nodded. "That would explain it, I suppose. I imagine that makes you stronger so that when you Slide alone it weakens you less."

He nodded his acknowledgment, having noticed it himself in recent days.

She smiled at him. "I see that it has."

"I still don't know if I could Slide like I saw Josun Elvraeth."

"I think he practiced constantly to reach that level. There is no question you could reach the same level of skill."

"When I first met him in the warehouse, I think he Slid with every step."

"And you wonder about doing the same?"

He'd considered it. The way Josun had moved, each step a Slide so that he practically flickered forward, made him seem… something more. Rsiran couldn't do that. Not with every step, and certainly not with Jessa along with him. He wouldn't make it through the day if he did that.

"Did you feel those ripples?"

"Every Slide makes ripples. The size of the Slide is what determines how far out they spread. Think of dropping a stone in the bay. A small stone sends tiny waves." She tapped the side of her mug with a bent finger, softly at first. The tea rolled to the edges and stopped. "But a larger stone creates a bigger disturbance. Your Sliding is much the same." She tapped more strongly this time, and the tea sloshed around, swirling for a moment before settling.

"So when I came from Ilphaesn?"

"I had not known it was you, but I felt it."

Rsiran thought of all the Slides he had done over the last few days. Traveling to Firell's ship. To Ilphaesn with Jessa. Throughout the city. Had Della felt them all?

"How many ripples can you feel?" And he had thought Sliding left his traveling invisible, but if Della knew when he Slid, he was not as unseen as he thought.

"Not all are felt the same way. Most Sliders do not even know what they do. But those with strength, like you and the Elvraeth, make larger ripples." She leaned toward the fire. Light from the flames reflected from her deep green eyes. "I cannot tell how many like you there are, Rsiran. There is no signature to Sliding. It just doesn't work like that. But know that you are not alone with your gift."

He took another sip of the mint tea. After meeting Josun, he hadn't thought that he was alone with his gift, but it was reassuring that there were others like him. Reassuring… and frightening. How many other Elvraeth could Slide? They were the most likely to manifest the ability. Josun claimed the council had worked to eliminate it, but if Rsiran could do it—and Josun—it seemed likely others of the Elvraeth could as well. And what if there were others like Josun, those who sided with him in his rebellion?

"Why did you pull me here tonight?" he asked.

"There is much you have yet to learn about your gifts. It is different from some of the other gifts, different from Sight or Reading. Mistakes can happen. You can get hurt. Practice, simply using your ability can help but may not be enough. Ignorance can kill you as easily as a misstep."

"I know."

"But you do not yet know how to control your abilities. Not fully. That is what you must practice."

Other gifts were well enough known. One with Sight could help another with Sight learn the intricacies of the gift. But with Sliding, Rsiran did not know who else to ask. Just as he'd learned of his ability by chance, he had to learn how to control it the same way. Doing so put him in a certain type of danger. "I do what I can."

She watched him. Rsiran had the sense that she wanted to say something but did not. Instead, she shifted her scarf and settled into her chair.

"There is something else you must know about your gifts," Della said.

"What?"

"You have learned that you cannot Slide everywhere."

He nodded slowly.

"Long ago, barriers were constructed to prevent Sliding without warning. A safeguard, though it should not have been necessary, not if the gifts had been used as the Great Watcher intended. But these barriers impede one with your gifts. I do not know how you managed to escape from the palace. From what I know of your ability, that should not have been possible."

"Why?"

"There is a reason the Elvraeth claimed Ilphaesn as their own. That the earliest Elvraeth built the city so near the mountain is no coincidence."

"The lorcith? I can Slide to the mines, and can carry lorcith with me." He thought of the knives he carried, of the lorcith he'd taken away from the mines. How many times had he Slid before he had even practiced much? And, many times, injured. Had he not been able to Slide with lorcith, he would have died in the mines.

"Not the lorcith alone. There is a process that turns it into something more, something the early Elvraeth smiths created." She saw his face. "You think the Elvraeth always secluded themselves in the palace? That they never did any work?" She laughed softly. "Such seclusion is a new thing, and Elaeavn is the worse for it." She took a long sip of her tea. "But as to the lorcith, I cannot tell you what it is, or how you could make it, but the change creates a barrier those who can Slide cannot pass through." She looked over at him. "Or so I thought."

"It's an alloy of lorcith," he explained.

Della looked at him, mug pausing as she raised it to her mouth. "You already know of it."

He nodded, realizing this was the real reason that Della had pulled him here.

"How did you Slide through the palace barrier, Rsiran?"

They had never spoken about it before. When he'd emerged in her home, he said nothing of *how* he had escaped the palace. But why ask now?

"I have a connection to lorcith," he explained. "It helps me with my forgings. The lorcith seems to speak to me."

Della studied him for a moment. "You have told me that."

"Once I've made something, I seem to have a different connection." He took a deep breath and *pulled* one of the knives from his pocket. His work at the forge had strengthened the connection. The knife hung in the air until Rsiran grabbed it and *pushed* it back.

"Yes. Haern spoke of this. If I hadn't known you were descended from the earliest smiths, this ability would tell me all I needed to know." She shifted the scarf set around her shoulders and sighed. "A gift long thought lost, but like in so many things, the Great Watcher surprises me." She sipped her tea and closed her eyes. "So that is how you escaped the palace?"

"I sensed something I'd made. The knives in your home, I think. I used that connection as a sort of anchor to pull myself here."

"And did you do the same within the palace?"

"Josun had stolen a sword I'd made. I think he Slid into the smithy after he learned of my ability." Rsiran remembered his surprise at learning that Josun had stolen the sword and how easily Josun had managed to Read him. Since he'd learned to fortify his mental barriers, he wondered how easily he had been Read *before*. How had Josun not known of his connection to the lorcith? Or had he known, but just not understood what it meant? "He had it with him. Without the sword in the palace, I don't think we would have found him."

She leaned back in her chair and placed her fingers on either side of her head, rubbing her temples. "I cannot tell what that means," she admitted. "I did not know that a connection to the lorcith would allow you to overcome the barrier it created. I suspect that he did not, either. It is a mistake that will not be made again."

Rsiran froze, the cup of tea halfway to his mouth. "He died that night. Whistle dust coated my knife…"

Della looked at him carefully. "One can survive being poisoned with whistle dust. Difficult, but not impossible."

Rsiran suppressed the fear he suddenly felt. Josun knew of his abilities. All of them. "But he hasn't come for us."

Della leaned back and took another sip of her tea. Lines deepened around her face, shadows from the fire flickering around her. "Are you certain he hasn't?"

CHAPTER 19

R SIRAN STOOD IN THE ALLEY OUTSIDE the Wretched Barth, shade from the overcast sky protecting him as he emerged from his Slide. The air held a chill to it and smelled of a coming rain. Somewhere, a cat yowled. Rsiran listened and did not hear an answering cry.

He shivered, wishing he had his cloak. After what Della had told him, he no longer felt safe. Even Sliding no longer left him feeling safe, especially if someone could feel the ripple of his Slide, or worse, draw him toward them. Just thinking of what could happen left him uncomfortable and anxious.

He wanted to ask Della more questions. He had the sense that she would answer them willingly. As far as he knew, that was the reason she had drawn him to her. In all the time he'd lived in Elaeavn, he'd never had someone able to answer questions about his ability, or willing. Whatever Della's secrets, she knew more than anyone he'd ever met.

But he hadn't been willing to stay behind any longer. Jessa expected him. And while he'd been at Della's, he'd felt the shifting of the lorcith charm and knew she was closer. He couldn't keep Jessa waiting much longer.

Too much had changed. More than he felt capable of answering alone. Jessa tried helping, but he had the sense that she felt just as overwhelmed as he did. Haern might have Seen something, but if he had, wouldn't he have come looking for them? And Brusus... Brusus had something else he didn't fully share.

But when he finally found Brusus, what would he tell him? Which came first? Did he share that they'd found someone in the warehouse? Or did he tell him that Firell had crates of unshaped lorcith on his ship? Lorcith that Firell smuggled for someone else. Or that Shael had delivered one of the crates of lorcith to his smithy—managing to sneak past the lock meant to keep him safe—so that he now had enough lorcith for whatever it was Shael wanted him to make?

Then there was Della's fear that Josun Elvraeth still lived. And if he did, if *he* was the person, the part of the rebellion, that Firell aided, then none of them were safe.

Part of him simply wanted to return to the smithy. To work the forge. Tonight, he felt as if he particularly needed to work through what he'd learned. But he would not leave Jessa waiting any longer. That, more than anything, pulled him to the Barth. Waiting did nothing other than keep her worrying. Rsiran hurried out of the alley and through the door to the Barth.

As soon as he did, he sensed something was off.

A lute player strummed near the back of the tavern. The fire crackled as it always did. The scent of roasting meat and bread crowded out the stink from the street outside, but a pall hung over everything, a hushed sense of quiet.

Jessa perched on a stool along one wall. Haern sat across from her. Neither spoke. The cup of dice rested on the table, untouched.

"What's wrong?" he asked as he approached.

Relief washed over Jessa's face. "You're here. When you didn't meet me…"

"I'm sorry, Jessa. I… I went to see Della." That hadn't been his intent, but perhaps that was why Della had pulled him to her. He needed to know doing so was possible.

Haern frowned, his eyes going distant.

"I told you I would be there," she said. "Were you…" She looked at Haern, but he shook his head.

"You know that I can't See him like the rest of you. That ability of his masks him."

Rsiran sat next to her and reached for her hand, only to find it trembling. "What happened?"

Jessa turned and looked toward the end of the tavern. Normally, Lianna would be bustling behind the counter, running out food or drinks. "It's Lianna, Rsiran. Brusus found her…"

"Lianna?" He looked toward the kitchen, practically expecting her to come out. And then the words sunk in. "What do you mean that Brusus found her?"

Haern met his eyes. "Near the docks. He does not think it chance that he was the one to find her."

"When?"

"Just now," Jessa said. "He won't leave."

"Is she hurt? Should I get Della?"

Haern shook his head. "It will not matter."

Understanding washed over him, explaining the pall over the Barth, and why everyone seemed so subdued.

Lianna was dead.

Everything started to jumble together. Connections that he had feared began stringing together. He and Jessa had been attacked in the warehouse. Lorcith on Firell's ship. An Elvraeth or part of a rebellion possibly involved. And Della's fear that Josun might live.

No longer could he doubt that they were related.

Rsiran stood and started toward the door of the tavern.

"Where are you going, Rsiran?" Haern asked.

He paused, nearly at the door. "Brusus needs us now." Rsiran pushed open the door and didn't bother to listen for it to close.

Outside, the wind had picked up, whipping through the streets and carrying the heavy scent of rain. Waves crashed along the shore. After what Della had told him about Sliding, he considered walking to the docks to find Brusus. If Della could pull him as he Slid, it stood to reason that someone else could as well. With the possibility of rain, he decided against it.

"Rsiran!"

He turned to see Jessa. Wrinkles pulled at the corners of narrowed eyes, and her lips tightened in a pained expression. A bright yellow flower was tucked into the charm he'd made her.

"I need to see if there's anything I can do."

"Haern says he just needs space."

Rsiran thought about how he had felt after his father banished him. He thought he'd wanted space then, that he wanted nothing more than to be left alone. But when Brusus welcomed him to the Barth, it had meant more than anything.

More than that. Rsiran knew Brusus, knew what he might try to do. If there was any possibility someone had hurt Lianna, Brusus would not rest until he learned who. Rsiran would feel the same if Jessa were involved.

"He might think he needs space, but I need to see if I can help."

Rather than arguing, Jessa just nodded. "I'm coming. Take us past the north dock. The rocks there." She held out her hand and waited until Rsiran took it.

They Slid, stepping from in front of the Barth to the rocks near the shore. The docks were shadows along the shore, moonlight unable to filter through the clouds rolling down from the north.

"Do you see him?"

Jessa pointed to a spot down the shore.

"I don't see anything."

"Just past the rocks. Before the point."

Rsiran Slid again, pulling Jessa with him.

When they emerged from the Slide, the wind whistled around them. Massive waves crashed along the shore. Rsiran wondered what happened to ships in the bay during storms like this, but couldn't see them as anything more than dark smears against the night. Firell's ship loomed in his awareness at the pull of lorcith, though it felt far enough away that he wondered if he'd left the harbor.

Over the sound of the wind, came a quiet sobbing. Two shapes huddled together on the ground about ten paces from them. Rsiran recognized Brusus's heavy brown cloak as it fluttered in the wind. He leaned over the other figure—Lianna—cradling her head.

"Brusus?" he asked, stepping toward him.

Jessa stayed back. Brusus didn't look up.

Rsiran crouched next to Brusus and looked at the body lying on the rocks. The decorative lorcith fork she'd used to hold her hair up lay on the stones. He understood why Haern said Della couldn't help.

"Brusus?"

"She's gone," he whispered.

Sorrow filled his voice; pain that Rsiran recognized. This was how he would feel if anything happened to Jessa.

"What happened?"

Brusus shook his head and looked behind him at massive towers of rocks, slowly rising to the north as they climbed out of the city. Rsiran knew of no way to reach the top of those fingers of rock. No way other than Sliding there. Even that carried the same dangers he experienced while making his way along Ilphaesn.

"She fell."

"How could she fall?"

"She was meant for me to find. This is a message to me. I have been digging too deep, pushing too hard." He swallowed and looked down at Lianna. "She should not have been here. But they knew I would understand."

"Would she have come here on her own?" he asked.

Brusus shook his head. "I don't think she did."

"Then how did you find her?" Without Sliding, Rsiran had no idea how they could reach this strip of shoreline easily. And knew of no reason to come here otherwise.

"We were supposed to meet here," Brusus said softly.

Brusus did not need to explain any more than that. This was their spot. A place for Brusus and Lianna to be together. A place that should have been safe.

"You think she was killed."

Brusus looked at him for a moment before turning back to run his hand through her hair. "I'm certain of it."

Rain started then. First soft, but quickly picking up strength until it sleeted down on them like sharp needles. Distant thunder rolled in over the harbor, washing across the water. Flashes of lightning streaked through the clouds.

Rsiran shivered. "You can't stay here, Brusus."

"I'm not leaving without her."

Rsiran would have felt the same were it Jessa. Now, more than ever, he knew he could not let her be a part of whatever happened. Regardless of what she said, how angry it made her, he would keep her safe. "At least let me help."

Brusus sucked in a big shivering breath as he nodded.

Together, they scooped their arms underneath Lianna and lifted. "Where should we take her?"

Brusus swallowed. "The Aisl. That is where she would want to go."

The Aisl was where all of their people were buried. A tradition that had not changed, though they had moved away from the trees and out to the edge of the water. But Servants of the Great Watcher would not let them just appear in the midst of the burial grounds. "I don't know if that's a good idea."

The look Brusus gave him nearly broke his heart.

"Where else is she to go? She needs to be returned to the forest. That is custom."

Jessa settled her hand on his arm. He hadn't noticed her coming up behind him.

"I don't think Rsiran should Slide us there. We can walk her out. Take her to the Servants. They will see her properly buried."

Brusus shook his head. "And then they will ask questions. Constables will come." He looked at Rsiran, eyes pleading. "I will not be allowed to be there as she is returned to the earth."

"There is a place I know," Rsiran said. He'd been there before and often enough that he should be able to reach it again.

Jessa pulled on his arm. "This is too much for you," she whispered. "There are times when taking the two of us taxes you too much. Let's find another way."

Rsiran had never tried Sliding this many at once. It would stretch him, and possibly he could not do it. But watching Brusus, seeing his devastated face, tears mixing with the rain, he knew he needed to try. For Brusus, he was willing to risk it.

"I can do this."

Jessa gripped his arm. The way she squeezed told Rsiran, *Be careful.*

"I can do this," he told her again.

Jessa didn't say anything. The look in her eyes was a quiet warning that she feared for him. But she did not let go of his arm. She wouldn't leave him alone for this. And he wouldn't let her, even if it might be easier.

Rsiran and Brusus both held onto Lianna as he Slid.

The effort felt unlike anything he had ever tried. The closest he had to compare it to was the effort of Sliding into the palace. And that had felt as if something pushed against him, trying to keep him out of the palace.

It felt as if a massive force pressed down upon him, like the weight of the ocean. And yet... Rsiran feared stopping, not knowing what would happen if he ended the Slide too soon.

He forced himself forward, *pulling* them with him. Were he to linger too long, he feared he might get stuck in the space between Slides.

Had he not been relatively rested, he would not have managed. Every ounce of strength he had went into completing the Slide.

Slowly, they Slid forward, practically oozing.

But it was not enough. Already he could tell that he didn't have the strength he needed. They would be trapped, stuck someplace in the city or, if lucky, perhaps he would reach the outskirts of the Aisl. Or end up stuck in the space between. Rsiran did not know what would happen then.

Fear coursed through him. More than for himself or Brusus, he would not condemn Jessa to that fate.

Rsiran surged his effort, *pulling* them with him.

With a sudden *pop*, they emerged from the Slide. Rsiran crumpled to his knees.

Brusus took Lianna and carried her to a small clearing just past the edge of massive trees towering over them. Rain pattered against leaves overhead, though didn't reach the forest floor. Soft leaves and grasses grew underfoot. The air smelled different, the salt of the sea changed to one of earth and rotting leaves. Something howled distantly.

The Aisl, at least as close as he could come. He hadn't Slid as far as he'd intended. He'd meant to reach the clearing where Brusus carried Lianna, but the effort had been too much, and he hadn't managed to reach it. What would have happened had he not even made it this far? Where would they have ended up?

"How do you know of this place?" Jessa asked.

He didn't answer at first. He didn't know if he *could* answer.

"I used to come here." His voice sounded weak and distant to him. Rsiran rested his head back on the ground and looked up at the canopy of trees above, rain gently filtering through. "When I was young. Before." He shook his head, unable to explain how it had been before he learned to Slide, before his father had decided he had a dark ability, before his family condemned him to the Ilphaesn mines. Jessa didn't need him to explain. "My sister and I used to love coming to the Aisl. Our mother," he started, wondering what had happened to her after his father lost his smithy, "thought it was important for us to know where our people used to live. She brought us here often. I think she liked the quiet."

He took a deep breath and looked up into the trees, trying to envision a time when their people would have lived there. Hundreds of years before, when Elaeavn still did not exist, they lived in the heart of the Aisl. When they were children, Alyse used to play at living in the trees, climbing through the forest, pretending to build her home, while Rsiran romped through the forest floor, unable to reach Alyse in the treetops while their mother wandered alone. Even then, he had not been allowed in her home. Those were some of Rsiran's happy memories, a time before Alyse manifested her gifts and he manifested his.

"Never really understood how we once lived among the trees. But we used to play here, running along the river..." He sighed and closed his eyes. "Did I ever tell you about how I got lost here once? Cried and cried until Alyse found me. Then I cried more when she scolded me for not having the sense to stay near her. But she wouldn't let me up into the trees with her." He never knew where his mother had gone, and by the time she returned, Rsiran had stopped crying.

"You should rest," Jessa said, touching his head and smoothing back his hair.

He looked up at her and smiled. His head felt full, almost as if he'd drunk too much ale or stayed awake all night, though it mostly reminded him of the way he felt as the poison from the mines set into his body. Della had almost lost him then.

Another strange howl echoed deeper in the forest. When he had come as a child, he never heard those cries. Only once he learned to Slide here did he begin to hear them. They should frighten him—Jessa tensed every time she heard one—but he felt differently, knowing he could Slide to safety. At least, most times he could.

Some of his strength had returned, and he pushed himself up. In the clearing, Brusus knelt before a heaping mound of dirt.

"Would she have wanted more?" he wondered. "The Servants would offer a prayer..." Rsiran didn't really know what else the Servants did. He'd never attended a burial. Few were allowed access, only those closest to the deceased.

"I don't think so. Other than Brusus, the Barth was the most important thing to her."

Brusus didn't move as rain washed over him.

"I… I never knew how close they were."

"Still just a babe." Jessa leaned and kissed him on the cheek. "But some things don't need Sight to see."

"I see you."

Jessa laughed softly. "Only because I make certain you do. Only because I know how little you see."

Rsiran debated whether to be offended but decided that it didn't matter. "Della pulled me to her house tonight."

"What do you mean she 'pulled' you?"

Jessa watched him, a worried frown on her face. "She said she can feel it when I Slide. I create… ripples, she called it. Somehow, she was able to use this and pull me to her."

"Has she done this before?"

Rsiran shook his head. "I didn't know it was possible. I've never been pulled someplace I didn't intend to Slide." At least, he didn't think he had, but what if that was what had happened when he first Slid out of Ilphaesn? He didn't think Della had a hand there, but she said others also could feel the ripples. How many could influence his Sliding?

"What did she want from you?"

"To warn me, I think."

"Warn you?" Jessa frowned. "Della doesn't simply warn. There must have been another reason for her to pull you."

Rsiran shrugged. The rain lightened somewhat, slowing to a soft pattering in the branches overhead. "I think she meant for me to know that it is possible to influence Sliding."

"Everything has a weakness. That is how the Great Watcher intended."

Rsiran laughed, though it felt hollow. With everything that had been happening around him the last few days, he struggled appreciating value in weakness. Besides, being Sighted didn't seem to have much weakness. He didn't think Listeners had one, either. Readers could be blocked, but that didn't seem the same.

"Della said something similar."

"And that was it?"

Rsiran thought about what Della told him. As far as he could tell, the most important message had been that she could detect him Sliding, could influence it. "Well, she also warned me that Josun Elvraeth might still live."

Jessa squeezed his hand. "She can't know, Rsiran. If he lived, he would have come after us—"

"I told her the same thing, but Della figures that if he had died, the Elvraeth would have come looking for me. Or the others with him. That they didn't…" That wasn't quite right, he realized. She said a "faction" of the Elvraeth would have come looking for him.

His heart fluttered, and he very nearly didn't hear the next thing she said.

"What if he's the Elvraeth I overheard on Firell's ship? What if he's the one smuggling lorcith out of the city?" And what if there was more to what Josun did than what Rsiran had known?

"But if he's alive, why would he go after Lianna? I'm not saying I agree, but he already knows of your abilities and knows you were the one who nearly killed him, so why not just attack you?"

"Because he is smart."

Brusus stood near them. His eyes were still reddened, but an angry determination crossed his face. Vibrant forest-green eyes, the whites now streaked with red, stared at them. For once, Brusus didn't mask his abilities.

"And he almost died underestimating you once. He will not make that mistake again."

CHAPTER 20

"Y OU THINK JOSUN STILL LIVES?"

Brusus reached out dirt-stained hands to help pull Rsiran to his feet. Brusus's eyes flashed with more heat than Rsiran had ever seen from him. "I have wondered that for some time, yes."

"You told me not to worry about him. That Haern saw him dead. That the Elvraeth fight among themselves so often that he would not be missed, that—"

"I did. When I thought him gone."

"But you don't know." Jessa ignored Brusus's extended hand and scrambled to her feet.

"No. I began to suspect shortly after I recovered. No rumors came from within the palace of a deceased Elvraeth. Nothing that indicated he had ever died. And no word of a rebellion," he said, looking to Rsiran.

"And you would hear from the palace?"

Brusus hesitated, glancing at Jessa. "Why do you think I've asked you to make so many knives, Rsiran?"

The question took him aback. "I thought you wanted the money."

Brusus breathed out heavily. "That, but there is another reason."

Rsiran thought about what Jessa had told him about Brusus, how he had spent time in Upper Town. "You used the coin for bribes?"

Brusus shook his head and Rsiran frowned. "I've used the *knives* for bribes," he said. "The Elvraeth have enough money, but they don't have knives like you make. A thing like that... well, a thing like that is worth information. After what happened with Josun, after what he showed me when he took me to the warehouse and *used* me, information was worth more than anything."

"And you haven't heard that Josun died."

He shook his head and sighed. "We need to get back. Can you..."

"Not for a while. Getting us all here took too much out of me."

"Then we walk."

Brusus started into the forest, heading west, back toward Elaeavn. Rsiran didn't question how he knew which direction to go. Standing in the dense forest, for most, one direction looked much the same as the other. But Rsiran felt the lorcith in the city like a distant awareness in his mind, just enough that he knew which direction to go to. Either Brusus simply guessed right, or he knew a different way to determine how to reach the city.

They walked a while in silence. Jessa kept near him, careful to ensure he had enough strength to keep going. Brusus stayed ahead of them, picking his way through the forest. At times, they had to climb over massive tree trunks or weave around thick thorn bushes. Once, they were forced to wade through a wide stream. From when he was a child, Rsiran knew the streams eventually all ran together, twisting into the Lneahr River that eventually dumped into the sea.

"How long have you known?" Jessa asked Brusus when they stopped at one stream.

Rsiran cupped water to his mouth to drink. Fatigue from the walk mixed with his exhaustion from Sliding to the Aisl, but he felt his strength returning, slowly building back to where he might be able to Slide himself if needed.

"I didn't know, not with any certainty."

Brusus stood near one of the massive sjihn trees common to the Aisl, one hand resting on the trunk. His face still had an anguished look to it, but he had taken the time to make his eyes a pale green. Rsiran hadn't learned how he managed the trick of masking his true abilities. Some method of Pushing, though he hadn't learned quite how.

"You said you suspected from the time you recovered?" she asked. "You didn't think we had a right—a *need*—to know? And that he might come after Rsiran?"

"But he didn't! He came for Lianna, didn't he?"

Rsiran laid a hand on Jessa's arm. "I'm sorry she's gone, Brusus. We all cared for Lianna. You know that we did."

Brusus took a deep breath and then sighed. "I know you did. I… I shouldn't let emotion take me like that. It's just…"

"I know," Jessa whispered.

Brusus looked at her with an unreadable expression that slowly softened. "Tell me what you remember from the night you broke into the palace."

"We told you everything that happened already. What more do you want to know?"

"I know you did. Just tell me again. I want to know how much fits with what I *have* learned."

"Which part? The part where Rsiran Slid me to the top of Krali Rock where I nearly fell off and died or the part where we snuck into the palace?"

"Yes."

"You're unbelievable! You've been hiding a danger to us—to Rsiran—when you *knew* what we went through. And you know why we did it!"

"*Do* you know why you did it?" he asked.

"Because you were lying at Della's, trying not to die."

"But you know Josun planned that. Once he learned of Rsiran's ability, he planned that attack to encourage Rsiran to play a role."

"What if he hadn't?" Rsiran asked.

She turned to him. "No, Rsiran. I've told you how I feel about this. Brusus needs to know the same. We can't keep helping him if he wants to keep us in the dark. How many people need to get hurt by Josun? You? Me? Haern?" She shook her head angrily. "No. No more secrets."

"If Rsiran hadn't agreed to go to the palace, I suspect Josun had another plan in place."

"What if we hadn't gotten in?"

"But you did."

"Brusus—"

"Then he would have staged it to look like you did."

"Is that why he poisoned the council?" He knew little about the poison that Josun had given him to use, other than what Della told him. Whistle dust would have made the council sick, but would not have killed them. But, introduced into the blood as Rsiran had done by pushing one of his knives through the powder and into Josun's leg… that was supposedly deadly. Only maybe it had not been. Della said it was possible to recover from whistle dust poisoning. And somehow Josun had found the antidote.

Unless he had it all along.

Rsiran hadn't considered that before, but Josun *had* been the one to give him the poison.

"You were able to Slide within the palace?" Brusus asked.

"Short distances."

"And Josun?"

"He Slid."

"And he told you that he poisoned the rest of the council?"

"He thought he had us trapped. Damn, Brusus, he practically killed me while we were waiting!" Jessa snapped.

"But he didn't."

"Only because Rsiran threw one of his knives at him."

Brusus ran his hand through his hair and shook his head. "But that's what I'm getting at. What if none of it happened the way we thought it did?"

"Why do you think that, Brusus?" Rsiran asked.

Brusus let go of the sjihn tree and started pacing. Rsiran had seen him do the same when trying to work through a problem or when he was having a particularly bad string of luck with dice. "After you escaped from the palace, I kept waiting to hear that something had happened. I suspected some of it would be covered up. Either the Elvraeth council getting poisoned or the death of one of the Elvraeth. Maybe even both. But too much happened that night for *all* of it to be suppressed. Nothing leaked out of the palace about the attack on Josun. Nothing about the council. And I heard nothing about a break-in." He stopped pacing and looked at Rsiran. "And I should have heard something. When I didn't, I started to wonder what I might be missing. That's when I started using the knives to trade," he told Rsiran.

"So?" Jessa asked. "What did you find?"

"That's just the thing. I didn't find anything. No evidence of anything happening that night. As if none of it happened."

Jessa reached for her neck where Josun's knife had drawn blood. "It happened."

"I know it happened. But I don't know why I can't learn more."

"Then what? What does Josun want?" Jessa asked.

Rsiran thought he knew, just not why. If Josun lived, and he was the same Elvraeth he'd overheard on Firell's ship, then he wanted lorcith. But what for? Lorcith would not be useful for Josun, not as it was for Rsiran. How did that help his rebellion?

"I don't know. And that bothers me. You wonder why I've been so secretive? Well, I don't want either of you to get hurt. If Josun is still out there, he knows about Rsiran, knows what he can do, and…"

"Why send us to the warehouse?" Jessa asked.

"I sent *Rsiran* to the warehouse."

Jessa frowned. She gripped the charm he'd given her. "Do you know what we found?"

Brusus's eyes narrowed slightly. "You know which crate was missing?"

"Not missing," Rsiran answered. He would let Jessa tell Brusus her theory on a crate added to the warehouse. "Just my knives."

"Josun?" Brusus said.

Rsiran shrugged. "Someone used my knives. It was dark. They were probably Sighted. Lorcith suddenly appeared. Then I felt the knives." At the time, he hadn't connected it to Sliding, but it made sense now.

"He Slid and then attacked?" Brusus said. "I had been there just the day previously. Never had a problem. I didn't even notice any sign of someone else there."

Jessa still didn't say anything about how a crate might have been brought onto shore rather than from the warehouse. What was she hiding from Brusus? Rsiran wouldn't say anything—not without knowing why she remained silent—but she clearly had a reason.

"What have you been doing?" Jessa asked Brusus. "You said you're trying to understand what Josun wanted with the warehouse, but this is more than that."

"It's always more than that."

"Is that why he went after Lianna?" Jessa asked.

Brusus didn't answer. He simply turned and started back into the forest.

* * * * *

The walk back to the city took most of the night. None of them spoke much. As they neared the outskirts of the city, as the trees begin to thin, massive sjihn trees slowly giving way to elms, Rsiran felt strong enough to Slide.

When he told the others, Brusus turned to him and said, "There's something I must do. Please take Jessa. Return to your smithy. Wait for me."

"What are you going to do?" Jessa asked.

He smiled at her sadly. "Nothing foolish."

"Brusus—"

"Just promise that you'll wait for me."

As Brusus started away from them, Rsiran realized that he hadn't told him anything about Firell or the lorcith he'd felt on his ship. "Brusus... there's something else I haven't told you that you need to know."

Brusus turned and waited.

"We went to Firell's ship."

Brusus's eyes still looked reddened and deep wrinkles lined his face. "Why?"

Jessa frowned. "When we couldn't find you and you didn't come to the Barth, we went looking for you. I'm sorry we cared enough to be concerned."

Brusus seemed to bite back a response and let out a soft sigh. "And what did you find?"

"Crates of unshaped lorcith. Some of my forgings." At least now, he knew how the forgings might have ended up there. If Brusus was using his knives to trade, Firell could have gotten them anywhere.

"Lorcith?" Brusus seemed puzzled by that. "What would Firell need lorcith for? The only value is in Elaeavn."

"That wasn't—"

"Just… wait for me," Brusus said, interrupting. Then he turned and headed into the city.

Jessa stared after Brusus. She sniffed softly at the flower tucked into her charm. "There is more here than we know."

"Why do you say that?"

"If the knives he has you forge are so valuable, then why wouldn't other smiths outside the city value the pure lorcith?"

"It's the same reason that I can hear the lorcith, the same reason my father wanted to send me to Ilphaesn," he suggested. "Our smiths can use lorcith and others can't."

But what if there was more to it than that? Rsiran could hear the lorcith, could shape it into whatever form it demanded of him, but that didn't mean other smiths couldn't simply work with it too. He remembered the one conversation he had with his father when he learned that others heard the lorcith, that most within the smith guild could hear it. Did that ability make them better smiths? That didn't seem likely, especially since his father had wanted him to ignore the song of lorcith… unless other smiths *didn't* ignore it. But if that was the case, why was Rsiran the only one to make weapons with it?

Jessa squeezed his hand. "You know more about it than I do. Are there any other uses for pure lorcith?"

"Not that I know. The metal itself is pretty hard. And as you know, it takes much higher heat than any of the other metals I work with to get it to the point where I can even shape it. But lump lorcith? I can't think of any reason."

"Other than to limit supply?"

"It's already limited—"

"How?"

"The mining guild controls what comes out of Ilphaesn. They are the only guild directly controlled by the Elvraeth. Once it reaches the city, lorcith is distributed to the smiths by orders. Even lump lorcith is expensive, though, so there are a few smiths who won't work with it. My father figured they didn't want to risk a forging not working. But if you can secure a commission, the return is more than enough to pay for what you've used."

But lorcith was even more limited than that. The supply depended on actually successfully mining it from Ilphaesn, and when he had been there, the boy had stolen lorcith from him to prevent larger nuggets from being found.

"So maybe Firell just had it to sell?" Jessa said. "But to who if not the guild?"

Since learning about the lorcith on Firell's ship, he'd wondered what it could be used for. At first, he'd thought it might be meant for him. When it became clear that it was not, he wondered if maybe lorcith had been moved to drive up the price. But if Josun was involved, it changed the possibilities.

He remembered how Brusus had described Josun the first time he'd mentioned him. Layers. If he could peel back the layers, they could reach better understanding. Only, he had no way of knowing what layers to peel back.

Then there was the issue of the lump of soft metal he'd found. If Rsiran was right, if it was meant to be used in the alloy of lorcith, how would that help Josun? The alloy created a barrier, but was that all that it did? What if Josun had a darker intent?

There was one place to find out more about the alloy, but it was a place he didn't dare go: the alchemist guild. He had never met one of the alchemist guild willing to share anything they knew. They were secretive, nearly as protective of their secrets as the Servants. Yet, if he didn't find the answer, he feared they would continue to be one step behind Josun, always looking over their shoulders, fearing what he might do next.

CHAPTER 21

Rsiran Slid them to the smithy. Doing so drained the rest of his strength, but not nearly as much as when he'd Slid with them all to the Aisl. Jessa let go of his hand and hurried to where he left the lantern hidden and covered, pulling the sheet off of it. Soft bluish light filled the smithy.

"Why do you think it's blue?" he wondered. The color of light the lantern emitted always seemed strange to him, so different from the one in the mines. The lorcith of the lantern pulled at him, an awareness different from what he felt from lorcith he shaped.

"Sight. It doesn't hurt the eyes of someone with Sight like orange light. Even as bright as it is, I can still see clearly."

"The lanterns in the mines let off orange light."

She shrugged. "Orange makes it harder for someone with Sight. Everything becomes dulled. Probably done on purpose so the miners wouldn't run."

"There wasn't anywhere to go," he said softly. His time in the mines had scarred him, and not just physically. The long scar on his neck still throbbed at times, but not nearly as much as the nightmares he had of being stuck in the depths of the mines, left wandering and injured. "They kept the entrance locked."

Jessa slipped her arm around his waist. "You got out."

"I did."

"What now?" she asked.

"Brusus wanted us to wait for him."

"I'm supposed to believe you intend to comply with his request?" A grin spread across her face. "And I never said that *I* would. Besides, you want to know what Firell is up to."

He let out a long breath. "Just let me—"

"You need to rest. I know how hard that Slide was on you. And getting us back here surely took whatever energy you had left." She pulled her arm away from him and checked to make sure the knives he'd given her were still tucked into her belt. "At this time of night, I can move easily. And there are things that only I can see."

"I… I don't know if that's safe."

She smiled. "Probably not. But neither was you Sliding us onto the ship." She leaned up on her toes and kissed him on the cheek. Her lips felt warm and wet and tingled where she'd touched him. "We all take risks, Rsiran. That's the price of what we do."

"I don't like it."

"I didn't ask you to."

* * * * *

Jessa locked the door behind her, leaving Rsiran standing alone in the smithy. He needed rest. His body felt weak and run down, but his mind rolled through what he had learned. Too much had happened, too much that he had no answers for. And he should feel scared—just knowing Josun Elvraeth still lived should worry him—but partly, he felt relief learning he hadn't killed someone.

Working the forge would help clear his mind, but he didn't have energy enough to do that now. He didn't want to simply sleep, either. If Josun *was* the one who attacked Lianna, that meant he was ready to reveal that he still lived. And maybe ready to move forward with whatever else he had planned.

Rsiran would need to be ready. That meant practice.

To reach the level of skill Josun had, he needed to build up his stamina to the point where Sliding no longer exhausted him. Even if that meant practicing when he felt overwhelmed with fatigue. So he Slid.

Just a step. Taking small steps required little energy, but after what he'd done earlier, he felt the effects. Another step, then another. Each step a small Slide, each taking him around the shop.

Small steps would not be enough. For him to build his endurance, he needed more. As tired as he felt, he had a sense of urgency to do this. What if Josun Elvraeth Slid to the smithy? What if Rsiran was too weakened to do more than simply Slide himself to safety? He needed to have the strength to defeat Josun. But he didn't know how hard he could push.

So many questions and he had few enough answers. There was one person he could ask, but he worried about the timing. The Great Watcher knew he had imposed on her enough since meeting her... but she had imposed on him, as well, though he suspected she meant it to help him.

Before thinking about it too much, he Slid, emerging in Della's home. All the times he'd Slid there made it almost as easy as reaching the smithy. After the attack in the palace, he'd made certain to leave a small candleholder he'd forged in her home, an anchor of sorts so he could make the Slide even when weakened.

Della sat before the fire, rocking in her chair. She did not look up as he entered, simply waved a hand at the other chair. "Sit."

"You felt me Slide."

She adjusted her scarf and nodded. "The ripples."

"Can I learn to do that?" he asked, sitting in the chair as she instructed. How useful would it be for him to *feel* when Josun Slid near him? Then he would have less reason to fear him.

"What do you feel when you Slide now?"

Rsiran leaned back in his chair. Fatigue from the day was starting to catch up to him, but this was the time when he wanted to push himself, use it to build his endurance. "I feel the sense of wind. Sometimes colors flash when I step."

Della nodded. "Do you know how it is that you Slide?"

When it first happened, Rsiran did not know how he had Slid. Even now, he still didn't know what he did to make traveling from one place to the next happen as he did. He simply saw it—or imagined, if he had been there before—and was able to step there. In his mind, he considered it stepping between planes, because he knew there was *something* in between, but did not know how he did it.

"I just Slide."

"You just Slide. And I feel the ripples. That is all I can tell you about *what* you do. Just as you cannot explain how you Slide, I cannot explain how I feel the ripples. But still—the ripple happens with each Slide. Especially tonight. There were great ripples around Elaeavn earlier. I suspect that was you?"

Della turned and stared at him. Deeper lines etched the corners of her eyes than the last time he'd seen her. Redness rimmed them. Rsiran suddenly knew that she had been crying.

"Brusus came to you."

She nodded slowly. "He came. Told me what happened to Lianna."

"There was nothing he could have done."

Della closed her eyes and sighed. "I know that. And I think he does too. But Brusus is one who sometimes lets his heart get in front of his head. I worry about what he plans."

"What is he going to do?"

She shook her head. "I don't know, though I suspect it involves him finding a way to draw out Josun. It is a dangerous game that he plays, one I fear he does not fully understand."

"With Josun, I'm not certain there is anything Brusus can do."

Della took a deep breath and turned back to the fire. "You see why I am concerned."

Rsiran shared the same concern. The fact that Josun was one of the Elvraeth put Brusus at a disadvantage. That Josun could Slide... well that left Brusus in danger. "I thought I had killed him once."

"And how do you feel now that you think you did not?"

The emotions were difficult for him to explain. Did he admit that he felt some relief? That the idea of having killed one of the Elvraeth frightened him? If the council learned, what would they do to him? Rsiran would never be safe in Elaeavn, he'd always need to remain vigilant, constantly worrying what would happen next, whether Jessa would suffer for him, whether his other friends would suffer for who he was...

"How would that be any different than it is now?" Della asked.

She had Read him. And if Della could Read him this easily, Josun would be able to as well. More than simply working to increase his strength for Sliding, he would have to practice keeping the barriers built within his mind, fortifying them with the image of lorcith.

Della looked over and smiled. "It is good you recognize that."

He decided to ask the question that had brought him to her house in the first place. "How much can I push myself?"

"As much as you can tolerate."

"You said doing so will make me stronger?"

"Not stronger," she answered. "You are not a weak Slider. This is not like Sight where there are gradients of strength. With Sliding, you either are or you are not."

Was that completely true? He could Slide, but there was no doubt that he had barely been strong enough to Slide everyone to the forest. Had he practiced more, would such Slides get easier? Was that not the same as strength?

"Are there dangers if I push myself?"

"The danger is in the traveling. You risk getting careless, coming out where you do not intend. Such things place you at risk."

Rsiran thought about what happened when he Slid all of them to the Aisl, how he hadn't quite reached where he intended. What would have happened had one of them emerged inside a tree? Or worse, if he would not have been able to pull them all the way to safety had they encountered danger of some kind? As tired as he had been after attempting the Slide, he might not have been able to do anything more.

"I have seen you push yourself. Is that how you got stronger?"

Della smiled sadly. "There are times when you have no choice but to push forward. When failure means death."

Rsiran considered her words. If Brusus ran into trouble with Josun, his failure would very likely mean death. Maybe his. But worse, others he cared about. He could not allow that to happen. Given what he knew now, he was certain Josun would continue to harm those Rsiran cared about to push them all in the direction he intended. First Lianna, but what would happen if he reached for Jessa? What would Rsiran do then?

Yet… he knew the answer already. Josun had tried to harm Jessa, had threatened her in the palace. If the same—or worse—happened, Rsiran would do whatever he could to protect her.

"He will see your caring as a weakness," Della warned. "That is why he chose Lianna. He knew how Brusus would react. That makes Brusus predictable. But also dangerous. I do not think Josun will expect that."

"You seem to know quite a bit about Josun."

"I have lived in Elaeavn a long time, Rsiran. There are many things I know."

Not for the first time, he wondered about what Della didn't share. Like Brusus, she had secrets. She had strength unlike any other person he'd met and unlike most in Lower Town Elaeavn, she was gifted in many areas. Healing. Reading. Probably Sighted as well. Normally, he would assume that made her Elvraeth, but he had no proof of that.

"I… I don't know what I should do." He had come to Della hoping for answers, but now he had only more questions.

"You think I should be able to tell you what to do."

"I don't want to lose anyone else."

Della rested a hand on his arm. "That is why I know you will do only what you must."

CHAPTER 22

JESSA DIDN'T COME TO RSIRAN THE NEXT MORNING. He awoke slowly, and his body ached as if he had actually carried everyone the day before rather than simply Sliding them. His head throbbed and lines streaked across his vision. His mouth felt thick and dry.

After leaving Della, he continued to Slide. He went from the city to the clearing in the Aisl to the docks and back to the smithy, repeating until exhaustion made it so he could no longer focus. And then, he made small Slides, taking no more than a few steps at a time, determined to push himself until he could no longer stand. At one point, he staggered to the mattress and fell onto it, plunging quickly into sleep.

Normally, Jessa joined him, but the empty mattress next to him said that she had not. He needed her to return. That was his next step in practicing—taking her with him until he reached the point of exhaustion. Rsiran was determined to build up his stamina so that Josun would not catch him unaware.

A skylight set into the repaired roof of the shop let some light in. They had patched over all the windows on the front of the shop, not wanting anyone wandering by able to see what he might be doing inside. That kind of exposure risked drawing the attention of the guild, something Rsiran was determined to avoid. In many ways, the guilds were as powerful as the Elvraeth.

He turned to the small basin of water resting near the table and took a long drink, trying to determine how he would spend his day. Brusus needed more weapons, and he now had the lorcith Shael had brought. The crate drew his eyes, but he didn't even need to see it to know it was there. The sense of lorcith packed into the crate pulled on him, and there was enough to create whatever weapons Brusus wanted, enough to not worry about where he'd find the next supply of lorcith for quite some time.

Before leaving, he checked his belt to ensure he had a pair of lorcith knives with him. After the attack in the warehouse, he didn't want to be caught without a weapon, and knowing he could throw his knives without touching them lent him a particular kind of safety. The lorcith in the knives pressed against his awareness. Before doing anything else, he made sure to grab the spyglass Jessa had given him and slipped it into his pocket.

Then he Slid to the docks.

Rest had done him some good. Sliding after a full night's rest was almost easy. Emerging on the rocks along the shore, careful to remain concealed, Rsiran looked out over the water toward the ships. Rsiran hoped to catch him before he set sail. Otherwise, it could be weeks before he returned.

The bay looked nearly empty. Waves crashed steadily along the rocks of the shore, but other than that, the gulls were silent today. Where he stood smelled of spoiled fish and rot, but he didn't dare emerge too close to the docks and risk one of the workers seeing him simply appear. A few of the flat-bottomed boats that he knew primarily fished within the bay dotted the far horizon. Smaller boats, mostly transport vessels, sailed close to shore. At first, he saw none of the massive ships that he had seen the other day.

Pulling the spyglass from his pocket, he scanned the bay, looking for signs of Firell's ship. Not for the first time, he wished he had Jessa's ability. Sight would be incredibly useful for this kind of thing. Besides, it would make Sliding distances easier, taking away some of the need for familiarity to ensure a safe Slide.

Instead, he had to work with what he had available. The glass brought everything into sharper focus. Oranges and reds from the setting sun gleamed off small waves cresting in the bay. A triangular sail on the nearest boat—barely larger than a dinghy—puffed out with the wind. A long rod hung over the side, but Rsiran didn't see anyone on the boat. Shifting the spyglass, he looked farther out over the water and caught sight of one of the massive flat-bottomed fishing boats that could sail into the docks.

At that distance, he couldn't make out much in the way of detail. What must it be like working the lines, reeling in fish day after day? How could anyone enjoy standing being surrounded by that much water? Much better to spend his time hammering at the forge, feeling the heat of the coals press against your cheeks, sweat running down your back as you hammered until the metal began to take its shape.

As he turned the spyglass further, he realized he had been mistaken about what he thought was another fishing boat. It had a pair of enormous masts, its square sails filled with wind, pushing the ship forward, drifting it slowly back toward the city. It turned and Rsiran recognized the shape of the figurehead on the bow. Firell's ship, and now returning toward shore.

Rsiran was too late. Firell might only have been gone for a few days, but the fact that he'd left at all made it likely he'd unloaded the lorcith he had stored in the hold. Safer that way, he knew, better to keep what he smuggled away from the guilds, but he still couldn't come up with a good reason why Firell would have that much lorcith in the first place. As far as he knew, taking it served no purpose, other than to deprive the Elvraeth. And if he had that much lorcith, why wouldn't he have it brought it to Rsiran, or Brusus at least, to have it shaped into something saleable? If it *was* Josun that he'd overheard on Firell's ship, then what did Josun want with the lorcith?

Rather than Sliding, he made his way along the shore road, walking slowly past a series of shops. Most were run down, paint faded or peeling. None had signs hanging outside, not like the nicer shops found in Upper Town, or even those on the border like his father's. At least, like it had been. Before.

Rsiran sighed. Wind pressed against his face, cool and crisp. Aches from yesterday slowly worked out of him as he walked, leaving him feeling better than he had in a few days. Yet… he couldn't escape the threat hanging over him. Josun Elvraeth lived and had come for Lianna. That he went after Brusus didn't make much sense, but what if Brusus was not his intended target? What if Josun simply wanted Rsiran to be aware that he lived? A message.

He reached the wide road heading up through the city when he collided with someone.

Rsiran bounced back a step, quickly stuffing a hand into his pocket as he reached for one of his knives. The woman in front of him looked offended that he would even touch her. The basket she carried fell from her hands, dropping to the cobbled street. Rsiran hurried to help her lift it but she waved him off.

"Don't bother." She pulled the basket away from him and turned back up the street.

He recognized the voice, but not the dress or the posture. "Alyse?"

Only days before, he had thought he'd seen her. But she should not be here, not in Lower Town and not dressed like this in a white dress stained with several day's worth of grime. Once sleek black hair now hung at her ears, cut short. Only the lorcith chain hanging from her neck told him it was she. It pulled on him, and he recognized the craftsmanship that had gone into making it. If nothing else, his father had been skilled.

She froze. Then she turned slowly, bright green eyes widening slightly. "Rsiran?" She looked around the street, and Rsiran wondered if she looked for someone to call to for help. When she turned her attention back to him, she studied him a moment. "You look... different."

He didn't know whether to take that as a compliment or not.

"Father said you were banished."

"By him. Not the council. Why are you here?"

Her face darkened. "You suddenly care what happens to your family?"

He took a step back, startled by the heat of her words. "I always cared. It wasn't always returned."

The corners of her eyes softened. "Go back to wherever you live now, Rsiran. We'll be fine."

Alyse straightened her back and turned away from him.

As she started back up the street, he blurted out, "What happened to the shop?"

She did not turn back to him. "What do you know of it?"

Rsiran hurried toward her, stopping in front of her. "I know that it's empty. After generations of Lareth smiths, now it stands shuttered."

Her eyes narrowed slightly. "That was always going to be the case."

He tried to ignore the barb, but it cut too close to what he felt. Had he stayed with his father, had he just been willing to serve out his sentence in the mines, would he have been able to return home? To apprentice with his father?

To suppress the gifts the Great Watcher had given him. Never know the call of the lorcith or the freedom he felt with each Slide? No… returning home had not been the answer. But that didn't change how he wished there had been another way.

"What happened?"

Alyse's eyes drifted to the basket she carried. Rsiran smelled the stink of fish coming from it and realized the basket carried more than just the three of them would need.

"You're working?"

Her eyes flashed and a flush came to her cheeks.

"But why? Why would you need to work?"

Even as he asked, he understood. The shop had always provided enough for the family, but the last year had been difficult. Jobs were less plentiful, especially those that paid well, and their father had fallen into the arms of ale. When Rsiran had still lived at home, he'd known that money grew more and more scarce.

When she looked up, her eyes were red. "Why do you suddenly care?" she whispered. "You would not do what he asked. You became—"

"Nothing," he snapped. "I became who the Great Watcher intended me to be. My ability is no darker than you trying to Read me." He made certain to *push* his reinforced barriers firmly in place so that she couldn't Read him. When he'd been younger, it had always been an expectation that she'd Read past his barriers. He no longer feared her as he once had.

Her face flushed more.

"Don't bother. I have learned much since we last saw each other. I doubt you will crawl through my mind as easily as you once did."

She glared at him.

"But, since I can't Read you, what happened to our father?"

Alyse glanced up the street. "I can't…"

Rsiran grabbed the basket from her. "I'll carry this. You walk."

She opened her mouth to argue, as if to scold him like she always had when they were younger, but closed it. Then she nodded. "You *have* changed," she said softly.

"It seems we all have."

Alyse studied his face for a moment as they walked. "He lost the shop," she began. "But you know that."

"I found it empty."

Alyse continued up the street, veering off onto a side street Rsiran didn't know, one running along the length of Lower Town. Rows of narrow buildings crammed together. The smell of bread and roasting meats mixed with the smells near the shore, reminding him of the market.

"Business trailed off after…"

When she didn't seem like she would continue, he asked, "After what?"

"After the mining guild accused him of stealing lorcith."

Rsiran almost tripped and without thinking what he was doing, Slid forward a step to steady himself. Alyse glared at him.

"Why would the guild accuse him of stealing lorcith?"

She cast a sideways glace at him. "You really think you need to ask that question?"

Rsiran nodded.

"Because he wanted to protect you."

"Protect me? He never did anything to protect me. Only punish me." The heat in his words surprised him. After all this time, he still felt anger at how his father had treated him. Even after getting away, he still felt that emotion. "You can't imagine what it was like being in the darkness of the mines. The way the stone presses down around you. The threat of the other miners willing to hurt you at any time." He said nothing about the lorcith calling him, demanding that he free it from the stone. Alyse didn't understand him Sliding; she would understand that ability even less.

She drew her back straight. For a moment, with the way she looked at him, she reminded him of the Alyse of his youth. "Yes, protect you. When the guild came to him demanding to see proof that he used lorcith, he claimed failure rather than reveal that you had been stealing from him."

"I did not steal lorcith from father's shop."

They had stopped on an intersecting street. The buildings lining the street reminded him of the alley outside the smithy, stone cracked and crumbling, and halfhearted attempts to repair it having failed. Pale painted walls faded, nothing like the more vivid colors found near Upper Town. Even the drains in the stone meant to divert rainwater out into the bay were plugged like they were near his smithy, fetid water pooling. It was a place he never would have expected to find Alyse.

A few others made their way along the street, most dressed in the same rough fabric that made Alyse's dress. Rsiran's finer clothes, finely woven cotton Brusus had procured for him, seemed just as out of place here as it did near his smithy. At least along the shore, the variety of people making their way kept him from standing out. Here, he felt as out of place as he would if he were to Slide to Upper Town in the daylight.

"We know what your ability makes you."

"What it makes me? You really believe that my ability to Slide…" He lowered his voice and glanced down the street. For a moment, he thought he saw a flash of bright red fabric that reminded him of Shael, but it disappeared. "That it changes me? What of Father's ability? Did it push him to drink? Did it push him to hit me?"

Alyse took a deep breath. "But he saw you in his shop. Do not deny that."

Rsiran wouldn't deny that he had. "I came for something else. Not lorcith."

Alyse sniffed. "If not you, then someone else? Will that be your story when the guild finds you? When you are brought by the constables before the Elvraeth?"

The Elvraeth might punish him for many things, but stealing lorcith from the guild would not be one. "The guild does not care about anything other than production. And I do nothing that impedes production."

"After all this time, you do not need to convince me, Rsiran."

Still, that someone had stolen lorcith from his father's shop worried him. That was the one thing Rsiran had made a point *not* to do. "You think I needed to steal from father?"

She shrugged and then nodded. "You have as much admitted that you did."

"I told you that I went to his shop, not that I took lorcith. Besides, why should I have the need when he gave me all the access I could ever want?" He had told his father the same thing when confronted.

Her eyes widened. "That is forbidden!"

Forbidden. "Just like sending his son to work the mines? Sentenced as if I were some criminal needing to be punished?"

Alyse stared at him but said nothing.

"Why are you here?" Rsiran asked.

"Where else am I to go?"

"Not here. Home?"

She laughed bitterly. "Still so foolish, aren't you Rsiran? After Father lost his shop, we had no place left to go. When he left us… This is home now."

"What do you mean he left you?"

"I thought you said you went to his shop?"

Rsiran nodded, unable to suppress the strange sense of emptiness he'd felt when he found his father's shop abandoned. "I did. It was empty. Nothing remained except a few scraps of paper."

"And why would Father clear out the shop?"

Rsiran sighed. He did not want to argue with Alyse. But seeing her brought back all the old memories he had. "Where did he go?"

Alyse only shook her head. "One day he was here. Coming home, drunk as usual. The next day, he never came home. Mother did not do well. So I had to do what I could to keep us fed. Had you… had you…"

Her face twisted as she trailed off. Whether embarrassed or angry, he couldn't tell.

Alyse grabbed the basket from him and turned, running away from him down the street.

Rsiran didn't bother to Slide after her.

CHAPTER 23

After Alyse left him, Rsiran wandered through Lower Town. Seeing her like that, knowing that she had taken to working at the market, was strange. Alyse had always expected to marry into wealth, especially after her abilities manifested. Both Sight and Reading. Gifts to make any in Elaeavn proud. Now she lived no better than he did. Worse probably. At least he didn't work carting fish up from the markets. He had the forge, and Sliding didn't restrict him.

The sun tilted toward the horizon as he walked. He debated returning to the smithy and working on Shael's project, but without a way to follow the plans, there seemed little he could do.

Thoughts of the alloy lingered. If Josun Elvraeth lived, having access to the alloy would be a way to keep him and his friends safe, but he had no idea how to mix the metal with lorcith. From his experience, there wasn't a way to mix anything into lorcith. It had to be worked in its pure form. All the master smiths thought that the case, including his father.

But did the alchemists? If anyone in the city—outside the Elvra-eth—were to know, it would be the alchemists. Their location in the city was a carefully guarded secret. Supposedly none but the guild masters knew how to find the guild house, but Rsiran had an edge that others did not. Wherever the alchemists resided, they would have lorcith. He could use his sense of lorcith to guide him.

The problem was sensing the lorcith. Here in the city, he felt too close. There was another place he could go, one that he did not visit as often as he once had. The last time had been when he'd needed a way to clear his head after visiting Firell's ship. This time, he needed the distance and view of the city he couldn't get anyplace else.

Rsiran made his way into a narrow alley. He checked to see if any-one else wandered nearby, but needn't have bothered. Even the street had been empty. Nothing but refuse and the stench of filth lined the alley.

He Slid and emerged atop Krali Rock.

No wind rustled his clothing tonight. As before, he looked down at the city. Candles flickered in some of the windows. He made a point of not looking toward the palace, ignoring the blue lantern light shining through the windows there. Nothing good would come of turning his attention to the palace, of getting mixed up in the Elvraeth politics. Already he had learned that lesson well.

He sat on the rock and closed his eyes. Then he listened.

Lorcith called softly. Some he recognized quickly. His smithy had a mixture of raw ore and that which he'd already forged. It drew on him, calling with a distinct voice. Were he to want to, he thought he could *pull* the sword to him even from here. Strange that he should have such a connection to it. He remembered its making, the way the metal had drawn him along, pulling its shape out more quickly than any other forging he'd made before. And none had gone quite the same since.

He pushed away the sense of the sword. It drifted to the back of his mind, willing to let him ignore it for now. Other forgings of his scattered about the city. These pulled on him, as well, almost as if simply to announce their presence. Rsiran acknowledged them and pushed them away too.

Then he felt the strange sense of the alloy at the palace. With the other sense of lorcith ignored, this threatened to overwhelm him, as if it urgently demanded his attention. Rsiran took several slow breaths before he managed to push this sense away, burying it deep in his mind.

All he had left were scattered senses of unshaped lorcith. A few seemed focused between Lower Town and Upper Town. It took a moment to realize that they likely came from the smiths there. Not nearly as much lorcith as he expected to sense. The smiths together had less than he had stored in the crate Shael had brought him.

Rsiran shifted his awareness away from the smiths. A few other small collections existed in the city—barely more than nuggets—but otherwise, he didn't feel anything. As he considered giving up, he felt something else. Something unexpected.

The alloy.

The lorcith of the alloy pulled on him differently than in the pure form. As the alloy, he had no sense of awareness, none of the pleading desire that he felt when working with lorcith. This felt muted. Had he not pushed away all the other lorcith, he might never have felt it.

The alloy in the palace called to him, but it wasn't the only source. There was another, small and near the palace, though separate. Firmly in Upper Town.

Few of the guilds were in Upper Town, but if any would be found there, Rsiran suspected the alchemists would find a way to be near the Elvraeth. Or perhaps it was the other way around. Would the Elvraeth allow the alchemists to be too far from them? Wouldn't they want their secrets protected?

Rsiran Slid off Krali and toward the palace. When he emerged from the Slide, he kept the other lorcith pushed into the distance and listened for the alloy. This close to the palace, he struggled ignoring the alloy found here, but he hadn't wanted to emerge too far away. Rsiran knew parts of Upper Town better than Lower Town, but there was no telling who might be out on the streets. There weren't the interconnected alleys all about Upper Town like were found in Lower Town, and streetlights lit the roadways with wide swaths of orange light.

Hidden near a stilted corbal tree, he listened. And then he heard it again, the soft faded sense of the alloy, just enough to trail. He hesitated, searching for evidence of lorcith as well, and noticed it near the alloy. Lorcith would be easier for him to detect, so he followed this, hoping it led to the same place.

Rsiran moved away from the tree and walked. Dressed in a navy shirt of decent cut and brown trousers only slightly stained from the day, his clothing wouldn't make him stand out. Likely he'd stand out less here in Upper Town than he did at night in Lower Town.

As he followed the sense of lorcith, the road took him past a line of taverns, some with soft music drifting through closed doors. Most had signs hanging from eaves, decorated with names like Trusted Lute or Sleepy Watcher painted with bright colors. A few smelled like bakers, their ovens now cool, but the scent of breads and sweets still drifting into the street, smells so different from what he knew in Lower Town. He passed dressmakers and candle makers and potters and weavers. All had shops better appointed than even his father's had been, places suited for the wealth found in Upper Town. These were places Rsiran had never visited in his youth. Even then, he'd felt separated from the people of Upper Town.

He turned, making his way onto a smaller street. Bright streetlamps still glowed here, no space along the street left in shadows. The orange light helped his eyes but from what Jessa said, wouldn't help those Sighted, not like the blue lantern light found in the palace.

Homes lined this street. Most were massive, rising two stories and separated from the next by stretches of green or groomed corbal trees. Some had candles glowing in their windows. A few had soft blue light. All demonstrated wealth unlike anything he could ever imagine, from the exquisite stonework of the buildings, to the way the trees were shaped, groomed into patterns.

The muted sense of lorcith came from the end of the street. Rsiran stopped before a wide house. Nothing about it seemed different from the others along the street, other than the fact that no candles lit the windows.

Rsiran hesitated, considering Sliding into the house, when he became aware of lorcith near him. One of his forgings.

Rsiran turned, readying to Slide away. Haern stood in between a pair of streetlamps, watching him.

Rsiran Slid to him. "Haern?" he asked carefully.

Haern glanced at him before looking over at the house Rsiran had been studying. He held a slender knife—made of lorcith that Rsiran had felt—and twisted it idly in his hand. A light cloak hung about his shoulders, covering a black shirt and pants that practically disappeared into the thin shadows. If Rsiran had ever had doubts about Haern's previous occupation, seeing him dressed like this erased them.

"What is it you seek here, Rsiran?" Haern's voice came out as little more than a harsh whisper.

"How did you know I'd be here?" Haern wouldn't have been able to follow him—not with how Rsiran had Slid to Krali Rock before Sliding toward the palace. And he couldn't See Rsiran the same way he could others. Sliding masked him.

"Something changed."

Rsiran frowned. "What changed? You can suddenly See me?"

Haern looked over at Rsiran. Shadows caught along his eyes making his face appear darker. "Yes."

That troubled Rsiran. Had pushing away the sense of lorcith shifted something? "Is that why you came?"

Haern flipped the knife so that the point faced down. "You should not have been this clear to me, Rsiran."

"What did you See?" He slipped back so that he stood with his back facing the row of houses behind him. The streetlamps on either side cascaded thin light onto him. Dressed as he was, he didn't blend into the darkness nearly as well as Haern.

"Normally, only swirls of color. Even that is muted. Most of the time, I cannot tell what that means." He shrugged, as if that should make sense to Rsiran. "But I had a sudden sense of the colors about you coalescing. There was darkness and danger around you when before I saw nothing."

"What does that mean?"

"Why were you planning to enter that house?" The knife stopped moving in his hand.

Rsiran tensed. The last time Haern had come to him like this, he had tried to injure him with Rsiran's knife. He claimed he'd only done it to help save Jessa, but Rsiran wondered how much truth there was in that.

Haern watched him, and a tight smile pulled at his mouth. Then he stuffed the knife into the waist of his pants, pulling his shirt up and over it. "It isn't me you need to fear."

"You think I need to fear entering that house?"

Haern looked across the street, and his eyes narrowed. "I Saw... changes for you—and others—if you do. Beyond that, I can't tell. The fact that I can See anything worries me. What's in there? Why have you come here?"

How much should he share with Haern? As a Seer, if Haern saw something that might make what he needed to do easier, then shouldn't he take advantage of it?

"I think it's the alchemist guild house."

Haern turned slowly away from the house and looked at Rsiran. "The alchemists? How could you know? I don't think even Brusus could learn the location of their house."

What did it mean that Brusus was so connected throughout Elaeavn that he should be able to learn secrets from the Elvraeth, to bribe constables, and yet still not know the location of the alchemist guild house?

"You know I sense lorcith?"

"I think I have heard that," Haern said. His hand moved away from the knife he carried.

"There is an alloy of lorcith which blocks my other ability."

"I thought you told us that lorcith could not mix with other metals."

Rsiran nodded. "Until I—" He glanced up toward the palace and lowered his voice. From here, the palace did not float as it did lower in the city, but the towers still stretched high overhead, as if reaching for the Great Watcher. "Until I tried Sliding into the palace. Windows are barred with this alloy. It kept us from easily Sliding inside."

"But did not prevent you completely."

"No." Rsiran chose not to explain.

Haern turned and gazed back at the house. "Strange that lorcith should prevent you from Sliding."

"Strange? How so?"

Haern just shook his head. "Contrasting abilities do not pair, at least not strongly. No Sighted can Listen. Readers are never Seers."

"But the Elvraeth—"

"Even within the Elvraeth, there exists this balance." Haern shrugged. "I don't know what it means—I can't See anything to explain it—only that it intrigues me. Perhaps Della would know more."

"I don't think my ability with lorcith is the same as being Sighted or a Reader."

Haern looked at him, eyes arched. "No? From what I've seen, it's just as useful. And likely gifted just the same as the others."

If that were true, then Rsiran could no longer feel as if he'd been shorted somehow by the Great Watcher. If he truly had two abilities, how was that any different from what Alyse possessed?

"You still haven't explained how you have come to believe the alchemists are here. Or why you would seek to find them."

"I wanted to understand the alloy. Something like that might help keep us safe from…" He hesitated. Did Haern know about Josun?

"From another Slider?" Haern finished.

Rsiran nodded. "The alchemists would know more about the alloy. That's why I'm here."

"Seems to be a dangerous thing you've pursued. When Brusus told me about Josun, I didn't know whether to believe him at first, but after Lianna…" He breathed out softly. "I wish I could See him more clearly. Then we could know what he was after and what it has to do with us in Lower Town." Haern tilted his head as he considered Rsiran. "And you think to protect yourself from him. That this alloy would keep you safe?"

The alloy *could* keep him safe, if Rsiran could only find a way to use it to block Josun. "I think I need to understand it."

"And the alchemists know how to create this alloy?"

Rsiran sighed. "I don't know. Before visiting the palace, I'd never heard of the alloy. Without the ability to sense lorcith, I don't think I'd even know it was a lorcith mix. And my father didn't know of it."

At least, he didn't think that he did. What reason would his father have had to potentially waste lorcith trying to create an alloy without any guarantee of success? Lorcith was far too valuable to the smiths to experiment with it like that. Testing alloys could be time consuming, and sometimes, each batch required a different amount. That was the value of the alchemists.

"A shame we cannot simply ask a master smith," Haern said.

Rsiran just nodded. He didn't say anything about the fact that his father's smithy had been abandoned. And he had no interest in searching for other smiths. Doubtless they would recognize him, but what reason could he give for asking about an alloy of lorcith? Better to seek answers from the alchemists.

"I See that I haven't changed your mind."

Rsiran just shook his head.

Haern nodded. With a quick flick of his wrist—faster than should have been possible—the knife came out from his waist and twisted in his hand.

Rsiran readied to push it away.

Haern offered a tight smile. "Then I will come with you."

CHAPTER 24

R SIRAN GLANCED UP THE STREET just to make certain no one
else approached. Then he grabbed Haern's arm and Slid them
to the edge of the house. Something about Haern's shirt seemed to
throw off the light, leaving him more shadowed than Rsiran.

Haern held tightly to the knife. No longer did it flip softly through
his hand. The lorcith of the knife pulled on him, drawing him with
a gentle call. With nothing more than a nudge, Rsiran could *pull* the
knife to him. Haern seemed to sense this and kept it in his outside
hand.

"Interesting," Haern muttered as they emerged from the Slide.

"What?"

"The colors. Much like what I usually See swirling around you."

Rsiran nodded. The colors were there every time he Slid. That and
the soft bitter odor that always reminded him of lorcith. He no longer
even noticed it as he once did.

"Why didn't you Slide us into the house?"

"I'm not sure I can. The alloy is there, enough that I feel it pushing against me. A barrier of sorts."

"And you can't Slide through it."

"Not easily." Even were he to manage to get through the barrier, getting back out would be difficult. Better to save his strength for the return Slide. At least then, he could anchor to lorcith he felt, either the sword in his smithy or one of the countless other items he had stored throughout Elaeavn.

"Then it's good I offered to come."

Haern took the lead, making his way between the neighboring houses, slipping into the shadows and quickly fading to be practically invisible. Rsiran hurried after him, wondering where Haern might lead him. Stones crunched too loudly under his boots. Each step seemed to send small debris cascading down the gentle slope that existed between the houses. The air felt heavier here, as well, and mixed with an undercurrent that seemed almost sickly sweet.

Haern stopped near the back of the house. A flat expanse of stone and grass fitted between this house and the one behind it. Two small trees struggled to grow, strangled by the height of the houses. One bloomed with a half-dozen limp flowers, the color of the petals bleached by night and lack of sunlight. Rsiran couldn't help but think that Jessa wouldn't even bother with those.

"Where are you going?" Rsiran whispered.

"Can't go through the front door now, can we? Raises too much suspicion if we're seen trying to pick the lock and sneak through. Besides, I wouldn't be surprised if the alchemists left some sort of surprises for anyone who tried to come in that way."

Haern glanced at the other houses visible to them from where they stood. No lanterns lit the homes, and no candles flickered in windows. And, hopefully, no one Sighted watched them.

"Still certain this is the alchemists?" Haern asked.

Rsiran listened. Since encountering Haern, he hadn't spent as much energy trying to suppress awareness of the rest of the lorcith around him, but by not doing so, the distant sense of lorcith he'd heard had faded to little more than a murmuring, barely scratching at the back of his consciousness.

As he had before, he focused on the sense of lorcith he felt, pushing each piece away one by one, until all he felt—all he heard—was that faint sensation of the alloy. As he did, he knew it was here, somewhere behind the walls of this home.

"Not certain, but it's the most likely," he said.

Haern nodded and then slipped away, drifting along the back of the house. Rsiran followed closely. He considered Sliding, but the lorcith warned against it, almost as if speaking to him. And then Haern stopped before a small door.

Rsiran had seen Jessa and Brusus pick their way through locks with skill. What Haern did next looked less refined, but went more quickly than what either had managed. Taking the slender lorcith knife, he shoved it into the lock, twisted once, and shoved a shoulder against the door. It popped open.

Neither moved for a moment, listening, but nothing came but the whispers of the hidden lorcith.

Haern ducked inside the door. Rsiran waited for a moment before following him in. As he did, he thought he heard the quiet cry of a distant cat. He didn't wait to hear if it repeated.

* * * * *

The darkened building seemed to swallow him, even more when he pulled the door closed behind him. Haern hovered nearby, barely

more than a presence, the lorcith of his knife pushing on his awareness. The heaviness he'd smelled between the buildings was thicker
here, filling his nostrils with the odor.

"Where do we start?" Haern whispered.

Rsiran pointed down what he thought was some sort of hallway.
Without any light, he didn't know with certainty. "I can't see much."

Haern sighed out a soft laugh. "My Sight is not much better. Should
have brought Jessa."

"I didn't want to risk her."

"Good," Haern said. "Stay close to me."

Rsiran couldn't tell what else might be in the building. For all he
knew, they might be surrounded by dozens of people, or it could simply be an empty house. Haern let Rsiran lead as they moved deeper
into the house. Rsiran held onto the muted sense of lorcith he felt and
let it guide him as he made his way down the hall.

As he drew nearer, he felt aware of something else. Only when he
reached a door blocking him from going any further did he notice
what he felt. Unshaped lorcith.

"What is it, Rsiran?" Haern whispered.

"Something changed."

"What?"

Haern slipped to stand alongside him. Rsiran felt the knife in
Haern's hand pointed toward the door.

"I feel lorcith. Different from before."

"Do you think someone else is here?" Haern asked.

"I don't know."

Haern turned toward him. He felt it more as a shifting of his cloak,
the soft fabric rustling quietly as he moved. Haern grabbed his shoulder and pulled him gently until the wall pushed back against him.

"Wait."

Haern reached for the door and twisted, pushing it open just enough for him to slip through. He didn't close it completely. Cool air breathed out through the crack.

And, suddenly, he no longer sensed Haern's knife.

Rsiran pushed back against the wall. Haern couldn't have simply disappeared. The distant sense of lorcith stayed with him, and he let it go, drawing on other lorcith around him, listening for Haern. At first, it came back to him faintly, hidden and soft. Then he felt it more strongly. Only it didn't move.

He waited, but still the sense of the knife didn't change. Had Haern dropped it? That seemed unlikely. Haern had gripped it tightly as he made his way through the door, not to mention that he was a skilled assassin. Losing his weapon didn't seem likely.

The only other thing he could think of was that Haern was in danger.

Haern wouldn't be here if not for him. He wouldn't have followed him into the house, risked angering the alchemists, if not for Rsiran. All the time he'd wondered where Haern's allegiance really lay, and now he might have sent him into danger.

Rsiran stepped through the door. A whistle of bitter air hit his nose, and for the briefest second, colors seemed to swirl. Then past the door, he saw nothing. A soft shimmering crossed over his skin, like a tingling cool touch. For a moment, he wondered if water dripped across his skin but didn't feel anything else. The sensation passed, but left a knot of nausea in his stomach.

Darkness surrounded him. But through it, he felt lorcith all around him. Just as he had in the mines, Rsiran used that sense to navigate through this space, sensing for voids in the lorcith to move carefully.

Where was Haern?

He didn't sense the knife. Rsiran hesitated and listened again. Distantly, the knife called to him, as if recognizing he sought it. But from what he could tell, there didn't seem any way to reach it. Walls of lor-cith blocked him.

If he couldn't reach him, he couldn't help Haern. Rsiran did the only thing he could think of. Anchoring to the knife, he Slid.

He emerged in a flat, open area. Blue light from four lanterns on the walls lit the space. Walls were smooth stone, not lorcith or the alloy but something different, and not simple rock. It took him a moment to realize that the ground under his feet was made of large sheets of the alloy, hammered flat and pieced together. There seemed a pattern, but he couldn't tell what it might be. The air in the room tasted stale and still.

Haern lay on the floor, unmoving. The knife he carried had fallen just out of reach.

Muted voices drifted as through a thick door, though he saw no sign of a door. As far as he could tell, no one else was in the room with them.

He hurried to Haern and checked if he breathed. His chest rose slowly.

Glancing around, he saw drawers lining one wall, practically built into the stone, with twisted handles that seemed to have grown from the drawers themselves. He hadn't seen them before. Nothing else marred the walls.

Where was he? Some area deep below the alchemist guild? Or someplace else?

Other than the knife on the ground, and the lorcith around him, he felt no other lorcith. Not even the distant and muted sense that had brought him to the house.

This must be where he needed to go, but how could he learn the secrets of the alchemists here?

He hesitated, listening to the distant voices. They hadn't come any closer.

He should grab Haern and get out, especially if others could learn he'd been there, but... would he have an opportunity like this again? He needed to understand the alloy, and seeing how much the alchemists possessed, he knew that he'd come to the right place. Would the alchemists learn that they'd entered their guild? Haern had jammed open the door; surely they would see it. And had he closed the door before coming through? Rsiran didn't think he had.

That meant he had to learn what he could now.

He ran toward the far wall and toward the drawers. His feet slapped with a muted sound as he ran. It seemed to take longer than it should to reach the other end of the room, almost as if he moved more slowly than normal. He considered Sliding again, but hesitated. What if someone on the other side of the wall felt the ripples of his Slide? Della said that skill was not very common, but it didn't mean others weren't aware. And if any would know, wouldn't it be someone like the alchemists?

Finally, he reached the wall. Small marks etched into the stone face of the drawers. Nothing with letters or numbers, nothing that identified one from another. Nearly two-dozen drawers. He didn't have time to look through each one.

Rsiran studied the drawers, scanning them quickly. One of them jumped out at him. The edge of the drawer seemed off, as if it had been opened more than the others.

The voices moved. He didn't have much time to spare.

Rsiran grabbed the handle and pulled. The drawer didn't budge.

He tried again and again nothing changed.

Rsiran tried a different approach. Pushing on the lorcith in the handle, there came a soft *click* and the drawer slid open.

It was deeper than he would have expected.

Rsiran leaned over the edge and looked inside, holding his breath as he did.

He didn't know what he expected. Items of power or gold and silver or even strange shapings of lorcith. Instead, the drawer contained a stack of parchment. Hundreds of pages.

Rsiran pulled out a few and started thumbing through them when the voices he'd heard became more distinct.

He pushed and the drawer closed. Only then did he remember that he still held the pages of parchment. He stuffed them into his pocket.

The sound of something heavy sliding slowly rumbled toward him.

His heart skipped. Without thinking, he Slid toward Haern. Then he scooped up the knife and grabbed Haern.

Someone gasped. Rsiran didn't dare turn and look.

Feet pounded across the floor. The sound was muted and distant but quickly became louder.

He did not wait. Pulling Haern with him, he anchored to the sword in his smithy and Slid from the guild house.

CHAPTER 25

R SIRAN EMERGED FROM THE SLIDE into the smithy.
Haern flopped onto the floor, still not moving. The effort
of the Slide had been much like Sliding from the palace, and Rsiran
suspected that only the familiarity of the smithy and the sword he used
to anchor to had helped him reach it safely.

He dropped down next to Haern, breathing heavily. He glanced at
Haern's chest to make sure he still breathed.

Almost caught. And certainly discovered. Whoever had come into
the guild house knew that someone had Slid from there. How long
would it be before the alchemist guild sent the constables for him? Or
something worse?

Everything seemed to be cascading out of control. And it all point-
ed to Josun Elvraeth. Had they not gotten mixed up with him, had
Rsiran never tried entering the palace, how much would be different?
Now he had violated another place nearly as off limits as the palace.
And brought Haern with him this time.

For what? For pages of parchment? He still had no idea about the alloy, no way of knowing what it took to make it, only that the strange silver-like metal was involved somehow. Firell still took lorcith away for an Elvraeth—likely Josun—and he had no idea what Shael wanted from him. Then there was Brusus. Whatever he tried to learn by bribing the Elvraeth was about more than Josun. Rsiran was certain of that.

He pulled the parchment from his pocket. Lines of script scrawled across the pages in a neat hand. Rsiran couldn't read the writing, but didn't know if it was a different language or some sort of code. Each page was much the same.

He stuffed the pages back into his pocket. Whatever else, he had now stolen from the alchemists as well. How long before they learned what he took?

Not long. And then none of them would be safe. This time, because of what he did.

Haern moaned softly. Rsiran turned and saw him trying to sit up. One hand grabbed his head. He blinked, looking around, before suddenly seeming to understand where he was.

"You got me out." His voice sounded rough and dry.

Rsiran nodded. "What happened? You went through the door... and then nothing."

Haern's eyes shifted, the green in them going distant. "Can't See you again. Just colors."

"What happened to you?"

Haern shook his head. "Don't know. Stepped through the door. Felt like I was falling. Saw a wash of colors like I did around you. Then I hit something. Can't remember anything after that."

What Haern described was different from what Rsiran had experienced. He'd had none of the sense of motion. Just the colors, almost as if Sliding, though he hadn't Slid. Then there was the cool tingling across his skin, unlike anything he'd ever felt before. He still didn't know what that meant.

"How'd you get me out?"

"I… I followed you after I realized you weren't moving anymore."

Haern's eyes narrowed. "How did you know?"

"The knife," he answered. Rsiran handed the knife back to Haern who twirled it briefly in his hand before stuffing it back into his waistband in a quick flourish. "It stopped moving."

Haern grunted. "Good thing Brusus suggested we carry these."

"That was Brusus's idea?"

Haern shrugged. "I wasn't sure it was a good idea, especially after how easily you *pulled* that knife from me the last time. Not sure I want someone able to kill me before I have a chance to act."

"I'm not a killer."

Haern's eyes narrowed. "We're all killers if given the right motivation."

Rsiran remembered what he'd done to Josun, how he'd almost killed him in the palace—in fact thought he had. But that time hadn't been intentional. He hadn't meant to poison him. He'd only done what he needed to free Jessa.

"Then why'd you keep the knife?"

Haern's eyes softened and he pushed to stand. "Times like this, I guess. Think you would have gotten to me otherwise?"

Rsiran wouldn't have. Without the knife to anchor to, he didn't think he would have even known where to find Haern. "No."

Haern nodded. "What did you find?"

Rsiran pulled the pages out of his pocket, and Haern took them with a frown. He scanned the pages for a few moments. "You know what these say?"

"Not a bit. Can you read it?"

Haern frowned. The scar on his face tightened as he did. "No. Looks to be some sort of code. Nothing I See about it makes any sense."

Rsiran found the comment strange. Could Haern really use his ability to See something about the parchment? "Either that or another language."

Haern shook his head. "None that I've seen. And these numbers seem to correspond, but I'm not sure how. Brusus is pretty good with this kind of thing. Mind if I show him?"

"I'm not sure that anyone should have that."

Rsiran reached for it and Haern held it away. "You fear the alchemists."

"I worry what will happen if they learn it was me who entered the guild house. I... I was seen, Haern. Someone came into the room before I had a chance to Slide us out. I know they saw me. There aren't many who could Slide out of there."

Haern took a deep breath and let it out slowly. His eyes lost focus as they did when he tried to See. He blinked once and shook his head. "Nothing. Just the swirls of color around you. Doesn't mean anything."

"What about Brusus? Or Jessa?" He hated that he had to worry about what effect he might have on Jessa. That he might have put her in danger again.

Haern clapped a hand on his shoulder. "Don't worry, Rsiran. I have seen nothing to indicate they are at risk." Haern pocketed the roll of parchment and turned toward the door. "Find Brusus. He needs to know what happened tonight. There are steps he can take."

"And you? Where will you go?"

Haern's mouth tightened into a narrow line. "There are steps I need to take as well."

* * * * *

Rsiran sat in the Wretched Barth alone, waiting for the others. He slumped on the stool at their usual table, leaning over the lukewarm mug of ale that didn't taste quite the same as usual.

As he sat, he let his sense of lorcith wander. All around him were forgings he'd made. Some intentionally given, like the bowl in the kitchen or the knife Haern still carried. Even the charm Jessa wore pulled at him. Others he felt were different. The pot here in the Barth. Knives at Della's home. The decorative fork buried with Lianna in the Aisl.

Thinking of Lianna put him into an even darker mood than he had already been. Now he didn't have to fear just Josun Elvraeth, but the alchemist guild learning of someone who could Slide. Haern might think he didn't have to worry, but how long before someone realized that it had been he in that room?

And then what would happen? Would he be brought before the council? That would be the traditional route to sentencing. But if Josun Elvraeth were involved, he might face a different penalty. Rather than just facing banishment, he might be subjected to something worse.

He shivered, trying to push away the dark thoughts. Sitting alone, nothing but the ale for company, made it hard to do.

The rest of the Barth seemed different too. A bandolist played, and the songs seemed appropriately mournful, nothing like the usual cheery tunes played here. A few others sat along the bar, but no one really talked. Without Lianna, the Barth seemed to have lost some of its vibrancy.

As he sat at the table, another thought came to him of his conversation with Alyse earlier. For the last few months, he hadn't given much thought to his family or what happened to them since he'd disappeared other than to feel thankful that his father apparently hadn't reported him to the constables. But between finding his father's smithy abandoned and meeting Alyse on the street, he felt drawn back to them.

And there was what Alyse had told him. Had his father *not* reported him to the constables after all? Alyse claimed their father had protected him from the guild. But if that was the case, why? Why would his father have protected him? He'd been the one to banish him to the mines, to try to teach him a lesson, either to ignore the call of lorcith or simply to punish him for Sliding. He'd been the one who'd said he didn't want to see Rsiran again.

But now that his father had lost the smithy, Rsiran wondered what happened. Where was his father? Alyse made no mention of where he'd gone, if she even knew. If he was still around, he couldn't imagine a time when he would simply have abandoned the smithy. And Alyse now lived in a part of Lower Town that even Rsiran wouldn't have wanted to live in. Did his mother live there too?

He took another sip of ale. If he didn't think Alyse would attack him for visiting—or worse, report him—he might try to learn more. As it was, he had enough worrying about those who actually cared for him.

The door opened and Jessa guided Brusus through. He was dressed in one of his finer cloaks, heavy embroidery worked along the edge. He wobbled, as if he'd already had too much to drink. Rsiran leapt to his feet to help.

"What happened?"

She shook her head. "Not sure. He won't tell me."

Brusus looked up at him and frowned. "What did you do, Rsiran?"

The words froze Rsiran.

Brusus looked at him through reddened eyes. "What did you do?" His words slurred heavily. Brusus was already drunk.

"A little help?" Jessa said.

They dragged him to the table and propped him on a stool. Brusus leaned back against the wall, but at least he had strength enough to keep from falling. A young server came over—one Lianna had only recently hired—a scowl painted onto her round face.

"Black tea," Jessa snapped.

The serving woman glared at her before turning and making her way to the bar.

"She'll probably spit in it now," Jessa muttered.

"What happened?" he asked, already fearing the answer.

She inhaled deeply before answering. A deep crimson flower tucked into the charm, and she'd changed into clothing nearly as fine as what Brusus wore. "Found him wandering near Upper Town like this. I'd think he was just mourning Lianna, but not there." She looked around the tavern, eyes skimming over the bandolist and the pair of elderly men sitting along the bar. She frowned as she watched the serving girl. "Nearly fell a dozen times as we made our way here. Wish you had been with me. It would have been easier."

Brusus's eyes had drifted closed. Had Brusus been there when he'd met Haern? With his Sight, they might have had better luck in the guild house.

The serving girl returned and practically dropped the mug of tea onto the table. Unlike the ale, it steamed with a heady scent. Jessa pushed it toward Brusus and his eyes opened. Heavy lids revealed dark green eyes as he looked at the tea.

Jessa tipped the mug toward his face and helped him take a few sips. "Careful," she warned when he tried taking a deeper drink.

Brusus blinked again, and his eyes started to clear. He looked at Jessa for a moment before turning to Rsiran. "What happened to you?" His words slurred, but less than when he'd first come in.

"What do you mean me?" Maybe Brusus did know where he'd been. If he'd been in Upper Town, it made sense that he would have heard something, especially as connected as Brusus seemed to be to anything that happened in the city. "What happened to you? Why are you already drunk?"

"Not drunk," Brusus slurred.

Jessa pushed the tea at him. "Drink this."

Brusus blinked again. "Looking for answers. Told you to wait for me at the smithy."

"How long did you think we would wait?" Jessa asked.

"Longer than you did. I came by last night, and neither of you was there. Foolish to go running around the city after what happened. More foolish to do what you did, Rsiran."

Jessa's head snapped around to Rsiran. "What did you do?"

"I… Only did what needed doing."

Brusus took a long sip of tea. Focus came back to his eyes, and the color faded, his eyes regaining the muted green color, masking his abilities. Even drunk as he was, Brusus managed to Push them, and did it so subtly that they didn't know he'd even done it. If what Della said was right—and he had no reason to think it wasn't—Brusus had been Pushing that image for a long time. Just as Sliding had been as easy as walking for Josun, Pushing to mask his ability came easily to Brusus.

Brusus shifted on the stool, sitting up straighter. He pulled off his cloak, frowning as he realized how soiled the ends had become. When he looked back up, his face had regained his usual quiet intensity. Wrinkles pulled at the corners of his eyes.

"I was in Upper Town to see what rumors I could find."

Had word already spread about Rsiran entering the alchemist guild house? "Did you find anything?"

Brusus swallowed another gulp of tea. "After what you told me you found on Firell's ship, and what Jessa told me about your father's shop, I needed to know if he had made the mistake of stealing lorcith from the guild, or if it was mined like you thought." He fixed Rsiran with a hard gaze. "You made it clear how the guild would react if lorcith were stolen from them."

"The guild tracks lorcith closely. It flows from the mining guild to the smith guild. From there to whoever commissioned the work."

"Usually Elvraeth."

Rsiran nodded. There were occasions when others beside the Elvraeth had commissioned lorcith work—rare and only done after consulting with the Elvraeth—but most of the time, it was an Elvraeth request. "Did you find something?"

"Not about lorcith. No rumors floating. Or if there are, I didn't hear." His tone made it clear how unlikely he thought that to be. "You certain you saw lorcith on his ship?" Brusus glanced around the tavern, his eyes lingering for a moment where Lianna used to watch over the place. He took a long drink of his tea before setting the mug down carefully. "Not just things you'd created, but the un-shaped lorcith?"

"I'm certain." He didn't say anything about the lorcith Shael had brought to him. Not yet.

Brusus inhaled deeply and turned to look at Rsiran. "And you are certain that he was taking lorcith *away* from Elaeavn?"

That was what he'd assumed, but what if that was how Shael got lorcith? The idea was unlikely—one of the reasons lorcith had such value was that it could only be mined in Ilphaesn—but not entirely impossible. Maybe Firell had found another source, and *that* was what Josun had been after.

"I guess I'm not," Rsiran admitted.

Jessa squeezed his hand under the table. "You asked Rsiran what he had done. What do you mean by that? What else did you find in Upper Town?" After rattling off these questions and getting only a worrisome gaze from Brusus, she added, "And why were you drunk?"

Brusus looked over to Rsiran. "Some things you don't speak openly about. Especially in Upper Town. Things like the Elvraeth. Or the palace. And I wasn't drunk."

Rsiran tensed, suddenly fearing what Brusus had learned. "Did you find anything about Josun?"

"I tried, but the tchalit will not speak of individual Elvraeth. Getting one to speak at all takes great convincing."

The tchalit.

Rsiran had heard that term only once before. After Sliding into the palace, Josun had claimed the tchalit were coming for Rsiran. Palace guards of some kind.

How would Brusus have managed to get one of the tchalit to speak, unless…

"You convinced them you were Elvraeth," he realized.

"You say that as if it would be difficult for me to do so."

Brusus's eyes had flared a dark green, revealing the depths of his ability and his connection to the Great Watcher.

"Of course not, Brusus. I didn't mean any offense—"

Brusus laughed softly. The edge of heat to his eyes faded slightly but did not disappear entirely. "I know you didn't, Rsiran. Since Lianna, I've been…" He didn't finish.

They all understood. Since Lianna passed, they'd all been on edge, Rsiran especially. Mostly, it was the idea that Josun could come for one of them next; that he could simply appear, Sliding into place and attacking, made him fear more for Jessa than himself. She was so stubbornly independent. But he didn't know what he would do if anything happened to her.

"What did you learn from the tchalit?" Jessa asked. She touched Rsiran's arm, as if Reading his fears. "Why did you ask what Rsiran did?"

Brusus sighed. "The tchalit do not like to speak to the Elvraeth. I had to be... persuasive."

"So you had drinks with him?"

"Not drinks. They live in the palace. They think themselves more refined than that."

Jessa's eyes narrowed. "Then what?"

"Most of the tchalit prefer orphum vapor. Faster drunk than ale and wears off more quickly. And less likely to have other effects."

Rsiran hadn't heard of orphum vapor. "Do you need to see Della?"

Brusus glared at him. "Do you? Foolish thing you did."

Jessa turned and looked at him.

"I... I needed to find answers. Haern came with me."

Brusus slammed a fist down onto the table. The elderly men at the bar turned to look and watched them for a moment before turning away. "Haern went with you? One of you is foolish, but two is simply asking to get caught."

Brusus was right. Rsiran should have gone alone, Sliding if needed. But had he done that, it was unlikely he would have gotten very far. The alloy would have blocked him from Sliding. If not for the anchor Haern brought, he wouldn't have been able to get through.

Even then, it hadn't been worth it. All they got was a few useless pages of parchment. Scrambled words. Numbers that meant nothing. And the guild learning of his presence and already sending word to the palace for Brusus to have heard about it. Not the secret of the alloy as he had hoped, a way to keep his friends—Jessa most of all—safe.

"I know they saw me. There wasn't anything I could do at that point."

Jessa squeezed his arm painfully. "What did you do, Rsiran? Where did you go?" Her voice hid the other accusation: that he'd gone without her. She didn't need to say anything for him to know how much that hurt her.

Brusus answered for him. "The tchalit told me that someone broke into the palace. They found them walking through the courtyard in the center of the palace carrying a lorcith sword."

"The palace and a sword?" Rsiran glanced from Brusus to Jessa, confusion surging through him. "I didn't go into the palace tonight."

Brusus frowned at him. "Rsiran—"

"You think I'd be foolish enough to return to the palace? I'm worried enough the Elvraeth will notice how much lorcith I've forged. I wouldn't dare try breaking in again."

Brusus studied him. "The sword would have been bad enough. From what I can tell, they are so rare that the tchalit had never seen one before. Even your knives are a rarity, though other lorcith knives exist in the city. That's why they're so valuable." Brusus leaned forward, eyes growing more intense and flaring a darker green for a moment. "That wasn't all the tchalit said. He said when they approached the person, he simply *disappeared*. They have the constables searching throughout the city for this person. With as close as you got to the Elvraeth, the constables will not rest until you're caught."

Rsiran didn't know what to say. Someone—and Josun was the only person he could imagine doing something like that—had entered the palace carrying a lorcith sword. His sword. As attuned to it as he was, shouldn't he have felt it moving?

Not with what he'd done tonight. He'd buried the sense of lorcith in order to find the guild house. And in doing so, he hadn't even felt for the knives he'd brought with him.

But it was more than just lorcith. By Sliding from the palace with a lorcith sword, the Elvraeth would be looking. The alchemist guild too. Now he didn't have to hide from only Josun; he had to hide from all the Elvraeth. And if he didn't, everyone he cared about would be in danger.

"Wait… if you didn't go to the palace," Jessa started, "then where did you and Haern go?"

He met her eyes, knowing how hurt she would be that he would risk entering the alchemist guild without her. "I went looking for a way to keep us safe from Josun Elvraeth, a way to make the alloy."

She frowned and her eyes narrowed. "Did you find anything?"

He'd gone to the alchemists, thinking to find a way to keep Josun from reaching him, but what if that wasn't the answer? He wanted to keep Jessa safe—to keep all of his friends safe. From what he'd seen, Josun was after *him*, not the rest of them.

That meant he would have to do something drastic.

If Josun, the Elvraeth, *and* the alchemists were after him, what choice did he have left?

Brusus watched him as he finally answered. "Not the answer I wanted."

CHAPTER 26

R SIRAN LET THE COALS OF THE FORGE cool on their own. A stack of new lorcith blades rested on his table, different from the usual knives he'd made. Not only in the shape—these were smaller and more compact, better for concealing within a cloak or stuffing into his pockets—but also in how he'd made them. For the second time, he had *asked* the lorcith to help him create the knives, rather than listening to what the lorcith wanted to become. And the lorcith had complied.

Was this what his father had wanted him to learn to do? What he had done seemed different from how his father described demanding the lorcith take a certain shape. Rsiran felt more of a cooperation with the lorcith. When he felt it calling to him, pulling on him to make it into a certain shape, he had asked if it would help him make the knives. Rsiran still didn't know how he did that.

Each knife had the same small mark on the end. *His* mark. And now his connection to them felt if anything stronger than it usually did.

Rsiran *pushed* on the top one. It slid along the table until he stopped it. Then he *pulled*, drawing the knife to him and caught it out of the air.

Collecting the other knives, he tucked two into his waistband. The rest went into pockets in his cloak. He grabbed the lantern, making certain to keep it covered, and looked around the smithy one more time. Possibly for the last time.

An ache pounded through his heart.

He looked over to where the sword he'd made months ago leaned against the table. When he'd returned after meeting Brusus in the Barth, he'd found it sitting atop the anvil. Somehow, Josun had snuck in after Rsiran had been here last, after returning from the guild house with Haern. A message or a threat from Josun. Either way, Rsiran no longer had a choice.

How much longer before Josun learned that Rsiran had entered the alchemist guild? Or did he already? He'd use that knowledge, along with the fact of his lorcith forging, to force his hand. Others would be harmed as Lianna had been. And he wouldn't allow that.

The door to the smithy clicked, and he turned, expecting Jessa. She stood in the doorway, watching him with a deep frown, her Sight taking in everything in the smithy, before closing the door behind her and locking it.

"Were you going to leave without me again?" Anger hung in her voice over how he'd Slid into the alchemist guild without her.

He swallowed a lump in his throat. He didn't dare tell her that he hoped he could have. "I don't think it's safe for you to come."

She stormed across the shop, her eyes flashing angrily as she scanned the smithy. Today she wore simple black pants and a shirt without embroidery. The lorcith charm hanging around her neck blended into her clothes. Only the dark red flower stuffed inside contrasted with what she wore. "Why do you think you need to go?"

"You know why. Josun Elvraeth will not rest until everyone around me is hurt. I thought that if I could find a way to keep us safe…"

If only he understood the secret of the alloy. Then he could use it to… to what? Did he really think he'd be able to find a way to prevent Josun from reaching him? If the Elvraeth decided you did something, you did not argue. Even if it meant your life.

"And since you didn't, you think leaving will change that? You think that if you leave, it changes anything about his plans?" She grabbed his hand and made certain to hold on tightly. He could not Slide without taking her with him.

Rsiran wasn't certain that it would. "You've seen what's already happened. And now he's coming after me. I need to go where he can't find me."

She shook her head. "Only what Josun wants to happen. We got past him once before. We'll do it again."

"We were lucky then. We both know what nearly happened."

He pulled her close, and she didn't fight. Her warmth pressed against him. Any other time, it would have felt reassuring. Now it only made him anxious, knowing that he would be the reason something happened to her.

"Only Josun knows where we are," Jessa said. She pressed her cheek up against his chest and wrapped her arms around him.

"For how much longer? The constables are on alert. Already they've begun patrolling Lower Town."

"They've always had a presence—"

"Not like this. Not this late. When was the last time you saw a constable after dark? And now, suddenly, we've seen three?" That, as much as anything, told him that what Brusus had heard was true. More than that, he wondered how much influence the alchemists had? "And if the alchemists haven't made the connection between what Brusus heard and what happened in their guild house, they soon will. And then I'll never be safe here." He squeezed her. "We'll never be safe here."

How was it that he would already lose what he'd only just gained? "Brusus can fix this."

Rsiran sighed. "Not this." They couldn't bribe their way past this. Not anymore. It had gotten too big for that. Too many pieces. And now, too many people knew about him. About his ability. Better just to leave. Exile himself as his father had once done to him. Only this time, it wouldn't be safe for him to return to Elaeavn.

"Leaving will keep you safe," he said. "That's all I want. You shouldn't suffer because of me. Haern will be fine, and Brusus…" Brusus apparently had enough connections that he would be fine as well.

"How would leaving me help anything?" The hurt hung heavy in her voice. "You're an idiot sometimes. You won't know anything if you go without me. You'll be just as in the dark as you always are without me." She punched his chest and her voice caught. "And besides, I seem to remember how much you needed me the last time you decided to do something on your own."

That she was right did not make what he had to do any easier. But she needed to know everything. This time, he wouldn't hide it from her. "I intend for him to come after me."

She frowned. "Who? Josun?"

Rsiran nodded. He hadn't fully worked out how he would manage to do it, but he needed to try. He still didn't understand the connections, and how they worked into whatever Josun planned with his rebellion, but the parts were there. They had been from the beginning. Lorcith disappearing from the guild. His father's shop closing. The lorcith on Firell's ship. Maybe even what Shael asked him to forge. And now Josun had made it appear like Rsiran broke into the palace.

"Then you're a fool. Dying won't help any of us."

"I don't intend to die."

"None of us intend to die. Sometimes the Great Watcher turns away just long enough…"

Rsiran sighed. Arguing with her did no good. "After what he did to Lianna—"

Her grip softened on his hand. "Is that what you think? That I'm some delicate girl who needs you to watch over me?"

"I know you're not delicate." He met her gaze and looked away, his eyes catching the flower hanging in the charm. "That doesn't mean I want to be the cause of you getting hurt."

"I did pretty well before I met you." She sniffed at the flower and her eyes calmed slightly.

"I know."

She hung onto him for a while, saying nothing. Rsiran kept his arms around her. They swayed in place. Just holding onto her felt comforting. Felt right. Maybe Jessa was right. He always had been stronger with her.

"Why do you think you have to draw Josun out anyway?"

"I think he means for me to come after him. He took the sword," he started, pointing to where it rested, "and brought it back as a message for me."

And he thought it hidden. Nothing was really hidden from someone who could Slide. He might be able to lock the door, but that wouldn't keep Josun out. But once in the smithy, Rsiran hadn't thought anyone would easily find the sword.

Jessa let go of his hand and picked up the sword. After twisting it carefully, she looked at him and frowned. "Why would he take this?"

"That's the second time he's taken it. The first time, I went to him and took it back. This time, he returned it here. Both times tie me to what happened in the palace."

"And the third time?"

"I don't mean there to be a third time."

Jessa nodded slowly. "But he already knew about the sword since he'd taken it from you before. Others would have seen him wearing it."

Rsiran took the sword out of Jessa's hands. The jeweled hilt made it more valuable, but its real value came from the lorcith of the blade. And from the fact that such creations were forbidden by the council.

"I don't know that he did. Brusus said the tchalit had never seen a lorcith-forged sword, but we know Josun had this sword in the palace. He wore it when we saw him in the warehouse, but maybe that was the only time."

"Rsiran—we can't win when we're dealing with one of the Elvraeth. They don't just rule over the city. The Elvraeth are revered in the other great cities as well. Places like Asador and Thyr where we still trade. They can make whatever decisions they want. And going after Josun is… well, it's just dumb."

"But I don't intend to go after Josun. I just want to get him away from the city. Keep him from people I care about. Brusus. Haern. Della." He pulled her toward him and hugged her tightly. "But mostly, from you. Then we need to prove his rebellion is real. That's the only way we can get out of this. The only way to keep us safe."

"Do you really think you can prove his guilt to the council? Think about what you're saying!"

Rsiran sighed. "Even if we don't prove his guilt, I need to get him away. Maybe that will be enough."

"You think that by leaving, he'll come after you for some reason. That you can keep the rest of us safe." When he nodded, she pulled her hands out of his and rested her palms on his chest, pushing lightly against him. "You're an idiot."

"Why? Because I think I can do something to help? That I want to do whatever I can to keep everyone safe? How is that so different from what Brusus does?"

She laughed. "Have you considered that leaving is what he *wants* you to do *because* you know he plans something? What if all of this is a way to simply scare you into disappearing?"

"If that's all he wanted, he could have just attacked me like he did with Lianna. But that's not what he's done."

"But if Josun has decided to reveal you, why now?"

Rsiran shook his head. "I don't know. I haven't figured that out yet."

"Like I said, you're—"

"An idiot. I know. I just can't shake the feeling that if I leave, he'll come after me." And, at least then, he wouldn't have to fear the alchemists coming for him. There were so many reasons for him to leave. And really just one to stay.

"Or just keep doing whatever he wants you to do. Only now, he's the only person in the city with the ability to Slide."

Maybe Jessa was right. Maybe he *was* foolish to think that leaving would keep them any safer. But staying only kept them in danger. "What would you have me do?"

Jessa smiled and kissed him on the cheek. "Well, at least now you're thinking straight. If Josun wants you to leave, make him *think* that you left. And we can keep working to figure out what he's up to."

"What if he learns what we're doing?"

"How would that be any different from the situation we find ourselves in now?"

Rsiran didn't want to tell her. If Josun learned what they were trying, he might do more than simply make it look like Rsiran Slid into the palace. Josun already knew how much Jessa meant to him. As Della said, Josun would consider that a weakness. But Rsiran would do anything to keep his friends safe.

"I see what you're thinking."

He laughed softly. "I would almost think that you can Read me."

She pushed on his chest again. "Don't need to Read you. I can see the way your eyes change. Or how the corner of your mouth twitches. You give yourself away when you do that. I know you're thinking something you don't want me to know."

As much as he could fortify the barriers in his mind, he couldn't prevent Jessa from knowing what he was thinking. And even if he could, would he want to?

"What about the alchemists?"

"Did they see you?"

Rsiran frowned. "They saw me Slide away. But if they learn of someone Sliding out of the palace, they'll make the connection. Eventually it will come back to me."

Jessa patted him on the chest. "Eventually. That means you don't have to worry about it now, so let's take care of one problem at a time. Maybe we can even tie them together, convince the alchemists that Josun was the one to enter their guild house."

Rsiran took a deep breath and let it out slowly. She was right. The alchemists should be the least of his worries right now. Once they figured out what to do about Josun—*if* they managed to figure out what to do—then they could focus on the guild, maybe even do as Jessa suggested.

"Besides, if we fail, you don't really have to worry about them," Jessa said with a laugh. "So... where now?"

"We have to make it look like we've left. I've already cleaned up what I can from the smithy. I want to move a few of these other lorcith items so that it looks like I've really gone. And then..."

"Where do you want to take the lorcith?"

"Well, we want to play into his expectations, right? Wouldn't he expect me to take it to Brusus?"

Jessa smiled and nodded. "Good. And since he's still sleeping off the orphum, you have time."

Rsiran bundled up the remaining lorcith-forged items scattered across the table, not bothering with anything made of iron or steel. Only the lorcith would be valuable if discovered, and Josun would expect him to take it. After stacking them, he looked at Jessa.

"Wait for me."

She frowned. "You're not leaving without me."

"No. Just going to take this to Brusus. Then I'll be back for you and we can decide what we need to do next."

"Together."

Jessa's eyes flickered brighter as she studied his face. He wondered what she saw there. But he wouldn't leave without her. More than anything, he needed her.

He nodded. "Together."

CHAPTER 27

RSIRAN EMERGED FROM HIS SLIDE EMPTY HANDED. Thankfully, Brusus had been asleep. He made certain to hide the items in a corner where Brusus would see them, but not so openly that anyone could discover them. Then, as promised, he returned to his smithy.

"Jessa?"

He didn't see her. Daylight started to fade, leaving a hazy gray light, but not nearly enough for him to see. He turned to the table, searching for the lantern, but didn't find it. Rsiran frowned. Why would Jessa have taken the lantern? But as he turned, he realized something else was off. The sword that had been resting alongside the table was missing.

With his focus on Sliding to Brusus's house and returning, he hadn't paid any mind to the sword. Jessa wouldn't have taken the sword from the smithy; he had intended to keep it with him.

Worry knotted his stomach. Jessa had been the one to want him to wait for her, but now she was gone. Rsiran had only been gone a short while. Long enough to drop off the lorcith items at Brusus's home, but not long enough for her to have gone far.

What if someone had come by the shop? Shael had come by several times over the last few weeks. Could he have stopped by? Or Haern, returning from whatever he intended? When he'd stopped at Brusus's house, he'd heard him snoring off the effects of the orphum vapor. And Della had never visited his smithy. She likely didn't even know how to find it.

Rsiran steadied his breathing. He could find Jessa easily. Pushing away all other distractions, he listened for the lorcith in her charm. Normally, he sensed it easily.

There was nothing.

His heart skipped. What would make him unable to find the charm? The alloy could mask it, but she'd have to have gone some place with enough of the alloy to hide it. And coals hot enough could probably destroy it, but Jessa wouldn't do that.

But there was another possibility. One that scared him the most.

He would not be able to feel the lorcith from a great distance. Certainly not a piece as small as the charm.

Hurrying to the table, he sorted through it until he found one of the iron lanterns he'd made. After quickly filling it with stale fish oil from a dusty bottle in the corner, he lit it. Soft orange light flickered to life, pushing back some of the shadows within the smithy.

He carried the lantern over to examine the door. It was unlocked. He frowned, twisting the lock until it clicked. Jessa would not have left without locking the smithy. Unless she didn't leave of her own accord. But he still should be able to detect the charm he'd given her.

The sword. Of all the things he'd made, he could always feel the sword.

Closing his eyes, he listened for the sword. Long moments passed before he finally heard it, someplace far away.

He almost Slid, chasing the sword, but then he thought better of it. Jessa's warning sounded in his mind, reminding him to think things through more carefully. No answers came. If someone like Haern, or even Shael, had come, she would have waited for him, knowing that he would soon return.

As much as he hated to think it, he knew Josun had taken her. Hell, he might even have been hiding near enough to Read or Listen to them as they planned. If she were still in the city—and she couldn't have gotten too far on foot in the short time he'd been gone—then he would have been able to sense the charm. That he couldn't meant Jessa was in danger.

He needed advice. What he considered doing—following his sense of his sword, Sliding blindly until he found it—would be dangerous. But who could he ask?

Brusus still slept. And even were he to wake him, he didn't know whether he trusted Brusus's judgment right now. With what happened to Lianna, would Brusus remain able to carefully consider what he needed? For that matter, could Rsiran?

But he knew who could.

Rsiran glanced around the smithy for a moment, debating whether he should take anything else with him. Other than the crate of lorcith, mostly untouched since Shael brought it to him, there was nothing that couldn't be easily replaced.

Then he Slid.

Rsiran emerged in Della's house. A soft smoky scent hung in the air, mixed with a sharp, clean odor. Nothing like the soothing scent of mint he'd noticed when last here. He glanced at the chairs angled in front of the hearth, but they were empty. The fire glowed a warm red rather than crackling wildly in the hearth. Rsiran spun, looking for where she might have gone. He doubted she would leave her home with the fire still burning.

Noise near the back caught his attention. He waited, one hand slipping near his pocket to remind him of the lorcith knives hidden there. Della came from the back, grey hair standing up all around her head, a turquoise shawl hanging loosely around her shoulders. She frowned when she saw him.

"You were not to come tonight."

He thought the comment strange, but ignored it. He had other concerns. "Jessa is gone."

She paused and crossed her arms over her chest. "Gone?" Her eyes went distant. "Tell me what happened."

Rsiran shook his head. "We were… we were planning on making it look like I'd left the city. I had taken some of my projects to Brusus, and when I returned to the smithy, she was gone."

"You intended to engage Josun Elvraeth."

"I intended to do what was needed to keep my friends safe. One of the tchalit told Brusus about a palace break-in."

"Only now they are speaking of this?" Della seemed puzzled. She stepped behind her counter and began pulling out small glass jars from some hidden shelving.

"This was different. They saw someone with a lorcith sword who then disappeared."

Her hands faltered, and she fixed him with a hard gaze. "And this was not you."

"I would not have gone back to the palace, and certainly not with my sword."

She closed her eyes and her breathing changed. "You think this was Josun."

"Who else knows how to Slide? Who else knows of the sword?"

Della let out a soft sigh. "You also went to the alchemist guild."

"Did Brusus tell you?"

She shook her head. "Not Brusus. He didn't need to." She sighed out a long breath. "A dangerous thing you did. The alchemists… You should know they are not like most other guilds. Ancient—as old as the smith guild, and there are those of the smiths who can trace their bloodlines back to the first of our kind. What did you hope to learn?"

"I wanted to learn a way to protect myself from Josun."

Her eyes narrowed. "And you think going to the alchemists would aid you in this?"

"If I can keep him from Sliding to me…"

Della turned away, tipping one of her jars for a moment. "That is what the Elvraeth once thought." She picked up another jar off the counter and looked over at him. "And did you find anything?"

"Haern was injured, and I think they saw me and—"

"So not only does Josun Elvraeth pursue you, but now the alchemists will as well."

He nodded. "Jessa thinks that we can figure out a way to tie Josun to the alchemists." But first he had to find her.

"Rsiran," Della started. "I wish I could tell you how this will turn out. Unfortunately, I cannot See anything other than a danger swirling around you."

"Della—" She had just revealed that she was a Seer to him.

Her eyes opened. They were a bright green, deeper and darker than anyone he had ever seen before. "Do not ask, Rsiran. These are questions with answers you are not yet prepared to hear."

If Della didn't want him to ask, then he wouldn't. "What sort of danger?"

She smiled at him tightly. "Would that I could answer that, Rsiran. But as Haern has told you, your ability to Slide masks you in certain ways. There are things about Sliders not easily Seen. That is why he struggled as he did with Josun when Brusus first began working with him, though he did not understand it at the time."

"Don't the Elvraeth have all of the gifts of the Great Watcher?" That was what he'd learned as a child, the reason the Elvraeth could rule. They were given that right by the Great Watcher.

Della just shook her head. "Each of the Elvraeth has some small amount of the gift, even if they never learn how to use it. This makes all the Elvraeth difficult to See, though it is nothing compared to one strongly gifted such as yourself."

"Haern Saw me more clearly when I went to the alchemists. That's how he knew where to find me."

Della frowned. "Haern is a gifted Seer. What did he See?"

"Just where I would be. And that I attempted something dangerous. I'm not sure what else."

Della tapped her spoon on the glass jar. "Do you know what changed?"

"To find the alchemists, I pushed away the sense of lorcith. I listened for the alloy instead."

"You can do that? Just… ignore it?"

"I'm not sure how I did. I've never been able to just ignore the call of lorcith before. I just sort of pushed it to the background, far enough away that I could listen for the muted sense of the alloy."

"That is how you found the alchemists." Della's eyes went distant, flaring a bright green. "And did you Slide at the same time?"

He tried to remember. Had he Slid while listening for the alloy? He didn't think so. Each time he'd emerged from a Slide, he had to reconnect with the alloy. "I don't think so."

Della nodded, brow furrowed. After a moment, she shook her head. "This is not why you come tonight. You have questions."

Had she Read him? Della was the only one who seemed able to work past his lorcith-fortified mental barrier. "I need to know if Josun took Jessa."

His mind provided enough answers, visions of Jessa lying as Lianna had lain, broken on the rocks. He would do anything to find her, including chasing down the sword, wherever it might be.

"I can't See that."

"Did you feel any ripples earlier?"

Della scooped a small spoonful of powder out of one of the jars and tapped it into a cup. Then she added a scoop from another jar. Before answering, she stirred them together and poured water from a small pot into the cup. Rsiran smelled the heady fragrance of mint from the mug. At first, he thought she intended to give it to him, but then she took a long drink.

"I felt ripples, but I cannot tell you who made them. That is what you want to know, is it not?"

He nodded. That she felt ripples wouldn't be enough to help. But she had known when he Slid all of them to the Aisl after Lianna died. Those ripples were larger, like a boulder thrown into a pool of water. If Josun had taken Jessa, she should have felt something more than him simply Sliding. "Did you feel anything that would have been from more than one person? Like when I Slide with Jessa?"

Della took another sip. "I felt something similar. You did not travel with her?"

"No."

"Then she is gone."

There seemed a finality to the way she said it. After what happened to Lianna, he understood. Della had already made it clear that Josun would see Jessa as a weakness to exploit. That was what he had done with Lianna, using her as a way to get to Brusus. But there had to be more to what he planned.

He sagged against the wall, leaning his head back. The sword flitted very distantly against his senses. "I can feel the sword I made," he said softly.

Della frowned at him. "The one he used to implicate you with the Elvraeth?"

"I wouldn't sell it. Brusus has asked, but…" He shook his head. "I should have let him. Then Josun couldn't use it against me."

"Then where is it now?"

"Gone from the city. I don't know where. It pulls on me."

Della's eyes went distant for a moment. Haern's did the same thing when he attempted Seeing. "Dangerous to go to it. I cannot See more than that."

"Isn't it dangerous for me to simply stay in the city?"

Della looked at him. Eyes deeper green than the Aisl forest held him. "Since you first came to me, danger has always been all around you. I have never known what it means. And now… now what you have done makes it worse."

"I only did what I needed to—to protect us."

"I wish I could tell you what it means, Rsiran. But it is vague. Just a sense of darkness."

"It means that I need to search for Jessa."

"And if you find him with her? Then what? Are you prepared to do what might be necessary?"

He touched the knives in his pocket. The lorcith had responded to his request when he'd forged it, almost as if it understood what would be needed. "I will do what is needed to protect my friends."

Della took another sip of her tea. A tight smile came to her lips. "And that is where I think Josun Elvraeth has underestimated you."

"Don't tell Brusus. He will only worry."

She looked at him. "And if I did? Do you think there is anything he can do?"

Rsiran felt for the sword. How far away would he have to travel to reach it? How far from him had Josun taken the sword? Rsiran didn't have the strength with that connection to know.

"Not where I must go."

Della just nodded. She did not look over at him as he Slid away.

CHAPTER 28

THE FIRST TIME RSIRAN LEFT ELAEAVN had been when his father had banished him to the mines. Leaving this time felt different, but no less painful. Then he'd thought he had a chance of returning to what he'd known before. That if he did what his father wanted, if he could learn to ignore his abilities as his father asked, he could return to his apprenticeship. This time, even were he to find Jessa, there would be no return to the safety that he once knew.

And maybe that had been his biggest mistake. Had he ever really had a chance to return to what he once knew? The safety of his time living with his parents had been mostly illusion born of ignorance. He'd thought he had to live under their rules, follow the pathway that his father laid out for him during his apprenticeship. Only… he'd learned that the Great Watcher had another plan for him.

Meeting Brusus had changed everything. For the first time, he found a reason to leave home, friends who wanted him around, and a skill they found useful. For the first time, he didn't have to hide who he was.

But now that was gone. Elaeavn had changed. Josun Elvraeth would not stop until Rsiran did what he wanted… or Josun was dead. Would he take that step? Would he really commit to killing if it came to it? Would it even stop then, or was Josun part of something larger?

But Jessa needed him. He didn't need to be a Seer to know that.

And then what? Return to Elaeavn and always fear the alchemist guild searching for him? How long until they learned of him and acted to recover the coded secret he'd stolen from them? Even returning it did not mean he would find safety. There would be no constable for Brusus to bribe this time, only a determined guild. And more than the guild, what happened when whatever Josun was a part of spilled out into the rest of the city? What would he do then?

Those were questions for later. Whatever happened, he would find Jessa first.

Rsiran emerged from the Slide atop Krali Rock. Standing there, he looked over the city. Night began falling as the sun dipped below the horizon, just sheets of orange and red bouncing off the water. Gulls circled over the water in the distance, cawing occasionally. Behind him, deep in the Aisl, an animal howled, the sound deep and low, almost mournful.

Looking down on the city from Krali, he no longer felt a sense of peace. Now he only felt unrest.

The air smelled different here where the distant sea air mingled with the scents of the Aisl, and with none of the bitter tang of lorcith he always smelled within his shop. With the wind whipping around him, he could almost feel free of the city.

Krali had always been a place for him to go to relax. The first time he'd Slid, he'd somehow ended atop Krali Rock. Perhaps he'd ended here because of how often he'd looked up, wondering how hard it would be to climb. Or maybe there had been another reason. Could he have been pulled, drawn to Krali as Della pulled him? That line of thinking only frightened him.

Yet, none of that was why he'd come. He needed to be free of distractions, free of anything that would affect his ability to sense the sword.

Rsiran closed his eyes and listened. As he did, he pushed away the lorcith he felt all around him. That coming from the knives in his pockets. The lorcith now hidden in Brusus's home. Even the unshaped lorcith that called to him from within his smithy. He pushed all of it back. In the distance far to the north, he felt the pull of the lorcith buried there. This was pushed deep and away too. Nothing remained other than the muted hum of the alloy in the palace and the faraway sense of the sword.

Before Sliding, he let worry slip through him for one last time. How long had Jessa been gone? Would he be able to reach her in time? Had Josun already harmed her?

But then anger seethed within him. That Josun thought to manipulate him—to harm someone he cared about again—left him practically shaking. Rsiran took a few calming breaths, pushing those emotions down to hide near the other sense of lorcith.

And then he Slid.

This time, he emerged atop Ilphaesn, standing along the narrow path that he'd stood on with Jessa. The wind changed but still whistled, pulling on him and tearing at his clothes. A few spindly trees lined the low road leading up to the peak. On the road below him would be the small village outside the mines, but Rsiran had been careful not to emerge too close to the village. The only time he'd been through it had been on his way to Ilphaesn, and that had been during the day. He wouldn't risk someone out at night seeing and reporting him.

Standing this close to Ilphaesn, he felt the pull of the lorcith deep in the mines more strongly than ever before. How much of that came from working with lorcith, forging it into shapes the metal preferred, and how much came from him focusing on using the lorcith, anchoring to it over the last few weeks?

He focused his thoughts again, quickly shoving away all sense of lorcith as he had before. Each time he did it, the process became easier. Always he knew it would return. After Sliding, the sense of lorcith always returned.

And then he felt the sword again. Still farther north.

Rsiran had never traveled any farther than Ilphaesn. Sliding from here carried more risk, just like Sliding blindly onto Firell's ship or into the space between the crates. Only this time, if he emerged someplace he didn't intend, he could be trapped and Jessa would never be freed.

He couldn't risk Sliding all the way to the sword. If Josun sat waiting for him, expecting him to follow the pull of the sword, then he might have something planned. Rsiran didn't intend to fall into Josun's trap.

He would have to Slide slowly, carefully. It would take more strength than a single Slide, but he couldn't risk Sliding blindly.

At least all the times he'd been Sliding with Jessa had built his strength. Even now, Sliding to Krali and then to Ilphaesn left him barely feeling the effects. Though the sword was closer, it was still not significantly closer. To reach it, he would have to Slide greater distances than he'd ever attempted.

Rsiran scanned the horizon. To his left, nothing but wild land stretched from the base of Ilphaesn. The rock of the mountain slowly rolled toward grassy plains stretching as far as he could see. If there had been more light, he might have been able to see farther into the distance.

To the other side of him rolled the angry Lhear Sea as it crashed against distant rocks. Somewhere nearby, he felt the muted sense of the alloy barricading the other mine entrance.

And then there was Elaeavn. Standing atop Ilphaesn, he saw it as a twinkle of distant lights, no more than stars in the sky. From here, the city looked small and safe, nothing like what he knew it to be.

Rsiran hesitated, but waiting did nothing except leave Jessa in danger. Holding onto the sense of the sword, using it as a compass to guide him, he Slid as far as he felt safe.

This time, he emerged standing in a clump of massive dry grasses. The wind swished them around him. The air smelled of dirt and dust, tickling his nose. A low howl rose into the air, and a dark shape circled overhead.

Rsiran fixed his eyes to the north and Slid again.

And again. And again.

Each Slide took him closer to the sword. In spite of Sliding, he felt as if he moved slowly, barely drawing closer to the sense of the sword. With each Slide, he had to focus, push away the sense of the other lorcith he felt, until all he knew was the sword. At one stop, he sensed the distant awareness of unshaped lorcith nearby, but ignored it as he moved on. At another, he knew several of his forgings were close.

He paused near a wide river burbling over rocks. A few short trees lined the river, twisted limbs covered with long, thin leaves. He had used the trees to guide his Sliding, emerging alongside one. Rsiran rested his hand on the trunk. The bark felt smooth, similar to the sjihn trees of the Aisl, but these were nothing like those massive trees. He leaned and took a drink from the stream, his heart beating as if he'd just run a long distance. The effects of Sliding as far as he had began to strain him.

As he pushed away the lorcith again, the sword loomed closer.

So far, he hadn't seen sign of anyone else. No other villages or cities since Sliding past Ilphaesn. That should reassure him, but a nagging worry sat in his mind. What was Josun's plan in drawing Rsiran out of the city, away from Elaeavn? There had to be something else, more than simply taking Jessa. With Lianna, he had killed her. Whether as a message or for another reason, Rsiran didn't know. Might he have already done the same with Jessa?

He stepped away from the trees to Slide across the river. The ground sloped down and away, giving him a better vantage. Far in the distance, a soft glow seemed to dome up from the ground, spreading out around in each direction like a massive lantern. It took him a few moments to realize what he saw: Light, rising up from a city.

He paused, listening again for the sword. Still distant, but not *that* distant anymore.

The city. That was where he'd taken the sword. But why?

Rsiran Slid, emerging far from the river. Now the lights from the city burned brighter. Shadows from buildings contrasted with the darkness of night, rising from the flat land like dark fingers.

Now he sensed lorcith of all kinds. His forgings. Unshaped lorcith. Even the muted draw from the alloy. All of it he pushed away until he sensed only the sword.

Now it was close.

He Slid again, more cautiously this time, and emerged near a clump of strange trees with sharp needles. They smelled sharp and reminded him of the powders in Della's home. A flock of birds resting in the tree fluttered to flight as he emerged. A lone howl erupted to the south.

The fat moon hung low and bright in the sky, finally freed of the clouds that had been blocking it for most of the night. Nearby, a wide road twisted around a low hillside, winding down into the city. A low wall ran around the outer edge of the city, disappearing in either direction over the slowly rising hills. Low grasses filled the fields, swishing softly in the gentle breeze. A few wide bushes dotted the field, some with flowers blooming bright against the moonlight. The sight of the flowers made his heart clench.

In only a moment, he pushed away all sense of lorcith. The sword felt nearby.

Rsiran almost Slid to it. Now, he no longer needed to suppress the other lorcith he felt. He sensed it as easily as he did in Elaeavn. So close, and he could simply Slide to it. If Jessa was there, he would rescue her and Slide back to Elaeavn.

Then the hard work would begin.

But Sliding now meant going blindly. Jessa depended on him reaching her, so he needed to be cautious. It wasn't just that he didn't know where he would end up, but what if he emerged only to find a group of people?

As much as he hated it, he needed to move carefully.

Rsiran took a deep breath. The air tasted cool and clear, different from in Elaeavn. Then he Slid past the wall and emerged in the city.

The low buildings on the other side of the wall looked nothing like those throughout most of Elaeavn. None butted against another. Each looked low roofed and built of thick timbers rather than stone. Slate roofs with overlapping seams arched high over him. Some were nearly as tall as the two-story homes he'd seen in Elaeavn. Small windows in each home were thrown open, letting the night breeze blow in. Down the street, a candle flickered. Stout doors blocked entrance to each building. Homes, but nothing like what he saw in Elaeavn.

Rsiran Slid down the street, not bothering to mask his ability. No one else walked the streets, leaving him in an eerie sort of silence. The breeze blowing from the west caused the buildings to groan every so often, but for the most part, all he heard were his steady breaths.

The buildings began to run together, their peaks rising higher than those nearest the wall. Chimneys rose from the top of most. Smoke billowed out of some, lazily winding into the sky before disappearing. Unlike nearer the outer wall, windows were shuttered.

The sword was closer.

Again he Slid. This time, he emerged in a grassy clearing. Signs hung in front of the surrounding buildings, reminding him of the shops in Upper Town, most painted with pictures and scrawling letters that he couldn't quite read in the dark.

Rsiran listened again for the sword. Closer, but he wasn't there yet. He Slid.

When he emerged, he could tell that the sword was close.

Rsiran walked. The cobbled street felt strange beneath his feet after all the time he'd spent Sliding through the night. He'd lost track of how many times he'd Slid. More than he'd ever done all at one time. How much longer could he keep it up? How much longer before he pushed himself too far?

Fatigue began to threaten him, but he refused to let it overwhelm him. Once he found the sword—and Jessa—he would need strength enough to Slide her to safety. Whether that meant back to Elaeavn or simply out of the city, he didn't know. He would do what he needed.

At the building with the wide chimney, he felt the sword on the other side. Rsiran moved out of the street and walked toward the long window running the length of the building. Thick shades covered the glass, blocking his view. He set his hand on the window and listened. Other than his sword, he felt nothing. Heard nothing.

Here was where he would have to take a chance.

After taking a deep breath, Rsiran Slid past the window.

The building was darkened, but enough light from fading coals in a massive hearth lit the room. A bench ran along the far wall on which familiar tools were neatly hung. A gleaming anvil rested near the hearth. Even the air smelled familiar, that of hot coals and metal mixed with sweat from a hard day's work.

A smithy.

Rsiran hesitated. Why had Josun brought the sword here?

Nothing moved in the smithy. Coals crackled softly, a bin of charcoal and thick logs stacked along one wall near the forge. Otherwise… nothing.

He looked around, listening for the sword. The sense of the lorcith guided him to where it rested on the table, lying out in the open as if it should be there. Rsiran knew without looking that this was his sword. The soft curve to the blade, the way the metal folded just enough to make it appear that it flowed. Even the jeweled hilt told him it was his. But his mark confirmed it. His initials, tightly inscribed along the lower edge, a clear sign of his work.

But no sign of Jessa.

After successfully Sliding this far, following the sense of the sword, he'd expected to find Jessa here too. But he should have known it wouldn't be that easy. Not with Josun involved. But if she was not here, why had Josun left the sword here?

No answer came to him.

Rsiran grabbed the sword. He would not leave it. He needed a sheath, some way to carry it, though unlike the Neelish sellswords, he had no idea how to use a sword. Were anyone to find him, he'd be better off throwing the sword at them than trying to fight them off with it.

Where was Jessa?

And why had Josun brought the sword to this city—so far to the north that it was likely Asador? Had Josun just wanted him out of the city? But why, and was this where he sent the lorcith? If so, how did that help him?

And if Jessa wasn't here, then where? Would Josun have taken her back to Elaeavn?

Rsiran leaned against the table in the smithy. He could return to Elaeavn. Maybe search for Jessa there. Better to find Brusus, have him help. Or Haern might be able to See something.

But a nagging worry told him that Jessa had already been gone too long.

The only other thing he could think of was the charm he'd made her. Could he sense the charm now that he had the sword? Only if she was still nearby, if at all.

The darkness of the smithy helped put him back in the mindset of being back in the mines, nothing but darkness around him, the sense of lorcith all around. He took a few calming breaths, struggling to push back the fear and anger raging through him, and listen only for the lorcith.

He felt the sword like a fiery beacon in his mind. And then… nearby he sensed other lorcith he'd forged. Knives mostly. Somewhere in the city. Could they be knives Jessa carried? But no… the lorcith sounded different, sang to him differently.

Then he started pushing back the sense of lorcith. The sword went first. Now that he possessed it again, he pushed back the awareness of it in his mind. The knives he carried went next. And then the other shaped lorcith throughout the city. All pushed into the background.

He listened.

There was a sense of unshaped lorcith, calling to him. Not large quantities, nothing like he felt near Ilphaesn or nearly as much as he'd felt on Firell's ship, but unshaped nonetheless. Some was very close. This *was* where Firell brought it, he was certain. He pushed that away as well.

The muted sound of the alloy thrummed against him too. He heard it nearby and frowned as he pushed that back as well.

And then there was nothing. No sense of lorcith. Not even a tiny dredge of a sense.

Rsiran held his breath. Waiting.

The charm would not pull on him very strongly, if at all. And possibly, he was too far away to sense it anyway. But he strained, listening, listening, listening for the barest hint.

There was nothing.

He took a deep breath. Lorcith flooded around him, filling him again with awareness. Each time he pushed it away, it seemed to bounce back stronger.

Something that he'd realized when listening for the charm made his eyes snap open.

This smithy had lorcith.

Following what he'd sensed, he made his way toward the stacks of metal. Shuffling past steel and iron, he came across square blocks of grindl and copper. Another block of brown that he didn't recognize. And then a large rectangular block of metal.

Rsiran grabbed the block and pressed his thumb deep into the metal. It felt soft, just like the lump he'd found in the warehouse. He slipped it into his pocket.

Beneath it was a dull grey lump of lorcith larger than many he'd seen while working for his father in the smithy, but not as large as those he'd found in the mines. Rsiran hefted it, twisting it in his hand. Light from the coals caught the dull surface.

But why would lorcith be found in a smithy unless the smith could work it? Outside of Elaeavn, there shouldn't be any smiths that *could* work with lorcith.

Several other lumps of lorcith sat beneath it. These weren't the only ones he sensed in the city. That meant other smiths had unshaped lorcith. Did they have the silver-like metal as well?

Whatever this metal was, it combined with lorcith to create the alloy.

But if that were true, did that mean these smiths tried to make the alloy? Would they know the secret the alchemists guarded?

Even if they did, he still didn't know why. Why would Josun and those with him need the alloy? For what purpose? It prevented Sliding, locked out Josun just as easily as it locked out Rsiran. And if that were the case, why would he want that?

Had Rsiran been wrong? Was it *not* Josun he'd overheard on Firell's ship? Did he chase a different Slider? But if that was the case, how would they have known about Jessa? How would they have known about the sword?

And then there was the other sense he felt when he'd pushed away lorcith. The alloy was somewhere in the city. With a sudden fluttering in his heart, he wondered…could it be enough to mask the lorcith in the charm? Enough to hide Jessa from him?

He would not leave this city until he knew.

CHAPTER 29

Rsiran Slid from the smithy. The metal block in his pocket weighed heavily, almost dragging him as he attempted the Slide. When he emerged, he stood again on the street in front of the smithy. Nothing moved. A cat meowed once and he waited, but the sound didn't come again. Would the luck be the same here as it was in Elaeavn?

Rsiran held the sword in one hand, feeling awkward standing in the street with a full sword. If caught in Elaeavn with it, there would be consequences. Only the constables were allowed swords, and apparently, the sellswords, but would it be the same outside of Elaeavn?

He checked down the street and then pushed away all awareness of lorcith, listening for the alloy. Within moments, he felt it. First as a soft tug upon his senses, then stronger.

The sense came from nearby. Rsiran trailed after it, listening. Were he to Slide, he might lose the connection to it.

Darkness shrouded the street as he made his way along it. The alloy pulled him, calling softly, its voice muted like coming through a thick wall. As he followed the sense, he allowed himself the hope that Jessa might be trapped inside. If his sword had been here, why not Jessa?

At an intersection, the sense of the alloy pulled him to the right. Overhead, the heavy moon began to sink past the peaked slate rooftops. A shadow flickered along one and he paused, but nothing else moved. Maybe a bat or the cat he'd heard earlier now prowling.

The sense of the alloy felt closer. Buildings made out of the same rough timbers lined both sides of the street with small doors and narrow windows. One door in particular drew him and he stopped in front of it. The muted call of the alloy came most strongly from behind it.

When he reached it, he saw a faint metallic inset on the door that practically disappeared into the wood. Had he not shifted his stance while staring at it, he didn't think he'd have seen it.

Unable to help himself, he touched it, running his hand across the smooth surface. The metal felt cool and made his hand tingle. The intricate work impressed him. Few smiths in Elaeavn had the skill to achieve such fine detail. When he leaned to one side, the inset faded. Only when standing in a particular position could he make out the detail.

Rsiran moved down to the window. Crisscrossing the window were narrow strips of metal. He touched these, as well, and felt the same tingling sensation.

Why should he feel that?

Yet the feeling reminded him of what he'd felt when he went through the door at the alchemist guild house. With a sudden certainty, he knew this was the place he needed to be.

Rsiran focused on the sense of the alloy. Even standing in front of this building, the sense was faded and muted. Had he not focused as he did, he might not have felt it. Nothing about the home looked otherwise different from any others on the street. The inlay on the door might be different, but for all Rsiran knew, such things were common here. Just the strange tingling on his skin and the awareness of the alloy.

He returned to stand in front of the door. With the sword in his hand, he Slid.

And was pushed back.

He slipped on the cobbled street before catching himself. The sensation had been no different from the resistance he'd felt when trying to Slide into the palace, or into the hidden cavern on Ilphaesn.

Now he had no doubt that this was the place.

Could Jessa be on the other side?

Letting go of the sense of the alloy, he listened for lorcith. If he had an anchor of some sort, he could pull through the alloy, but would there be anything inside this building for him to use?

The sense of lorcith hit him with a sudden awareness blazing in his mind. The sword and the knives he carried. The unshaped lorcith from back in the smithy. A few other shaped items scattered throughout the city. But not Jessa's charm.

If only Brusus were here. He'd unroll his lock-pick set, find the right combination, and have the door open in moments. Still slower than Jessa, but faster than Rsiran could manage. Then there was what Haern had done. Physical and quick, but effective.

That Rsiran could do.

He grabbed one of his slender bladed knives and shoved it into the lock. It met resistance at first, but then slid inside with a soft *click*. He tried twisting, but the door still didn't open.

Frustration rose inside him. This was not the palace to block him out. There should be no reason for this simple door—this building—to barricade him as it did.

With a surge of anger, he slammed his shoulder into the door. It popped open.

Rsiran grabbed the knife out of the lock and stuffed it back into his pocket. Then he slipped into the house, pushing the door closed behind him. The tingling sensation washed over him as he did.

The house was dark. No streetlight shone through the narrow window, nothing of even moonlight. Again he felt useless, blinded by his lack of Sight.

He might not possess the same Sight as Jessa, but he had other ways to see. Letting out a slow breath, he listened for lorcith.

As he did, he felt a strange absence of lorcith, so different from what he felt other places, even standing on the other side of the door. It took a moment for him to realize that the absence came from the alloy blocking him.

Through the void, he felt a tiny shimmering awareness. Almost as if the metal had been here once but was no longer. Now, nothing was here. Certainly not answers.

Time to return to Elaeavn. He would regroup. Find Brusus and Haern. Seek their help in searching for Jessa. Then he would go after Josun.

As he neared the door, a soft shuffling sounded behind him.

Rsiran spun, pushing one of the knives from his pocket away from him almost as soon as he did. It hit with a soft thunk.

Someone cried out.

Rsiran Slid, using the knife to guide where he went. Whoever had approached lay on the ground, sprawled out. In the darkness, he couldn't tell where the knife hit.

But he needed answers. This person dying would not help him find them.

Rsiran leaned and reached for a wrist to grab onto. The person fought him for a moment, trying to pull away, but Rsiran resisted. Whoever this was could answer his questions. Why was the house protected by the alloy? Why did the smith have unshaped lorcith? Had it been Josun who had stolen the sword and brought it to the city?

The person grunted and fell silent. Rsiran pulled. If he was too heavy, he wouldn't be able to drag him all the way back to Elaeavn. Thankfully he was not.

Then he Slid.

CHAPTER 30

Rsiran Slid back to Elaeavn in a single Slide. Anger and frustration gave him strength.

The distance—especially bringing someone else with him—should have made the Slide difficult, but he emerged feeling no weaker than when he Slid with Jessa.

He emerged at Della's house, standing just inside the door. The hearth crackled softly as if she'd been waiting for him. Rsiran stood, knowing that whatever ripples his Slide made would draw her attention.

Within moments, she came out of the back of her home. The bright shawl shifted on her shoulders, and she seemed to know immediately what had happened. Rsiran no longer cared if she Read him.

"Where did you find him?"

He shook his head. "Asador, I think." He waved the sword with his free hand. "Found it in a smithy."

She glanced at the man. "And him?"

Rsiran looked down, seeing him for the first time. A thick beard covered his face, long and scraggly. Streaks of grey shot through it. His wide nose was reddened. Black hair peppered with grey ran nearly to his shoulders. He wore baggy brown pants smudged with black stains. His grey shirt hung open, revealing a scarred chest.

"Found him in a different building. Protected by the alloy."

Della looked up quickly. "And you? How did you get in?"

"I didn't Slide, if that's what you're wondering. No anchor on the other side." Though once he'd been inside, he didn't have any trouble Sliding. "Just used a technique I picked up from Haern."

Della grunted. "Haern. Nothing subtle about that man."

"Subtle doesn't always work."

"No," Della said, motioning toward the cot near the fire. "It does not."

Rsiran carried the man to the fire and set him atop the cot. When he did, the man stirred a moment, his eyes flicking open. Panic surged through green eyes as he looked at Della. He turned his head, and when he saw Rsiran, his eyes widened.

The man started to tremble. One leg kicked. The other didn't move. Rsiran realized that his knife stuck through the middle of his thigh. Blood pooled around it, more than he would have expected for a thigh injury.

He reached for the knife, but Della caught his hand. "Don't. Could lose too much blood if you do that." She let go of him and put both hands on either side of the man's face. Her eyes went distant.

Then the man sagged, his eyes falling closed.

She moved around the cot and touched the knife. One finger ran across the blade, following it down to where it pierced his flesh. Her eyes flashed a bright green. "You may take your knife now."

Rsiran grabbed it, pulling it out of the man's leg. Blood spurted briefly as he did, soaking into his pants and splashing onto Della's hands, before the wound just closed on its own.

"This will take some time."

"But he might know where—"

Della looked up at him sharply. "You may question him later, Rsiran," she snapped.

He hesitated long enough to wipe the knife on the man's pants, cleaning the blood from it. Then he stuffed it back into his pocket. Rsiran made his way to the door, glancing again at Della. Her hands ran over the man's pants, along his leg, before pausing when she touched his stomach. Della did not look back at him.

Rsiran stepped out into the night.

* * * * *

The sounds of Elaeavn surrounded him, suddenly strange and foreign. The waves crashing along the rocks seemed angry and violent. Gulls cawing overhead swirled with dark shadows. It seemed as if a dozen cats yowled at once, though it could not have been more than one or two. He no longer cared to count.

Rsiran didn't want to Slide. He should be exhausted. After everything he'd done tonight chasing down the sword in the hope of finding Jessa, he should be so weary that he couldn't stand. Instead, he felt only emptiness.

She should be with him.

And he had failed her.

He glanced at the sword he carried, feeling disgusted by it for the first time since forging it. Not because he had made it, but at what it represented. He should have left it with Josun. What did Rsiran care whether one of the Elvraeth had a sword he'd forged? As far as he knew, there were knives bearing his mark in the palace as well. He'd been very productive, yet the only thing he'd felt an attachment to had been the useless sword.

Rsiran turned onto one of the side streets and started toward the shore.

More than anything, he needed answers. And who better than Brusus to help with that? The Great Watcher knew Brusus was connected well enough.

Rsiran wandered through the streets as he made his way to Brusus's home. He debated Sliding, but chose not to. What did it matter how quickly he reached Brusus? Jessa was gone. Taken. Likely left broken, just like Lianna.

When he finally reached Brusus's home, he hesitated. He had been here earlier, but that had been to leave the lorcith-forged items. It seemed so long ago that he'd been here. A lifetime. Back when he and Jessa planned to leave Elaeavn. Draw Josun out. Before Jessa disappeared.

Still, in the time since he'd been here, something had changed. The small room stretched barely five paces wide. A draft blew in through the tiny hearth in the corner. A plush rug with a red and green checked pattern abutted the hearth, the edge slightly singed. A wooden chair angled in front of the hearth when he'd been here before had tipped over. The bundle of lorcith he'd forged was gone.

A candle flickered in the room off to the side. Rsiran had never been back there. Even though his ability let him travel freely, there were places where he felt uncomfortable going without permission. Brusus had secrets, true, but didn't they all?

But Jessa needed him. Now was not the time to worry about violating privacy. He would do anything to help Jessa.

He stepped through the shadowed threshold. The room on the other side surprised him. Instead of a mattress or rolled blanket or anything that would make the room a place of rest, there was a large, hinged chest along one wall. A narrow desk against the opposite wall.

The candle he'd seen flickered there. A small block of the silvery metal sat atop the desk, a twin to the one he still had in his pocket.

Rsiran froze.

Instinctively, he listened for the sound of lorcith. In the house should be the collection of lorcith he'd brought earlier in the evening, the sound of his forgings calling to him, pulling on his senses. He heard nothing.

Instead, he felt the pull of unshaped lorcith.

Slowly, he made his way to the trunk. This was where the lorcith pulled at him the strongest. Long wooden slats formed the lid of the trunk, squeezed together by bands of iron on each end. The body of the trunk seemed to be made from solid wood, as if milled in a single sheet, but wider than anything he'd ever seen. Rsiran frowned when he noticed faded writing on one end that reminded him of the crates in the warehouse.

He lifted the lid, dreading what he might find. Inside were nearly a dozen massive lumps of lorcith. Each about the same size as the one he'd seen at the smithy in Asador. He lifted one, holding it in his hand, and turned to the desk where the block of metal rested.

Only then did he realize he wasn't alone.

"Where's Brusus?"

Della stepped through the doorway. Her hair stood wild, and deep wrinkles pulled at the corners of her vibrant green eyes, making her look weary. The first time he'd met her, he'd been the cause of that fatigue.

"The man will live," she said.

He looked from the trunk back to Della. "Is he awake enough to answer some questions?"

Della blinked slowly. "Rsiran... do you know who you brought back to Elaeavn?"

He didn't. Someone bearded, which those living in Elaeavn never were, but his green eyes said that he possessed the Great Watcher's gift. "Who is it?"

"When you visit with him, you must remember—"

"Who is it?"

She crossed her hands over her stomach as she faced him, considering her response. "Someone who will not know where Jessa was taken."

He nearly collapsed. The effort of the day seemed to be catching up with him. After everything, the man he'd brought back with him to the city had been his last hope that he'd find Jessa. And now... now he had nothing.

"Where's Brusus?" he asked again. "Why does he have lorcith?" The questions spilled out of him, mixed with the hopelessness he felt.

Della sighed. Her breath smelled of mint and reminded him of his visit earlier in the day. "I cannot claim to know you as she does, but anger does not suit you."

"What else could I be? He took Jessa from me. The one person I counted on as a friend hides lorcith from me. And you seem to know why."

"There is much I know. And there are things I wish to forget. Many things. That is something I think you begin to understand."

The words touched a nerve, and he bit back what he started to say. "What's this about, Della?"

She stepped closer. One hand reached for him, touching his arm. A wave of relaxation started through him, the tingling in his skin reminding him so much of how it had felt entering the barricaded house. "This is about Brusus."

"I don't understand."

"And you should not. I don't think you were ever meant to be a part of it."

"And Brusus?"

"It's different with him."

"He means to exclude me from what he plans?"

Della shook her head. "From what I can See, neither of you were to have been involved. What happened to Lianna was meant to hurt Brusus, and it did. Josun took something very personal from Brusus. All that managed to do was make him angry. Then he targeted you. Tried to implicate you in a palace break-in. And took Jessa from you."

"After what happened in the palace, he wants to use me in his rebellion."

"Possibly."

Rsiran set the lump of lorcith into the trunk and closed the lid. He felt the effects of his Sliding, growing so weary that he couldn't stand. He sat atop the trunk and looked up at Della.

"Brusus did not react as he expected when Lianna died. He expected Brusus to back away, but he did not. That is not how the Great Watcher made him."

Rsiran wondered how much of what had happened was his fault? He and Jessa had been the ones to go to the warehouse. To Firell's ship. Rsiran had been the one to find the space between the crates and the strange silver-colored metal. What if Josun blamed Brusus when he should blame Rsiran?

Wrinkles deepened as she looked at him. In spite of having the mental barriers he built in his mind, he felt it as she Read him, as if crawling around or over them.

"You still do not understand. You've been sheltered too long. First your family, and then with Brusus."

"You think that I've been sheltered?" His parents had not sheltered him. If anything, they tried to discourage him from using his abilities.

"You have lived in Elaeavn your entire life, Rsiran. Yet you do not know Elaeavn." Her smile meant to soften the blow of her words but did not. "I saw that when I first met you. Many who live in the city do not really know it. They know the city, places they call Lower Town and Upper Town, but they do not know Elaeavn. And they cannot, not without knowing the Elvraeth." She tottered to the desk and looked down at the silvery block of metal on the table. "What has Brusus told you about Josun?"

"That he's one of the Elvraeth. And that he didn't always know what Josun wanted."

Della looked up from the desk and nodded. "And did he tell you how he knew Josun?"

"Only that he'd worked a few jobs for him."

"Brusus would make it seem that Josun hired him rather than how it actually happened." She lifted the metal block off the desk and held it in her hands.

"How did it actually happen?"

As he asked, he felt the sudden pull of lorcith he'd forged.

Rsiran turned toward the door. Brusus stood watching them, gaze flicking between Della and Rsiran. He wore a deep blue cloak with heavy embroidery clasped at his neck. Grey hair slicked back over his head. Deep green eyes flared bright.

"He used me."

Rsiran jumped to his feet as Brusus entered. "You know what happened tonight? You know that Josun took Jessa?"

Brusus stiffened. "He has her?"

"Earlier. I left some of my forgings here. We… we were going to draw him away from the city." Saying it aloud to Brusus left him feeling foolish.

Brusus narrowed his eyes. "Yes. I moved them to a safe place. But why would you think you could draw Josun?"

"To keep him from coming after us. All of us."

Brusus stepped forward. "Great Watcher," he swore softly. "And while I was gone this evening."

"Gone?"

"There were… things… I needed to learn."

"Yes? Well, there were *things* I needed to learn too. Like why does Firell have lorcith on his ship? Why do you suddenly have a trunk full of it? Are you a part of this rebellion too?" His voice rose with each question, and he couldn't mask the hurt in his voice.

Without meaning to, he pulled on lorcith all around him. The knife hidden under Brusus's shirt *pulled* free and floated toward Rsiran. The knives in his pockets shook, threatening to come flying out. Even the lorcith inside the trunk wobbled, vibrating with an almost eager energy.

"Easy, Rsiran." Brusus put his hands up, palms facing outward.

Rsiran let out his breath. The knife he'd taken from Brusus fell to the ground with a clatter.

"Share what you know, Brusus," Della said. "He has come in too far already. And now… I See only more danger if he remains in the dark. If he is to help, you must share with him the reason why."

Brusus looked at Della and nodded slowly. He motioned to the end of the trunk next to Rsiran, waiting for him to sit. He grabbed the knife off the ground before sitting alongside him. "There are not many who know of my past," Brusus began.

"I haven't shared your secret," Rsiran said.

"No. I know you haven't." He looked over to Della as he began. "You know that my mother was born in the palace. One of the Elvra-eth. Descended from the first families, those first gifted by the Great Watcher with what we know as our abilities. She was banished… Forgotten… while pregnant with me."

Rsiran looked over at Della. He had often wondered if Della was Brusus's mother, but Rsiran had never asked her pointedly whether she was. There was no doubting that Della had gifts like the other Elvraeth. Sight. Reading. Healing. A Seer. Perhaps more.

But she shook her head. "I have already answered that question once."

Brusus followed Rsiran's eyes and laughed softly. "Were it as simple as that, Rsiran. Then perhaps none of this would have happened." He looked at Della standing by the desk and his eyes danced past the block of metal atop it. "Like so much in Elaeavn, everything comes back to the Elvraeth. Not just for me. Even if I didn't share their blood, the decisions they make impact us all."

"What are you saying?" Rsiran stood and turned to face Brusus who remained seated on the trunk.

Brusus sighed and motioned to the trunk. "Sit, please."

Rsiran shook his head. "I don't have time to sit. I need to find Jessa."

"Unfortunately, there isn't anything I know that will help with that."

"Then what are you hiding? What do you think to protect us from?"

Brusus chuckled. It sounded dark, with none of the mirth he usually had. "The Elvraeth," he started. "Always back to the Elvraeth. I have shared how five families, each claiming descent from the first Elvraeth, live within the palace."

"And each family sits one person on the council."

Brusus nodded. "That is right. Each family. All separate, yet each claims they are descended from the earliest Elvraeth, those first five who left the Aisl with the gift from the Great Watcher. And since I was attacked, I have been trying to understand what Josun wanted. Why did he ask you to poison the council?"

"He claimed it was a demonstration, but there was more to it."

Brusus nodded. "Perhaps a demonstration. And maybe that is all it was to him, nothing more than quiet rebellion from one who would never sit among them. Each member of the council serves as the head of their family. Each is powerful, but that does not mean they are irreplaceable. I told you that the Elvraeth fight amongst themselves? That even were Josun dead, the Elvraeth likely would not search outside their walls for the killer. And even searching within their walls would be unlikely. You see, the Elvraeth fight for position within each family, all striving to sit on the council. It is there the real power exists."

Rsiran didn't fully understand even the simple answer. "And if it was more than a 'quiet rebellion'?"

Brusus sighed and looked up at him standing in the middle of the room. His eyes flared a deep green. The only other time he'd revealed his abilities had been when sick. "That is a different matter and for a different time."

"Are you so certain?" Della asked.

Brusus's eyes narrowed. "I find it unlikely."

"Just as you thought it unlikely that Josun Elvraeth lived. And because of that, Lianna died," Della said.

"I know what happened to Lianna."

"Do you? Just as you knew his mind when he led you to the warehouse? Did you intend Rsiran get drawn into it?"

Brusus looked away. "You know I didn't."

"Then tell him," Della whispered. "You may not have wanted him drawn into this, but it doesn't change that he is." Della made her way to stand in front of Brusus and grabbed his chin. "You cannot do this alone, Brusus t'Elvraeth." When she said his name, the air practically snapped. She held his gaze before releasing his chin and turning away.

Brusus looked after her before turning to Rsiran. "I thought to stay out of this, but learning of the warehouse, learning what it stores, well… I couldn't."

"What are you talking about?" Rsiran asked.

"My mother was not the first of the Elvraeth banished. Since the founding of Elaeavn, there have been others. Many others. Many scatter, settling in quiet villages or finding a place of seclusion in the great cities. Thyr. Cort. Asador."

Rsiran stiffened with the last, thinking of the smithy and his sword he'd found there, and the man he'd brought back to Elaeavn. Did Brusus imply the man was one of the Forgotten Elvraeth?

"As you can imagine, banishment does not set well with them. They were Elvraeth, used to power. Used to ruling. While some faded into obscurity, others took a different tact and banded together."

"Banded together? What do they think to do?"

Brusus shrugged. "Who is to know exactly? You think me well connected, but there are places my connections fail."

Della turned. "And times when you fear to speak, it seems. Avoiding does not change the truth, does it?" she asked Brusus. Looking over at Rsiran, she frowned. "What Brusus fears telling you is there are some who think to return."

"Return? But the Forgotten cannot return."

An edge came to Brusus's face. "Only because the Elvraeth make it so. We wonder what Josun wanted, what he had planned? For the longest time, I struggled to understand what he hoped to accomplish with his poisoning."

A chill worked up Rsiran's spine. "What do you think he wanted?"

"These others will do whatever they can to return. Even if it means poisoning the council. That was the beginning, but I didn't know it at the time. Now... now with what I've learned, I realize that the real fight is only starting, only I don't know why now."

"What does that," he said motioning to the desk, "have to do with it? What is this metal?" Rsiran grabbed the block of metal off the desk. He didn't say anything about the other he'd found, but it weighed against his pocket.

Della took it from him. Her eyes softened as she looked it over, twisting it in her hand. One long, crooked finger ran along the smooth surface. Her voice shifted, coming more distant. "Before tonight, I had not seen it in that form in many years."

"It is called heartstone," Brusus said, taking the metal from Della.

Rsiran turned and looked at him. "But it's metal."

Brusus nodded. "It is. And rare. Rarer than lorcith. For years, most thought the last of it had been seen."

Brusus glanced at Della before pinching off a small piece and held it in the palm of his hand. His eyes flared a brilliant green for a moment and then the small piece of metal began glowing with a soft blue light.

"The warehouse brought me into all of this, but not only me. I think Josun didn't even know what all was stored there. When he discovered..." Brusus sighed. "Heartstone is valuable, and I don't think even the Elvraeth knew they had this any longer."

"But if it's so valuable, why would it have been stored?"

Della smiled sadly. "So much of our past has been lost, Rsiran. Much that once mattered, not just to us, but the rest of the world. Elaeavn is just one place in the world. There are other places, massive cities—"

"Like Asador?" he interrupted. "You know that's where I found the sword. That's where Josun took it when he took Jessa." But not her. Jessa wasn't there. She might not be anywhere, anymore. That didn't change the fact that he would search until he knew.

Della sighed. "Yes Asador. And others. Most would need to travel for weeks to reach the great cities, but you can simply *step* there." She looked into his eyes. The color seemed to swirl, almost as if alive. "There are not many with you gift, not many who can Slide. Ahh... how I wish you could have lived in a time when someone could have taught you. You do not believe, but it's a great gift you've been given, one that you never should have been ashamed of."

She looked over his shoulder, her eyes going distant. He wondered if she Read him or was attempted to See something.

"Once the ability to travel was not like now. Not common, but not rare as it is today. And never quite like Sight. Most of our kind have some small ability there. But what you do—Sliding"—she said the word as if she disagreed with the term—"would be like Seers now. A useful skill. And those who could travel went all over the world, as if the Great Watcher had gifted them with the ability to see all that had been made. A time when our people had influence and knew peace. Those with your gift who went outside our boundaries were known as Travelers. And they were respected for what the Great Watcher had given them." She shook her head, focus returning to her eyes, the distance fading. "But that was a long time ago. Before we left the trees. Before we felt the need to live along the water, looking out toward the distance. Before." Della sighed, and it seemed as if she remembered those times.

Rsiran wondered what it must have been like to live when Sliding was common. What must it have been like not to fear Sliding openly? To be respected for it? Or what it had been like living in the Aisl, knowing the protection of the trees, feeling comfort rather than the anxiety he felt when he'd been among the ancient sjihn stretching high overhead, blocking out the sky?

Brusus looked from Della to Rsiran. "You wonder why the warehouse is full of treasure?"

"You said they were sent for the Elvraeth."

"And they were. From the great cities. You have seen what the crates contain. Ceramics from Valen. Textiles from Bris. Strange crates from places even Firell hasn't seen. But it was not the treasure the Elvraeth care about."

274

"I still don't understand. What is this heartstone?"

"Something the earliest of the Elvraeth knew to respect. A temper to the power hidden within lorcith. Only later was it twisted." Della ran her finger across the block of metal and shook her head.

Comments Della had made over time left him with a question. The Elvraeth moved their people out of the Aisl. The Ilphaesn Mountain rose as a backdrop, full of lorcith that when combined with the metal, created an alloy that could prevent Sliding. And the palace used this alloy throughout.

What reason would the Elvraeth have to create a barrier from Sliders? Unless they feared those they'd banished.

He looked at Brusus. "The palace. They use that," he said, pointing to the heartstone, "to keep out the Forgotten?"

Brusus glanced to Della before nodding. "Now you begin to understand." Brusus took the heartstone and set it back atop his desk. "There are enough Elvraeth within the palace that the barriers built can't protect them from each other. They fight. Some are exiled, sent from the city to be Forgotten. Others die." Brusus laughed, a soft, dark sound. His hot breath smelled of ale and tea. "In that, they are little different from the rest of us. And now the Forgotten seek to return."

"How long have you known?" Rsiran asked.

Brusus glanced at Della. "Not at first. And after what Josun had you do, and your suspicion of a rebellion... it made me question whether rumors of the Forgotten are more than I had believed."

"And that's why you wanted the knives. You're trading for information about the Forgotten, about this rebellion, not only about Josun."

Brusus made his way to the trunk and tapped on it. "They had been quiet before. I've never been able to learn. But now there is activity. I needed to know why. Josun brought me in. I don't think he intended me to play this part, but now that I know what I do, how can I not?"

"Why Jessa? When I went to Asador, there was a smithy, and lorcith there." He looked over to Della. "And the alloy. That was where I found him."

"I still don't know. But if Josun is after lorcith, and now we've found heartstone…"

"You think this is all about the alloy?"

Brusus slammed his fist on the trunk. "That's just the problem. I don't know *what* this is about. And Josun is the only connection that I *can* find."

With a dawning understanding, Rsiran realized what Brusus really wanted. "You *want* to find the Forgotten?"

Brusus didn't back down at the accusation. "Yes. My mother would be among them, Rsiran. What would you have done?"

Rsiran didn't know. "I'd have been honest with my friends."

"I have been as honest as I could be."

"Really? And now Jessa is gone because you have been honest with us."

"As I said, neither of you was ever to be a part of this. It was supposed to be me."

Rsiran turned to the door, anger surging through him. Brusus had kept them in the dark about his true plan, and in doing so, had endangered them even more. "Had you told us from the beginning, we would have helped. Now… Now I have to find where he's taken Jessa, if there's still time."

The only thing he could think of to find her now was learning where Firell went.

But that meant Sliding to his ship. And even with an anchor, supposing Firell still had some of Rsiran's forgings aboard, he wouldn't be able to reach him if he had already sailed out of the harbor.

"What you plan is dangerous," Della said.

Rsiran hadn't even felt Della Reading him. He looked at her, releasing his useless barrier as he did, pushing his thoughts at her. If he could hide nothing from her, then he would hide nothing.

Della winced but didn't look away.

"What else can I do?" he asked.

"You should rest. Think before you act. You will be better able to help her if you get some sleep first."

He glared at Brusus who only watched him. "No," he decided, "I don't think I can wait any longer. There is nothing more to learn here."

Brusus looked from Rsiran, to Della. "You mean to Slide to his ship?" When Rsiran nodded, he shook his head. "No. I can't let you do that. If you miss, you risk ending up in the water. Disappearing. Let me figure out what to do next. We'll get her back, Rsiran."

"I'm not asking permission, Brusus."

"Think about what you're saying!"

Brusus took a step and only stopped when Rsiran raised his hand. The knife that had fallen to the ground when Rsiran's anger flared now floated up, hovering in the air and not moving. Brusus's eyes went to the knife. "Listen. Della is right. You're in this now. No more secrets. After where you've been, I don't think I can protect you anyway."

Rsiran shook his head. He had decided. He needed to reach Firell. Get answers to what he knew about the Forgotten. And then he would find Josun.

"I'll tell you everything that I know. Then we can find Josun. Give me a chance—"

"Like how he gave Lianna a chance?" He regretted it as soon as he said it.

Brusus's face twisted. Anguish returned to his eyes. But he swallowed and pushed it back. "Please…"

The one word said it all.

"I will bring her back. He will not take another of us. After that, you'll tell me everything about what you've pulled us into."

Brusus breathed heavily before finally nodding.

CHAPTER 31

Rsiran hid the sword within the lumps of lorcith in the smithy. If Josun were determined to take it again, it wouldn't matter where else he hid it. But not knowing where he might find Firell, he wanted to ensure he knew the sword's location in case he needed an anchor to return. Then he Slid away from the smithy.

He emerged standing on the rocky shores. Thick clouds filled the night sky, swirls of pale yellow from the obscured moon making them shadows overhead. Waves splashed around him, the sound chaotic and unsettling. The rocks felt slick beneath his boots. At least here, near the shore, he felt better connected to the water. Hopefully, he would be able to reach out his senses far enough to find Firell.

Rsiran closed his eyes. Doing so was not necessary, but the darkness seemed to increase his sensitivity to the lorcith. All around him were forgings he'd made. Knives and bowls and even the spoon Haern preferred to keep for himself. But farther came other senses. The call of the lorcith in the smithy, that hidden in the trunk at Brusus's home, and even the softer sense of lorcith from far to the north. If he let it, Ilphaesn would practically fill his senses.

He pushed them all away.

Had he not had to search for the sword in Asador, had he not learned how to ignore the sense of lorcith, he might not have been able to do what he needed.

Distant senses of lorcith pulled on him. Some he recognized, like the knives far to the north. Likely Asador, but they could easily be in Thyr as well. The unshaped lorcith, familiar only because he'd held it. Even the muted sound of the alloy. Everything he'd touched before called back to him.

Rsiran pushed it all away, stuffing it into the deep recesses of his mind.

Beyond that, *out* and away from him, came the call of lorcith. First as a soft tickle, just at the edge of his awareness, like a pinprick of light mixed with a soft familiar call.

Not knowing what he'd done, Rsiran latched onto it. The sense came to him more fully, as if dragged across a great distance. For the briefest of moments, he let himself hope that he felt the lorcith charm Jessa wore. But then he felt more lorcith with it, unforged and with a different call.

That would not be Jessa.

He pushed away the twinge of hope. It did no good, not with what he needed. Or with what might be necessary.

And what he planned was risky. Della had been right about that.

For Jessa, he would take any risk.

Opening his eyes and clinging to the lorcith, he Slid.

Distance blurred past him. Sounds and colors mixed with the familiar bitter scent of the Slide. And then he emerged.

At once, he knew he stood in the hold on Firell's ship.

Waves rocked against the ship, sending him sliding across the slick deck of the hold, crashing painfully against one wall. Rsiran bit back a cry of pain and held onto his shoulder, wincing.

Again there was no light in the hold, and he felt a moment of fear at the darkness. But he had known the dark, and here in the hold, it was not dark, not like he'd known. All around him came the awareness of lorcith.

As before, he used this to know where he stood, feeling for the void in the darkness where no lorcith existed to find the door.

When he reached it, he flexed his injured arm. Nothing appeared broken, but it throbbed with a steady pain. This kind of pain he could tolerate. And strangely, pain in the darkness like this felt familiar to him. At least he had not been poisoned as he had in the mines.

Rsiran checked his knives. Three and each small, meant for pushing rather than throwing. Other knives were stacked inside some of the crates. He thought for a moment about grabbing those, before deciding against it. He would not harm Firell unless he had to. All he wanted was answers.

And then he would Slide away—hopefully, to Jessa.

The cold metal doorknob slipped beneath his hand. Rsiran turned it, prepared for whoever might be out in the hall.

Lantern light streamed through the cracked door. A single orange lantern hung along the wall, the same kind as found in the mines. The steady light brought back unwelcome memories. His heart fluttered, and a surge of anxiety twisted his stomach.

He needed to control those emotions to help Jessa.

He stepped into the hall. The ship rocked under him and he swayed with it. One hand trailed along the smooth wooden wall to keep balance. At the first door, he paused, listening for any voices. Unlike the last time he'd been aboard the ship, he heard nothing.

He continued onward and stopped at the bottom of the stairs.

Lantern light behind him made it difficult to see out into the darkness. The ship creaked and someone clomped across the deck. Wind snapped against the sails, whistling loudly. Soft patters of rain or spray splashed down the stairs. Rsiran tensed, considering Sliding onto the deck before deciding against it.

He started up the stairs, taking each step carefully. The second step creaked loudly, and he froze. For a moment, he thought he heard someone coming. But then nothing more.

By the time he reached the top of the stairs, tension made his shoulders ache. The last time he'd been on the main deck had been with Jessa. Then, lines had been coiled against the rails. Sails were rolled and tucked. Wooden planks underfoot had been dry.

Now the lines were pulled taught as wind filled the sails. The ship swayed more violently here, and Rsiran struggled to keep his feet. Rain splashed down, striking his face like sharp needles.

Footsteps hurried across the deck. Rsiran crouched in the shadows, hoping to stay hidden. One of Firell's sailors, a man named Tagas who he'd met before, grabbed a coil of line and threw it over his shoulder before hurrying out of view again.

Rsiran didn't know anything about sailing. How many men would be on the ship? Firell certainly. And Tagas. But who else did he sail with? How many others would he find?

"What is this?"

Rsiran stiffened as the voice boomed behind him.

He turned, prepared to either Slide or push his knives, whatever it took to escape if needed. Firell stood at the bottom of the stairs. Shadows obscured his usually affable face. Deep green eyes flickered. His hand slipped to the knife at his waist.

One of Rsiran's.

Footsteps thundered across the deck of the ship. Toward him. Tagas had heard.

Without waiting, Rsiran *pulled* on the knife. It jerked free and flew across the distance. Rsiran grabbed it out of the air.

He Slid to the bottom step and grabbed Firell, turning him toward the knife.

Firell watched him with less uncertainty than Rsiran expected, especially after he'd just demonstrated rare abilities.

Rsiran pointed the knife toward Firell and glanced up the stairs. Tagas looked down, watching with a tight expression. Firell shook his head and Tagas disappeared.

"Brusus send you after realizing that crate on the dock was mine?" Firell asked. Somehow he didn't seem surprised to see him.

It wasn't the question he'd expected. Firell didn't seem surprised. "No. He didn't want me to come."

Firell pointed down the hall. "Might as well put that knife down. I'm not going to hurt you."

His voice seemed so different than the Firell he'd known. "I don't think you can. And I have questions."

"Of course you do. That's why you're here. But we can at least sit and share a mug of ale while we talk." Firell didn't wait for his answer. He started down the hall, pausing briefly at the door of the room where Rsiran had overheard him the last time. "Come on. Rain is picking up. You don't want to be out there when it really starts. No sea legs. Might get nasty. Ale will help calm your stomach."

As he said it, the ship swayed again, throwing Rsiran against the wall. A tight smile crossed Firell's lips.

Rsiran made his way down the hall after him and entered the room on edge.

He needn't be. Firell stood with his back to him, facing a long table. A low bunk rested against the far wall. A small trunk rested on top of the table, and Firell twisted, showing him a small flagon before pouring it into a metal cup. The room stunk of faded perfume and bitter ash.

Rsiran shook his head. He had not come to drink.

"Go on. Ask your questions. Then it'll be my turn."

After closing the door—he didn't need Tagas or one of the others surprising him—he moved toward the bed. "Why do you have lorcith? Are you working for Josun? For his—" he almost said rebellion, but he knew that wasn't right anymore "—for the Forgotten?"

Firell took a long swig of ale before answering. "The lorcith was the job, Rsiran. Some of it went into town like that crate Lianna saw. The rest goes out. Didn't Brusus take enough for you to use?" When Rsiran hesitated answering, Firell laughed. "I know Brusus was here. Not much happens on my ship that I don't know about."

He said it so off handedly that Rsiran almost missed it. But he recognized the implications. Firell knew that they'd been to his ship. "I know about the lorcith. That you have some of my work that Brusus hadn't asked you to move. Where did you get it?"

Firell laughed again. "That girl of yours isn't the only one who can sneak."

"You?"

He shook his head. "Not my gift," he said, but he didn't elaborate more.

Shael, then. The man had proven capable of sneaking into the smithy, so why wouldn't he have been the one to take some of Rsiran's forgings? "You didn't answer the second questions. Who asked you to gather lorcith?"

Firell's eyes tightened. He took another drink of ale and refilled the mug. "So many questions. Don't I get to ask any?"

"No."

Firell looked at the knife Rsiran still held out toward him. His eyes danced dangerously. "Fair enough. For now. But I'll have answers before you leave."

Rsiran didn't intend to stay on Firell's ship long enough to answer his questions, but he didn't argue. "Who has you gathering lorcith from the mines?"

Firell studied him, his eyes flickering a deeper green for a moment. "I see you already seem to know."

Rsiran tensed. Did Firell Read him? He hadn't worked out his ability yet. He should have asked Brusus. Likely he'd know. But the lorcith-fortified mental barrier he managed to keep in his mind kept most Readers out. All except Della, and he began to think her abilities were somehow different from most.

But no. There had been no sense of someone trying to crawl through his mind. He'd met delicate Readers—Della Read him without him knowing—but that wasn't it.

If not a Reader, what did that make him?

"I heard you talking to someone on your ship," Rsiran admitted. "Warning you to continue with your job."

His eyes flicked past Rsiran and toward the door. "You were here."

At least Firell hadn't known that he had been on the ship a second time. Perhaps he didn't know everything that happened on his ship as he claimed. "I was here."

Did it matter if Firell admitted that Josun had him smuggling lorcith? Rsiran already knew Josun was the reason Jessa went missing. He needed Firell to help find him.

"Then you know I don't have much of a choice, don't you?" Firell asked.

"He took someone you care about, didn't he?" Rsiran asked again. He finally lowered the knife. If Firell came at him, Rsiran would have to push the ones from his pocket. He hoped it didn't come to that. "Or did you do this only for money?"

Firell took another drink of ale. Something in his voice changed. "If you overheard him, you already know. Don't play the fool, Rsiran. It does not suit you."

The comment reminded him of one Della had made. Just like that one, he ignored it. "You have lorcith you are getting from the mines. More than the city has seen in quite some time. Why does Josun have you taking lorcith *away* from the city?"

Firell refilled his mug. Then he set down the flagon of ale, pulled the sole chair in the room out from the corner, and sat, lounging with his legs kicked out. He sighed deeply. "I wondered at that for a long time. Couldn't understand why he'd want the ore taken away from the city. After all, not many who know how to work with it." He nodded toward Rsiran and tipped his mug. "Though to be honest, I didn't really know who I worked for." Firell shook his head, and Rsiran frowned at him. "Don't look at me like that. In my line of work, that's not uncommon. You ever ask who Brusus be sending those knives of yours off to?"

He hadn't. Not as he should have been, especially when the demand continued to increase. Now that he knew about the Forgotten Elvraeth, he wondered what questions he *should* have been asking.

Rsiran sank onto the only other surface available—the bed. "When did you learn who it was?"

Firell sighed again. "I been working this job for months. Taking crates of lorcith away. Asador. Nheal. Cort. Thyr. Valen." He tapped his fingers as he named the cities. "I sailed where I was paid. And he paid well. *They* paid well. Shael made certain of that."

Rsiran frowned. Shael set up the job. But if that was the case, then it meant Shael knew from the beginning about the lorcith. Was that how Josun learned of him, or was it really only the meeting in the warehouse?

"Didn't know 'bout Shael?" Firell said. "Don't feel bad. Don't think Brusus knows, either. That's sort of how Shael likes it. Works all angles, you see, and each side pays. Took me a long time to learn. And that's what makes him dangerous."

As he said it, the door to the room burst open.

Shael stepped inside, his massive form filling the doorway. Whatever had once seemed friendly about his face had disappeared. Water or sweat stained his bright yellow shirt and plastered down his thick beard.

He lunged for Rsiran, faster than he should have been able to move. In that instant, he slapped a thick chain around Rsiran's wrist, and it closed with a *click*. He held Rsiran by the wrist, gripping him with a strength that reminded him of the time Haern had tried to kill him.

Just like then, Rsiran tried to Slide, tried to *pull* Shael with him, but could not.

Shael's other hand swung around and struck Rsiran on the side of the head, and he crumpled to the ground.

Chapter 32

Rsiran awoke with his head pounding. For a moment, he didn't remember where he was. Pain pierced his skull like a hot lance. He tried to move but couldn't.

He lifted his head. Soft blue light glowed near one corner like the lantern Jessa had found in the warehouse. Something gripped his arms, encircling his wrists and ankles, pinning him painfully to the wall.

Nausea washed over him. Where was he? A steady rocking told him he must still be on the ship, but this didn't look like any place he'd seen. How long had he been unconscious? Moments? Hours? Long enough to chain up. But how had Shael surprised him like that?

He needed to get away. Could he Slide out of the restraints? He'd never tried anything like it before, but he didn't know why it wouldn't be possible.

Just a short Slide. Just enough to escape. Then he could return to Elaeavn and get Brusus and… then what? Still not know where Josun had taken Jessa?

He would have to return to Firell. But he'd be ready.

Rsiran tried to Slide and couldn't. It was as if the ability had been taken from him.

Unlike the barriers around the palace or Asador, rather than pushing him back, it felt as if he simply could not start the Slide.

He was trapped.

Hopelessness different from what he had ever known when working in the mines settled into him. At least there, he had known he could always escape. He might not have been willing to use his ability, but there had always been the sense that he could Slide away if needed.

Now... there was nothing.

And worse than that. He had failed Jessa.

* * * * *

A door creaked, the sound barely more than the sound of the ship groaning as it moved. Rsiran hung in place, dark thoughts the only thing keeping him company. He had drifted, losing time. No one had come to see him.

Now soft footsteps thumped along the floor, moving steadily.

Rsiran should be scared but did not have the energy needed to fear what came next. What energy remained, he needed keep in reserve to help save Jessa.

And he recognized the gait. The steady sound of boots across the wood, the lumbering steps. Without looking, he knew who he would see, so he did not lift his head. There seemed no point in looking at Shael again.

"I be knowin' you're awake there, Rsiran." In spite of what he did, his voice had some of the friendly lilt to it that he'd always had.

Rsiran worked the thick sense of cotton off his tongue. "Why did you let him take Jessa?"

"Don't be knowin' that he'd take the girl. A damn shame that he did. You won't believe this now, but I do be likin' her more than most your kind."

His kind. Is that what drove Shael? "What do you want with me?"

Shael stepped in front of him. The scent of his sweat mixed with grease. He grabbed Rsiran's chin with a vice grip and lifted his face. "Same as I always wantin', though you never make that forge that I ask."

Rsiran blinked, confused. "Forge?"

Shael laughed softly. "Never figure out that schematic?" He leaned forward. "Guess you didn't, else you wouldna gone to the alchemists, now would you."

Rsiran's mouth felt thick. "What did you do to me?"

Shael released Rsiran's face. His head lolled back down, and he didn't have the strength to fight.

"I do know 'bout your ability, Rsiran. No one travels that I don't know 'bout."

Through the thickness in his head, it took a few moments for Rsiran to understand what Shael was saying. "You feel it?"

Shael stepped away. His boots scuffed along the ground softly. "S'pose you'd call it an ability. I never met any others with it. Jus' know when you be steppin' all over Elaeavn." His eyes took on a strange tilt. Was there a faint hint of green there? "And farther."

Rsiran managed to turn his head enough to where he could see Shael. He stood looking out a small, barred porthole. "Why are you doing this?"

Shael tapped on one of the bars and then turned. "Why you think, Rsiran? Why do I be doin' anything I do? There's coin in it." He sniffed out a soft laugh. "And with that one, plenty of coin."

"How long have you worked for him?"

"Long enough to know he pays. Not everyone pays, you see."

"You mean Brusus? Is that why you took me?"

Shael laughed again. "Brusus do be a tough one. Smart, just like this other, just not quite smart enough. Mos' of the time he be paying on time."

"What do you want from me?"

"Not what I be wantin'. It's what *you* be wantin'."

"I just want Jessa. Bring her safely back to Elaeavn." He didn't care about anything else. Brusus and his plots could be damned for all he cared. Even Josun could wander if he left them alone. All Rsiran wanted was Jessa back safely. He would do practically anything to see her safe again.

"There no be safety in Elaeavn, Rsiran. Never been, not for a long time. That be somethin' Brusus do keep from you. Thinks he can protect you, he does. But he knows the truth. Haern, too, though he got a different view. Comes from livin' like he did. Things he saw and did." Shael pushed himself away from the bulkhead and stood near him again. "You do be knowing about Haern?"

"Brusus only tried to help me."

Shael snorted. "Brusus do be a fool. And that's goin' to get him pinched."

"Why has Brusus been a fool?"

Shael laughed softly. "Brusus don' know he be playing in a game bigger than him. Only now, it's too late for him to understand. Now we got you *and* your girl. You'll be doin' what we need without him interferin'."

A bigger game. The rebellion. The exiled Elvraeth. Forgotten.

"Doing what?"

Shael stepped toward him, and Rsiran caught the glint of light off of metal. A distant part of him recognized it as one of the cylinders that they'd found in the crate in the warehouse.

"Gonna help me find the rest of these, too, you are."

"Brusus has them. Why don't you go get them from him—"

Shael tapped him on the cheek with the open palm of his hand. So much like his father had slapped him.

And just like then, he couldn't do anything.

Rsiran swallowed. His throat felt thick and dry in a way it hadn't since he had been forced to work the Ilphaesn mines. And there, working at mining all day, his body ached from a day of hard work rather than the beating he'd experienced. At least in the mines, he'd been able to Slide. At least when his father had mocked him, he'd been able to escape.

"Why can't I Slide?"

Shael laughed and stepped out of sight. Rsiran's arm suddenly jerked, pulled as if Shael meant to tear it from his socket.

"For someone from Lower Town, you do be so sheltered. Probably not your fault here. Not sure even your Brusus do be knowin' about these. Elvraeth like their secrets."

Elvraeth then. After what Della told him about the Elvraeth, and what Josun had alluded to the last time they'd met, he should not be terribly surprised, but finding something that could physically restrain him, that could prevent him from using his ability still felt strange. Did the Elvraeth have the same for other abilities? Could they wear something that prevented Reading? Limit Sight? Diminish a Listener? Or did they only fear Sliding?

"What is it?"

Shael stepped back around him. He leaned forward so Rsiran could see his eyes. "Chains. Best you be getting' used to 'em."

"Why?"

"Told you back in Elaeavn. You be needed." He turned away, his feet shuffling across the wood until he reached the door. It creaked open, the sound mixing with the soft groaning of the ship. "Lucky for you that you really do be a skilled smith, Rsiran."

With that, he left Rsiran alone.

CHAPTER 33

Rsiran drifted again. The steady rocking of the ship lulled him. At least when he slept, he did not feel the pain throbbing in his head. At least then, he was not as aware that he couldn't Slide. Surprising that after spending so much time wishing for a different ability, now that he couldn't use it, he missed it as much as he did.

But each time sleep pulled him under, dreams came. Strangely, most of the time, he dreamt about the Ilphaesn mines. The darkness and sense of lorcith all around him. The steady tapping that kept him awake. The pain in his back and neck from the attacks.

Other dreams drifted in. Dreams he couldn't explain. At times, he felt the distant pull of the alloy. Once he thought it came from the lantern, but he realized what he felt was larger. There was a vastness to it, a sense that he could lose himself were he to listen too long. Floating in the dream as he was, he didn't care. Let the lorcith pull on him, draw him to it, so the muted sound came louder, closer, until it seemed all around him…

Rsiran jerked awake. His arms and legs hurt. During the awake periods, the dull ache gradually worsened. Much longer, and he would not be able to stand on his own. Then, only the chains would support him.

Shael had not returned. Rsiran lost track of time, the steady rolling of the ship and creak of the wooden planks his only company. Occasionally, he thought he heard voices or footsteps, but they never ventured where he could see them.

In a moment of clarity, he listened for lorcith. If he could only *pull* a knife or one of his forgings to him, he might be able to work his way free. But there was nothing. As if he suppressed it, pushing the sense of lorcith away.

More than anything, that sent shivers of fear through him. Firell's ship carried massive amounts of unshaped lorcith. He should feel *something*. Or even the forgings Firell had taken from him, smuggled onto his ship. Instead, there was nothing.

Had Shael taken him off Firell's ship? Like Firell, Shael was a smuggler, but Rsiran had never seen his ship. It wouldn't be impossible to think Shael could have moved him. But he didn't think so.

That meant that these cuffs somehow blocked his sense of lorcith.

Only... not completely.

As he listened, blocked from everything as he was, he recognized the distant sense of the alloy much as he had when he intentionally pushed away the sense of lorcith.

With lorcith so completely blocked from him, he heard it clearly.

With nothing but the steady creaking of the ship and the constant rolling beneath his feet, he listened. As he did, the sound of the alloy became clearer.

It reminded him of his dream. Muted and steady, and both farther and closer than he'd ever felt before. Almost as if he could simply anchor to it and pull himself. Only, he'd never managed to anchor to the alloy. Even Sliding disturbed the tenuous connection he managed with it.

He tried latching onto it as he did when anchoring, but the sense flickered and faded, disappearing into the blackness of his mind. Almost as if by reaching for it, he pushed it farther away until the sense of it faded.

Rsiran let go. As he did, the muted sense returned.

He remembered sitting in front of the anvil when he'd listened to the lantern. Then he'd almost had an understanding. Had he sat longer—or listened better—he had the sense that he might learn some deep secret.

Instead of latching on, he just listened.

For long moments, he felt nothing. But—slowly, so slowly—awareness came to him, just as it had when sitting and listening in his smithy. And he thought he knew what to do.

This time, Rsiran didn't reach. He *pulled.*

Slowly, like a difficult Slide, the sense came closer. Yet it felt nothing like any Slide he'd ever experienced. Almost oozing toward him, the faded sense began to change, shifting into something else. No longer did it seem like it called quietly. Now it filled him.

Different from lorcith. Where lorcith had an eager quality to it, this had an edge. Lorcith sometimes sang to him. This demanded his attention. Lorcith knew it needed him. This knew he needed it.

Rsiran almost let go, but if he did, he suspected he wouldn't have a chance to listen again.

He knew he should be scared. But chained as he was, locked upright in Firell's ship, separated from Jessa with no way to help her, at least he no longer felt alone. Whatever the strange sense of the alloy demanded, he would comply.

His breathing eased, and he dropped his head, welcoming the sensation.

Fatigue overwhelmed him, like after an onerous Slide, and he drifted again toward sleep.

CHAPTER 34

RSIRAN AWOKE TO THE SOUND OF FOOTSTEPS ON WOOD.
He jerked his head up and turned to see who might be
there, only he saw nothing. Even the lantern had been extinguished.
Darkness swirled around him, a pure black night so much like the
mines. Lorcith burned all around him…

His heart hammered.

Lorcith.

This felt different from the muted sense he'd noticed earlier. That
was still there, just at the back of his mind, but he could call on it if he
wanted.

For the first time, he felt the chains holding his wrist and ankles,
the bars covering the porthole, the lantern across the room. And not
muted, but rather as a steady call. As lorcith normally would.

Rsiran probed the alloy encircling his wrists. It felt hot and tight,
and scraped the flesh nearly to the bone. Dried blood caked along his
arms. Fire burned through his skin, up toward his injured shoulder

where it threatened to separate. Through it, he *felt* the way the chain had been forged, almost as he felt it when his own forgings called to him.

And he knew how it had been made. That knowledge filled him in a way that he never had when working with lorcith. With lorcith, he simply let the ore take him, guide his hammer, and show him what it wanted to become. This was knowledge. The perfect combination of heartstone mixed with heated lorcith. The way to mix it together so the lorcith accepted the heartstone. The technique of shaping the chain in just such a way that when clasped and locked, it prevented Sliding. And the way to trigger the lock.

Boots scraped on wood again. Not in the room, but just outside. A guard, or did Shael patrol?

Rsiran sensed for lorcith. Chained as he was, he still couldn't feel it. He had the vague sense that if he pushed hard enough, he could almost reach it. Still trapped.

The heavy gait came closer. Almost to the door.

Rsiran *pushed* on the lock of the chain, not expecting anything to happen. Lorcith only reacted to him when he had been the one to forge it. Only then did he have the connection needed to control it.

The lock clicked.

Rsiran pulled his hand free.

Pain shot through his arm, but he still let out a soft sigh of relief. Acting quickly, he released the other locks. As he did, the sense of lorcith flooded him.

His knives, the unshaped lumps stacked in crates, even the sword in Elaeavn. All filled him as it did when he pushed away the awareness of lorcith. That rebound sense practically filled his mind, nearly staggering him. Yet this felt different. Had the sense always been this strong or had something changed while he'd been separated from it?

The door jiggled. Rsiran couldn't wait any longer or risk getting caught again.

Needing to know if he could, he Slid forward a step.

There were colors, twisted and bright. The air smelled sharp and crisp. And then he emerged. Relief filled him. Surprisingly, the sense of the alloy remained.

What had changed?

It was a question for another time. Now he needed to reach Firell. Find Josun. And then Jessa.

The chains hung from a hook on the wall. Rsiran examined them. Made of twisted lorcith that slowly spiraled around before reaching the clasps that had held his wrists. The alloy felt different from what he'd encountered so far. He listened to it—doing so no longer felt difficult or muted, no longer did he have to push away the sense of lorcith to hear the alloy—and understood that more heartstone had been used in their making than was used in the lantern, or even the bars covering the port-hole. With a forge, lorcith, and heartstone, he could recreate the chains.

The chain came off the hook easily and felt surprisingly light. Coiling it so that he could carry it easily, he slipped it up and over his arm. He removed the leg bindings from the wall and rolled them until they coiled easily to fit into his pocket. He wouldn't leave these behind to trap someone else.

Then he grabbed the lantern from the floor near the corner. The soft blue glow created just enough light for him to see clearly. He felt the sense of the alloy used to create the lantern. Deeper inside, heartstone burned, creating the pale glow.

With the lantern, at least he wouldn't be stuck in darkness.

Rsiran Slid.

He emerged from the Slide inside the hold. For the first time, he could see what it held. The sense of lorcith all around him practically overwhelmed him. If he closed his eyes, he would see where each crate rested, where each forging he'd made hid.

His knives were here.

Not the knives that he'd made initially for Brusus. What he wanted were the smaller knives, those that he'd *asked* the lorcith to let him create. Dropped into one of the crates, he didn't need the lantern to see that they rested atop a bowl he'd made. They would fit in his pocket, hidden away. And they didn't take much thought to push.

Or pull.

Rsiran *pulled* them toward him.

The knives floated up from the crate, and he grabbed them out of the air as they neared. Then he stuffed them into his pocket. A few other knives were here, as well, but he wouldn't worry about them now. Even the unshaped lorcith, its call so loud in his mind making it so that he had to push it back, would be left behind. If everything went well, he would return for it later.

Then he Slid.

This time, he emerged in Firell's quarters. The room stood empty. The small trunk where Firell stored his flagon of ale rested on the floor. The lid partially closed. Bed sheets crumpled atop the bed. Blood stained the pillow. A stack of paper rested atop the table. A knife jabbed through one corner, holding them in place. Not lorcith, but finely made.

Rsiran pulled the knife out of the paper and twisted it in his hands. Something about it looked familiar. There seemed a sense of flow to the steel made by the folding of the metal until it tapered to a sharp point. Finely balanced, it was more functional than decorative. He set it aside.

A series of numbers scrawled across the top page. Rsiran studied the page, reading through the tight script along the left side. A logbook, recording lorcith. Weights and quantity of lorcith delivered. But he couldn't tell where it was delivered to. He folded the sheet and tucked it into his pocket.

He flipped through the other pages. Some were more logs, others were notes. He didn't have the time to sort through it all. Instead, he took the stack and rolled it, stuffing it alongside the other sheet. When he returned to Elaeavn, he would take more time to read through it. Only when Jessa was finally safe would he care.

The door opened.

He had expected it.

Rsiran looked up. Shael stood in the doorway. Surprise lined his wide face. Eyes narrowed and his arms tensed.

"Don't know how you be escaping. Felt the traveling, though. Someone come let you out?"

"Where's Jessa?" Rsiran asked. The anger in his voice surprised him. So, too, did the rage. He would not hesitate to harm Shael if it meant getting Jessa back. The knives thrummed in his pocket, ready for whatever he asked of them.

"Don't be makin' me hurt you again, boy."

Shael lunged.

He moved quickly, but Rsiran anticipated it. As Shael came at him, he Slid and emerged just long enough to grab onto him.

Rsiran pulled him up to the main deck of the ship. He emerged in bright sunlight. The ship rocked gently beneath him, nothing like the angry waves he'd felt before. After all the time he'd spent chained and trapped in the room, nothing but the motion of the waves for company, he did not struggle with his footing as he had initially.

Shael staggered and Rsiran released him. He went sprawling across the deck.

Someone leapt from a rope and landed on the deck with a thud.

Rsiran didn't turn to see who it was. He didn't need to. The sense of lorcith flooded him, telling him that the attacker carried a knife, though not one of his. Strange that he should feel it so strongly. Without giving it another thought, he *pulled* on it and the knife went flying.

He twisted it so that it hung over Shael, tip pointing down toward his throat. And then left it hovering there. The lorcith responded as if forged by his hand.

"Don't," he said.

Shael froze. Only then did Rsiran turn.

Firell stood behind him. A large gash lined one cheek. Deep green eyes had reddened around the sides. He looked weary. "You continue to surprise me, Rsiran. No wonder Brusus values you as he does."

"Someone will tell me what they know."

As he spoke, he *felt* people moving about below deck. They carried lorcith on them or else he wouldn't have noticed. With a pull on the lorcith, a distant moan sounded. And then silence.

"How many others?"

Firell's eyes narrowed.

"How many!"

"Two more. But they should be sleeping. Had their shift last night."

"Over by Shael," he said.

Firell obeyed, keeping his eyes fixed on Rsiran as he made his way toward Shael, careful to give Rsiran a wide berth. "Thought you said he was restrained."

Shael laughed bitterly. "Thought he be. Don' know how—"

Rsiran *pushed* the knife down until the tip rested on Shael's throat. A spot of blood bloomed where it touched. Shael stiffened but did not move any more.

"You will tell me what you know of Josun Elvraeth," Rsiran said. "And of the Forgotten."

"Rsiran—careful with what you ask. There are things you don't know about, things Brusus has kept from you. Thinks he's keeping you safe, but really bringing you deeper," Firell said.

"He's told me what he knows about the Forgotten. And I don't care. All I want is Jessa."

Shael didn't move. "Aye, boy, but you should."

Rsiran surveyed the deck, making certain that no one else might attack him. Bright sun hung overhead. A strong sea breeze fluttered the full sails, sending spray up and over the deck as the ship cut through the water. In the far distance, flat land stretched out, sweeping away from the ocean in a field of gold and brown.

Everywhere around him he felt the soft sense of lorcith.

What had happened to him chained in the hold? Had the separation from the lorcith simply made him more aware of it now that he could sense it again, or was it something different? Had something about him changed? And why could he suddenly feel the alloy so sharply?

"Just tell me about Josun."

Firell sat next to Shael, looking up at him. "You think you will find your girl. I understand that. I've been through it myself. But that's not how his kind works. You've got to earn them back. Do their bidding—"

"I tried that once," Rsiran said. "It didn't work out for either of us too well."

"You're not dumb, boy. Think about what you do be doin'. What this Elvraeth be having you do. Do you really think you be getting the upper hand here?"

"I just want to get her back. Have him leave me in peace."

Firell pushed himself to his feet. Rsiran turned. One of the knives hidden in his pocket flashed up and streaked toward him. Firell held his hands out in front of him, eyes wide as he stared at the knife. "That's what I'm trying to tell you, Rsiran. What Brusus either hasn't or won't tell you. And maybe you've been sheltered. Most in Elaeavn are. But there isn't peace—not really—and not where the Elvraeth are concerned."

"I only care about one of the Elvraeth. He's the one who took Jessa, the one who thinks to use her to get to me."

Lying on the deck, knife pointing to his throat, Shael still managed to laugh. "You be thinking you the only one to be used? You do be sheltered, boy!"

Rsiran frowned at Shael and turned to Firell. The knife hung in the air between them, just out of Firell's reach. Who had Firell lost? How did he understand what Rsiran went through?

Rsiran remembered what he'd overheard. Josun had taken someone Firell cared about as well. And maybe that was the reason Firell helped him smuggle. Wouldn't Rsiran do the same for Jessa? If there were a chance that he might get her back, wouldn't he take it?

Except… he knew that he couldn't trust Josun. He'd been used once already, meant to take the blame for whatever poisoning Josun intended. As much as Firell and Shael might know of the Elvraeth, whatever Josun had over them, Rsiran would do anything to keep away from him.

With a quick *pull*, he dragged the knives back to him and caught them. The smaller of the two—the one he'd asked the lorcith to let him make, he stuffed back into his pocket. The other he quickly pushed into the band of his pants.

"Tell me, then. Tell me why I'm sheltered."

Shael pushed up to sit. He rubbed his neck before leaning back against the rail, not making any other attempt to move. Rsiran didn't trust him not to attack again, but at least he knew to be ready. And now, he suspected he could pull Shael with him. If he had to, he would drop him off the rocks near Ilphaesn.

"What do you know of the Elvraeth?" Firell asked.

"They rule Elaeavn."

"And before?"

"They were gifted by the Great Watcher with abilities granting them authority to lead."

Shael laughed softly. "Foolish customs," he said. "And most you people do be believing them too."

"Why shouldn't we believe?" Rsiran asked. He Slid toward him a step, and Shael's eyes darkened.

Firell only shifted, crossing his legs. He flexed his arms and rubbed at the gash on his cheek. "You think the Great Watcher cares who rules? They might have been gifted more strongly than the rest of us, but what gives the Elvraeth a right to rule?" Firell smiled, his mouth little more than a tight line. "Most never even question. Never question why the Elvraeth exile people from the city. But there are some who know the world is larger than Elaeavn. Who have seen beyond the Aisl and the Lhear Sea. And they know there is more than just the Elvraeth. Gifted by the Great Watcher. Perhaps that is true. Once I believed my Sight was a gift. Once I believed as you do—that the Elvraeth were given their gifts by the Great Watcher. But I see how they use their gifts. How they exile those who compete for power. How they hurt or kill their own people. And now... now that comes back to haunt them."

"I don't care about your lectures. Or about who rules—"

"Who rules be the most important, now don't it?"

Rsiran frowned at Shael. "Why?"

But Shael just shrugged.

"You should focus on what you *can* do, rather than what you cannot. You don't know where she is. And we can't help you." Saying that seemed to pain Firell.

Rsiran swallowed. What did Firell know? "Is she dead?"

Emotion crossed Firell's face. Anger? Sadness? A mixture of both? "I doubt that he'd take her from you like that. No way to motivate you otherwise. And trust me when I tell you that he wants to use you."

Shael had said the same thing. Had mentioned Rsiran forging. "Taking Jessa is the way to motivate me?" Rsiran Slid a step closer. "I've seen what happens when Josun tries to use people. It nearly killed Jessa the last time. Lianna wasn't as lucky."

"Lianna?" Firell asked.

Rsiran nodded. "Didn't know about her? Josun killed her. Let her go above the rocks. It was Brusus who found her."

Firell frowned. "Lianna is gone? But it makes no sense to harm her. Doing so only aggravates Brusus and would…" He looked up at Rsiran, eyes going wide. "Listen to me, Rsiran. You must keep Brusus from getting more involved. Doing so only serves their purpose!"

"I can't keep Brusus from his plans any more than he can keep me from mine."

Firell swallowed. "Not Josun. Don't you see, Rsiran? It's never been about you or me or Brusus or Jessa or even Josun. It's about the Elvraeth and the Forgotten. And they will use us however they choose all in the name of acquiring power."

Rsiran felt the lapping of waves as they pushed against the ship. "Just tell me when he's meeting you."

"Would now work?"

Rsiran turned. Josun Elvraeth stood leaning against the railing. A wide smile crossed his face.

CHAPTER 35

I THOUGHT YOU SAID YOU HAD HIM CONTROLLED?" Josun said, his deep blue shirt open wide across the chest, with slashes of crimson ribbon lacing it together. Black pants fit tight over his boots. Rather than anger, amusement crossed his face. If he worried that Rsiran was not chained, he did not show it.

"We do be having him chained. He escaped," Shael said. He nodded to the chain wrapped around Rsiran's arm.

Josun Slid past him as another smaller wave made the ship shudder. Now he stood next to Firell and knelt. "You told me those chains were genuine."

Firell shook his head. "They *are* genuine. You said you tested them yourself!"

Josun laughed and stood, turning to face Rsiran for the first time. "I suppose that I did. Interesting that he should escape. He continues to surprise me."

Rsiran shifted the chains as he listened for lorcith, curious if Josun kept any forged lorcith on him, but there wasn't anything.

Josun smiled and looked at Rsiran. "The blacksmith. You look different than when last I saw you."

"I do be saying that the last time I saw him," Shael said. He stood and leaned against the railing of the deck just as leisurely as Josun managed. "You do be knowin' of his knives?"

Josun tilted his head and sniffed. "I do be knowing. I just have not worked out *how*."

"And you no be concerned?"

Josun turned to Shael. "And why should I be concerned about Rsiran? Were he to want to harm me, he would have attempted it by now. And besides," he went on, a dark smile deepening on his face, "if I am gone, how would he find his... friend?"

Rsiran bit back the rage he felt, pushing it away. Hurting Josun would do nothing to return Jessa to him. "Where is she?" he asked.

Josun looked over and shrugged. "That is not how such negotiations should go. You see, you bargain from a position of weakness. I have what you want. And she is somewhere even you will never find her."

With a thought, Rsiran *pushed* one of the knives hidden in his pocket toward Josun.

It whistled past. Somehow, he'd managed to Slide just as a wave pushed on the ship and the knife went splashing down into the water.

"Careful, Lareth, or one could think you don't truly care what happened to your friend."

"What did you do with her?" Rsiran asked. He readied another knife. If Josun wanted to taunt him, he wouldn't hesitate to use the knives to incapacitate him. The last time, the knife he'd used had been poisoned. This time, they were not. That didn't mean he couldn't still be deadly.

Josun shook his head. "First, we will begin with what you can do for me. And then, if you complete what I ask, we will speak about what I can do for you."

"What is it you think I can do for you?"

Josun leaned away from the railing. Wind ruffled his shirt and sent his chestnut hair fluttering. "I wouldn't ask you to do anything you do not do already. A simple forging, is all."

"What kind of forging? You're the Elvraeth. Why do you need me?"

He shrugged. "There are some things even one of the Elvraeth cannot get made. And then there's your unique ability," he said, glancing at the knife Rsiran held. "A smith like you has uses. So first, I need a demonstration."

"I've already seen what kind of demonstration you want."

Josun smiled. "Nothing like that, and nothing that you would not do anyway."

"What is it?"

"Just a sword. I believe you already know how to make one?" His smile twisted his mouth. "Something similar to that. Only, I would require a personal flourish. You know of heartstone?" He watched Rsiran as he asked and then nodded. "I see that you do. And as you have no doubt learned, heartstone can be worked into your lorcith. The combination is really quite beautiful. This is what I would like my sword made from. This will be your demonstration."

If Rsiran needed any more proof that Josun was after the alloy, this request confirmed it. "Why do you need a sword like that?"

His eyes hardened. "I want it so that your Jessa can be returned to you intact." Then he shrugged. "Is that not a good enough reason?"

Firell watched Rsiran and shook his head.

"Not for the lorcith," he said. Already he had the feeling that he couldn't make such a sword. Mixing the alloy might be difficult enough. Even with the ability to listen to it, the knowledge he gained there, he didn't know if what Josun asked was even possible, at least for him.

"You want me to believe the metal cares what shape it takes?" He laughed, his head shaking. "You Lower Towners are so much alike. So quick to believe in such things. It really does make ruling much easier." His laughter died, and he fixed Rsiran with a dark expression. "Now. As I have said. What I require is the sword. I believe Shael provided you plans for a way to mix the two metals?" He smiled. "Yes, you know what I mean. Once you demonstrate your ability, you will have her back."

Rsiran hadn't realized that was what the plans were for, and now that he was more tightly connected to the alloy, he doubted that he would need them. "And if I can't?"

"Then I will take one of your lovely lorcith knives and drag it across her throat. Her last thought will be of how you failed her. And how you killed her."

Rsiran tensed but realized that Josun wanted him angry. "How long do I have?"

Josun fixed Rsiran with a dark smile. "You ask the wrong question. How long does *she* have?"

"How long?" he repeated.

Josun shrugged. "Perhaps a day. Perhaps longer."

"And then?"

"And then I move on. I am sure I can find other ways to motivate you. Do you think you can complete this task in time?"

Doing so meant forcing lorcith into forgings it would not want. That felt too much like what his father did when working with lorcith, and nothing like the collaboration he had when he worked with the ore. But what choice did he have? To save Jessa, wouldn't he do anything?

"You will bring Jessa with you when we next meet," he said.

Josun frowned. "And risk you attacking like the last time? I think you will leave the sword for me, and then I will decide if your work is satisfactory. If it is not, then I might have another task for you." Josun Slid just as the ship rocked in the waves, moving only a step. "I will find you tomorrow night, Rsiran. And you know what will happen if you are not there."

With that, Josun Slid.

CHAPTER 36

O NCE MORE, RSIRAN STOOD IN THE SMITHY. The blue lantern rested atop the table, now devoid of anything he'd forged, spilling cold light around it and pushing back the shadows of the night. Night was for forging. Since claiming the smithy, his best work had been done at night and in the darkness, the thick stone trapping the sound of his hammer. And now, he'd have to do his best work yet, even if he didn't understand why.

Coals flared hot and angry, heat raising a shimmer of sweat on his arms and face. The orange glow reflected off the gleaming anvil. A massive lump of lorcith sat atop it, waiting for him to place it into the coals, but he had not. Not yet.

Heartstone sat on one of the back shelves. Rsiran could not bring himself to set it any closer. Now that he understood what it did, how it *changed* the lorcith—and more than any simple alloy—he didn't want to look at it.

But he had the night. Long enough to create the sword Josun wanted. And if he could do it, then maybe Jessa had a chance.

The schematic Shael had left for him lay folded open on the table. Rsiran still didn't know how to make what the plans indicated—some way of forcing lorcith and heartstone, he now knew—but did that even matter when he could *hear* from the lorcith what it would require?

Rsiran sighed. Even if he did this thing, there was no guarantee that Josun would return Jessa to him. Like Firell, he would continue to serve him, praying for the chance that he could see her again as he made more and more of the alloy for Josun.

"You are right to doubt his intentions."

Rsiran spun. He should not have been surprised to see Della standing behind him, but he hadn't heard her enter. For a moment, he wondered if she had Slid to the smithy, but she had denied that ability. And he'd never known Della to lie to him. "You knew I had returned."

She glanced at the fire as she made her way over to him. One hand touched his arm and her eyes closed. She left it there for a long moment. "Something has changed," she said softly.

He shook her arm off. "Nothing has changed. Only what I must do to reach Jessa."

"You saw Josun Elvraeth."

He nodded. "He wanted me to Slide to Firell's ship. Or expected me to." Either way, the end result had been the same. It was the only way he could explain how Shael knew to trap him. And he'd thought Firell didn't know of his ability, but Josun likely told him.

"You have been gone for many days."

He'd thought as much. Days during which Jessa suffered, wondering if he would come for her. Days spent hanging from the chains in Firell's ship, cut off from his ability to Slide. From the ability to sense lorcith.

Della gasped.

"You know of them? The chains?" He did not question how she Read him. His barriers were nothing to her, even reinforced with lorcith. Perhaps if he added heartstone to the mix...

"Don't," Della said sharply. "Such a thing is dangerous."

He lifted the chains from the ground where he'd set them upon returning. Rsiran hadn't wanted to have them touch him any longer. For some reason, they had not prevented him from returning. Only when they pierced his flesh did they seem to work that way. "I'm not sure that it does," he said softly. The alloy might change the lorcith, but it was not dangerous, not by itself. "What are they?"

"Those chains are an ancient creation, born out of fear and one that never should have been."

Rsiran felt the pull of the metal on him. Whatever had changed while he stood chained in the darkness let him feel the alloy just the same as he did the lorcith. Only... it gave understanding with it.

"That should not be possible," Della whispered.

"Nothing I do should be possible," Rsiran muttered. "So what are these chains?"

"There once was a time when the Elvraeth needed a way to protect themselves. To keep safe from those who could travel. Those"—she waved toward the ground—"were created. And even then, they were rare. Only the greatest of the master smiths could make them. I had thought them long destroyed."

Rsiran looked down at the chains. "Not destroyed," he said. "And they work."

Della nodded. "Many Elvraeth felt their bite. But how did Josun get them?"

"Shael found them for him. I didn't ask where," he said bitterly.

"And you? How did you escape?"

Rsiran laughed, the anger and frustration he felt bubbling to the surface. "I'm not sure I did."

Della watched him, her eyes unreadable. "What does he ask of you, Rsiran?"

"He asks me to make something for him. He says that if I do, he will release Jessa back to me. And if I don't…" Rsiran shivered, thinking of how Josun described what he'd do to Jessa.

"And you think he will hold true to what he says? That he will release Jessa once you demonstrate your ability to make the alloy?"

From her tone, he knew there was something else. "If I do this thing for him, he says he will release her."

"Once you do that for him, will it stop there?"

Rsiran hadn't noticed Della nearing him. Now she stood almost alongside him. She smelled of the mint tea she preferred and looked small and frail. Different from the healer he'd met only a few months ago. That time had changed her, twisted her back, and taken some of the vibrancy from her eyes.

"I don't know."

"Can you even do it?"

Rsiran sighed, pointing to the schematic on the table. "That shows how to create the proper forge, only I can't follow it." Relief surged behind her eyes. "Doesn't matter. I think I can ask the lorcith to mix."

She looked at him strangely. "Is that how it works for you? You must ask the lorcith?"

"For something like this. I could not force it into the alloy, not easily."

Della frowned, eyes flickering a darker green. "No. I don't think that you should."

"Even if it means Jessa's release?"

Della looked at him. "Once you prove that you can make what has not been seen in centuries, do you truly believe he will release her?"

From the look Firell had given him when talking about Jessa, Rsiran didn't think it likely. What else could he do?

"I need to get her back."

"Is this the only way?"

When he looked at her, he saw the fatigue lining her face. The way her eyes wrinkled more than they once had. The tightness to her lips. Even her posture looked more stilted and bent. She waited for his answer, not saying anything. And he knew she was right. This was what Josun wanted.

"I don't know."

Della nodded. "Then find another."

CHAPTER 37

R SIRAN HELD A LONG LENGTH OF LORCITH shaped almost into a sword. It had none of the grace the other sword possessed, none of the smooth lines made by the steady hammering, the continued folding of the metal. But it was what he'd asked of the lorcith.

No heartstone mixed into the sword, not for Josun. He had the sense that the lorcith would have mixed with heartstone, if only he had asked, but he didn't risk it, not now when he had a plan to get Jessa back.

Coals heated the forge. An orange lantern taken from Della's house cast harsh light, nothing like the clean blue light of the heartstone lanterns. He hammered noisily but without any real intent. Waiting.

A soft tremble almost sent a shiver down his spine. A boot scuffed the stone floor. Rsiran turned.

Josun watched him. Deep green eyes flared as he looked through the orange lantern.

Rsiran made certain to fortify his mental barriers. He couldn't have Josun Reading him. He stepped partially in front of the sword.

"Is it ready?" Josun asked.

"Only if I know she's safe."

Josun Slid to the table. To Rsiran, it felt as if a breeze fluttered through the smithy. Josun looked at the different items spread out across the table. None were lorcith made. Those had all been given to Brusus. Only Shael's crate of unshaped lorcith remained.

"As I believe I said, that isn't how this works."

Rsiran turned, holding the sword in both hands. He could do nothing other than swing it, but it felt right holding it as he stared down Josun. "And I will not give you anything without knowing she lives."

Josun Slid a step. "She lives. That's all you need to know. If you wish to see her again, you will do what I say."

For a moment, Rsiran wondered if what he planned would work. Josun moved too quickly. Each step a Slide. Rsiran had no way of knowing when Josun would Slide, or where he would emerge when he did. He considered pushing one of the lorcith knives at Josun, but didn't think he'd fall for that again.

"The sword, Lareth. Then we will talk about what you need to do to get your girl back."

"You said that if I made the sword, I could get her back."

Josun's smile widened. "I said we would talk." He looked at Rsiran's pockets. "And don't think to send your knives at me. I will see it if you do. Know that if I don't return by morning, she is dead."

At least he knew how Josun intended to escape the knife. "I don't want to hurt you. I just want her back."

"You can't hurt me, Lareth. You couldn't even kill me. Don't you know that it takes more than a smith to kill one of the Elvraeth?"

"You only want the alloy," Rsiran said.

Josun smiled. "Now you begin to understand."

"Why? What is it about the alloy that you care about?"

Josun shook his head. "Someone like you cannot begin to under-stand," he said.

Rsiran bristled at the contempt that Josun demonstrated, but he had to play along, if only long enough for him to find Jessa. "And once you have the sword?"

He shrugged. "There might be other tasks asked of you." His gaze swept around the smithy. "It seems you enjoy your work. I would only convince you to continue. How is that wrong?"

Rsiran feared what Josun asked, the tasks that he would be forced to complete. It might start with the sword, but there would be other requests. And then others. All while he was pulled deeper into the de-mands of the Elvraeth, both Forgotten and not.

If he left Josun to his plans, they could never be safe. His friends—his family—could never be safe.

"The sword, Lareth."

He nodded, then leaned to hand him the sword. Josun reached for the blade, and as he did, Rsiran *pulled* the chains from where they rest-ed beneath the table. The cuffs snapped around Josun's wrist. He tried to Slide—Rsiran *felt* him trying—but couldn't.

Rsiran *pushed* a pair of knives toward Josun's throat and snapped the chain around his other wrist.

Josun's face twisted in a mask of rage. "She's dead now. Whatever you think you will achieve. She is dead."

Rsiran dropped the half-made sword into the coals. It would heat and deform, turning into a useless lump of lorcith. A change it had agreed to for him. He Slid to Josun and grabbed the chain. Josun tried to kick, but Rsiran grabbed the hammer resting next to the anvil slammed it down onto his leg, ignoring Josun's scream.

"It is time we talk."

And then he Slid.

* * * * *

They emerged near Ilphaesn. A steady sea wind whipped around him, violent and angry. Rsiran held Josun by the chain, standing along the path leading to the peak of Ilphaesn. The sense of lorcith all around him pulled on him.

"Where is she?" he whispered.

Wind threatened to steal his words, but he leaned in, making certain Josun heard him.

"You won't find her. Your only chance is to release me and hope that I—"

Rsiran gripped the chain and Slid.

He wasn't entirely certain what he planned would work. When he stood on the path, he sensed the alloy barrier blocking access to the upper mine. Since chained and trapped on Firell's ship, he felt the alloy differently than before. He still didn't know if he could Slide past it without an anchor.

He felt the barrier, but it had changed. Or he had changed. He didn't care.

Rsiran pulled Josun through the barrier.

They emerged into the darkness of the hidden mine that he and Jessa had discovered. Lorcith pressed all around him, giving him a different kind of sight. He pushed Josun away from him and heard him stagger, his injured leg giving out as he fell to the ground. The chains told Rsiran where he lay.

"Where is she?" Rsiran asked again.

Josun laughed darkly. "To feel truly threatened, I need to believe that you'll carry through with it. You're just not believable, Lareth. You may think you sound dangerous, but you have already shown me that you'll do anything to get her back. And to see her alive, you will not harm me."

Rsiran stepped toward him. The darkness of this mine didn't frighten him as it once had. With lorcith all around, it practically glowed in his mind. "You assume I don't already know where she is."

Josun didn't answer at first. When he did, he laughed again. "Were that true, you would have gone to her first. No. You know that you need me. She is already dead, as sure as if you made the kill yourself."

Rsiran Slid to Josun and kicked. He didn't care where he hit him, only that he did. Josun grunted as Rsiran's boot connected. "And you will stay here, trapped as she has been."

Rsiran walked deeper into the mine, leaving Josun lying on the ground.

As he did, he listened to the lorcith, letting it guide him.

When Della told him to find another way to reach Josun, it had gotten him thinking. Everything had revolved around the lorcith. First the access—the extra mine he'd discovered, the lorcith on Firell's ship, even the lorcith scattered around the other great cities. Where else would Josun have taken Jessa that Rsiran wouldn't be able to find her?

He made his way quickly. At one point, a soft wind began gusting through the mine, blowing at him with the bitter odor of lorcith. And then he felt it as he expected. Jagged edges to the mine where lorcith had been taken from the walls. Voids where the ore once had been.

He paused and listened. Did he hear the soft pulling of forged lorcith or was that his imagination?

As he walked, he felt a growing certainty. Forged lorcith. Done by his hand.

He Slid with each step, hurrying toward it.

And then he reached her.

She jerked back when he touched the charm tucked into her shirt and tried to kick out toward him.

"Jessa," he said.

She stopped moving. Her body tensed. "Rsiran?"

He lifted her, scooping her up and cradling her in his arms. She did not fight. "It's me. I found you."

Jessa coughed. "Took you long enough."

Then he Slid her from the mine.

EPILOGUE

Rsiran sat in Della's house drinking a mug of the mint tea. Jessa leaned back in the chair, warming herself in front of the fire. She hadn't said much since he'd brought her from the mines.

"Where did you leave him?" Della asked. She pressed her hand onto Jessa's forehead, feeling for a long moment.

"The mine. I left the chains attached so that he couldn't Slide."

"You didn't kill him," Della asked.

"No. Not that he didn't deserve it. Only… I didn't need to." Rsiran discovered that he had been willing to kill Josun if that was what it would have taken to free Jessa. He hadn't known that darkness—that anger—was in him before.

Della nodded slowly and turned away.

Jessa looked up and blinked slowly, as if finally understanding. "What chains?"

"The alloy. Another Elvraeth gift," he answered.

Jessa looked back to the fire. Her eyes had a flat expression. Rsiran hoped it was only fatigue that made her look as she did.

"Someone will free him."

"Why do you say that?" Rsiran asked.

She took a deep breath. "I overheard them while they had me. Josun was just a part of a bigger plan with the Forgotten."

"I know."

"You know?"

He glanced to Della who pretended she wasn't listening. "Brusus has been looking for signs of the Forgotten. For his mother, I think."

Jessa sighed. "And instead they found us."

"They found us," he agreed.

"They wanted you for some reason."

"To make the alloy," he said. He still didn't know how it fit into Josun's—and the Forgotten—plans. But now that he had Jessa back, did it matter? All he wanted was to fade into obscurity, only… only he wasn't sure that he would be given the chance.

"Did you?" Jessa asked.

He shook his head, clearing the worry from it. "No. And I won't."

Jessa breathed out slowly. "Maybe that was it. I don't know. And it doesn't matter. There are others they've pulled into it. That was part of their plan. The Forgotten Elvraeth were rounding up smiths, forcing them to work in other cities. Asador. Cort. Thyr." She shook her head. "They're everywhere."

"What do you mean they're rounding up smiths?" Rsiran asked.

Della looked at him. "That was what I hadn't told you yet. That man you found in Asador?" Rsiran nodded, already dreading what she would say. "That was your father."

DK HOLMBERG is a full time writer living in rural Minnesota with his wife, two kids, two dogs, two cats, and thankfully no other animals. Somehow he manages to find time for writing.

To see other books and read more, please go to www.dkholmberg.com

Follow me on twitter: @dkholmberg

Word-of-mouth is crucial for any author to succeed and how books are discovered. If you enjoyed the book, please consider leaving a review online at your favorite bookseller or Goodreads, even if it's only a line or two; it would make all the difference and would be very much appreciated.

Others Available by DK Holmberg

The Dark Ability

The Dark Ability
The Heartstone Blade
The Tower of Venass
Blood of the Watcher

The Cloud Warrior Saga

Chased by Fire
Bound by Fire
Changed by Fire
Fortress of Fire
Forged in Fire
Serpent of Fire
Servant of Fire

The Lost Garden

Keeper of the Forest
The Desolate Bond
Keeper of Light

Made in the USA
San Bernardino, CA
07 July 2020

75095227R00207